W9-BZA-844

CYBER
ATTACK

Pinnacle Thrillers
by TIM WASHBURN

Cyber Attack

The Day After Oblivion

Cataclysm

Powerless

CYBER ATTACK

TIM WASHBURN

PINNACLE BOOKS
Kensington Publishing Corp.
www.kensingtonbooks.com

PINNACLE BOOKS are published by

Kensington Publishing Corp.
119 West 40th Street
New York, NY 10018

All Kensington titles, imprints, and distributed lines are available at special quantity discounts for bulk purchases for sales promotions, premiums, fund-raising, educational, or institutional use. Special book excerpts or customized printings can also be created to fit specific needs. For details, write or phone the office of the Kensington sales manager: Kensington Publishing Corp., 119 West 40th Street, New York, NY 10018, attn: Sales Department; phone 1-800-221-2647.

This book is a work of fiction. Names, characters, businesses, organizations, places, events, and incidents either are the product of the author's imagination or are used fictitiously. Any resemblance to actual persons, living or dead, events, or locales is entirely coincidental.

PINNACLE BOOKS and the Pinnacle logo are Reg. U.S. Pat. & TM Off.

ISBN-13: 978-0-7860-4252-4
ISBN-10: 0-7860-4252-4

First printing: December 2018

10 9 8 7 6 5 4 3 2 1

Printed in the United States of America

Electronic edition: December 2018

ISBN-13: 978-0-7860-4253-1
ISBN-10: 0-7860-4253-2

This book is dedicated to:

Loren and Frances Washburn

and

Jack and Sue Cress

CHAPTER 1

Washington Dulles International Airport

The skyline around Dulles International Airport changed significantly in 2007, thanks to the construction of a new air traffic control tower that soars 325 feet above the surrounding landscape. With a panoramic view of the entire airport, the air traffic controllers are now able to visually see the runways and taxiways that funnel nearly twenty-two million passengers in and out of the airport every year. With that many people coming and going, Dulles is a busy place, especially for the air traffic controllers responsible for safely organizing the chaos that comes with two thousand daily flights. And if that wasn't enough to cause heartburn, the air traffic controllers must face the reality that the tiniest mistake could lead to a major catastrophe.

But for Adam Baldwin it's just another day at work. He's accustomed to the pressure working as a flight controller inside the tower at Washington Dulles. Nine years on the job, Baldwin has seen a little bit of everything, from aborted takeoffs to emergency landings.

The one thing Baldwin has never witnessed is a passenger jet crash and he has no desire to see one, especially on his watch.

Today Baldwin is working departures on runway 1C. He glances out the window to see how many aircraft are lined up for departure. The airport had a small hiccup earlier that put them behind and now he'll need to play catch-up to get back on schedule. Baldwin does like the unfettered view from the top of the tower, but all that glass also allows the sun in, creating a hotbox the air-conditioning unit is struggling to cool on this hot August day. Glancing up at one of the large video screens hanging from the ceiling, Baldwin checks the scheduled departure times and compares it to the current time. They're fifteen minutes behind, something he'll hear about at the end of his shift, but he can't make the planes fly any faster. He triggers his radio and says, "AirExpress 1423, you are cleared for takeoff. Please contact Potomac departure at 125.05."

Baldwin leans back in his chair and pulls the headset from his head to dry moisture collected in his ear canal. Inside the tower, Baldwin sweats on even the coldest days of the year. The sweating is in direct relation to the extra fifty pounds he's packed on since college and the intensive nature of his job. After swabbing his inner ear with a pinky finger, he repositions his headset and stacks the paper strip for the next departure at the bottom of his flight board. They're still using the paper strips because the last significant computer upgrade for the Federal Aviation Administration's flight systems occurred in 1999. And even then, the software was already outdated. In 2003, the FAA began the process of upgrading the nation's air traffic control system with their NextGen system, but like most government programs, it's years behind schedule and billions of dollars over budget. Installation of the new system did start last year at Dulles, but it's not yet operational, leaving Baldwin and his team with their pencils and paper strips.

Baldwin scans the radar as the last plane to depart makes a right-hand turn. He triggers his radio. "Transjet 1536, Dulles Tower. You are next for departure." He watches as the heavy jet taxis into the center of the runway and holds, waiting for Baldwin to give the all clear. He glances at his departure board and radios another jet to tell them they're clear to taxi. As the planes continue to back up on the runway, the sweat begins to roll down Baldwin's back in waves. He checks the radar to make sure the last departure has cleared the airspace and triggers his radio again, saying, "Transjet 1536, Dulles Tower. You are clear for departure." He follows the plane's progress through the window as the pilot pushes the throttles to the stops and the jet picks up speed. Baldwin slots his next departure and then, without warning, the power in the tower flashes off. Shift supervisor Elise Carleton steps into the center of the room and takes charge. "Where the hell is the generator?" she shouts. "Hold all departures and have all aircraft maintain current positions."

"How the hell are we supposed to do that?" Baldwin shouts, removing his headset. "The radios are down."

Carleton mutters something about how much she loves her job and pulls the microphone away from her lips, snatching up the phone. She punches in an extension and waits for the call to be answered. After several seconds of silence she realizes the phones also aren't working. "Somebody"—she looks around and points at another supervisor—"run downstairs to check on the generator."

The supervisor hurries to the door and begins the long climb down.

There's a roar as Transjet 1536 passes by the tower, zooming toward takeoff speed.

"Who's taking off?" Carleton shouts.

"Transjet 1536," Baldwin says. "They were cleared."

"How the hell are you going to track them, Adam?" Carleton says.

Baldwin stares at his dead headset. "I don't know. I can't radio them to abort."

"Jesus Christ, what a mess," Carleton says.

Seconds later, the generator kicks on but they have to wait for the antiquated systems to reboot. Baldwin snaps on his headset and waits for the radio to power up, his eyes glued to the jet now lumbering down the runway. He hears a beep signaling the radio is up and running and he relaxes a little when the plane lifts off. Baldwin triggers his microphone and says, "Transjet 1536, please contact Potomac departure."

"1536. Roger, Dulles Tower—what the hell? Dulles, we seem to be having engine—damn, dial back the engi—"

Baldwin triggers the radio. "Repeat, Transjet 1536." Baldwin waits for a reply and when it doesn't come, says, "Transjet 1536. What is the problem?" He pumps his right leg, mentally begging the pilot to respond.

Baldwin nearly jumps out of his chair when a massive explosion rattles the building to its core. Every eye in the room is drawn to the end of runway 1C, where a fireball is blooming high into the sky. Baldwin's hands begin to tremble as he triggers his microphone again, saying, "Transjet 1536? Dulles Tower to Transjet 1536, please respond."

He pauses to listen for a response, knowing there won't be one.

CHAPTER 2

Calvert Cliffs Nuclear Power Plant
Lusby, Maryland

Located approximately fifty miles from Washington, D.C., Maryland's only nuclear power plant is perched along the western shore of Chesapeake Bay. Two massive concrete cylinders front a long, three-story building that houses the necessary equipment used to generate electricity. Situated inside this building is the nerve center of the plant—the control room. The walls of the room are lined with muted yellow metal cabinets, reminiscent of the harvest gold appliances that were all the rage back in the '60s and '70s when the plant was constructed. Although ugly, the cabinets do serve a purpose and they're outfitted with more switches and gauges than you'd find in an Apollo spacecraft. Phones, buttons, red lights, green lights—you could spend two days looking and still not see it all. In the center of the room is a U-shaped desk equipped with more phones and an array of computer monitors. Manning the desk is David Roark, the leader of the day shift. Presently, Roark is closely monitoring the incoming voltage levels from the power grid on his computer screen. If the voltages drop to a certain level the two nuclear power generating plants could shut down, one of a dozen or so safety measures designed to protect the surrounding civilian population.

The facility is equipped with backup diesel generators and a pair of emergency generators if those backups fail to start, a scenario that appears unlikely but has happened in the past. Two months ago, the two nuclear reactors shut down due to a weather event and the backups failed to start, as did the emergency generators. Roark and his crew had to scramble to keep the water flowing to the pool where the fuel rods are submerged. But according to the maintenance logs Roark scans every morning, the generators are now up and running and in tip-top shape. Roark will have to see it to believe it.

Both units at the plant are pressurized water reactors, and the fission of uranium heats the water to produce steam that is then used to spin massive turbines, generating electricity. Roark pedals his chair across the floor to check the computer display for turbine speeds. A tall, lean man with a shock of wavy red hair, Roark's most noticeable feature is his oversized Adam's apple. That big ball of cartilage is now bobbing up and down as he dry swallows repeatedly while watching the turbine speeds continuing to ramp up. "What's up with the turbines?" he shouts to his four coworkers.

"Both started speeding up a moment ago," his coworker Charles Lewis says while looking at a video screen at the front of the room. A cascade of alarms begins to sound and the front wall lights up like midnight in Times Square. "David, shut the turbines down!" Lewis shouts.

Roark begins typing the shutdown sequence on his keyboard and looks up to see his monitor frozen. He reaches across the desk and grabs the keyboard of a second computer only to find that one is also unresponsive. "The damn computer is locked up," he shouts. "Try for a manual override."

"Trying manual override," Lewis shouts, pounding his palm on a button that's supposed to cut the power to the turbines. "The manual override won't enga—"

A loud shrieking noise pierces the room, followed closely by two loud explosions. Inside the plant, the turbines, spinning ten times faster than they were designed for, rip apart, launching a wave of shrapnel that rips through the other equipment, including two critical pumps used to transfer water from the bay.

"Pressure's droppin' like a rock on two of the water pumps on unit one," Lewis shouts over the continuing wail of alarms.

"Bypass them," Roark shouts.

"I'm trying. None of the controllers on the bypass valves are responding."

Just when Roark thinks things couldn't get any worse, the control room is plunged into darkness. "Where's my backup generator?" he shouts into the black void.

"Checking," another coworker, Emily Edwards, says.

"Check faster," Roark shouts. The battery-powered emergency lighting kicks on, providing some light, but it's no help for the rapidly failing pumps. He can hear the radio chatter between Edwards and the technicians, but can't distinguish the actual words.

"Emily?" Roark asks.

She holds up a finger and moments later Roark sees her shoulders slump. "Both backups failed to start," Edwards says, "and the emergency generators are offline for maintenance. They're trying to get the generators started."

"They better hurry the hell up," Roark says. "We're about two minutes from disaster."

After a very long two minutes with no word from the techs and the power still off, Roark reluctantly picks up the phone and pushes a preprogrammed button on the console. When the call is answered, he says, "This is shift supervisor David Roark at Calvert Cliffs. The emergency code is 746W3. Please initiate evacuation procedures."

Daily News Website

—BREAKING NEWS—All air travel halted after a series of accidents. More details to follow . . .

CHAPTER 3

FBI Special Agent Hank Goodnight has his feet up on the desk and a keyboard in his lap, his eyes glued to the computer screen as he scrolls through the latest surveillance reports on a suspected hacker. Hank doesn't have a clearly defined role within the agency and his job description has been reduced to two words—*special projects*. He does have a boss, though—Assistant Deputy Director Elaine Mercer—who decides which projects would best fit Hank's unique abilities. The two have been a team for the last eight years and for the last four years they've been working on a joint task force focused on cyber threats. It's a field of investigation that didn't even exist twenty years ago. But that's all changed and now the general public is bombarded by daily news reports about data breaches and stolen identities. Hank's office phone rings and he leans across the desk and glances at the caller ID to see Mercer's name. He picks up.

"My office, now," Mercer says before hanging up.

Hank lowers his feet and stands, lays the keyboard

on the desk, grabs his cell phone, and strolls out of his office. The official name of the agency Hank and Mercer are assigned to is the National Cyber Investigative Joint Task Force (NCIJTF), which occupies two floors of an unassuming building in downtown McLean, Virginia. A multiagency task force, it is run by the FBI and includes members from nineteen other government agencies—Homeland Security, the National Security Agency (NSA), Secret Service, Justice, Energy, State—along with a passel of military people mostly from the intelligence and special investigation units. According to the task force's mission statement, not only do they coordinate, integrate, and share information about cyber attacks, they are also tasked with hunting down the perpetrators. And that's where Hank comes in.

Hank places his palm on the scanner by the elevator and waits for the car to arrive. He dislikes the endless security gauntlet the agency installed when the space was remodeled for the agency's use. He understands the need for security, but it's a little over the top to suit him. He does, however, like the location and that's the reason this building was chosen—it's a short trip to both CIA Headquarters and the National Counterterrorism Center, with the added bonus that Dulles International Airport is just down the road.

The elevator car arrives and Hank climbs aboard. When he arrives on three, the doors open onto a sparsely decorated corridor devoid of any signage. Hank hangs a right and heads down the hall. In this building you're supposed to know where you're going. Of course there aren't many slackers roaming around when you have to run through an onslaught of security measures just to enter the building. Hank supposes the government saved a few bucks by not springing for signs, but he doesn't know that for sure. He sighs as he comes to a stop in front of a plain wooden door and positions his face in front of the iris scanner attached to the wall. Hank did a little research on the scanner and learned that it can detect two hundred unique points of reference on the iris as opposed to a fingerprint, which offers sixty to seventy points of reference. And much like a fingerprint a person's iris is unique. He didn't find anything in the stuff he read about repeated exposure to the damn things, but Hank wonders if he's doing permanent damage to his eyes every time he puts his face up to the scanner.

The computer, satisfied that the person standing in front of the scanner is Hank Goodnight, triggers the door lock and he steps through, the door closing silently behind him. In the center of the large room is a cubicle farm that houses junior personnel who are doing the bidding of those people in the private offices that line the perimeter of the space. A set of double doors on the far side of the room leads to another large workspace with access to some of the fastest computers in the world. Hank bypasses everything and heads for the door tucked into the far corner of the room. This time there's no scanner or security device to please and he pulls open the door and enters a handsomely decorated reception area, complete with leather wing chairs and a comfy leather sofa. Hank moves deeper into the space and waves at the older, silver-haired woman manning the reception desk. "How're you doin', Darla?" he asks.

"I'd be doing better if you'd take me out for a drink, Hank." This is a game Hank and Darla play often. In her late fifties, she's been married thirty-some years and has pictures of her grandchildren lined up across her desk.

"Name the time and the place, Darla. But you might better check in with Big John before we go." Hank has been out of his native state of Oklahoma for years but, despite focused attempts, can't seem to shake the accent.

Darla laughs. "You let me worry about John. I swear he turns into a bigger fuddy-duddy every day." Darla waves a hand in dismissal and glances at her phone console "She's on the phone, Hank. It's been ringing off the hook. Have a seat."

Hank settles into one of the wingback chairs and crosses one long leg over the other. Noticing a smudge on the toe of his ostrich cowboy boots, Hank licks his thumb and rubs the smudge away.

The door to the reception area opens again and a tall, lean brunette enters. Outfitted in distressed jeans, Doc Martens, and a black T-shirt with *COEXIST* printed across the front, she waves at Darla and plops down in the chair opposite Hank. Hank studies her out of the corner of his eye. Her dark brown hair, highlighted by shades of lighter browns, is cut shoulder length and, when she turns to look at Hank, he's instantly mesmerized by the color of her eyes, a Caribbean Sea green. Hank has seen her around the building at a distance, except for that one time, weeks ago, when he was close enough to get a glimpse of her name tag. He says, "Paige Randall, correct?"

Paige gives him the once-over. "Have we met?"

"We have now." Hank leans forward and offers his hand. "Hank Goodnight."

Paige makes a fist and Hank matches her and they fist-bump. She glances at the digital watch on her wrist. "I'm way behind. Are you also waiting to see Assistant Deputy Director Mercer?"

"Yep."

Paige glances at her watch again. "Any idea how long you'll be in there?"

Hank smiles. "Nope."

Darla glances at the phone console on her desk. "She's off the phone. You two can go in now."

Paige glances at Hank. "We're going in together?"

"Appears so." Hank and Paige stand. At six-two, he has about four inches on her and he does the gentlemanly thing and holds the door open for her before following her inside.

Assistant Deputy Director Elaine Mercer glances up from the stack of paperwork on her desk. "You two have met. Good. Have a seat at the conference table, please." Mercer stands, grabs a file, and strides across the office, taking a seat at the head of the table. Fifty-two, Mercer is a wiry, petite woman with shoulder-length salt-and-pepper hair and dark, intelligent eyes. Today, she's wearing navy trousers and a button-up light blue shirt tailored to fit her slim profile.

Mercer, who always appears to be in a hurry, gets right down to business. "Within the last hour there have been two possible cyber attacks. The first involved a passenger jet crash at Dulles. That's bad but the second incident is of greater concern."

"What's worse than a plane crash?" Paige asks, still confused as to why she's there.

"A nuclear disaster. The people manning the Calvert Cliffs nuclear facility are on the verge of losing one of their reactors. I don't want to risk sending a crew to the plant, but I've got people headed to the corporate headquarters of the parent company in Atlanta."

"What makes you think it was a cyber attack?" Hank asks.

"Both of their computer systems crashed after several unusual anomalies. We have unconfirmed reports of other jet crashes and the FAA has grounded all air traffic until we can get a handle on what's happening. I have other people on the way, but I want you two to head for the airport."

"I'm a computer programmer," Paige says. "Not a field agent."

"Today you're both," Mercer says. "It's all hands on deck."

"What are the anomalies?" Hank asks.

"That's what I need you two to find out," Mercer says, turning to look at Hank. "And I need you to put that big brain of yours to work."

CHAPTER 4

McLean

After returning to their offices to grab whatever items they need, Paige and Hank meet in the lobby and head outside. The August heat, mixed with the thick humidity, makes the air feel soupy, and both begin to perspire only seconds after exiting. Wiping the first beads of sweat from his forehead, Hank leads Paige through the parking lot to his car, a black-on-black 2014 Mustang Shelby GT500 Super Snake. He chirps the locks and they pile in. Hank fires the engine and cranks down the air conditioner. The car was a splurge for Hank, who usually keeps a tight rein on his money, a holdover from his childhood, when money was so tight they struggled to eat sometimes.

Paige looks around at the interior. "Boys and their toys. Does this muscle car make you feel like a *real* man?"

Hank smiles. "No, but it is fun as hell to drive." He exits out of the parking lot and gooses the gas, the whir of the supercharger whining as he shifts to second and then third. He glances over to see Paige white-knuckling the armrest and shifts to fourth and eases up on the throttle as he hits the on-ramp to Interstate 66.

"Does she do this kind of thing often?" Paige asks.

"Elaine?"

Paige nods.

"Depends on the situation," Hank says, clicking on the radio and lowering the volume as Jason Aldean sings about fly over states. "But she's not afraid to send an expert into the field with me if it's merited."

Paige glances over. "What's your role?"

"Multifaceted."

"That's obscure as hell. What did she mean when she referred to your big brain? Are you some type of genius or something?"

Hank smiles. "Nope, but I might be a tad smarter than your average bear."

"What the hell does that mean?"

Hank flips on his signal and steers into the fast lane. "Do you think the FAA's air control system has been hacked?"

"Changing the subject, huh?" Paige scowls then says, "To answer your question, Mr. Big Brain, maybe. The software is beyond outdated and probably has more holes than a prairie dog town. But what I don't understand is how that would be responsible for a single jet crash. A midair collision maybe, or a jet is told to take the wrong taxiway and gets slammed by another plane, but that would involve two planes."

"Elaine said it was *a* passenger jet crash, I assume meaning only one plane is involved," Hank says. "I guess we'll find out when we get to the airport. Any ideas about the culprit?"

"Take your pick. Iran, North Korea, Russia, maybe even China. I'd lean toward the first two. Russia and China would be concerned about our response; the other two probably not so much."

"So a nation or state and not a group of bad actors?"

"Yes. Even though the FAA's software is outdated, if that was indeed the target, the hackers would have had to penetrate numerous firewalls to get that deep into their system. That's not easy to do and would probably require enormous resources. And hacking a nuclear power plant is much more difficult. How much do you know about hacking?"

"I'm competent."

Paige shakes her head. "Which means you're probably a freaking expert."

Hank smiles as he slows for traffic. Now within a mile of the airport, they're close enough to see a cloud of black smoke still lingering above the runway. A little ways farther on there's a break in the trees and traffic grinds to a halt as the rubberneckers ahead crane their necks, hoping for a quick peek at someone else's tragedy. While they're stopped Hank takes a moment to study the scene. The terminal building blocks their view of the actual crash site and all Hank can see are the emergency vehicles that are parked haphazardly around the tarmac, their lights flashing.

Paige leans forward in her seat to look out Hank's window. "Can't see much from here. I wonder what type of plane it was."

"No telling," Hank says. "Let's hope it's not a Boeing triple-seven or an Airbus A380. If it was, the death toll will be somewhere north of five hundred."

Paige settles back in her seat. "Even if it was one of those smaller planes, the death toll will still be significant. Can you imagine? All of those people lost in an instant."

Hank glances at Paige. "I hate to be the bearer of bad news, but if this is some type of cyber attack I don't think we're done yet. Not even close."

CHAPTER 5

Upstream from its more famous cousin (Hoover Dam) and one of the nation's most visited national parks (the Grand Canyon), the Glen Canyon Dam towers over the downstream side of the Colorado River. Built between the sandstone cliffs of Glen Canyon, the dam stands over seven hundred feet tall and required nearly five million cubic yards of concrete to construct when work was finished in 1963. The damming of the river created Lake Powell, the second-largest man-made reservoir in the United States. The largest reservoir resides farther downstream—Lake Mead, which was created with the construction of the Hoover Dam.

The control room inside the dam is a sparsely furnished place containing two desks, which are staged in the center of the large, circular room. The walls surrounding the desks contain an amalgamation of buttons, rotary dials, and old analog dial clocks that appear to be original equipment—which they are. There have been upgrades over the years though they've been few and far between. Although the dam contains eight massive hydroelectric turbines that turn twenty-four/seven, the room often contains only a single occupant. That's because, today, after the last major upgrade, most of the dam's operations are controlled off-site via computer in Montrose, Colorado.

Today's lone occupant is twenty-four-year-old Brian Hunter, who is busy refining his résumé. His sole job is to act as the fail-safe—the one person who can operate the ancient levers and dials in case of an emergency. It's a boring task and Hunter, dissatisfied with the job's lack of stimulation, is on the hunt for a more challenging work environment. With a degree in hydrodynamics, he took the job with the U.S. Bureau of Reclamation hoping to explore the West and to help the western states manage their most scarce resource—water. But so far the only things he's explored are the buttons, switches, and levers on the walls of the control room and the local bar scene.

Pen in hand, he scratches out a phrase in the previous employment section of his résumé and leans back in his chair and closes his eyes, deep in thought. He's searching for the right word or combination of words—something other than *monitoring*—he can use to describe his present job duties. Moments later, the correct word is just on the tip of his tongue when an alarm bell begins ringing. His eyes snap open and he lurches to his feet, searching for the source. Lights on the far wall begin sparking to life just as the phone rings. Momentarily flummoxed, he stands transfixed as more bells begin ringing. He stares at the lights, then his eyes dart to the phone as a loud humming sound begins to penetrate the room. Finally, Hunter acts. He grabs the phone and can hear voices shouting in the background as he puts the handset to his ear. "Hello?"

"Brian, this is Dan McCoy in Montrose. You need to do an immediate manual shutdown of the turbines."

Hunter drops the phone and it clinks to the floor as he races to the far wall and begins flipping switches to shut off the turbines, the humming only growing louder. His actions appear to be having little effect and he nearly pisses his pants when there's a tremendous crash that sounds like a freight train plowing into a semi stalled on the tracks. Hunter hurries back to the desk and quickly reels in the phone. His hand is trembling when he puts the phone to his ear and says, "Turbine manual override is . . . is . . . inoperative."

"Screw the turbines," McCoy says. "They're toast. Listen closely, Brian. The spillway gates are stuck open. You have to close them."

"H-h-how?" Hunter asks, his entire body now quavering.

"Hit the emergency release. The gates are heavy enough they might close."

Hunter hurries over to the near wall, stretching the phone cord to the limits. He slams the big red button with the palm of his hand. "I hit the emergency release."

"Goddamn it," McCoy shouts, nearly piercing Hunter's eardrum. "You sure you hit the right button?"

"Yes. Wha . . . wha . . . what's happening, Dan?"

"The damn computers are locked up. We've lost control." McCoy sighs, sending a hiss of static down the line. "Okay, Brian. You need to grab who you can from the turbine room and go manually close the spillway gates."

Hunter steps over to the observation window that looks out over the turbine room, the phone cord nearly strangling him. "Oh God. Oh God. Oh God. There's . . .

there's . . . there's blood . . . everywhere." The phone slips from his grasp and rebounds off the desk just when the lights flash off.

Below, the spillway's four 8-foot-diameter pipes are shooting out water at a rate of 208,000 cubic feet per second, or nearly 94 million gallons of water per *minute*.

Daily News Website

—BREAKING NEWS—Nuclear power plant on verge of meltdown.

Residents around the Calvert Cliffs Nuclear Power Plant in Maryland are being ordered to evacuate. At the moment the cause of the accident is unknown. More details to follow . . .

—BREAKING NEWS—All air travel halted after a series of deadly accidents.

Investigators are scrambling to find the cause for several deadly airline crashes that have occurred across the United States. All commercial flights have been grounded until further notice. More details to follow . . .

CHAPTER 6

Dulles

Hank and Paige finally make it to the turnoff to the terminal only to find the exit blocked by two state troopers, their cars parked diagonally across the asphalt. Hank rolls down the window and holds up his credentials. The closest trooper climbs out of his car and walks over for a look. He glances at the badge and nods at the other trooper to move his car. "Any idea how the crash happened?" he asks Hank.

"Not yet," Hank answers, "but you're probably in for a long day."

"Tell me about it," the trooper says. He steps back and waves Hank forward.

At least with the roads blocked there is no incoming traffic, but that changes the closer they get to the terminal building. Hank weaves the Mustang through an obstacle course of emergency vehicles and pulls in behind a police car parked near the entrance to baggage claim. After killing the engine, he pulls a placard with FBI printed on it from the back pocket of the passenger seat and tosses it onto the dash.

"What now?" Paige asks. "Are we heading out to the tower?"

"No, the airport's servers are in the basement of the terminal building."

"How do you know that?"

Hank shrugs. "Read it in a report, somewhere." Hank's phone dings and he pulls it out of his pocket to see a text from Mercer. "I hate to say I told you so, but I told you so."

"What happened?" Paige asks.

"Appears the hackers hit a dam."

"Which one?"

"Glen Canyon Dam."

"Damage?"

"Plenty. Worst thing is the floodgates are stuck open."

"Jesus. That could spell disaster for those downstream. They couldn't have picked a more dangerous dam to target."

"I think that's what they had in mind." Hank leans forward and opens the glove box, pulling out his holstered Glock 22.

"*You* carry a service weapon?" Paige asks.

"Never leave home without it," Hank answers, climbing out of the car. He pops the trunk and takes a moment to clip the holster on his belt. "There are a couple of FBI Windbreakers in the trunk if you want to grab them."

Paige does and closes the lid. She hands the larger jacket to Hank and slips the other one on.

"Might want to wait to put that on," Hank says.

"Why?" Paige asks. "It'll allow us to move through

the crowds easier." She ducks back inside the car to retrieve her backpack and slings it over her shoulder.

Hank shrugs and heads for the entrance, his jacket
inside out and draped over his arm. Glancing at the
chaos through the windows, Hank takes a deep breath
and steps up to the automatic door, Paige right behind
him. They're barely through the door when people begin
swarming Paige like a pack of hyenas moving in on a
fresh kill. Paige tries to make herself smaller as the
crowd swells, the shouted questions hitting her like a
barrage of bullets. People are jostling for position, stepping on her toes, and grabbing her clothing. Paige slaps
at the hands grabbing her clothes and looks pleadingly
at Hank, who's standing off to the side leaning against
a support column.

Hank raises his brows and tilts his head in an *I told
you* look and allows the melee to continue for a few
more seconds before wading into the crowd. He grabs
Paige by the arm and pulls her free. Once they've created some space, Paige peels off the Windbreaker—in
world record time—and folds it so that none of the let-
tering is visible. "Why didn't you tell me that was
going to happen?"

Hank takes Paige by the elbow and steers her down
the corridor. "If you recall, I suggested you wait to put
on the jacket."

"You could have been more forceful with your suggestion," Paige says, glancing over her shoulder to see
some of the same people following. "I feel like I'm
leading a conga line."

Hank and Paige make their way to the elevator.
Hank debates calling the director of airport security to
intercept the followers, but decides the man has enough
on his plate and Hank doubts anyone will go to the trou-

ble of making the trip downstairs. He and Paige hop on the elevator car when it arrives and take it to the basement. Just as they exit the elevator the lights flash out.

A collective groan can be heard echoing through the terminal upstairs.

"I think things just went from bad to worse," Paige says. "Let's hope the server room is connected to a backup generator."

They remain where they are until the emergency lighting kicks on. When it does, the fixtures are so widely spaced the battery-powered bulbs do little to dispel the darkness. Hank and Paige wait for their eyes to adjust and then proceed. An area not frequented by passengers, the basement is cold both in temperature and feeling. Posters about workplace safety are plastered on the walls, and the dingy linoleum floors are worn through in spots, the walls practically begging for a fresh coat of paint.

"Where's the server room?" Paige asks.

Hank glances at the room numbers tacked over the doors. "Room B203."

"You remember the room number from a report you read ages ago?" Paige asks.

Hank shrugs. A little farther down the corridor, they find the correct room and are glad to see the lights are on and the servers up and running. The steel exterior door is outfitted with a numeric lock and a camera is positioned in the upper-left corner of the wall. Hank knocks and holds his credentials up to the camera.

The door is answered moments later by a man in his midforties, dressed in khaki pants and a blue button-down shirt streaked with sweat. "I'm Daniel Copeland, the IT manager," he says, ushering them into the room.

Hank introduces himself then Paige. "Tough morning?" Hank asks.

"To say the least," Copeland says, leading them deeper inside. The far wall is mostly glass and it looks over a large room jammed with computer equipment.

"Does the rest of the airport have backup generators?" Paige asks.

"Yes and no. There are generators to activate the emergency lighting and a few other security features, but you'd need several generators the size of a semi truck to power the entire terminal building." Copeland leads them into a control room that's currently occupied by three other people. In the center of the room is a large banana-shaped desk bristling with computer monitors, and hanging from the ceiling are more monitors displaying the current status of the computer network. Copeland turns his chair around and plops down, waving at two unoccupied chairs.

"What have you discovered?" Hank asks, pulling up a chair and sitting.

"Not much," Copeland says. "How much do you know about hacking a computer network?"

"Enough, but Paige here is an expert," Hank says.

Copeland turns his gaze on Paige. "Then you know how difficult it is going to be to find out how they entered the network much less find who might be responsible."

Paige nods and takes a seat in the other vacant chair. "What software are you running?"

"Windows Server 2008 R2."

Hank holds up a hand. "Before we get into the technicalities, can we hear the audio recording from the tower at the time of the incident?"

"Of course. The tower lost power shortly before the

accident occurred so we don't have much lead-in on the radio recording." Copeland swivels around to face his workstation.

"That happen very often?" Hank asks.

Copeland glances over his shoulder. "Losing power?"

Hank nods.

"They've recently been doing a lot of construction around the airport, so yeah, it does happen occasionally. The tower is equipped with a generator, but for some reason there was a delay before it started. Do you think that's significant?"

"Won't know until we hear what you have," Hank says. "Let her rip, Daniel."

"This is fifteen seconds before the incident. The first voice is the air traffic controller Adam Baldwin, followed by the captain of Transjet 1536."

"Transjet 1536, please contact Potomac departure."

"1536. Roger, Dulles Tower—what the hell? Dulles, we seem to be having engine—damn, dial back the engi—"

"Transjet 1536, what's the problem?"

There's a pause on the tape and then: "Transjet 1536? Dulles Tower to Transjet1536, please respond."

"That's it," Copeland says, swiveling his chair around.

Paige asks him to play it again and he does. After the second playback, Paige asks, "Any word on the flight recorders inside the plane?"

"No. Once it cools down a bit, I assume the NTSB will recover those."

"What type of aircraft was Transjet flying?" Hank asks.

"A 737-800," Copeland replies.

"How many 737s do you reckon are currently in service, Daniel?" Hank asks.

"What are you thinking, Hank?" Paige asks, tucking her hair behind her left ear.

Hank holds up a hand, waiting for Copeland's response.

"Gosh, I don't know," Copeland says, pausing to think. "There are several variants of the 737, but I would think, globally, the total number has to be in the thousands."

"'Bout what I thought," Hank says, standing. "I don't know if your flight control system has been hacked or not, but I don't think it had anything to do with the crash."

"What do you mean?" Copeland asks, a bewildered expression on his face.

"Most of today's aircraft offer some form of Wi-Fi and my bet is they hacked the aircraft's computer systems," Hank says. "And if that's the case we've got major problems."

CHAPTER 7

Lusby

The local golf club in north Lusby is located four miles south of Calvert Cliffs Nuclear Power Plant. Surrounded by a blue-collar neighborhood, the course attracts the barbers and hairdressers on Monday and the retired the rest of the week. The greens and fairways aren't manicured, but they are playable. If you're thinking Augusta National, this isn't it. Not even close. But to Roger Rinsky and his three pals who play there three times a week, it might as well be. And at ten bucks a round—including cart—it's affordable.

Playing for five dollars a hole, Rinsky and his playing partner, Harvey Moretti, are heading to the sixth tee down twenty-five bucks each. Yes, they'd heard the sirens a while ago, but when Rinsky's losing there's no stopping him. He squeals the tires when he slams on the golf cart's brakes at the sixth tee. Rinsky climbs out, yanks his driver from his bag, and stalks up to the tee box. A tall and thin man when he was younger, Rinsky's fondness for beer has finally caught up to him at the age of seventy-two. A round, firm potbelly protrudes from his midsection, and his friends—when Rinsky is in a good mood—will often tease him about the sex of the baby. But today is not the day for teasing Rinsky.

After the other twosome tees off, Rinsky plunges his tee into the ground and places his ball. He's in the middle of his second practice swing when the sirens sound again.

"Rog, maybe we should head to the clubhouse and find out what's going on," his partner, Moretti, suggests.

"Screw that," Rinsky replies. He steps behind the ball and works on picking a target farther down the fairway, waiting for the sirens to end. When they do, he steps forward, lines up his driver, shuffles his feet, and takes a huge, angry swing at the ball. His shot slices right and ends up in the trees. "Fuck!"

After Moretti hits his tee ball down the middle of the fairway, Rinsky stomps back to the cart and slams his driver into his bag. He slides behind the wheel, pops the top on a fresh beer, and guzzles half of it before hitting the gas. After driving through the trees for a few minutes, Rinsky spots his ball and mutters another string of curse words. The ball has come to rest behind a large oak tree, giving Rinsky no shot. He climbs out, grabs a club, and looks around to see if his two competitors are watching. They aren't, so Rinsky uses the nose of his golf shoe to nudge the ball out from behind the tree. He steps back to plot his next shot when the sirens sound again.

"Roger, that's the third time the sirens have gone off. We need to find out what's going on," Moretti pleads.

Rinsky steps to the back of the cart and takes a club from his bag. "Harvey, quit being a pussy. They're probably running some kind of fuckin' drill."

Moretti shifts uncomfortably in his seat. "But what if it's not?"

Rinsky points his club in the direction of the nuke plant. "Do you see anything wrong? Hell no. If there's a problem, don't you think you'd see steam, or smoke, or something?"

"There doesn't have to be visible evidence for them to be having problems, Roger."

"Yeah, well, until I see *any* evidence they're having trouble, I'm going to keep playing." Rinsky settles over the ball, takes a big backswing, and knocks the ball all the way across the fairway and into another grouping of trees. "Fuck!" He slams his club into the ground and turns, marching back to the cart. He takes the wheel and stomps on the gas pedal, driving over to Moretti's ball.

"I'll give you the twenty-five bucks, Roger," Moretti says.

"Screw you, Harvey. It's not the damn money and you know it. Hit your ball."

Moretti steps out, selects a 5-iron from his bag, and hits his ball onto the green before climbing back in the cart. "Jeez, Rog, it's not like we're playing the U.S. Open."

"I don't care." Rinsky zips over to the trees that swallowed his ball and finds it sitting on the edge of the fairway. "I must be living right." He steps out, selects a club, and swings, the ball dribbling onto the front edge of the green. "Ha. A par putt."

"From about sixty feet," Moretti says.

"Still a par putt, assh—"

His words are clipped when the sirens start up again. Rinsky drives up to the elevated green and scowls when he sees the other two players within six feet of the pin for a birdie. Balls are marked and the green repaired as Rinsky looks over his long par putt. He kneels down behind his ball to study the undulations of the green. The other three are huddled together, looking at the power plant to the north. Rinsky picks a line, takes a couple of practice swings, and addresses the ball. In the middle of his backswing there's a deafening explosion that shakes the ground beneath Rinsky's feet. He looks up to see the other three running for the carts then turns his head a few degrees to the left and drops his putter. The nearest concrete cylinder housing one of the nuclear reactors has been obliterated. The steam, smoke, and debris shooting high into the sky are picked up by the wind, pushing the cloud of radiation toward the golf course.

Rinsky runs for his cart. The major problem is that they're now at the farthest point from the clubhouse. The foursome is three hundred yards from the clubhouse when the cloud of ionized radiation particles sweeps over them.

CHAPTER 8

Dulles

Once clear of the terminal's basement, Hank's phone starts dinging like a slot machine hitting the jackpot. Surprised that he has a cell signal with the power out at the airport, he fishes his phone out of his pocket and sees over a dozen text messages and six missed calls—the calls all from Mercer.

"Somebody's looking for you," Paige says.

"Mercer," Hank says, holding his thumb on the home button to unlock the screen.

"I'm going to hit the little girl's room while you call her back," Paige says.

Hank nods, scrolling through his text messages. Two are from his grandmother wanting to know what's going on, the others from fellow agents looking for information. Hank types out a quick reply to his grandmother: **Call you shortly, Nana** and then punches Mercer's number and she answers on the first ring.

"Where in the hell have you been, Hank?"

"The basement of the terminal buildin'. No cell service. What's happened?"

"We've had reports of nearly a dozen more aircraft crashes and they were all landing after the grounding order was issued," Mercer says.

"All 737s?" Hank asks.

"Hold on," Mercer says. She comes back on the line a moment later. "Yes. How did you know?"

"The jet here was a 737 and, in the tower audio recording of the incident, the pilot's last words were something about engine speeds. My guess is they've somehow hacked the airplane's thrust management system. How, I don't know, but all these planes now offer Wi–Fi so that might be it. That's not to say they haven't infiltrated the FAA flight systems, too, but they'd have to have a lot of things break their way to create this much havoc."

Paige returns from the restroom and Hank says, "Hold on, Elaine." He covers the phone's microphone, saying, "More jet crashes all over the place. All 737s."

The blood drains from Paige's face. "How many?"

Hank shrugs. "More than a few. See what you can find out on your phone."

"I will. How widespread is the power outage?"

Hank takes his finger off the phone's microphone. "Elaine, how widespread is the power outage?"

"So far it's confined to the D.C. and Dulles areas, but I don't know for how long," Mercer says.

Hank passes the info on to Paige and says to Mercer, "That's strange."

"Why?" Mercer asks.

"Because there are basically just three power grids that cover the entire nation: the Eastern Interconnect, Texas, and the West Coast."

"Meaning, if they've infiltrated the D.C. power grid

they're also embedded in the Eastern Interconnect?" Mercer asks.

"Yes," Hank replies. "And I'd be surprised if they haven't hacked the other systems, too. That might be act two of this horror show. Are you picking up any chatter about the attacks?"

"Chatter about the incidents but nothing about, or from, the culprits," Elaine says. "We're liaising with the CIA and the NSA and even with all their resources we've failed to find a single shred of usable intelligence on who might be responsible."

"We're still only about three hours into this mess. Someone will start blabbin'. Human nature," Hank says. "Think Paige and I can get into one of the power companies to get a look at their software?"

"Probably not without a court order. They're all private companies and they're competitive as hell. I'll make a call to the secretary of energy to see if she can pull some strings."

"We're burnin' daylight, Elaine. Might be better to bypass all the bureaucratic bullshit and talk to the man that holds all the strings. Have him declare a national emergency or whatever he needs to do so we can get a look at some of this software."

"I'll talk to the director, Hank, and see if he wants to approach the president," Mercer says. "I'll also call the Chicago field office and have them send agents out to the 737's manufacturer. I doubt they'll be forthcoming, but all we can do is try."

"Maybe we could offer to limit their liability in exchange for cooperation. By the time the liability lawyers get through with them they'll be lucky to still have a company. Or better yet, start pullin' some of their Defense Department contracts. We need to drop the hammer on some folks."

"I'm on it, Hank. What are you and Paige going to do?" Mercer asks.

"We're goin' to do a little explorin'." Hank disconnects the call and looks at Paige, who is using her phone to watch footage from one of the air crashes. "How are your hackin' skills, Paige?"

Paige looks up from the screen. "Let's just say I'm better than your average bear."

Hank smiles. "Good."

CHAPTER 9

En route to Miami

The Hammond family is flying from drizzly Portland, Oregon, to sunny Miami for their first family vacation in five years. The children, ten-year-old Chloe and seven-year-old Camille, had lobbied hard for a trip to Orlando and its numerous theme parks, but had eventually come around to the idea of a seven-night cruise to the western Caribbean. The deciding factor: a chance to swim with the dolphins, an encounter that's going to cost their father, Martin, about five hundred bucks. And that's just for the three-hour shore excursion. The entire trip has put a major dent in the Hammond family bank account, but his wife, Lilly, insisted that they were building lifetime memories with their children.

Martin, stuck sitting next to Camille, is trying to keep her occupied with a coloring book. He switches crayons and begins coloring SpongeBob red.

"No, Daddy," Camille says, grabbing his hand. "He's s'posed to be yellow."

Martin puts the crayon on the tray table and squirms in his seat, trying to find a comfortable position. Something hard to do for a man who is six-four and weighs well north of two hundred and fifty pounds. Martin silently curses the makers of the 737 as he kicks his carry-on bag around beneath the seat in front of him, trying to stretch out his legs. He and his daughter had already colored five pages in Camille's coloring book and the plane can't get on the ground fast enough for Martin. He pulls out his phone. "How about you listen to some music on my phone?"

Camille shakes her head. "Your music sucks."

"I downloaded some movies to my iPad," Martin offers.

"Uh-uh. I want to color with you."

Martin sighs and glances across the aisle at Lilly and Chloe. Both have earbuds in, their seats reclined. He waves at his wife to get her attention. When she looks over, he pantomimes trading places, and his wife smiles and shakes her head. A few choice curse words zing around Martin's brain as he shifts around in his seat, again. He accidentally bumps Camille's elbow, creating a big yellow smear across the page of her coloring book.

"Daddy! Look what you made me do."

Martin sighs. "I'm sorry, honey. Why don't we start on a new page?" He grabs the red crayon in anticipation then spots a female flight attendant collecting garbage and waves her over.

She steps down the aisle. "Yes, sir?"

"How much longer until we land?"

The flight attendant glances at Camille and her coloring book then at the crayon in Martin's hand. She smiles and puts a hand on his shoulder. "We should be on the ground in about thirty minutes." With a wistful look at Camille, she says, "Enjoy them while you can. They grow up so quickly."

"I know. How about I pick up the trash and you color?" Martin asks.

The flight attendant laughs. "I'd take you up on it if I could. My baby girl is off to college this fall." She gives Martin a pat on the back and continues down the aisle.

Martin spends a moment studying his daughter. She's a redhead like her mother. The tip of her tongue is sticking out between her lips as she concentrates on her coloring. She glances up. "Daddy, you can color Squidward."

Martin smiles. "Okay. He's red, isn't he?"

"No, Daddy," Camille says, giggling. "That's Mr. Krabs. Squidward is turq . . . turq . . ."

"Turquoise?"

"That's it, Daddy." She digs through her box of crayons and hands the correct color to her father. Martin and Camille color until the flight attendant returns to instruct them to close the tray table and lift their seat backs.

Inside the cockpit, the pilot and copilot were informed about the possible breach of the aircraft's computer systems early in the flight, but at 35,000 feet, there's not a hell of a lot they can do about it. Now only three miles from touchdown, the copilot says, "Looks like we're going to make it."

"We're not on the ground yet," the pilot replies. "Flaps, thirty-five degrees."

"Flaps, thirty-five degrees," the copilot repeats as he shifts the flap selector to the required setting.

Two miles from touchdown, the plane's engines begin to decelerate. The pilot grips the wheel and shouts for the copilot to add more thrust.

Passengers inside the cabin scream when the plane suddenly loses altitude. Martin wraps an arm around Camille and reaches across the aisle for Chloe's hand. Camille is crying and Martin is praying when the plane slams into the ground, bursting into flames.

CHAPTER 10

Dulles

Hank chirps the locks and pops the trunk and he and Paige dump their Windbreakers into the back before climbing into the Shelby. "Back to the office?" Hank pulls his pistol and puts it back in the glove box.

"Hell, no. If we're going to be hacking, we're sure not going to do it at the office."

"Okay. Where?"

"My place."

"Okay. Which way am I going?" Hank asks.

"Head toward Tysons Corner mall and I'll direct you from there."

"Sounds like a plan." Hank threads his way through more emergency vehicles and heads for the airport exit. He digs his phone out of his pocket, pulls up his contact list, and touches his grandmother's picture before putting the phone to his ear. "Hi, Nana," Hank says when the call is answered. "Yes, I'm okay. Promise."

As his phone conversation continues, Paige takes a moment to eyeball her new partner. Hank has a headful of raven black hair and, looking at his face in profile, his broad nose has a slight bump right in the center. His high cheekbones pair well with his deep-set, dark eyes and, mixed with his olive complexion, it's difficult for Paige to determine his origins. Hank glances over to catch Paige staring and she can feel her cheeks warm.

"Yes, Nana, I will," Hank says into the phone. "One last thing, you might want to have Jerry pull the generator out of the barn and get her gassed up. Talk to you soon." Hank kills the call and drops his phone into a cup holder.

"Your grandmother?" Paige asks.

"Yes. My paternal grandmother, Ida Goodnight."

"I take it you two are close."

"We are. She's seventy-five and still going strong."

"Where does she live?"

"She lives on a hundred and sixty acres just outside of Ada, Oklahoma. Heard of it?"

"Can't say that I have. I know where Oklahoma City and Tulsa are, but Ada, not so much. Is that where you grew up?"

Hank nods. "Yep, lived there until I was seventeen and went off to college. It's about eighty miles southeast of Oklahoma City. The last time I checked the population was 17,143. Could have swelled some since then, though. The town's calling card is that it's the seat of government for the Chickasaw Nation."

Paige snaps her fingers. "That's it. So you're Native American?"

Hank nods. "I've got a good dose of Indian blood running through my veins. My grandmother, on the other hand, is full-blood Chickasaw." Hank flips on his blinker and moves into the right lane. "What exit do I need to take?"

"International Drive. My condo is just off the highway."

"Which building?"

"One Westpark."

Hank whistles. "Pretty rich digs."

"Have you been there?"

"Yep, dated a gal that lived there. Her condo was much nicer than she turned out to be."

Paige chuckles. "Not a good relationship?"

"You could say that," Hank replies.

"Goodnight is not a name you hear often."

"My grandmother married one of the Goodnight clan from out in the Texas Panhandle. I guess that makes Charlie Goodnight one of my great-great-somethin's."

"And who was Charlie Goodnight?"

Hank glances at Paige, his brows raised. "Western history not your thing? Charlie Goodnight was a big cattle rancher who developed the Goodnight-Lovin' cattle trail to drive longhorns north to the railheads. You can Google him if you'd like to brush up a little on your history."

Paige shows Hank her middle finger as he exits off the highway. At the stoplight, he makes a left on Westpark Drive then another left and pulls into the condo's visitor lot. A high-rise, the nineteen-story tower dwarfs the surrounding buildings. Hank finds a vacant parking place, pulls in, and kills the engine. Reaching across Paige, he pops the glove box and grabs his pistol.

"We're going upstairs to my condo. How dangerous could that be?"

"I'd rather have it handy and not need it, than to need it and not have it." Hank shrugs. "Could be somethin' passed down by my Native American ancestors."

They climb out of the Mustang and Hank holsters his weapon and grabs his backpack from the backseat before following Paige into the lobby, a handsomely decorated space that would be at home in any five-star hotel. The low-slung furniture is grouped into seating areas to encourage conversation and the walls are paneled in mahogany, stained a honey brown color. Hank eyes the furniture and the custom-made light fixtures, wondering if he could afford just one of the wall sconces. He nods to the doorman as he follows Paige down the hall to the elevators. Paige punches the button and the car closest to them opens. They board and Paige swipes a card key before touching the uppermost button.

"Well, hell," Hank says. "Here I thought maybe you could eke out a one-bedroom, maybe. But no, it has to be the fuckin' penthouse?"

Paige laughs as the elevator ascends toward the nineteenth floor. "I did some video game programming for a couple of buddies in college for a percentage of the profits. They sold the company three years ago for something like five hundred million dollars. I got lucky."

"Why the hell are you slavin' away at the FBI, when you could be island-hoppin' through the Caribbean?"

"That's boring. I like catching bad guys." The doors open onto Paige's condo, a wide-open space with floor-to-ceiling windows that look out over the Virginia landscape.

"Damn," Hank says, scanning the interior space. The living room and kitchen are one open space with a vaulted ceiling soaring high overhead. "It's gorgeous."

"Thank you." Paige puts her messenger bag on the entry table and Hank follows her deeper into the condo. "Would you like something to drink?"

"I'm good for now." Hank steps over to the windows to take in the view. "How many bedrooms?"

"Three. I converted one of them into a home office."

Hank turns away from the view. "Let's put it to use."

Paige leads Hank down the hall and into her office. Six computer towers are lined up on a credenza positioned along the far wall and six large video monitors sit atop a sleek steel-and-glass desk the size of most conference room tables. Paige steps behind the desk, waving to the two rolling chairs fronting her workspace. "Have a seat."

Hank sits and sinks into the soft leather of a chair that probably cost more than he makes in a month. He shakes his head as he pulls out his laptop. He places his computer on the desk, asks Paige for the Wi-Fi password, and logs in.

"Where do we start?" Paige asks.

"The aircraft manufacturer might be a tough nut to crack. Let's start with the power companies."

CHAPTER 11

Lees Ferry Campground
Marble Canyon, Arizona

The thirteen-mile stretch of the Colorado River that runs from Glen Canyon Dam to the Lees Ferry Campground provides some of the best trout fishing in the country. The cold, clear water is a consistent 50 degrees Fahrenheit year-round, making it a perfect breeding ground for one of the largest wild trout populations in the western half of the nation. Ranging in size from one to five pounds, the population of mostly rainbow trout along this stretch of the river number in the thousands per mile and many are awaiting the arrival of that wily fisherman with the perfect bait.

Two of those trying their luck today are best friends Tommy Thompson and Dale Schaefer. Retired from Fire Station 16 on the South Side of Chicago, the two friends have talked about this fly-fishing trip for the better part of twenty years. Though it was planned numerous times, their efforts to make the trip were often thwarted by work, family issues, or financial difficulties. Two months ago, they said screw it and booked the trip. Now they're on day two of their scheduled five-day trip. Yesterday, both caught their limit (four) and they're hoping for more of the same today.

"What fly are you using?" Dale asks as they huddle on the bank, preparing to wade out into the stream.

"Same one I used yesterday, the orange midge." Tommy makes a couple of practice casts, waiting for Dale to tie on his lure. Both were disappointed to discover they weren't going to have the river all to themselves. The campground is filled to the gills, and people of all shapes and sizes line the river, casting for the elusive rainbow trout. "You about ready?"

"Just about." Dale finishes tying on the fly and sticks a box of extra flies in the bib pocket of his waders. "I'm going to head upstream a bit and fish those riffles. You fishin' the deep hole you fished yesterday?"

"I think so. Hot as it is, they might be in the deeper water."

"Be careful. That current is a lot faster than it looks," Dale says.

"That coming from the man who worked on the water rescue team. I'll be careful, Mom."

Dale laughs and it echoes around the canyon. This stretch of the Colorado River is walled in on both sides by part of the original Glen Canyon and the ragged cliffs soar nearly a thousand feet overhead. The upper part of Glen Canyon is now underwater, flooded with the completion of the Glen Canyon Dam, thus creating Lake Powell. And it wasn't done without protest. Many along the river want the dam removed so that the Colorado River will return to a more natural flow, helping to reduce the sediment that builds up along the bottom, choking off some of the native wetlands. Dale

doesn't care one way or another as long as there are
trout to catch. He walks upstream a hundred yards and
ventures out into the water.

Though the waders are insulated, he can feel a chill
as the cold water swirls around his calves. The spot
where he really wants to be is occupied by a man and a
young boy who looks to be about ten years old, so Dale
drifts toward the middle of the river where the water is
waist-deep and begins casting. He glances over his
shoulder to check on Tommy and finds him midstream,
casting into a deep pool that hugs the far bank.

Dale has been fly-fishing exactly twice in his life—
including day one of this trip—and it's not long before
his line becomes a snarled mess. Muttering a string of
curse words, he strips the line from the reel and slowly
reels it back in, using his left hand to apply some tension to the line. Once he has everything squared away,
he begins casting again.

"Wrist firm, up, out, and follow through," he mutters,
mimicking the instructions from a fly-fishing YouTube
video he had watched endlessly before the trip. It's not
long before he's in a rhythm, landing the fly in the exact
spot he wants and letting it drift, hoping a trout will
charge to the surface and swallow his lure. Dale is so
focused on his technique that he's unaware the current
is growing swifter and the water level is rising. Slowly,
he realizes he's exerting greater effort just to remain
upright. He stops casting and looks around. The water
is now chest-deep and a tiny tingle of apprehension begins to nibble at the edges of his brain. He turns to look
for Tommy and spots his friend floundering in the middle of the stream. "Tommy," he shouts, "are you okay?"

"No," Tommy shouts, struggling to maintain his
balance. "Waders are full of water."

"Can you make it to shore?"

"I'm trying."

Before Dale can decide what to do about his friend, the man fishing with the young boy screams, "Ethan!"

Dale whips his head around to see the young boy drifting downstream, his arms churning. After twenty years of training, Dale's instincts kick in. He drops his rod and reel and lunges through the water, racing to grab the boy. The water level continues to rise, eventually filling Dale's waders with ice-cold water. He turns to find the boy and spots him drifting farther away. He shouts to Tommy, "Grab the boy," as he slips the suspenders over his shoulders, allowing the current to pull the waders free. Now unencumbered, Dale starts swimming, his stroke powerful and efficient. He swims toward the middle of the stream where the current is faster, hoping to shoot past the boy so he can grab him farther downstream. Screams echo around the canyon as others are swept away in the swift current.

Tommy is struggling mightily and is still a long way from shore. "Strip your waders," Dale shouts, now a hundred feet from his friend. Both had slipped since retirement—too much easy living and too many beers—and Dale can see Tommy fighting to catch his breath. He glances to his right. The boy is twenty yards ahead, but still afloat, his arms pinwheeling.

A sudden dilemma hits Dale like a slap to the face—save his friend or save the boy?

Dale focuses on controlling his breathing while his mind flips through scenarios he'd either been involved in or had trained for while part of the water rescue team. Now twenty feet from Tommy and closing fast, Dale is out of time. He takes two, huge, lunging strokes, snags Tommy by the shirt, and aims for the boy, dragging

Tommy along with his left hand. "Hang on, Tommy, I'm going for the boy."

Screaming continues to echo off the walls of the canyon, yet lurking underneath that noise, Dale can just make out a low sound that sounds a lot like a locomotive rumbling down the tracks. He glances over his shoulder, but doesn't see anything. He turns his focus back to the boy, who is still about ten yards away. Dale can't seem to make up any ground stroking one-handed and, to make matters worse, his right shoulder feels like someone is stabbing him with a hot poker. He glances toward the shore, praying someone will step in to help. Instead, he sees people running toward the road that leads out of the campground.

With a sinking feeling Dale looks back upriver and his heart nearly seizes: A wall of water and debris is jetting around the bend of the narrow canyon only three hundred yards upstream. He turns and swims for the boy, burning through his last reserves of energy as he churns his feet and stabs at the water, pulling with everything ounce of power he has left. He and Tommy are fifteen feet from the boy when the enormous wave engulfs them, pinning them to the bottom of the river and pummeling their bodies with debris.

CHAPTER 12

Paul and Irene Betkowski have been agonizing over this decision for weeks. Paul lost his job in automobile manufacturing last year when the parent company opened a new plant in Mexico. Irene lost her job two years ago when the auto parts manufacturer she worked for downsized. Fearing the companies would find some way to shirk their pension liabilities, their financial advisor, son Paul Junior, convinced both parents to take a lump-sum pension payment upon termination. Their son's advice proved golden when both companies filed for bankruptcy months later. But now, after locking their money up in a one-year certificate of deposit that paid a paltry 1 percent, Paul and Irene are struggling to find other investment options.

Paul and Irene sold their house last year for half of what it was worth ten years ago and are now renting an apartment in a small retirement community in St. Clair Shores. With the home sale proceeds added to their nest egg, Paul and Irene are sitting on $473,546. The figure represents every dime they could scrape together, excluding the ten grand they keep in their checking account for living expenses. Paul, sixty-seven, and Irene, sixty-five, have been resistant to putting their money in the stock market despite their son's assurances the money will be safe.

Now, sitting at the kitchen table, Paul is eyeing the computer screen displaying their current balance in an account he had opened with one of the large national discount brokerages. He shifts his gaze to Irene sitting across the table. "What do you think, hon?"

"I don't know, Paul. That's every dime we have to our name."

"Know how much we made on the CD last year? Four thousand measly fucking dollars. Hell, that doesn't even cover what we lost to inflation."

"Maybe we should call Paulie."

"Paulie's the one who suggested we put it in the market. And according to that guy that's worth a gazillion dollars out in Nebraska, we could maybe earn ten percent just by investing into one of those index funds."

Irene throws up her hands. "What the hell do you know about index funds, Paul?"

"I know they pay a good return. What do you want to do? Put the money under the damn mattress?"

Irene hangs her head. "I don't *know*, Paul. We lose this we're going to the poorhouse."

"We're not going to lose it. Jesus Christ, millions of people are in the stock market."

"At our age?"

"Hell, yes. It's the only way to make any money."

They sit in silence for a few moments, the only sound the whirring of the cooling fan on the old computer. Irene gets up, toddles into the kitchen, and returns with a glass of water. "Have you been tracking this fund's returns?"

"Every day. But I've got my eye on a couple of funds. Don't want to put all our eggs in one basket."

"How are they performing?"

"They're up. Hell, the whole market's up."

Irene throws her hands up again. "Whatever."

"Oh hell, no," Paul says sharply, "We're not playing that game. This has to be a mutual decision or I'd never hear the end of it."

Irene thinks it over for another minute. "You sure you don't want to put it back in a CD?"

"Hell, no. Didn't I just tell you what we made on it last year?" Paul peers over the computer screen, giving Irene a hard look.

"And you're sure the money'll be safe?"

"Hell, Irene, there ain't no guarantees in life. But millions of people do it every day with nary a second thought."

Irene takes a sip of water, thinking. "Does that mean you'll take me on that cruise?"

"When we start making some money, I'll take you on two cruises."

"Oh, stop, Paul. I'll be lucky to get you on one. Is the money already in the brokerage account?"

"Yep. Put in there last week. A few computer clicks and we can start packing for that cruise."

"And I can buy a couple of new outfits for the trip?"

Without even a second thought, Paul says, "Sure."

"Okay, Paul. Invest the money."

Unfortunately for the Betkowskis, Paul picks the exact wrong day, the exact wrong hour, the exact wrong minute to make the trade.

He finishes placing the buy order and switches over to his e-mail account to check for a confirmation. He waits. And waits. And waits some more. "That's strange."

"What?" Irene asks, a hint of panic in her voice.

"Paulie says the trades happen almost as quick as the order is placed, but I haven't gotten a confirmation e-mail yet."

The Betkowskis' wait stretches on for several minutes with Paul clicking the *get new mail* button every few seconds.

"Anything?" Irene asks.

"Don't you think I'd say somethin' if I'd gotten an e-mail?"

"Don't be short with me, Paul. Check the account."

Paul mouses the cursor over to the web page, logs out, and logs back in. "The money's not there. They must be in the process of making the trade."

"Paul, you better call them."

Paul scrolls down the page to the CONTACT US section and pulls out his cell phone, a knot forming in the pit of his stomach. He punches in the number and navigates through about ten menu options before being placed on hold.

Irene sits, wringing her hands. "I told you, Paul."

Paul glances over. "Don't start, Irene. I'm sure it's just a mix-up."

After five minutes on hold, a live human comes on the line and Paul explains the situation. He can hear the woman clicking away on a keyboard. She returns to the line, and Paul hears only the first part of her explanation before the phone slips from his hand.

"What is it, Paul?"

All the blood has drained from Paul's face when he looks up at his wife. "They have no record of the account."

Daily News Website

—BREAKING NEWS—Power out in nation's capital. More details to follow . . .

—BREAKING NEWS—Problems at Colorado River dam.

Details are sketchy at the moment but early reports suggest the floodgates at the Glen Canyon Dam are stuck in the open position. Experts are concerned about the effects on Glen Canyon's downstream cousin, Hoover Dam. More details to follow . . .

—BREAKING NEWS—Nuclear power plant on verge of meltdown. Emergency workers widen evacuation zone. Experts fear the worst. Potentially worst U.S. nuclear power plant disaster since 1979's Three Mile Island.

Residents around the Calvert Cliffs Nuclear Power Plant in Maryland are being ordered to evacuate as a cloud of deadly radiation continues to escape from one of the plant's reactors. At the moment the cause is unknown. As the story continues to unfold there is some speculation that the water pumps used to pump cool water to the reactor may have failed. More details to follow . . .

—BREAKING NEWS—All air travel halted after a series of deadly accidents. Possible engine failure may be to blame. Death toll could be staggering, according to one airline executive.

Investigators are scrambling to find the cause for several deadly airline crashes that have occurred across the United States. All flights have been grounded until further notice. Preliminary reports say all the aircraft involved are Boeing 737s. Early indications suggest it may have something to do with the planes' engines. We have not yet confirmed the precise number of crashes or the number of people involved. One airline executive says the death toll could be staggering. More details to follow . . .

CHAPTER 13

"Find anything?" Hank asks.

"Still looking," Paige replies. Each had chosen a power company in the D.C. area and it had taken Paige five minutes to break through the firewall and enter the company's computer network. Hank was a little slower. It took him nine minutes to hack the system of another power provider. Both are using software developed by a consortium of programmers at the FBI and NSA.

"I'm perusing some company e-mails to see if they had any indications or warning signs they were being hacked," Paige says, "but I'm not seeing anything. Someone wasn't doing their job because the hackers would have been lurking around on their network for months if not years."

"You're probably right. I wonder what else they've hacked. So far, they've targeted a dam, a flight control computer, and a portion of the power grid. The big question is, what's next?"

Paige continues scrolling through the company's e-mails. She stops and clicks on one from earlier in the day. It's an e-mail from a field engineer to the CEO of the company. She quickly reads through the contents. "Want some more bad news, Hank?"

"I think that's all we're going to be hearing for a while. Shoot."

"According to one of this company's engineers, portions of the D.C. power grid could be off-line for months. Not days. Months. Apparently the hackers did a number on some of the larger transformers."

"I'm not surprised. Does it say what method the hackers used? Was it an attack on the SCADA system or maybe a specific programmable logic controller?" Hank takes a moment to text Mercer the new information about the D.C. power grid.

"It's not mentioned in this e-mail. I'd vote for answer *C*—all the above. If the bad guys *have* been on these networks for months, there's no predicting how many vulnerabilities they've discovered. As for method of insertion, someone probably inserted an infected flash drive into their computer. Those damn things should be outlawed." Paige looks up. "You know that's probably how the NSA injected the Stuxnet worm into the Iranian computers that controlled the centrifuges, right?"

"Yeah. Unfortunately it got out in the wild. I wouldn't be surprised to find we're being attacked by some variant of Stuxnet as we speak." Hank launches a piece of software that will allow him to drill down deeper into the system he's working on. "I'm assuming the malware is a rootkit?"

"That's how I'd do it," Paige says, clicking out of the e-mail program. "I'm headed that way, myself. Look at all the device drivers and search for any anomalies. If the hackers are really good they've inserted it into the kernel where the most trusted functions of the operating system work. That's where I would put it. And putting it there makes it damn difficult, if not impossible, to find."

"But wouldn't that cause catastrophic system crashes?"

"If these were average hackers, yeah. But these people aren't your average hackers. Look, the software only does what it's told. It can't think for itself. So if you insert a piece of malware, in this case a rootkit, and it has an exploit to allow it the ability to modify the system's software, then the system is none the wiser. It doesn't know the malware isn't supposed to be there."

"Then how do we find it?"

"It's going to take time, Hank. And even then we may not find it. The source code for these power companies contains millions of lines of code. Even if the malware did cause a system crash, I can promise you these hackers created a back door that would allow them to come and go at will. If a system crash occurred they'd wait for it to be repaired then manipulate their software to keep it from happening in the future."

Hank's phone dings and he lights the screen to see a text from Mercer. "I told you the bad news is going to keep coming."

"What now?"

"Trouble at the stock exchanges. Surprise, surprise, they're seeing some computer irregularities. Mercer's thinking about sending us to Manhattan." Hank leans back in his chair and rubs his eyes. "The hackers have to know this country will respond with overwhelming force, either through cyber or conventional means."

Paige glances up. "We have to find them, first. And that's no guarantee."

CHAPTER 14

Somewhere near Boston, Massachusetts

Working out of an undisclosed location somewhere near Boston, twenty-five-year-old Hassan Ansari pulls up the list of malware exploits on his laptop screen. Pakistani in origin, Ansari is now a second-year Ph.D. student at one of Boston's major universities. As he scrolls down the list, he checks the scheduled times for the payload releases, making sure all is in order. And he's not working alone. Inside the building with him are five other people—four of whom are also Ph.D. candidates at various universities around Boston. All are of similar age and all are foreigners. All are extremely intelligent and all have elite-level computer skills. And, most important, all have a reason for being there.

The sixth man is a recent arrival. Ansari first met him six months ago. That's also the same time that he met the other four members of the group. The man identified himself as Basir Nazeri, but offered little else. Suspicious, Ansari put his computer skills to work, but after a frustrating two days, found no information on the man calling himself Basir Nazeri. He found a few Basir Nazeris, none with any approximation to this man's age or likeness. Whoever he is, he's now the guy ramrodding this show and Ansari doesn't really give a damn. After all, each and every one has the same objective.

Each member of the group was recruited to the universities with offers of lavish scholarships from entities with marginal backgrounds. In return for the scholarships, each man was asked to devote some time to work on a new piece of software that they would receive upon admission to graduate school. The only stipulation was that the work was to be done in private and had to be done on a computer with no connections to the Internet. Those people granting the scholarships did attach one caveat—if it were discovered that someone wasn't adhering to the rules, the scholarship would be rescinded and that person would be deported immediately back to their native country.

The new unit is a diverse group. In addition to Ansari, there is one other man from Pakistan, two men from Afghanistan, one man from Yemen, and one man from Somalia. Different countries, yes, but they all hail from the same region of the world. And it's an area of the world that has endured countless wars and atrocities that stretch back generations. And all five have faced hardship, some more than others.

At first, Ansari had difficulty finding a common denominator—the one thing that compelled each man to agree to take on this mission. The five men are not wrapped up in religious zealotry nor are they hiding behind a veil of racism or fanaticism. In fact, four members of the team espouse no religious views whatsoever. Only one, Ansari, claims to be a Muslim, but by no means is he devout. But to be clear—these aren't spoiled rich kids searching for a cause, nor are they attempting to start a movement or launch a crusade.

But they do have one very specific reason for their involvement.

In the country on F-1 student visas, the five, busy planning their dissertations, had little interest in that piece of software until Nazeri arrived six months ago. The timeline accelerated when the new administration in the White House announced that all student visas would be rescinded by the end of the year for students from a list of specific countries. The home countries of all five team members made the list and now it's the software taking center stage, while the dissertations are on hold.

Looking at the software now, Ansari finds it remarkable to see the changes each man made while working on it individually over the years. Some were changes Ansari had never thought to make, but many of the men made similar progress and, with some fine-tuning, the software program was meshed together. Now, months later, they have created a well-honed computer program unlike anything else in existence.

Ansari knew they were creating a piece of malware, but he had no idea how it was going to be used until Nazeri arrived. The mystery man appeared with a grab bag of goodies that must have taken years to assemble. How he amassed them and from whom has not been disclosed. But with his collection of zero-day exploits, back doors, and precisely mapped networks, the group now has administrator-level access to a broad array of military and civilian networks, as evidenced by the morning's events. Ansari has worries, though. They haven't been told the length of the mission nor have they been briefed about the exit strategy—all red flags in Ansari's book. But it is what it is.

In addition to his bag of software goodies, Nazeri also arrived with some computer hardware that can't be found in any store. The modest, unobtrusive building Nazeri leased came wired with fiber-optic lines and, judging from some of the trash left behind, the building once housed some type of tech start-up outfit that was either bought out or went belly-up. After pairing the fiber-optic lines with some of the hardware Nazeri brought, the team created a max secure wireless network with speeds nearing eighty gigabits per second, allowing them to operate in real time. To mitigate communication lag, a satellite uplink was installed on the roof of the building and was connected directly to the network.

Some members of the team are more exuberant than others, but none appear giddy about the hell they're unleashing, other than Nazeri. The reason for their stoicism is tied to their memories of the past—the explosions, the mangled bodies, the stench of death that lives on in their nightmares. The events they remember were often brushed away as collateral damage, but for these five who lost close loved ones to U.S. drone strikes, it's all too real.

And their reason for participating is one as old as time itself—revenge.

CHAPTER 15

McLean

After an hour of digging, Hank and Paige are no closer to finding out how the hackers infiltrated the power companies. "Think we should try the aircraft manufacturer?" Paige asks, rocking her head from side to side to loosen the kink in her neck.

"We're already inside here. I say we keep diggin'."

"I'm open to suggestions, Hank, because I'm not seeing anything. It could be the malware self-destructed after the exploit ran."

"You would think there'd still be some residual pieces driftin' around."

"You'll only find them by looking at the code line by line. If we had six months we might find something. But we don't. I say we take Elaine up on her offer to send us to Manhattan. Once the power's out, it's out. It's a whole different ballgame with the financial markets. They could manipulate those for months and really put the screws to us."

Hank picks up his cell phone. "Pack a bag. I'll call Elaine."

"What do I need to pack?"

Hank shrugs. "Clothes?"

"Just casual stuff?"

"I don't think we'll be attendin' any charity galas while we're there."

Paige scowls. "Smartass. How many days should I plan on?"

"You're the computer expert. You tell me how long it's going to take to find these people."

"Okay, maybe a week, then?"

Hank looks around at all the computer hardware, the expensive desk, and the expensive chairs. "I think you can afford to buy some clothes if it stretches longer."

Paige holds up a finger. "Good point. Give me twenty minutes." Paige disappears down the hall while Hank calls Mercer.

She picks up on the third ring and Hank says, "I guess we're headin' to the Big Apple. You have a jet for us?"

"You haven't made any progress?" Mercer asks, disappointment in her voice.

"No. We've been diggin' around, but Paige thinks the malware might have erased itself. That's why we need to scoot up to NYC. Any luck with the aircraft manufacturer?"

"We're waiting on the judge to give his ruling on the court order request."

"How long's that gonna take?"

Elaine sighs. "Who knows? You hear the latest?"

"No, we've been workin'. What happened?"

"Power's out in Chicago."

"I hate to say this, Elaine, but the entire country may be without power before this is all over. You get my text about the e-mail from the field engineer?"

"I did. Is it really going to take months to restore power?"

"That's what the e-mail said. And it was an internal e-mail marked *highly confidential*."

"I don't need any more information about the e-mail, Hank, or how you got it."

"Understood," Hank says. "So do you have a jet for us?"

"I will. Dulles is still a mess and Reagan National is without power. Where are you now?"

"Paige's place here in McLean."

"I'll have the plane meet you at Davison Army Airfield. Can you be there in an hour?"

"Depends on how long it takes Paige to pack."

"On second thought, let me check the jet's flight schedule."

Hank can hear Mercer tapping on the computer keys. She's back on the line a moment later. "Actually, you have forty-five minutes to make the plane. It has to be back in D.C. for an evening flight."

"We'll make it. I'll call you when we're wheels up." Hank kills the call, loads up his laptop, and exits the office, walking down the hall to the bedroom. Paige is staring at a couple of outfits laid out on the king-sized bed. "Scratch twenty minutes. You've got ten if we're goin' to make the plane."

"Ten? How am I supposed to pack in ten minutes?"

"Easy. You grab some clothes and stuff them in the suitcase."

"Don't we have to stop at your place for you to pack?"

"Nope. Keep a bag in the trunk."

"Of course you do. Okay, go drink a beer or something while I finish up. Looking over my shoulder is not helping matters."

Hank meanders down the hall to the main living space, bypassing the fridge and heading, instead, for the pictures lined up on the fireplace mantel. There are pictures of Paige with an older couple Hank assumes are her parents. A couple of pictures show Paige with a younger version of herself—a sister, Hank reasons. Other photos depict Paige with a group of friends, another with her parents and sister taken on a beach somewhere, but there are no pictures of Paige paired off with a significant other. "Huh," Hank mutters.

Eleven minutes later, Paige appears from her bedroom, rolling a large Louis Vuitton suitcase with a matching shoulder bag slung over her left arm. "You nosing around?"

"Just lookin'. How old is your sister?"

"Thirty-one, three years younger than me." Paige runs her fingers through her dark hair. "I'm ready when you are."

Hank steps over and rolls Paige's suitcase toward the elevator. "What's your sister's name?"

"Peyton. She lives in Chicago with her husband, Eric."

"You better call her and give her a heads-up."

Paige cocks her head. "Why?"

"Power's out in Chicago."

"Damn. Do you think they destroyed the transformers like they did in D.C.?"

Hank punches the elevator button. "Most likely. You need to tell her to get out of the city."

"And go where?"

"Anyplace will be better than a big metropolitan area. Where do your parents live?"

"It's just my mom now. They moved to Champaign after my dad retired."

"Then that's where Peyton and Eric need to go. And they need to leave today."

"They don't have a car."

"Probably wouldn't be able to get around, anyway. They'll have to rely on the oldest form of transportation."

"What's that? Walking? It's a hundred and thirty miles."

The elevator arrives and they load on. "'Bout the only choice they have. I promise you, they don't want to be in Chicago after a few days without power."

"I'll call her when I get off the elevator. You really think things will go downhill that fast?"

"Absolutely. It's probably already started."

"Will her cell phone be able to receive a call?"

"Depends on where she is. Some cell towers have battery backups that'll last a few hours, maybe a day or two, dependin' on the network activity."

The elevator stops at the lobby and the doors open. Paige digs out her cell phone and starts trying to call her sister as Hank leads them to the Mustang. He pops the trunk and nearly gets a hernia lifting and stowing Paige's overstuffed suitcase before taking the wheel. After firing the massive engine, he backs out and squeals the tires pulling out of the lot.

Paige wags her phone. "The call won't go through."

"Keep trying. That's all you can do," Hank says, steering up the on-ramp to Interstate 495.

CHAPTER 16

Chicago

The Chicago advertising agency Brown, Wright, Zuker, Tomlinson & Qualls occupies two floors of the high-rise office building One Magnificent Mile, located at the northern end of Michigan Avenue. The seventeenth floor is one large, open creative space for those who design the advertising campaigns while the eighteenth floor plays host to the executives and media buyers responsible for implementing those campaigns. One of those working on seventeen is thirty-one-year-old Peyton Lynch, a graphic artist. Peyton lights her cell phone screen, again, and groans—still no service. The Chicago skies are filled with angry clouds and it looks as if they could unleash a torrent at any moment. After they sat around looking at one another in near darkness for a good hour and a half, a bigwig came down from upstairs and cut everyone loose. But before Peyton can make any decisions about the rest of her day she needs to get in touch with her husband, Eric, who works in commercial lending at a large bank at the other end of Michigan Avenue.

With no landlines or cell service, Peyton would

spend good money right at this minute to send a message via a homing pigeon if one were available. Otherwise she's going to have to slog all the way down the street to see if Eric's free so they can start their walk home, which is in the exact opposite direction. For a long time they rented a small apartment in a building overlooking the lake, but at $2,500 a month for less than eight hundred square feet, the walls began to close in on them and they grew tired of throwing their money away every month. So after looking for months and being outbid on three of their dream properties, they finally settled on a two-bed, one-bath condo on the third floor of a three-story brownstone in Lakeview West. Given their thoughts of starting a family soon, the area's excellent schools sealed the deal. The problem, though, is rather than walk to work as they did for years they are now dependent on the city's subway system for transportation. Not a problem on a normal day but cut the electrical umbilical cord and it becomes a major issue.

Peyton checks her phone again with the same result—no service. Her mind clicks through possible scenarios. The easiest thing for her to do is stay where she is and wait for Eric to come, but if he works until six or six-thirty p.m. as he usually does, they'll be traipsing across Chicago in the dark. That wouldn't normally be a problem because the streetlights, the lights from the businesses, and the lighted residences would provide enough illumination for them to find their way. But the thought of traveling home in absolute darkness sends a shiver of fear down Peyton's spine. "Flashlights," Peyton mutters. "We'll need flashlights."

She stands and works her way across the room to

the "goody" closet. The ad agency receives a large assortment of products from companies wanting to hawk their wares. Some products get returned, but a majority of them either go home with the employees or end up in the goody closet, a large walk-in space filled with floor-to-ceiling bookshelves. Peyton opens the door, flicks on the light switch out of habit, and stares into the darkness. "Shoot," she says, the frustration over the loss of electricity already building. She walks back to her desk, grabs her cell phone, and returns, launching the flashlight app.

Wading into the closet, she's trying to recall if a recent ad campaign had featured batteries, or a camping scene, or maybe a night shoot. Inside, boxes line the shelves, each labeled with the name of the client. Peyton scans the boxes, hoping a name pops out. In the first row, there's a box for a soup company, a tire maker, a toy company, a national lingerie retailer—Peyton is currently wearing one of the bras from that campaign—an auto manufacturer, and a movie promotion. She stops and goes back, recalling a scene from one of the agency's earlier shoots. Pulling out the box for the auto manufacturer, she places it on the floor. The ad was a promotion for a new and improved version of one of their popular trucks. Peyton remembers one scene that was shot at night, something about difficult terrain that only their new truck could surmount—who knew?—and she's hoping to find a flashlight left over from the shoot. Pawing through the box, she smiles when she finds a flashlight at the bottom. She holds it aloft like it's a first-place trophy and clicks the button only to be disappointed—the batteries are dead. Standing, she starts rummaging through the boxes again.

Thirty minutes later, Peyton exits the closet with

two flashlights and a brand-spanking-new box of AA batteries. There's no one left in the office to celebrate her find, so Peyton returns to her original problem: What to do? She carries the flashlights and batteries over to her desk and dumps them in a reusable shopping bag she keeps handy in case she needs to lug something home. She stands there, hand to her chin, thinking. Eric's boss is an asshole of the highest order and the odds of Eric being released early fall somewhere between zero and 10 percent. Paige sits and wipes the perspiration from her forehead. It's suddenly stuffy inside with no air-conditioning. A bolt of lightning strikes nearby, lighting the room with a brief, blinding flash. That's followed a second later by a loud rumble of thunder that Peyton swears rattles the glass. She holds up a finger. "Umbrellas," she says to the empty room. She stands and heads back to the goody closet.

When she's halfway across the room, her cell phone rings and she thumbs the answer button without looking at the screen. "Eric, are you headed this way?"

"It's me, sis," her sister, Paige, says. "You need to get out of Chic—"

"Paige, you're breaking up. What did you say? Paige?" She hears the beeps that signal the call has ended and immediately redials her sister. All she hears is silence and she glances at her phone screen—NO SERVICE.

CHAPTER 17

"**D**amn it, the call dropped," Paige says, looking at her phone screen. She hits redial and puts the phone to her ear.

"How much did she hear?" Hank asks.

"No idea. Now the call won't go through."

"If there's only a few towers in the area with battery backup, it'll be a crapshoot for you to get another call through."

"Can't the FCC force them to install a backup power source on all the cell towers?"

"They tried back in May of 2007 after Hurricane Katrina and again in June of 2012. The industry took them to court to block it."

"Why in the hell would they do that?"

"Why do you think?"

"Money?"

"Yep," Hank says. "It's the number one driver for most business decisions. Forget what's best for the customer."

"But don't they lose money when their systems are not up and running?"

"How are they goin' to lose money? You're locked into a plan that charges a certain amount every month. Hell, they'd probably save money if the power went out every once in a while. Ever see a credit to your bill for lost service?"

"No."

"There you go." Hank glances in the rearview mirror to check traffic before pulling into the right lane. "What's our game plan when we get to New York?"

Paige glances out the side window and tries her sister again, ending up with the same result. "Call still won't go through." She turns to look at Hank. "I think we have to approach it the same way we did with the power companies."

"Why? Because that worked so well for us?"

Paige shoots him an angry glare. "Let's hear your plan."

Glancing ahead, Hank spots the exit for Fort Belvoir and pulls over into the far-right lane. He glances at Paige. "Do you think the malware really self-destructed, or is it still there and we just didn't find it?"

"I ran every software program in my toolkit and didn't find squat."

"Maybe we need a better toolkit."

"Hell, Hank, techies at both the FBI and the NSA worked on the software, including me."

"Let me reframe the issue. If you invite someone you've just met over for dinner are you going to serve them the very best wine in your cellar or will you pick, say, a midrange selection, savin' the best for yourself and your dearest friends?"

Paige thinks about the question for a moment. "You think the NSA is holding out."

"Of course they are. You don't give your best toys

away to someone that Uncle Sam says you have to play nice with. And I guaran-damn-tee you the folks at USCYBERCOM have software toolkits that'll put ours to shame."

"How do we get access to them?"

"Good question. I'm goin' to make a few calls after we board the jet."

"Do you have contacts at both of those places?"

"I've worked ops with other agencies. So yes, I have developed some contacts over the years."

"Do you have the type of relationships that they'd be willing to part with some of their most prized hacking tools?"

"Don't know. Won't cost anythin' to ask." They ride in silence for the next mile or so.

"I'm going off subject for a moment," Paige says. "Are you like a numbers savant or something? Was that what Elaine meant when she referenced your"—Paige makes air quotes with her fingers—" 'big brain'?"

"Is it really botherin' you?" Hank asks, slowing the Mustang for the gummed-up traffic ahead.

"No, not bothering me, I'm just curious. For instance, we were talking about making the government force the cell companies to provide backup power and you said May something and then another date."

"May 2007 and June 2012. That's not difficult to remember," Hank says.

"What about when you were talking about your hometown? You mentioned the population in precise numbers. Most people would say 'around such and such.'"

"The population of Ada is 17,143. Or it was the last time I checked."

Paige turns in her seat, now facing Hank. "Do you have hyper . . . hyper . . ."

"Hyperthymesia?"

"Yeah, that's it. Well?"

"No. People with hyperthymesia have an autobiographical memory of events that happened in their past."

"If not that, what? Did you get knocked in the head when you were little and it scrambled your brain?"

Hank sighs. "My brain is not scrambled, just wired a little differently. I'm not big on labels. I guess the closest thing—though some suggest it's hogwash—is that I have an eidetic memory."

"Like photographic memory?"

Hank nods.

"You remember everything?"

"Mostly," Hank says.

"Can you recall everything you've seen? Like scrolling back through a roll of film?" Paige asks, her voice incredulous.

Traffic is crawling. Hank checks the side mirror and waits for a gap before easing the Shelby into the exit lane.

"Am I being too nosy?" Paige asks.

"If I said *yes*, would you stop with the questions?"

Paige thinks for a moment. "Probably not."

Hank sighs—again. "Yes, I can recall most everythin' I've seen and heard."

"Wow. Everything you've heard, too? Wow, wow, wow." Paige lets Hank's revelation run around her brain for a few minutes. "Whew, man. That might drive me crazy."

Hank glances over. "It can if you let it. My grandmother taught me how to compartmentalize it."

"She has it, too?"

"Yes. Apparently this thing skips generations. Neither of my parents had it, but my grandmother's grandfather had it—or at least he did accordin' to the oral histories passed down through the tribe."

"You can't forget anything even if you wanted?"

Hank shakes his head. "With effort I can wall it off in my mind."

"Can you then remove the memory, or image, or sound from behind the wall if needed?"

"Yes." Hank exits off the highway and picks up a feeder road that'll take them to the airstrip.

"Amazing. You said you remember most everything. What can't you recall?"

"I don't remember."

Paige laughs as Hank pulls up to the guardhouse and holds up his badge. The man, dressed in army fatigues with corporal stripes on his left sleeve, grabs a clipboard and writes down the badge number and Hank's name. The guard points his pen at Paige and asks, "Her name?"

Hank relays the name and the corporal writes it down before waving them through. Hank follows the feeder road to the parking lot and slots the Mustang into a spot under a large oak tree.

"Aren't you worried about birds crapping on your precious car?"

"They do a good job of keepin' the birds away from here." Hank reaches over, pops the glove box, and grabs his pistol.

"What type of trouble are you expecting at the stock exchange?"

Hank pushes open his door. "It's not the stock exchange I'm worried about."

"Are you worried they're going to cut the power to Manhattan?"

He and Paige pile out of the car and Hank seats the

pistol in his holster. "If I was, I'm a little less worried now.

The roar of jet engines reverberates off the nearby hangars and Hank looks up to see their jet, a Gulfstream IV, touching down. He pops the trunk, busts a gut unloading Paige's suitcase, and grabs his bag and a couple of FBI Windbreakers. He puts his on and tosses the other to Paige, pausing before closing the lid, wondering if he should grab more firepower. He has another go bag in the trunk that contains another pistol, an M16, a Browning 12-gauge shotgun, and extra ammo for each weapon. He unzips the bag and reaches in, grabbing two extra clips for the Glock 22. He closes the trunk and drops the extra clips into the pocket of his Windbreaker as they head for the jet.

Hank feels a tad bit guilty when Paige struggles to get her suitcase up the steps, but she packed it, and the way Hank looks at it, it's a teaching moment. He follows her up the stairs and the pilot ducks his head out of the cockpit. He and Hank fist-bump. "How you doin', Donnie?" Hank asks.

"I'm good, Hank. New York's kinda tame for you, isn't it?"

"I bet I can still find my way into some trouble. Who's playin' second fiddle?"

"Theresa Slayton." Donnie steps aside and Hank sticks his head into the cockpit.

"How you doin', Theresa?"

"I'd be better if you'd take me on a date, Hank," Slayton says.

Hank chuckles. "Maybe one of these days our schedules will sync up. You keep a close eye on Donnie, here. He's gettin' mighty old to be drivin' these jet planes." Hank ducks back out.

Donnie laughs. "I'm not that damn old, Hank. We're ready when you are."

"Let's roll." Hank walks deeper into the cabin and takes a seat across the aisle from Paige.

Paige nods toward the cockpit. "Buddies of yours?"

"It's always good to make friends with the people who hold your life in their hands."

CHAPTER 18

Chicago

Peyton Lynch pulls her polo shirt away from her torso, hoping the faint movement of air through the lobby will dry the sweat dripping down her back. Descending seventeen flights of stairs in a building with no air-conditioning is a hot, tiring task, especially carrying an overloaded bag and two large umbrellas. And to make matters worse, Peyton picked today to wear that new pencil skirt and matching heels she bought on sale last week. She prowled through the goody closet looking for something else to wear, but the advertisers usually ship their smallest garments that are designed to fit the emaciated models and Peyton didn't have a prayer of finding anything that would fit. Even with that she thought about shucking the skirt several times on the way down, and probably would have if she hadn't decided to wear a thong to avoid the dreaded panty lines. Letting go of her shirt, she walks over to the window. The storms have moved on but they left behind a thick layer of humidity that seeps through every crack and crevice of the large lobby. Peyton still hasn't heard from Eric, so her plan is to camp out here until he arrives.

Standing next to the wall of glass, Peyton pulls out her phone to see if a change in location has improved her chances for getting a signal. It hasn't. The result is the same—no service. During her trek down, she'd mulled over the few snippets of conversation from the phone call with her sister. The words that Peyton dwelled on, and continues to dwell on, are when Paige said "get out." *Did she mean out of the building? Out of the condo? Or is it something more sinister, like get out of the city?* Peyton wonders about that for a moment. Paige works for the FBI and usually knows the scoop on what's going on. *Could the power be out for an extended period of time?*

Peyton grabs her bag and the umbrellas and drifts over to one of the sitting areas positioned around the lobby. She kicks off her shoes and gently massages her arches, keeping her hands well away from the nasty blisters that have bubbled up on both heels. She brushes her dark hair out of her eyes and scans the lobby. Usually bustling with people, the lobby now feels like a tomb. The two guards who usually man the large circular desk in the center of the room are either attending to some crisis or they've abandoned their post. The ground-floor space inside the building was carved up to attract high-end retail, but most spaces remain vacant and have been that way since Peyton took the job at Brown, Wright, Zuker, Tomlinson & Qualls five years ago. The only successful venture is the small sundry store and newsstand that occupies the northeastern corner of the building.

"Shoot," Peyton mumbles, thinking about the cramped

store and its small selection of food items. That's one thing she hasn't thought about. And if Paige's intent is for them to get out of the city, it's going to be a major problem because the pantry back at the condo is about as bare as the grocery store shelves before a blizzard.

Peyton digs through her overstuffed bag, pulls out her purse, and unzips it to retrieve her wallet. Knowing the probabilities are low for her having more than twenty dollars cash, she opens her wallet to check. Yep, a twenty-dollar bill is it. She has half a dozen credit cards, but they're just worthless pieces of plastic at the moment. *Unless* . . .

Peyton stands, throws her bag over her shoulder, and looks down at her shoes then at the blisters on her heels. "Screw it," she mutters. She leans over, crams the umbrellas and shoes under the chair, and pads across the lobby and down the corridor to the small store. She sticks her head through the door. "Ranjeet?"

"Yes?" a voice calls from the rear of the store. A moment later, Ranjeet appears. "Peyton. Come in." At five-six, Ranjeet might weigh 110 pounds if he stood in the rain for an hour before stepping on the scales. Immigrants from India, he and his family took over the lease and purchased the contents of the store about five years ago. He and Peyton became fast friends after only her second visit.

"Are you open?" Peyton asks, stepping inside.

"For cash customers, always open."

"That's what I want to talk to you about, Ranjeet," Peyton says, crossing her fingers. "I only have twenty bucks cash and I was wondering if you would be willing to take an imprint of my credit card and run it through the system when the power is restored."

Ranjeet thinks it over for a moment. "For you, Peyton, of course." He leads her over to the front counter and hands her a small shopping basket. "You think storms cause power outage?"

"Maybe. I just hope that it comes back on soon." Peyton feels a little guilty, but in reality she doesn't know any more about the situation than Ranjeet does, other than that very ambiguous phone call from Paige. She heads down the aisle with her basket.

Ranjeet doesn't stock a lot of food items, but he does have a can or two of various soups, some Spam and Vienna sausages, and a few tins of canned pasta that Peyton hasn't eaten since she was about six years old. Nevertheless, they go in the basket along with the other items. Peyton wanders up and down the aisles. Most of Ranjeet's inventory consists of grab-and-go items for the building's condo owners. She finds a small section of nutritional supplement items and loads up on granola bars and protein power bars. The rest of the store's inventory is mostly candy, chips, gum, and a rack full of tabloid magazines. Peyton walks to the front and places her basket on the counter.

"No water?" Ranjeet asks. "That is usually first thing to go."

"Damn. I didn't even think about that." That's when the magnitude of the situation hits her. There's not going to be any water, or air-conditioning, or lighting, or any way to use the bathroom for the foreseeable future, if she's interpreting Paige's few words correctly. "Do you have a couple of cases of the small bottles of water?"

"I can spare one, Peyton. I need water for my family, also." Ranjeet turns and grabs a case of water from behind the counter.

"Thank you, Ranjeet. You're a lifesaver."

Ranjeet smiles. He pulls out his calculator and tallies up the items and piles them into Peyton's bag. She passes him her card and he uses a pencil to shade the card's information on a slip of paper.

"You can have my twenty if you want," Peyton offers.

"No, you keep, Peyton. Credit card fine."

Peyton grabs the case of water and balances her bag on top then pauses before picking it up. "Ranjeet, how much water are you saving for your family?"

"Two cases."

Peyton knows there are at least six people in Ranjeet's household and maybe more. "You're going to need a lot more than that."

Ranjeet looks at her with a bewildered expression on his face. "Why?"

"The power may be off for quite a while."

"How long, Peyton?"

"I don't know. But you need to hang on to as much water as you can."

"How much?"

"Let me put it to you this way, Ranjeet—I wouldn't let another bottle of water leave the store."

"Oh my. Okay. Okay. Thank you, Peyton. You be safe."

Peyton leans across the counter and gives Ranjeet a hug. "I will. Same to you and your family." Peyton grabs her items and exits the store.

CHAPTER 19

Davison Army Airfield, Fort Belvoir, Virginia

Now aboard the jet as it taxis toward the runway, Paige makes one more attempt to call her sister, but, as expected, the call won't go through. She types out a quick e-mail to Peyton outlining what she knows about the power situation and hits send. She's hoping that Peyton's phone will eventually ping an active cell tower and the e-mail will automatically download. Options for contacting her sister exhausted, Paige scrolls to her favorites menu, touches her mother's picture, and puts the phone to her ear.

Her mother, Frances, answers on the second ring. "Paige, what in the world is going on? I've tried to call your sister several times after I found out Chicago was without power, but nothing happens."

"I managed to get a call through and talked to Peyton for a few seconds. I tried to tell her to get out of the city."

"Out of the city? Why? Surely they'll have the power back on soon."

Paige glances out the oval window as the jet accelerates down the tarmac. "Listen, Mom, there are a lot of strange things going on. We're dealing with some type of cyber attack and I'm now on a jet headed to New York City, so I don't know how long I'll have a signal. If Peyton manages to make contact, you need to tell her to get out of town as soon as possible. Tell her that she and Eric need to head for your house. The power in Chicago could be out for an extended length of time."

"Oh, my word. How long?"

"I don't know for sure, Mom, but it could be weeks—maybe months."

"Oh my." There's a pause then Frances says, "Should . . . should I drive up to Chicago and pick them up?"

The aircraft shudders slightly as the plane takes flight. "Absolutely not. You stay where you are. Peyton's smart. She'll figure it out."

"But they could be in danger."

"That's why I don't want you driving up there. Eric's resourceful. He can navigate their way out of the city."

"I hope you're right, Paige. And what are you doing? Can't you please just stay home? Why do you have to go to New York?"

"I'm working, Mom. I don't have time for specifics, but New York City might be our best chance to discover who's responsible for these attacks."

As Paige's phone conversation continues, Hank pulls his computer out and places it on his lap. Before raising the screen he takes a moment to study Paige. She'd changed clothes back at her place and gone are the Doc Martens, the jeans, and the T-shirt. Taking their place is a pair of tailored navy slacks, a sleeveless lightweight gray sweater, and a pair of navy peep-toe wedges that show just enough of her toes for Hank to see her nails painted a royal blue. The clothes are a perfect fit and, judging by the quality of the material, he has no doubt they were expensive. He allows his gaze to travel up her body. Paige's shoulder-length, straight, dark hair is blended with auburn highlights and, when she tucks it behind her ear—a habit he noticed quickly— he catches a glimpse of her simple, yet elegant diamond teardrop earrings.

Paige glances up and catches Hank staring. Embarrassed, he looks away, but it's not long before his gaze drifts back to her. With an oval-shaped face, her high arching eyebrows act as a perfect frame for her tantalizing green irises. She's tall and willowy thin, but Hank can see the ropy muscles in her forearms as she grasps the phone. Overall, she's very attractive and Hank wonders, again, about the lack of a significant other in the pictures on her fireplace mantel. Not that it's any of his business, but he is curious.

Paige looks up to catch Hank staring again. She arches her brows in a questioning look and Hank sheepishly lifts the lid on his laptop and hits the power button. Moments later, Paige wraps up her phone conversation and asks, "Do I have something on my face?"

"No," Hank says.

"What is it, then?"

Hank squirms in his seat. "Nothing. I guess I was daydreaming."

"Uh. Most people stare out the window or at something in the middle distance when they're daydreaming. You sure you weren't checking me out?"

Hank's cheeks flush red.

"That's okay. I did some checking out of my own while you were driving."

Hank is suddenly desperate to change the subject. "So your mom hasn't heard from Peyton, either?"

"No. She wanted to drive to Chicago and look for her and Eric."

"I hope you talked her out of it."

"I did. She can't navigate the Chicago traffic on a good day. I can't imagine what traffic is like now that the signal lights aren't working."

"It'll be a mess," Hank says. "But I think traffic problems will soon be way down the list of things to worry about for the Chicago PD."

"How do you know this? Can you see the future, too?"

"No, smartass. I was assigned to one of the agency's Critical Incident Response Groups when Hurricane Sandy hit. Lootin' began before the storm even passed. And it wasn't just the lootin'. You'd be surprised what humans can do to one another in enormously stressful situations."

Paige shudders. "I can only imagine. I just hope Eric and Peyton can get out of the city."

Hank's phone dings. He pulls it out of his pocket and lights the screen to see a text from Mercer. He unlocks the screen and reads through the message and mutters, "Jesus."

"What now?"

"The hackers hit several chemical manufacturers. Somehow they triggered the release of some pretty nasty stuff."

"Anything around Manhattan?"

"Not yet, but it's probably comin'."

Paige sighs. "What makes you think that?"

"They'll be targetin' the most densely populated areas," Hank answers, "hopin' to get the most bang for their buck."

"I just hope there's something left of this country when we do find out who's responsible."

"Stuff like this pisses me off," Hank says. "We've known for years that these chemical plants are vulnerable to either a conventional attack or a cyber attack, and no one's done a damn thing about it."

"Does that surprise you?"

Hank drops the phone on the empty seat next to him. "No. But that doesn't make it any less frustratin'."

"So far we haven't heard about the hackers attacking any of the federal government's networks, but you have to believe they've infiltrated those. And that frightens me way more than these chemical plants."

"What are you thinkin'?" Hank asks.

"What's the one thing that's been proven to be vulnerable by the government accounting office?"

"Some of the military weapons?"

Paige nods. "Yep."

CHAPTER 20

Mudiyah, Abyan Governorate, Yemen

July 14, 2011
TARGET: Al-Qaeda
CONFIRMED KILLED: 50
CIVILIANS KILLED: 30

Eighteen-year-old Jermar Bakal is enjoying his last few days at home before beginning his journey halfway around the world to a place he'd never been before—Boston, Massachusetts. All of the prep work has been completed online and all the financial documents regarding his scholarship have been signed. Jermar is both excited and apprehensive about his prospects. An excellent student, in sixth grade he was plucked from his local school by a ministry of education official and enrolled in a special program through the University of Science and Technology in Sana'a. That was the first time Jermar had ever been away from home and the adjustments in the beginning were difficult. But over time, Jermar flourished, finishing first in his class.

Today, the day is hot, the temps pushing close to 37 degrees Celsius with a light breeze out of the east. That's one thing Jermar is not going to miss—the oppressive, merciless heat. While Jermar is busy packing, his mother is out in the garden picking fresh vegetables for lunch. He steps over to his small desk, searching for his passport. When he doesn't find it he walks across the room and sticks his head out the door to ask his mother. And that's when he hears a peculiar whistling noise. Before Jermar's brain can interpret the sound, the house next door explodes, launching shrapnel in all directions and knocking him to the ground. He scrambles back up, shouting his mother's name. He stumbles through the door and hurries out to the garden.

With smoke and tears stinging his eyes, Jermar careens down the rows of tomatoes and squash and still doesn't find his mother. He cuts across two rows of sweet corn and sinks to his knees near his mother's lifeless body. Sobbing, Jermar cradles his mother's head and, between sobs, begins to mumble the Janazah prayer.

Present day, somewhere near Boston

Now twenty-five years old, Jermar Bakal recalls that fateful day as he pulls up the master list of targets. He's not a heartless man and he wonders about their actions today. But then he thinks about all the innocent lives lost, including his own mother, to American drone strikes and that sharpens his resolve.

Basir Nazeri has forbidden televisions in the building and also confiscated everyone's phone last night, leaving the five students in the dark about the death and destruction they are currently unleashing on America's citizens. And Jermar prefers it that way. He doesn't know how the others feel, but for him he has no desire to witness the horrors of their actions. For him, it's better the victims remain faceless and nameless. Not a strong-willed man, the less he knows the better. In his mind, he likens their activities to those of the faceless drone pilots who rain down death from afar.

"Bakal, why are you hesitating?" Nazeri asks, standing behind him and looking over Jermar's shoulder.

Jermar is surprised that Nazeri snuck up behind him. The man can do that sometimes almost as if he's a ghost. Jermar turns and looks up at Nazeri. "I am not. I'm attempting to find a suitable target."

Nazeri points at the computer screen. "A suitable target is the next one on the list. Get on with it."

Nazeri is always pushing, but this time Jermar pushes back. "Why are you here? We"—Jermar waves at the four other men—"are here for a reason. What is yours?" Jermar surprises himself by the sudden outburst.

"I'm here because I have paid your bills for the last eight years of your miserable, pitiful life." Nazeri glances at those gathered around the conference table. "And that goes for all of you. I now own you." Nazeri turns his penetrating gaze back on Jermar. "Did you think I was doing that out of the goodness of my heart? I was not. Do not ever question my reasons for being here. Is that understood?"

Seething inside, Jermar wants to stand and punch Nazeri in the mouth yet he knows he's no match for the much larger man. Instead, gritting his teeth, he nods.

"Good. I am glad we had an opportunity to get that small piece of business out of the way. Continue on, everyone. As for you, Jermar, select the next target and launch your attack." Nazeri moves back to his position at the head of the table and sits.

A tall, lanky young man, Jermar vows to get even and he begins plotting payback for Nazeri as he pulls up the next target, another chemical plant. After surveying the list of programmable logic controllers at the plant, Jermar launches two of the malware's payloads that will allow him control of the thousands of valves inside the facility.

CHAPTER 21

The WaveFront Water Park, a very popular summer destination for families, is located twenty-five miles south of downtown Seattle and two miles east of New Tacoma, a busy port and industrial complex. With no federal regulations and few local zoning ordinances addressing the siting of chemical facilities, the area around New Tacoma grew with residential neighborhoods and local businesses, such as the WaveFront Water Park. As Washington's only water and theme park, it draws people from all across the state.

Melissa (Missy) Dwyer is one of today's visitors at the seventy-acre wonderland. And she's not alone. Her son, Dylan, conned her into chaperoning a group of twelve-year-old boys for an end-of-summer shebang. And now Missy is trying to corral ten preteens with an overabundance of hormones who can't seem to stop gawking at the girls in their two-piece bikinis. And no wonder, Missy thinks. Some of the swimsuits are little more than dental floss and itty-bitty pieces of fabric. Missy shakes her head and clucks her tongue as another group of teenage girls prances by, their butts hanging out for the entire world to see. She wonders what the parents were thinking when they purchased the swimsuits.

"Mom, I'm hungry," Dylan whines, plopping down on the end of Missy's lounger.

"Go play. We'll eat later."

"But I'm hungry."

Missy is kicking herself for not smuggling in snacks from home, knowing that ten boys could eat through a grocery store and not leave a crumb behind. She sighs, digging through her bag of sunscreen and swim goggles to retrieve the small waterproof case holding her cash. She peels off a five and hands it to Dylan. "Try to find something healthy, please. No funnel cakes and no ice cream." Dylan is paying little attention to his mother, his gaze riveted on two scantily clad girls with long ponytails. "Dylan, did you hear me?"

Once the girls walk out of view, Dylan turns to look at his mother. "Huh?"

"Stop ogling the girls. I said, no sweets. Got it?"

"Sure, Mom," he replies before scampering away.

Missy sighs and opens the *People* magazine she'd carted from home. She's deep into an article on a high-profile divorce between two television stars—the second for her and the third for him—when one of her charges, Liam Grayson, comes running up. One of Missy's least favorites among her son's friends, Liam hovers over her, dripping water onto her magazine.

"Mrs. Dwyer, may I borrow five dollars?"

One of the deals Missy made with the other parents when she agreed to chaperone was that the boys would be responsible for paying for their own food and drink while at the park. But, as usual, Liam didn't bring any money. "What do you need the money for, Liam?"

"I saw Dylan eating an ice cream cone and it really looks good, Mrs. Dwyer."

Something about Liam just irritates the hell out of Missy. It could be that he's Eddie Haskell reincarnated.

Missy mutters a curse word under her breath, angry at Dylan's choice and angry at Liam's parents for not sending money—again.

Missy opens her case and peels off another five, handing it to Liam. "I want you to pay me back."

"Yes, ma'am," Liam says before racing off.

"You're welcome," Missy shouts to his retreating backside. She stands and pushes her lounge chair deeper into the shade. It took a dozen blistered burns during her early years to convince Missy, a redhead, that the sun isn't her friend. She did wear a bathing suit today, though—a tankini—but has yet to venture into the water. And not just because of the sun. Lithe and lean before birthing two kids, Missy is now carrying forty extra pounds on her small frame and she knows it's not a good look for her. Even with visits to the gym and a low-carb diet, the pounds refuse to leave now that they've taken up residence on her thighs and belly. Her husband, Mike, hasn't mentioned the extra weight— bless his soul—but their romps in the hay have tapered off over the last few years. Missy works hard to convince herself it's because they're busy with the kids' activities, both Dylan's and his older sister, Megan's, and not a result of her ballooning weight. She glances up and pauses to watch a well-chiseled older man parade by. She sighs and returns to her magazine.

She's into the meat of the article, finally finding out who cheated on whom, when there's a massive explosion not far from the park. Missy clambers to her feet to see what's going on. In the distance she can see a building engulfed in flames, the dark smoke roiling skyward. As the smoke drifts closer, blown by the coastal breeze, Missy's nostrils flare at the scent of chlorine. She glances around to see if the workers are adding chemicals to the pool, but doesn't see anyone with a bucket of chemicals in hand. People crowd against the fence, many with their cell phones out recording the scene, as the fireball rapidly expands. Missy looks around and notices that people are beginning to cough. She scans the crowd for her son and the other boys under her charge, but the crowd is too dense.

Now the chlorine odor is stronger, and Missy feels the first tendrils of panic inching down her spine. There are ten boys somewhere here that she's responsible for. She has to find them.

Now.

Missy wades into the crowd, elbowing people aside as the chlorine smell intensifies. Her eyes are burning as she scans the crowd, searching desperately for a familiar face. She breaks through an opening near the rim of one of the pools and spots Dylan near the entrance to the lazy river at the outer edge of the park. She waves her arms and shouts his name, but with most of the crowd now coughing, he can't hear her. Missy wades back into the crowd, her eyes now watering. Her sinuses are burning from the chlorine and she pulls her top up to cover her nose and mouth, leaving her belly exposed.

But that's the least of her worries at the moment.

She pushes through a group of young girls, many of them vomiting. In the distance, Missy can hear approaching sirens yet she doesn't know if they're on the way to the fire or on their way to offer medical support here. Her breathing ragged, Missy reaches into her bra, pulls out her cell phone, and unlocks the screen to dial 911. When the call is answered, Missy stops for a moment, trying to catch her breath. She mumbles out the details and disconnects the call, shoving the phone back in her bra. She bends over and puts her hands on her knees, overcome by a sudden wave of nausea.

The chlorine smell is stronger near the ground and she struggles to think why that's important. But she can't put her finger on it with her thoughts laser-focused on Dylan and his friends. She stands, sucks in a lungful of air, and regrets it immediately when her lungs begin to burn like she'd swallowed a flaming torch. She tries three shallow breaths and pushes through the crowd, nearly tripping over an older couple writhing on the ground. Her first instinct is to stop and help them, but her maternal instincts prevail and she sidesteps the two, elbowing her way forward. Finally, she reaches Dylan to find him kneeling and coughing uncontrollably. She does a quick head count of the other boys who are kneeling around her son.

Nine.

"Who's missing?" Missy shouts.

She counts again, this time really looking at the boys' faces. "Liam? Where's Liam?"

Could he still be over by the food court? While her mind spins with possible locations where Liam might be, she's hit with a sudden thought from moments ago. She grabs Dylan by his arms and lifts him to his feet. "All of you, stand up." She pivots from boy to boy, helping them all to their feet. She scans the park then squats so she can look the boys in the eyes. She waits for a momentary break in the coughing. "We have to climb to the top of the water-slide tower." She looks from one boy to another. "Understand?"

Those able to nod, do, and she begins herding them toward the tower.

"Liam?" Dylan asks, his voice raw.

"I'll find him, but I need all of you at the top of the tower first."

Dylan nods and reaches for his mother's hand.

Wading through the crowd like a rugby scrum, they finally reach the water slide that towers over the park. On a normal day, the line of waiting riders would stretch from the top of the tower to the kiddie pool two hundred yards away.

But today is far from normal.

Missy orders the boys to climb and they begin slowly ascending. Missy waits until they reach the top of the tower, then turns and hurries onward, wondering where Liam could be. When she reaches the other side of the kiddie pool area, there's another tremendous explosion that is so large Missy is hit with the pressure wave a second later. It's as if the explosion has sucked all of the oxygen out of the air, and Missy is struggling for the tiniest breath. Stopping, she leans against the wall of the Shake Shack. She does have the presence of mind to glance over her shoulder to make sure the boys on the tower are okay. Her eyes are watering and stinging so severely, all she can see are shapes, but from what she can tell they're still there. Missy pushes off the wall and continues on, desperate to find Liam.

A few moments after the second explosion, the chlorine smell increases tenfold and Missy's seared lungs begin to falter. Staggering forward, she has to grab on to the back of a chair to keep from falling. It feels as if someone has put an ignited blowtorch up her nose and Missy's vision is now so awful it's like looking through a pair of glasses smeared with Vaseline.

Missy staggers forward another few steps and trips over something that sends her crashing to the ground. After several moments spent trying to regain her strength, she rolls over to see what she'd tripped over and discovers it was a person. What little she can see of the colors on the swimsuit triggers something in her brain. Burning through the last of her energy, she pulls herself over to the body. She leans in until she's six inches from the person's face and discovers it's Liam. She tries to reach out to feel for a pulse, but her synapses begin to misfire and she becomes confused. She rolls over on her back, her entire body feeling like it's on fire. All Missy wants now is to die.

And that's exactly what happens a moment later when her throat swells shut, sealing her airway.

CHAPTER 22

Cruising at an altitude of 35,000 feet

Hank doesn't know which government agency actually owns the Gulfstream G550 they're currently cruising in on their way to Manhattan, nor does it really matter. Although he's flown on this aircraft multiple times, this jet, the newest in the fleet, is usually reserved for the bigwigs, like the director of Homeland Security or high-ranking congressional members. As such, the jet has all the trappings of a well-appointed living room, including Wi-Fi, satellite television, a well-stocked galley kitchen and bar, and comfortable, plush leather recliners. Paige and Hank raided the kitchen earlier and scored a couple of fresh sandwiches the crew had brought on board for them. Now sitting on opposite sides of the aisle, they're sharing a bag of kettle-cooked potato chips and sipping diet sodas with CNN on the television, the audio muted.

"I thought you were calling some of your contacts to get us a few new software toys?" Paige says around a mouthful of chips.

Hank grabs a chip from the bag, pops it in his mouth, and chews. "I am. I'm tryin' to decide who'd be best to call." Hank hands the chip bag to Paige and digs out his phone. After pulling up his contacts, he begins scrolling through the list. He knows the person he wants to call at the NSA, but the last time they were together things didn't turn out so well. He scrolls to the name anyway and pauses, debating. "What's the worst that could happen?" he mumbles as he touches the phone number.

The call is answered after four rings. "What?"

"Hey, Natalie. Long time, no talk."

Paige glances up when Hank mentions the name.

"You're not telling me anything I don't know, Hank," Natalie Lambert says, her voice dripping with venom. "What do you want, Hank?"

"Come on, Nat, don't be like that." Natalie is a computer programmer at the NSA.

"How would you feel if *I* didn't show up for a dinner and left *you* sitting at the restaurant?"

"I got called away."

"Yeah, well. They have these devices called telephones, Hank. Have you heard of them?"

"I believe I'm talkin' on one right now," Hank says. He gives Natalie a moment to cool down. He really had tried to call, but trying to get a cell signal on a helicopter is hit or miss.

"You could have at least called the next day to explain."

"I was on assignment. And if you'll recall, I did try to call when I returned but someone wasn't answerin' her phone."

There's a long pause and then Natalie sighs. "Okay, let's start over. Hi, Hank."

"Hi, Natalie."

"Okay, that's better. Now, what do want, Hank?"

"You guys workin' on the hackers?"

"That's all we're working on at the moment, even though we can't do shit until we get access to some of the software."

"C'mon, Natalie, this is me you're talkin' to. If you want access you can get access."

"It's different on this, Hank. The higher-ups are being real squirrelly about it. They want everything done all nice and legal like."

"Huh. What's that indicate to you?"

"I can't say over the phone, but you can figure it out."

Hank thinks about it a moment and the only thing he can think of is that Natalie is suggesting an insider may be involved. "That makes no sense and, frankly, I don't believe it. Most of those people want to steal classified information so they can release it to the world and get their fifteen minutes of fame."

"I don't know, Hank. Something's going on."

"Strange. Hey, we did a little pokin' around in . . ." Hank pauses, trying to frame his statement, knowing the conversation is being recorded "Well, I'll let you guess, but we didn't find much. My partner suggested the malware might have self-destructed."

"Whom are you working with?"

"Paige Randall. Know her?"

"Of course. All of us programmer chicks like to hang out once in a while. Paige knows her way around. Tell her I said hello."

"I will, but back to the reason for my call. We're headed to Manhattan to get a look at some of the stock market software and I was wonderin' if you'd be willin' to share a few of your special software tools."

"Are you going to share that source code with me?"

"Oh, so we're barterin', now? Sure, I'll ask Paige to send you everythin' we get."

"Deal," Natalie says. "What do you need?"

Hank thinks about it a moment. "I guess what we don't already have."

"Put Paige on the phone, Hank."

"She wants to talk to you," Hank says, passing his phone over to Paige. He scowls when the second thing out of Paige's mouth is a deep, hearty laugh. Hank has no doubt Natalie's comment had something to do with him. Paige glances over and smiles. Yep. No doubt. He glances up at the television to see a full-screen graphic: BREAKING NEWS. He digs around in the seat for the remote and cranks up the volume.

The graphic transitions to a dark-haired woman sitting in a studio. "As if this day couldn't get any worse— we're receiving word from our affiliate in Seattle that there are multiple fatalities at a local water park after some type of industrial explosion in the area. In addition to those killed, area hospitals are swamped with people who are reportedly having difficulty breathing. Nothing has been confirmed about the nature of the accident, but eyewitnesses reported smelling chlorine shortly after the explosion. We have crews on the way and will have further details when they become available."

CHAPTER 23

The town of McAlester is famous for one thing: it's the home of the Oklahoma State Penitentiary—the only supermax prison in the state with a death chamber and a long line of prisoners awaiting its use. But there's another facility in the area that deals in death yet remains unknown to most residents outside the McAlester area. In addition to making bombs, the McAlester Army Ammunition Plant is also one of the largest ammunition storage depots in the world. From 7.62-mm rifle rounds to five-thousand-pound bombs, the folks working at the plant can ship, when required, four hundred large containers of ordnance every day. And if that's not enough to get the job done, the manufacturing side builds the GBU-43/B Massive Ordnance Air Blast (MOAB) bomb, or, as it's known by its other moniker, the Mother of All Bombs. The MOAB bomb is the most powerful nonnuclear weapon in America's arsenal. Clocking in at over twenty-one thousand pounds, the bomb's blast yield is equal to eleven tons of TNT, only three tons less than the *atomic* bomb dropped on Hiroshima at the end of WWII. The weapon can be guided to a precise target using GPS and, due to its size, must be deployed via drag chute from a C-130 Hercules aircraft.

Those who live around McAlester are very aware of the facility's existence. It's hard not to be when the personnel that work there detonate bombs on a daily basis, destroying obsolete ordnance. The locals get a kick out of watching a newcomer's reaction when the first bomb of the day blows. The high school principal even swears he's had salespeople try to climb under his desk when it happens. For the local residents, the bomb blasts are part of everyday life and most will tell you they don't even notice them anymore, much like those residents who live near a hospital and claim they no longer hear the sirens.

The employees *not* blowing up bombs at the McAlester facility are busy building them. The workers on the production line inside the large warehouse can build twenty different types of ordnance, everything from missiles to mortar rounds. Today, they're constructing their favorite weapon to build, the MOAB bomb. For Darlene Watkins, it's a strange feeling to be working on a weapon whose only purpose is to kill or maim other human beings. It's something she tries not to think about too often, but she has added incentive to make sure the job is done correctly—her son is currently deployed in Afghanistan. And she's not the only one working at the plant with loved ones serving overseas. When her son's National Guard unit was activated, a good number of people from the McAlester area were pressed into service. Several of the fourteen hundred employees at the facility have sons or daughters, husbands or wives, or brothers or sisters who are now in harm's way. The feeling among most of them is the more bombs they build, the quicker their loved ones can return home.

Today, Darlene, a rail-thin woman in her late fifties with a two-pack-a-day habit, is working at the end of the line in the final assembly area. Her job is to test the bomb's inertial guidance components, a critical job to ensure the bomb arrives at the specified target. She attaches two leads to the guidance system's testing terminals and steps over to her old, yellowed computer. *The damn thing is nearly as old as I am*, Darlene thinks as she clicks the grimy mouse, initiating a program that will activate the sensors and gyroscopes to diagnose the components for errors or defective parts. As she waits for the computer to finish, she glances at the clock in the upper-right corner of the screen to calculate her next smoke break. Darlene groans. She'll have to wait another hour and a half. The program finishes and she studies the results. According to the computer the bomb is good to go.

Darlene walks back over to disconnect the leads and hears a clicking noise. It's a noise she doesn't remember hearing before, but they build so few of these particular bombs—maybe three or four a year—and she can't recall if it's normal activity or an anomaly. She steps away and scans the surrounding area for her supervisor and spots him talking to another employee farther down the line. Darlene cups her hands around her mouth and shouts, "Bobby!"

Bob Davidson looks up and Darlene waves him over. Bob, in his early forties and nearly as wide as he is tall, waddles over. "What's up, Darlene?"

"Hopefully nothing. I have a piece of ordnance making a strange sound."

"What the hell are you talking about, Darlene? They're bombs. They don't make noises."

"Come here, then," Darlene says, walking back over to the finished bomb.

Bob shuffles along behind her, and when he's close enough to hear the clicking sound, the blood drains from his face. "Oh shi—"

Before Bob can finish his statement, the massive bomb detonates, killing everyone within a mile of the plant.

CHAPTER 24

Chicago

Peyton Lynch is still parked in the lobby of her workplace building, silently cursing Eric's boss. There has been a steady stream of people leaving, including most of the big wheels from Brown, Wright, Zuker, Tomlinson & Qualls. Even the seventy-six-year-old J. Michael Zuker, the agency's founder, made it down seventeen flights of stairs without keeling over. Thrice divorced—the latest a young blond bombshell in her early thirties—the lecherous old bastard had offered Peyton a ride, which she kindly declined. The last place she would want to be is in a private, confined space with that handsy old fart and, with traffic gridlocked, he'll be lucky to get out of the parking garage.

Peyton lights the screen on her cell phone to check if she has service yet and finds she doesn't. No big surprise there. God, she'd kill for ten minutes of Wi-Fi time, just to send Eric an e-mail to hurry his ass along. She stands and walks to the closest window, the symphony of car horns growing louder. The streets are jammed with cars going nowhere and the sidewalks are jammed with people trying to get home. Peyton turns and paces to the other side of the lobby, still barefoot and still sporting blisters on both heels. The thought of walking home in her new heels makes her nauseous, but the thought of walking home barefoot makes her doubly nauseous.

There's a shoe store down the street and Peyton spends a moment fantasizing about breaking in to steal a pair of flats. She sighs and turns her mind, instead, to what may lie ahead.

The small parcel of groceries she purchased might last them three or four days, but then what? *What are we going to eat after that?* Peyton returns to her chair with that thought weighing heavy on her mind. *Hunt for game? With what?* She and Eric don't have any type of weapon at home and probably wouldn't know how to use a gun if they happened to stumble upon one. *Okay, no weapon and no game. What, then?* All the heavy thinking makes Peyton want to pee. She stands, looks down at her pitiful pile of belongings, and wonders if she can afford to leave them unattended for even a minute or two. A few hours ago it wouldn't have mattered. They could have stopped at the grocery store on the way home. But now their very survival may depend upon those oh so few cans of food and the lonely case of water.

What to do? What is it—thirty, maybe forty steps to the lobby restrooms? Peyton squats down and empties everything out of her overstuffed bag. *Looking at it now, am I really going to need the extra makeup or the shampoo and conditioner I'd pilfered from the goody closet? Of course not. What was I thinking?* Peyton reloads the bag with the flashlights, extra batteries, a pair of scissors, and the canned goods. The bag is not large enough to hold the case of water, so Peyton scoots it close to the chair and pops open one of the umbrellas to hide it.

Hurrying down the corridor, her need to pee is no longer an urge but an absolute necessity. Rounding the corner she finds the restrooms cordoned off, OUT OF ORDER signs stuck on the doors. Peyton mutters a few unkind words as she slips the strap from the stanchion and tries to open the door. It's locked. She steps over to the door for the men's restroom and finds the same. Muttering another string of unkind words, Peyton turns and scans the lobby. Holding it is no longer an option. She spots the door to the stairs and walks over. Stepping inside, Peyton squats on the first step down to the basement, pulls down her underwear, and empties her bladder. The relief is instantaneous, but it does little to tamp down the humiliation Peyton feels. She stands, pulls her panties up and her skirt down, and exits, her face still burning with embarrassment.

That embarrassment quickly transitions to anger when she returns to find the case of water and the umbrella gone. Usually one to avoid conflict at all costs, Peyton is now fighting mad. She hurries to the exit and steps outside, looking up one side of the sidewalk then the other. The sidewalks remain packed with pedestrians, and Peyton is not tall enough to see over the crowd. She turns left and walks down to the intersection, searching for the culprit. In her mind she's mentally calculating how long she was away. *Three, maybe four minutes? How far can a person walk in four minutes?* There are too many variables. If Peyton knew the direction the thief traveled, she might have a chance. Without that, it's a crapshoot. Dejected, she trudges back to the lobby, her mind spinning.

How long can we go without water?

CHAPTER 25

On final approach to LaGuardia Airport

Hank shuts down his laptop and closes the lid as Paige Randall disconnects the call to Natalie Lambert and passes the phone back to Hank.

"Jeez, I hope you didn't kill my battery."

"You have a charger," Paige says. "We had some catching up to do."

Hank, scowling, lights the screen to see the phone still has a decent charge. "She goin' to send us some software goodies?"

Paige points at the ceiling then her ear, miming the question of whether someone is eavesdropping or recording their conversations.

"Plane's clean. It gets swept for listenin' devices and cameras before and after every flight."

"Good. I didn't want to implicate Natalie if this turns into a shitstorm. Yes, she's going to send me the latest and greatest software she has."

"I hate to burst your bubble, but it's already a shitstorm. Did Natalie say anythin' to you about a possible insider bein' involved?"

"She's going to send me an e-mail from home when she gets off work."

"Do you think the NSA monitors her home computer?"

"They might try, but Natalie is one of the sharpest programmers I know. There's zero chance the agency has penetrated her network. Hell, she creates or has a hand in creating most of the software the NSA uses to infiltrate other networks."

"She's that good?"

The jet wobbles slightly before touching down and the cabin fills with the roar of the dual engine thrust reversers. As the plane slows, the pilot triggers the reverse thrusters off and the noise level in the cabin returns to normal. "Yes, Natalie's that good," Paige says. "What's the deal with you two?"

"We went out a couple of times, but it withered on the vine because our schedules never synced."

"Was this recent?"

"Last spring."

"So I take it there's not a Mrs. Goodnight waiting for you at home?"

Hank slips his laptop into his bag. "Nope. What about you? Is there a Mr. Randall?"

"As a matter of fact, there is."

Hank feels a . . . hell, he doesn't know what he feels . . . maybe a tad bit of something. He tries to wrap his mind around why because they'd just met for the first time early this morning.

Paige smiles. "He was my father. Other than that, no."

"Ever been married?" Hank asks.

"No. You?"

"Nope." When the jet comes to a stop, both Hank and Paige unbuckle their seat belts and stand.

"What's the game plan now?" Paige asks.

"Hopefully, Elaine has called the New York field office to arrange our pickup. Then I guess it's on to Wall Street."

"What about hotel rooms?"

Hank shrugs. "I assume we'll have a couple."

"But you don't know where?"

Hank looks at Paige. "Are you one of those people who needs a precise plan? Everythin' laid out in order— do this, then that?"

"Maybe. I like to know what lies ahead and I like having some idea of when it might occur."

"Well, that's not goin' to happen here. We go where the evidence tells us to go and we do it after examinin' said evidence and reachin' some type of conclusion on the best path forward. We'll eat and we'll sleep, but I can't tell you when or where."

"Thank you for the lecture, Hank," Paige says, her words laced with anger. "Are you finished?"

"Yes."

"Good. Fuck you." Paige grabs her suitcase and rolls it toward the front of the plane, where the pilot is opening the door. She stomps down the steps, her suitcase bouncing along behind her. Hank grabs his two bags and follows.

"I think you pissed her off, Hank," Donnie Davis says.

"I'm bettin' it won't be the last time." Hank ducks his head in the cockpit. "Safe travels, Theresa."

"It better be safe or we won't be around to pick you up. How long you staying?"

"Undetermined. I'll have the boss call ya." Hank

ducks back out. He and Donnie fist-bump. "See you on the rebound, buddy."

Donnie glances out at Paige, who's standing impatiently on the tarmac, a stern expression on her face. "Good luck. I think you're going to need it."

"Hell, I might need somethin' more than luck." Hank walks down the stairs and pauses to survey the area. He spots an idling black Tahoe near the entrance to the private flight terminal. "Ride's here," he tells Paige, pointing out the black SUV.

Paige glances over her shoulder, turns, and begins walking toward the truck without saying a word. When they reach the vehicle the driver pushes a button that opens the rear hatch and Hank piles his stuff in. Paige is struggling to lift her suitcase and Hank grabs it and tosses it in. Paige brushes past, a scowl on her face.

"You're welcome," Hank says to her backside. He closes the hatch and opens the passenger-side door and looks at the driver. "Well, hell. When the hell did they make assistant directors in charge taxi drivers?"

"Hi, Hank, climb in. We're burning daylight," Assistant Director Tomás Morales says.

Hank climbs in and shuts the door. "How ya doin', Tomás?"

"Busy. Very, very, busy," Morales says, dropping the shifter into drive and punching the gas. He glances at the rearview. "I'm sorry you got paired with Hank."

"Me, too," Paige says. "I'm Paige Randall, a computer programmer at headquarters."

"I know. I read your file. I must say you have a very impressive résumé. I'm Tomás Morales. Nice to meet you, Ms. Randall."

"Paige will do. And nice to meet you, also, sir."

"No *sirs* around here. It's Tomás."

Paige nods as Morales exits out of the airport and picks up the Grand Central Parkway for a mile before exiting onto Interstate 278 south.

"I don't suppose you've found out who the hackers are?" Hank asks.

Morales sighs. "No. Not even a whiff. I've got agents scouring the stock exchanges, agents out at their data centers in New Jersey, and more agents working with the Wall Street banks. And we still don't have a damn thing. You hear the latest?"

"No. What?" Hank asks.

Paige leans forward in her seat so she can hear.

"We don't have all the details yet," Morales says, "but apparently they somehow triggered the detonation of a very large bomb at an army ammunition depot. I think it was one of those MOAB bombs."

"Damn," Hank says, balling his hands into fists. "It had to be the plant in McAlester."

"It was," Morales says, "now that you say that."

"When we find these bastards, I'm goin' to stomp a mudhole in their asses and walk it dry."

"Where is McAlester in relation to Ada?" Paige asks.

"The plant is forty-nine miles east of Ada." Hank pauses, trying to keep his composure in check. After a moment or two he says, "There're a lot of people around town who work at the plant, includin' some people I've known since kindergarten." Hank turns and stares out the side window for a few moments, his mind clicking through images of friends who might have been at the plant. He eventually turns to look at his friend. "The death toll had to be staggerin', Tomás."

"It was, Hank. The blast radius extended out to a

mile or more. It could be days before they have a final tally."

Hank nods and takes another deep breath. "Any idea how they detonated it?"

"No," Morales says. "The plant is still burning and there's extreme concern the other ordnance will cook off. They've cordoned off a wide area around the plant. I guess they're going to wait and let the fire burn out."

"That's the only choice they have." Hank says. He pauses another moment before continuing, "That place has enough ammo to not only start a war, but end it, too." Hank, knowing there's nothing he can do for his friends, tries to refocus his mind. "Do we know if their computer network was interfaced with the Department of Defense network?"

"*I* don't know, but we can damn sure find out."

"I'm bettin' it was," Hank says. "Might be another avenue of investigation."

"I'll assign an agent to look into it," Morales says.

"I have a question, Tomás," Paige says.

Morales glances at the rearview and says, "Shoot."

"If they've detonated one of these bombs at the manufacturing plant, what's to keep them from detonating them elsewhere? Surely, some of these weapons are deployed."

"They are. The bombs are stored at several air force bases. The military is working to disarm the remaining bombs."

"That leads to my next question," Paige says. "If the hackers have access to this particular bomb why not other types of military hardware?"

"I think the military folks are hoping the ammunition plant is the weak link in the chain. An isolated event," Morales says.

"And what do *you* think?" Paige asks. "So far, they've hacked the power grids—which is not all that difficult to do—a dam, a series of chemical plants and nuclear power plants, a fairly sophisticated piece of aircraft flight software, and now some military ordnance. What's to stop them from escalating their attacks to other military weapons?"

Morales's eyes drift to the rearview mirror. "You think the military people are wrong, Paige?"

"Yes, I do."

Morales glances over at Hank. "You feel the same?"

"Absolutely."

"God help us," Morales mutters.

CHAPTER 26

Hoping to build the next great class of ships for twenty-first-century warfare, the U.S. Navy commissioned a trio of defense contractors to do just that. After years of design and building, the result of their efforts is the USS *Stark*, a Zumwalt-class guided missile destroyer. Designed to be stealthy, the ship is a marvel of modern technology. From her knife-edged bow to her totally enclosed superstructure, the 610-foot-long USS *Stark* has the radar signature of a 50-foot fishing boat.

The modern marvels continue inside the ship with racks of computer servers that run every system on the ship from bow to stern. The servers are enclosed in what the navy calls an Electronic Modular Enclosure (EME) and the *Stark* has sixteen such enclosures on board—each jam-packed with computer equipment. Everything on the ship, from the showers to the gun turrets, is controlled by what the navy calls the Total Ship Computing Environment (TSCE). And all that computing power and the sophistication of the ship's weapons and navigation systems require an enormous amount of software to operate. Even without several systems online for sea trials, it requires nearly six million lines of code to get the ship out of port.

The navy originally hoped to purchase thirty-two of these advanced war machines, but as costs ballooned to the point that each ship was going to cost over $3 billion to acquire, the order was cut in half. But similar to many other government programs, the costs didn't end there and the navy cut the total number of ships to seven. Flash forward to today, and the navy capped the number of ships at three and the whole program ran aground and was eventually canceled.

Today, Captain Bruce Hensley is commander of the USS *Stark*, a ship that is far from complete and years away from combat readiness. Despite the Government Accountability Office's assessment that only three of the ship's eleven critical technologies are fully operational, the U.S. Navy ordered the USS *Stark* out for sea trials, the navy desperate to show *something* from all those billions spent. Hensley glances at one of the camera displays hanging overhead. The view he's looking at is from the bow camera and there are storm clouds on the horizon. To say they have bugs to work out would be an understatement. The last time they were out to sea, both of the ship's propellers seized while they were traversing the Panama Canal and the ship had to be towed out of the canal and back to port. After eleven months waiting for repairs, they are now back out on the high seas and the captain is wondering if his career is going to crater along with this piece-of-shit ship.

The bridge on the *Stark* is small compared to the overall size of the ship, with room for only four or five sailors. Most of the work is accomplished in the navy's new-concept control room called the Ship's Mission Center (SMC), where the captain is now. A large room, it has space for dozens of three-video-screen workstations and is a total departure from the old concept when there was a radio room, a weapons station, or an engineering room. All of the ship's functions are now controlled from this one futuristic-looking control center. The one thing that aggravates Hensley is the fact that the room has no windows—apparently windows are bad things to build in a ship if you're trying to be stealthy. "Let's take her out a little further," Hensley says. "Helm, left rudder, fifteen degrees. All ahead full." They have been navigating a busy shipping channel all morning and the radar is on the fritz—again. Hensley wants out of the clutter. The last thing he needs is to collide with another ship.

The large ship begins to turn, veering east. They are currently sailing about fifteen miles east of Naval Station Norfolk.

The executive officer, Lieutenant Commander Kathleen Connelly, sidles up to the captain and whispers, "The farther out to sea we go, the farther we have to tow her back in."

"Hush, Kat," Hensley says. "You're going to jinx us."

"Bruce, this ship was jinxed the moment it hit the water." At five-six, Connelly is runner-lean with short blond hair and lake blue eyes.

"I'm praying we can make it through this tour without another breakdown." At forty-nine, Hensley is a tall man who wears the same size pants—a thirty-two waist—that he wore in high school. His dark hair is still more pepper than salt, but that could change, depending on how this portion of the sea trial goes.

Although this is another trial run, the USS *Stark* carries a full complement of weapons: everything from missiles to six-inch rounds for the two 155-mm deck guns. You can't be caught in a possible gun battle and be shooting blanks. And in today's pressure cooker of political uncertainties, a new enemy could be lurking just out of sight. "How long to fix the radar?" Hensley asks a sailor siting at the engineering station.

"Unknown, sir," the young man says. "It appears to be a software coding error, sir."

"What else is new?" Hensley mutters. He turns to Connelly and says, "I was hoping to run through some live-fire drills, but we can't do a damn thing without the radar."

"Patience, Bruce," Connelly says.

"That's one thing I'm about out of." He lowers his voice and says, "I'd love to ask for a reassignment."

"What? And leave me stuck with this albatross?" Connelly asks. "Don't you dare."

"It wouldn't do any good, anyway. Not until we finish these trials. No, let me rephrase—if we ever finish these trials, which seems highly unlikely at the moment." He takes advantage of the lull and pulls out his smartphone to check for messages from the family. That's another selling feature of this state-of-the-art ship—stem-to-stern superfast Wi-Fi via the *Stark*'s TSCE. The TSCE system links all of the ship's various systems—weapons, engineering, communications, etc.— using redundant servers running the Linux operating system. The fact that Linux has more holes (security vulnerabilities) than a paper target at a police shooting range seemed to matter little to the designers and builders of this new class of destroyers. Hensley finds no messages from family members and he takes a moment to check his e-mail.

An hour later, the ship's chief engineer assures Captain Hensley the radar is repaired. He turns to Connelly and says, "Order preparation for live-fire exercises. Let's see if we can get some action in before the radar craps out again."

Connelly steps away to organize the exercise and Hensley orders the targets deployed. The targets are large inflatable orange squares that get tossed into the ocean to give the gunners something to shoot at. The two large 155-mm deck guns, the first of their type, were designed to shoot a newly designed projectile that would achieve a new level of precision with a range of sixty miles. But after installation of the gun system, the navy discovered the costs of the new projectiles would be somewhere between $700,000 and $900,000 per round. After finding out the price tag to fill the two gun's 300-round automated magazines would be in the millions of dollars, the navy went looking for alternatives. They discovered some ammunition already in inventory that would work, but only if the new guns were retrofitted. The guns were worked over and the new rounds Hensley will be firing today have a range of about twenty-six miles and a more manageable price of *only* $68,000 per round.

Executive Officer Connelly returns. "We're locked and loaded, Skipper.

"Good. Let's see what she can do." The captain walks over to the combat center. "Chief, have you acquired the targets?"

"I have, sir," Chief Warrant Officer Ed Elliot replies.

"Light 'em up."

"Aye, aye, Skipper," Elliot replies, a large grin on his face. The all-electric guns are controlled entirely by computer through the gun system's master control unit. Elliot powers on the two massive guns and immediately notices the turrets rotating the exact opposite way than planned. "What the hell?"

"What's wrong, Chief?"

"I don't know, s—"

His last words are clipped by the roar of cannon fire. "Sir," Elliot shouts, "something's wrong."

"Shut it off!" Hensley shouts.

Each gun is capable of firing ten rounds a minute, and since they began firing they have shot off six rounds.

"The computer's not responding, Captain," Elliot say.

"Then shut the whole damn system down," Hensley shouts.

Elliot's fingers jab at the keyboard as the guns continue firing—boom . . . boom . . . boom—one round right after another.

"The computer's locked up, Skipper," Elliot shouts over the constant barrage.

"Unplug the damn thing!"

"I can't. It's all tied into the ship's systems."

"Hard left, rudder!" Hensley shouts to those on the bridge, hoping and praying the guns won't track whatever target the guns are shooting at.

He glances at the bow camera to see the turrets turning, the tracking system apparently working flawlessly.

"Mr. Elliot, I need answers!" Hensley barks as more personnel flood onto the bridge. The ship's weapon systems officer, Lieutenant Mike Griffin, comes racing in, out of breath. With this being the first planned firing of the guns, he had been doing an on-site inspection of their operation. He nudges Elliot aside and reaches for the keyboard, typing in command after command with no effect. "Skipper," Griffin shouts, "we're locked out of the computer."

"What the hell do you mean, 'locked out'?" Hensley hollers over the ongoing fusillade.

"I can't access any of the ship's weapon systems."

Everyone on the bridge startles when a barrage of missiles roars out of their launchers.

"What the hell!" Hensley shouts. "Cut the power to the guns and missile launchers!"

Before anyone can answer, another flight of missiles streaks high into the sky as the large guns continue to fire.

"The computer won't let me kill the power," Griffin shouts.

"Goddamn it!" Hensley turns to Connelly. "Call down to the engine room. Have them cut power to the entire ship."

Connelly snatches up the phone and makes the call as more missiles launch. Moments after Connelly's radio call, the computer monitors and the lights in the Ship's Mission Center wink off. The sudden silence is startling yet welcome—the guns have stopped.

"Mr. Griffin, how many howitzer rounds were fired?" Hensley asks.

"I won't know the exact number until we power up the computers. A rough estimate based on duration would be somewhere close to a hundred rounds."

Hensley shakes his head. "And missiles?"

"I won't know how many or type until the computers are back on."

"I'm not turning those sons-a-bitches back on until we find out what happened. Call downstairs and have someone count how many missiles are left on board."

Griffin grabs a radio and pauses. "Sir, I can't call down there with the power off."

"Fuck! Run downstairs, Griff, and tell your men to count the remaining missiles."

Lieutenant Griffin stands and hurries for the exit.

"Wait, Griff," Hensley shouts. "Any idea if there was a specific target?"

"I won't know that—"

Hensley cuts him off with a wave of his hand. "I know, I know . . . until the computers are back on." Hensley runs a hand across the top of his head and steps over closer to Griffin. "What the hell happened, Griff?"

"The only thing that makes sense is that someone hacked our weapons systems."

"Who?"

"Unknown, sir. Might find something when we power back up."

"While you're down there, put a crew together. I want those weapons immobilized."

"Yes, sir," Griffin says, hurrying out the door.

Hensley walks over to the communication's center. "Any luck with the radio?"

"Not yet, sir. But I think we were close before the ship was powered down."

CHAPTER 27

Chicago

Peyton is dripping sweat and her feet are aching as she climbs down the final few steps to the ground floor. She's uttered every curse word in her vocabulary on the trip back up to her office—all aimed at the sorry bastard who stole her case of water. Peyton had remembered seeing a case of water in the company's break room and she's now lugging it, and her heavy bag, back down the stairs. She hits the door and spills out into the lobby. After taking a moment to catch her breath, she hauls her stuff to a chair and plops down. Her new pencil skirt is in tatters after Peyton used the scissors to cut slits to allow for a wider range of movement. The slits grew to long rips during the journey, and it now looks as if Peyton is wearing a hastily cobbled together loincloth. She pulls her right foot onto her lap to pick the grit out of the scrapes and cuts on her sole. She'd love to use one of the bottles of water to wash the blood and grime off her feet, but the fear of not knowing what lies ahead wins out in the end. Instead, she wipes her foot with a section of her tattered skirt and does the same for her left foot and calls it done.

Sitting in the vacant lobby, she begins to worry about those same cuts and scrapes. *How many germs on those stairs?* She glances around the lobby. *And not just the stairs. How many potential bacterial infections are lurking along the surface of the lobby floor? A floor that gets trod on by shoes that have probably tromped through pigeon shit, or dog shit, or worse? Think how much trash and garbage collects on the sidewalks.* "Stop it, Peyton," she utters out load, surprising herself. She glances at her new heels lying on the floor, but the thought of having to put them on roils her stomach. Peyton turns her gaze from the shoes to the window, hoping to see her husband's familiar face. She doesn't see any sign of Eric, but she does see a nicely dressed woman stop midstride, pull her skirt up, and squat. The woman appears nonchalant as her urine puddles around her shoes. "At least I opted for a stairwell," Peyton mutters. The woman stands, lowers her skirt, and continues on, as if urinating on the sidewalk were an everyday occurrence for her, which, judging by her clothing and expensive handbag, it's not. *Jeez, if it has come to this after only a few hours without power, what's it going to be like after a few days?*

Before Peyton can give that question much thought, she's startled by the sound of shattering glass. She stands and hobbles over to the window as the cascade of breaking glass continues. Peyton gasps at the sight of people pouring in and out of the nearby stores, their arms laden with stolen goods. Peyton isn't that surprised that looting has already started, but she is surprised and somewhat unsettled by the people doing it. They aren't street thugs or gang members, they're people like her. People who have jobs, apartments, families—people who ought to know better. Peyton hears more glass shattering and steps closer to the window to see which place has been hit now.

It's the shoe store down the street.

She ponders that for a moment. *Huh. No, absolutely not. I'm not a thief. My parents raised me better.*

Peyton watches as men and women leave the store, their arms loaded with boxes of shoes. Two well-attired women spill onto the sidewalk, both clutching the same shoebox. They are shouting and spitting at each other, tugging on the distinctive black-and-white box that Peyton knows contains an expensive pair of shoes. When it looks as if one of the women is getting the upper hand, the other turns loose and Peyton thinks that's the end of that. She's shocked when the other woman winds her arm up and slaps the other woman in the face. The injured woman sags slightly and the box slips from her hands. The slapper leans over, grabs the shoes, and takes off while Peyton looks on, horrified.

More windows are broken and more stores are looted. Peyton cranes her neck to look up the street at Bloomingdale's. It looks like Christmas Eve as people exit the store carrying overstuffed bags filled with stolen bounty. Peyton's eyes drift away from the scene and down to her bruised and battered feet. *Is one more missing pair of shoes really going to matter to the owner of the store? Heck, they probably have insurance to cover incidents just like this.* Her gaze returns to the unfolding horror show outside. *Besides, there's glass everywhere and I'd have to put on those damn heels just to go outside.* She watches as two men square off in the middle of the street, about to come to blows over a Gucci bag that one has stolen from the high-end department store. Both are wearing khakis and button-downs, but that's where the similarities end. One is tall and overweight, his gut lapping over his belt; the other a head shorter and about sixty pounds lighter. The larger man makes the first move, throwing a big roundhouse punch that misses by a mile. The smaller man ducks the punch and delivers a short quick left to the larger man's solar plexus and he doubles over, obviously out of breath. Fight over before it even began. The man grabs the bag and melds into the crowd.

Peyton checks the shoe store again. More people are flooding into the store as others exit, one man carrying an armload of shoes minus the boxes. Peyton looks down at her poor feet again. *It's easier to put on the damn heels now and walk across the street for a pair of comfortable shoes rather than try to wear the damn things home. Besides, it's just one measly pair of shoes and these assholes are carrying them out by the handfuls. One pair. That's all.* Peyton remains frozen in place with indecision. *Plus, how much glass are we going to encounter on the way home? Probably lots, right? But wait . . . Shit. If I lug that food and water outside I'm going to be mugged.* Peyton turns and scans the lobby, looking for a better hidey-hole. She walks along the perimeter of the lobby, trying doors to see if any are unlocked. None are and she's back to square one. Standing in the center of the lobby, she places a hand on her hip, deep in thought.

Seconds later she nearly jumps out of her skin when a staccato of gunfire erupts outside. She drops to the floor and slithers behind the chair for cover.

CHAPTER 28

"Where do you want to start, Paige?" Morales asks, as they exit off the Williamsburg Bridge.

"I'd like to begin at Nasdaq headquarters."

"Why? Because they've been hacked before?" Morales asks.

"Yes. I'm thinking there might be a vulnerability or two still lurking around in their network."

"The company allegedly shored up their network," Hank says as Morales makes a left on Broadway.

"So what?" Paige says, now cooled off from the altercation with Hank. "All software has flaws. Even if they reconfigured their systems or built in new and better firewalls, there will still be vulnerabilities. Humans write code and humans make mistakes. You just hope, as a company, you find them first before the bad guys do."

"If you find the malware, Paige, how long to make an ID on the hackers?" Morales asks.

"I don't know, Tomás. How long did it take the agency to identify the bad actors from the first hack on the stock market?"

Morales scowls then says, "Four years. And even then the agency said they were only seventy percent certain the Russians were involved. I don't think we ever identified any of the individuals involved."

"Exactly," Paige says. "And, no, we never ID'd any of the hackers. We're in for a long slog, Tomás."

"Okay, we're a long way from identifying the hackers," Tomás says, "but how long to get a handle on this malware, Paige?"

"Well, we have to find it first," Paige says. "After that it's a matter of dissecting whatever it is and writing a piece of software to quarantine and kill it. That could take a while once we find it."

Tomás grimaces. "No way to speed things up?"

Paige shrugs. "I'm open to ideas."

Hank turns in his seat to look back at Paige. "Do you think they're usin' the same piece of malware for all of their attacks?"

"There's no way to know that yet," Paige says. "But I would find it highly unlikely the same virus is being used."

Hank shakes his head. "They might be the best hackers on the planet, but I doubt they've developed a grab bag full of exploits. I think it's more likely they're usin' multiple variants of the one piece of malware—malware they've probably spent years refinin'."

"I'm not arguing with you, Hank," Paige says, "but we shouldn't base future decisions on what we might or might not find here. We need comparison samples from the aircraft manufacturer or one of the other places that was hit. We'd be shooting ourselves in the foot if we create a piece of software to scan for this particular malware and find out they've been using multiple types of malware."

"Jesus," Morales says, "I feel like we're just waiting for the next bad thing to happen. We need to be more proactive. Why can't we create software to scan for what we may find here and ship it out? If we find they're using other malware, couldn't we just create more software?"

"In theory, yes," Paige says, "but in reality, no. The virus scan itself could cause the malware to execute its payload. Then we'd have an avalanche of bad things happening. We have no idea what else is in the works, but we need to be very careful how we proceed."

"It's hard to be careful when the body count continues to rise," Morales says dejectedly. He pulls into a parking garage a block south of Wall Street, takes his ticket, and begins the search for a vacant spot. Round and round they go, finally finding a spot down on the fourth level. They park, exit the SUV, and make their way to One Liberty Plaza.

After a brief, heated argument between Morales and the company's chairman over privacy issues, the administrator username and password were passed on to Paige and Hank and they were taken to a small office near the local server room. Morales opted to stay behind to return phone calls, so Hank and Paige grab chairs and start working. Using her laptop, Paige logs in to the company's Wi-Fi and navigates to an FBI-created virtual private network (VPN) and enters her credentials. She downloads the new toolkit that Natalie had sent and loads it onto a clean encrypted flash drive. She hates flash drives but it's the only way to insert the software into the company's system without hooking up her computer, something she won't do. The last thing she needs is for the malware to infect her computer.

"What do you want me to do?" Hank asks.

"Use one of the company's computers and log in to the system. See if the username and password they gave us will allow us access to the source code."

Hank steps over to a workstation and sits. The office door opens and a balding man who looks to be in his early forties enters. "I'm Kent Fitzpatrick, head of IT. I've been instructed to assist in any way I can."

"Pull up a chair, Kent," Hank says. "Have you had a chance to look at any of the source code?"

"No. I've spent most of the day putting out fires."

Hank recalls the admin username and password from a compartment in his brain and enters the information and logs in. "I assume access to your source code is tightly controlled."

"You are correct," Fitzpatrick says. "Most of it is proprietary software and unique to the industry."

Hank looks up at Kent. "If access is strictly enforced, how did you end up with malware in your system?"

"I'm not convinced it exists."

As the conversation between Hank and the new guy continues, Paige spends several moments examining the new software from Natalie. They are tools she's never seen or used before, but it doesn't take long for Paige to get up to speed on how they function. She ejects the flash drive and pulls it from her laptop, carrying it over to the computer Hank's working on.

Fitzpatrick spots the flash drive in her hand. "We don't allow external storage devices on our network."

Paige pins Fitzpatrick to his chair with a stern look. "Today, you do." She pulls up another chair and nudges Hank away from the computer.

Fitzpatrick rubs his forehead with his palm. "I object to your use of a flash drive on our system."

"Duly noted," Paige replies. She plugs the drive into

the computer's USB port and launches the first application.

"What program are you running?" Fitzpatrick asks.

"One you've never heard of. Let's just leave it at that, shall we?"

"Whatever," Fitzpatrick mumbles, kneading his neck with his right hand.

"Do I have access to every server on your network from here?" Paige asks.

"Not all of them. We keep redundant systems offline in case of emergency."

"How do you access them when you need to?"

"They have to be manually plugged in to the network at our server farm in Carteret, New Jersey," Fitzpatrick says.

"How often are they connected to the main network?"

"Not very. The last time was October of last year when we were doing some system maintenance."

"They might not be infected, but depending on what we find here we might need them online. Are you prepared to make that call?"

"Not really. Like I said, I'm not convinced our network has been infiltrated."

"Were you workin' here in October of 2010?" Hank asks.

Fitzpatrick rubs a hand across his balding head. "I was working in the IT department, yes."

"But not the lead guy?" Hank asks.

"No."

"What happened to him or her?"

Kent sighs again. "He was fired."

"Why?"

Fitzpatrick blows out a long breath. "Yes, we were

hacked in 2010, okay? But we did a major revamp and beefed up our security."

The program Paige had started ends with no infected files found. "Damn," she mumbles under her breath. She clicks on her flash drive and launches another application. It runs for several minutes and a piece of source code flashes onto the screen. "There you are, you little bastard," she mutters as she highlights the code and copies it to her flash drive.

Hank, looking over her shoulder, asks, "You find somethin'?"

"Yes. Not quite sure what it is, but it was found on a device driver in the system's memory."

Fitzpatrick pedals his chair over for a closer look.

"Does it look familiar to you, Kent?" Paige asks.

"No. But every driver we put on the network is accompanied by a digitally signed certificate of authenticity."

"Oh well, that's great. Those certificates are never stolen or compromised, are they?" Paige says, her voice filled with sarcasm.

Fitzpatrick shrugs. "It's damn difficult to do."

"Yeah," Paige says, "almost as difficult as hacking an allegedly secure network."

CHAPTER 29

Bardere, Gedo, Somalia

September 6, 2008
TARGET: al-Shabaab
CONFIRMED KILLED: 69
CIVILIANS KILLED: 41

Situated along the banks of the Jubba River in the Gedo region of Somalia, Bardere is one of the most fertile areas of the country. Palm trees line the riverbank and irrigated plots of land stretch across the Jubba Valley for as far as the eye can see. The farmers in the area grow sorghum, corn, onions, beans, and fruits such as watermelons, oranges, and mangoes. While unemployment for the rest of the country is nearly 70 percent, most of the 75,000 people who call Bardere home consider themselves quite prosperous when compared to others in this war-torn country.

One of those residents working in the fields this afternoon is fourteen-year-old Yuusef Yuusef Mohamed. In Somalia there is no concept of Western-style surnames. Children are given three names when they enter the world: his or her name, the name of the father, and the name of the grandfather or great-grandfather. To simplify things, Somalis will often create a nickname for the child that stays with him or her for life. Yuusef must have arrived during a period of low creativity because his nickname is also his first name. Yuusef climbs down the handmade ladder and carries it to the next orange tree in line and climbs back up, picking the oranges at the top of the tree and placing them carefully in the canvas bag slung around his neck. These orange trees or ones like them have been in Yuusef's family going back four generations. And Yuusef doesn't mind the hard work, but he has bigger plans for his life.

An excellent student with an uncannily sharp mind, Yuusef splits his time between high school and an accelerated learning program, including English, at the local university. That is, when he's not picking oranges. Thankfully, the picking season is short and Yuusef can't wait to get back to his studies. After a series of standardized tests over the years, Yuusef was discovered to have an extremely high aptitude for math and a Mensa-worthy IQ of 151. Teachers steered him toward all things computer related and Yuusef was off and running.

In addition to the small orange grove, the family also grows corn and watermelons and also owns a good-sized herd of goats. When not farming, Yuusef's father often transports their goods to the larger cities, where he and Yuusef's mother and his older sister and her husband set up shop at the local markets. Today is market day and the group of four rolled out long before daybreak with plans to return before dark when things often get dicey in Somalia.

His thoughts of upcoming studies are interrupted when he hears his grandmother ringing the dinner bell. *Before heading back to the house Yuusef finishes with that tree and moves the ladder to the next tree so it'll be ready first thing in the morning. Yuusef empties his bag of oranges into a larger crate, takes off his picking bag, and moves over to the well to wash up for dinner before going inside.*

The home houses three generations of Yuusef's family and quarters are tight. Yes, there are squabbles, but, in general, things run smoothly. Inside, Yuusef gives his grandmother a peck on the cheek and takes a seat at the table. His grandfather died two years ago and his grandmother now cares for Yuusef's two-year-old niece, Leylo, while her parents are away at the market.

With the sun riding low on the horizon Yuusef asks, "Have you heard from Mother and Father?"

"They called when they were leaving the market. I thought they would be home by now."

"Have you tried calling them again?"

"Yes, but you know cell service can be difficult."

His grandmother places a bowl of stew on the table for him and Yuusef digs in. He's hungry after a long day in the fields. Leylo takes a seat next to her uncle with a small bowl of stew and begins pestering him with questions as his grandmother sits. Moments later, dinner is interrupted when they hear the squeal of brakes coming from the front yard. Thinking it's his parents, Yuusef stands and walks to the front door to find a strange truck in the drive. Two men climb out and approach, asking to speak to an adult. Yuusef's grandmother comes to the door and meets the men on the porch. After a few minutes of discussion, Yuusef knows his world has been turned upside down when his grandmother bursts into tears and sags to her knees.

It wasn't until two weeks later, long after the funerals, that Yuusef found out what happened. His family had been at the wrong place at the wrong time. Stuck in traffic, they were directly behind a car that was targeted by an American drone. The ensuing fireball engulfed the family truck, killing everyone aboard.

Present day, somewhere near Boston

Now twenty-four, Yuusef is waiting for a satellite window to open to launch their next attack. Over the weeks, the team hacked numerous communication satellites and installed back doors in the software. The back doors don't allow them the ability to reposition satellites, but they do allow them to communicate with their targets across a wide swath of the country. The payload Yuusef is waiting to release targets a specific programmable logic controller that regulates speed.

"Where are we with target nineteen?" Nazeri asks from across the room.

"Waiting for the satellite window," Yuusef replies. He has no idea who the passengers are, but he does wonder if it's possible he might know someone aboard. As quick as the thought arrives, Yuusef pushes it from his mind. But, while he waits, his continuously active mind drifts to what might have been.

His professors at the university thought his research into artificial intelligence held great promise. There was mention of numerous published papers in the finest academic journals and a possible breakthrough in a field that has stumped scientists for fifty years. Not that any of his hypotheses had yet been proven, but Yuusef felt like he was on the cusp of a breakthrough that could advance machine-level intelligence to the next level. But that was before.

Yuusef sighs as he waits for the satellite. All of his research is stored in the cloud and on a portable hard drive he keeps in a hidden location, but to have an opportunity to work in an environment with that level of expertise and funding is now up in smoke. As he thinks about that, a tiny morsel of doubt begins to creep into his subconscious thoughts. He works to keep it at bay and, when the satellite comes online, Yuusef triggers the payload and takes control of the small computer-networked device that regulates speed.

CHAPTER 30

Two times a week, Gavin Minnick boards the noon Acela train from Washington, D.C., to New York City. The Acela Express is a high-speed train capable of traveling up to 150 miles per hour, but averages closer to 85 due to track conditions along the Northeast Corridor. On good days the trip usually takes two hours and forty-six minutes, gate to gate. That'll put Gavin in New York in time to make his late-afternoon meeting and enjoy a nice meal before returning in the morning. An international banker by trade, his twice-weekly meetings in New York are beginning to erode his home life. His wife and two daughters at home often complain they don't see enough of him. And at forty-six, the travel itself is a real grind even with the first-class accommodations aboard the train.

Gavin has made the trip enough times that he could probably drive the train blindfolded. He knows the slower sections of the track and the places where the train can accelerate to full speed. With four passenger cars bookended by two power cars capable of producing 6,200 horsepower each, the train's acceleration can be breathtaking.

Gavin turns from the window and unloads his laptop from his messenger bag. He logs on and opens a spreadsheet for this afternoon's meeting. Gavin has dissected thousands of corporate financials, accounting spreadsheets, and profit and loss statements, and it doesn't take him long to zero in on the important numbers. The board of directors at the company he's meeting with is hoping to slash payroll costs. Not their own exorbitant salaries, but the salaries of the hourly workers who make up the backbone of the company. If his bank didn't have a financial interest in the matter, he'd tell them to go to hell. But it does, and he can't.

Gavin removes his glasses and rubs the pressure points on the bridge of his nose. Once a basketball player at the small college he attended, his years spent behind the desk have sent his weight one way and his receding hairline the other, now extending to the back third of his skull. He cleans the lenses of his glasses with his silk tie and replaces them on his head, stealing another glimpse of the outside world. The bright sun is high in the sky, casting shallow shadows under the trees lining the track. He returns to his laptop, and, with a sigh, continues to search for cost savings.

After spending several more minutes crunching the numbers and finding no easy solutions—layoffs are the only option—Gavin closes the lid on his laptop and reclines his chair. The train begins to slow as the grimy underbelly of Philadelphia flashes past the window. The intercom chirps and the conductor announces the next stop will be at Penn Station. The train lurches as it rapidly accelerates.

An hour later, a pit the size of the Grand Canyon forms in Gavin's gut as he cranes his neck to look ahead. The train is less than half a mile from Penn Station, one of the busiest train stations in the country, and instead of slowing the train is *accelerating*.

A small girl screams and clambers onto her mother's lap as a pair of train conductors rush into the first-class car. "Please take your seats and brace yourselves," one shouts as they race past. Gavin doesn't know whether to stay where he is or find another place to take cover as the train continues to speed up. *Brace ourselves? What the hell does that mean?* Power poles flash past the window as screams fill the cabin. Gavin glances around at the other people aboard. Some people are weeping, while others sit, their eyes closed, their lips trembling out a remembered prayer.

Gavin sits and braces his legs against the seat in front of him. He grabs his cell phone and begins typing a message to his wife as the train sways violently from side to side. Before he can hit send, the train tips to the right and slams onto the ground. Gavin is aware of shrieking metal, sparks, and screams before the car he's in rams into one of the waiting trains. Slamming against the forward bulkhead Gavin's brain registers a sharp, intense pain before his world goes dark forever.

Daily News Website

—BREAKING NEWS—Stock trading halted because of computer irregularities.

All stock trading has been halted due to some type of computer glitch. More details to follow . . .

—BREAKING NEWS—Chemical plant explosion south of downtown Seattle. Some residents to be evacuated. Still no word on types of chemicals manufactured at the plant. Witnesses describe strong smell of chlorine. Reports of numerous fatalities at nearby water park. More details to follow . . .

CHAPTER 31

With the weapon systems disabled and completely severed from *Stark*'s computer systems, Captain Hensley crosses his fingers and orders the generators restarted and the power turned back on. The lights and computer screens on the bridge flicker back to life and the guns, for now, remain silent. Hensley breathes a sigh of relief. The ship's e-mail system still isn't operational and with the radio down, he's desperate to know who and what was targeted when the ship's weapons went berserk. He pulls his phone out of his pocket to check for a cell signal and finds no service now that they've sailed farther from port.

There had been much discussion during the design phase of this next-generation destroyer about enabling the ship's computers to allow Wi-Fi calling via smartphone. The lead admiral on the design committee, Rear Admiral Richard Malloy—who grew up watching three channels on a black-and-white TV back in the '60s—nixed that idea and wanted to limit or eliminate Wi-Fi capability altogether. His reason was an old one: loose lips sink ships. It wasn't until some of the younger officers, Hensley included, got involved later in the process that ship-wide Wi-Fi was put back in the plans.

The Wi-Fi signal is strong and operates at fast speeds when it works, which it does—sometimes. The big question now is, will it work at all after the system re-boots? This is the first time the crew has completely powered down the ship while at sea and those on the bridge are somewhat nervous to discover which systems will restart and function as they should and which won't. If the ship's track record so far is any indication of the outcome, they'll be lucky if they're not dead in the water. Hensley walks over to the communications desk. "Where are we on the radio, Lieutenant Taylor?"

"We're still waitin' for the systems to come online, Skipper," Taylor replies. A red-haired, blue-eyed young man out of West Texas, Taylor looks more like a defensive lineman than a sailor.

"What are the odds the radio is going to work?" the captain asks.

"Well, sir, we didn't do a lot of wagerin' back home, but I'd put the odds somewhere around fifty-fifty. In other words, sir, it'll be a crapshoot."

"If the radio doesn't work is your team capable of repairing it?"

"Yes, sir. We about had her whipped before we killed the power, Skipper."

"Is the satellite uplink operational? Could we send a flash message to Norfolk about our wonky weapon systems?"

Taylor shakes his head. "It's all part of this new computer system, sir. It's either all or nothin'. I don't know who designed it that way, but somebody needs to find out who it was and fire his or her ass. Sir."

"So what you're telling me is we are now aboard the most sophisticated warship ever built and we can't make a phone call, send an e-mail, or talk on the fucking radio?"

"That 'bout sums it up, Skipper," Taylor says. "If we had loaded on the helicopters we could have used one of their radios."

"Little late now," Hensley says.

Taylor glances over when his video screen powers up. He swivels in his chair and types out a series of commands and waits for the system to respond. When it does, radio chatter fills the speakers. "We need ambulances on piers fourteen, twelve, ten, nine, and eight, stat," a voice shouts.

Another voice, one the captain recognizes as belonging to the admiral designated as the commander of the Atlantic Fleet, says, "I want a fucking status report and I want it now. How many ships have taken fire?"

Someone starts reading off a list of ships and the blood drains from Hensley's face. "Is that radio traffic out of Norfolk?"

Taylor mouses over to check the radio frequency. "Yes."

Hensley hangs his head as the horror show from Norfolk continues to play out over the radio. Lieutenant Griffin returns from downstairs and approaches Hensley. "Sir, we have thirty-nine remaining missiles on board."

"How many missiles did we load on before leaving port?"

"Eighty, sir," Griffin says.

"This is the *Forrest Sherman*. We're taking on water," a voice shouts over the radio. Hensley winces at the name of the ship, one he'd served on early in his career.

Griffin nods at the radio. "Where's that from?"

"Naval Station Norfolk," Hensley says.

"Oh shit. Did we do that?" Griffin asks.

"Unless the Russians decided to attack in the last forty minutes, yes," Hensley says. "I need a detailed report of what went where, Mike."

"I'll get it, sir. Have you contacted Norfolk and told them our systems have been hacked?" Griffin asks.

"Not yet," Hensley says, and turns back to Taylor. "Is the radio transmitting?"

"I haven't tried, sir," Taylor replies.

"Try now. Contact Norfolk and tell them . . . Fuck, what am I going to tell them? Tell them . . . tell them our weapon systems are . . . ?" The captain pauses. "The weapon systems are compromised—screw it. I'll talk to them."

While the captain is occupied, Griffin takes the opportunity to slip away.

Taylor nods and puts on his headset. He tries hailing Norfolk and gets no response. He changes to an emergency frequency and tries again with the same results. Taylor grimaces as he looks up at the skipper. "No go, sir."

Hensley throws his hands up in the air. "Does anything on this ship work the way it was designed to fucking work?" He doesn't really expect a reply and one is not forthcoming. He glances up at the video screens to see a pair of heavily armed helicopters inbound on the stern camera. A moment later one of the chopper pilots hails the ship over the radio. "This is Seahawk one-niner-two calling the USS *Stark*."

Connelly returns from the engine room. After a quick briefing on recent developments Hensley says, "Send someone out to the helipad. Have them wave a white shirt before these helicopters blow us out of the water."

Again over the radio they hear another call from the Seahawk pilot requesting a response, his voice more urgent. The Seahawk is a highly modified version of the army's Black Hawk helicopter and just as deadly.

"Hurry, Kat," Hensley says.

"I'm on it. Maybe you should go out on the deck. Let the pilots see you."

"Good idea."

As Connelly picks up a ship's phone to convey the captain's orders, Hensley grabs a pair of binoculars and a portable radio in case it starts working again, and hurries down the steps to the rear deck.

CHAPTER 32

With no more gunshots echoing down the street, Peyton tiptoes back to the front window. She cups her hands around her face and leans in, closer to the glass. There is still no sign of Eric and she glances at her watch and mutters a curse word or two. Most are directed at Eric's boss but one or two are reserved for Eric, who obviously needs to grow a pair of balls. "What the hell does he have you doing when there's no electricity?" she mumbles to herself. Yes, Eric makes good money, but, jeez, does he earn it, having to put up with the asshole running the commercial lending department.

The streets are still clogged with cars, but Peyton notices that most of the autos are now empty, abandoned where they sit. No doubt some ran out of gas after hours of trying to get out of downtown. Peyton looks farther up the street to see delivery trucks, buses, taxis, and an assortment of other vehicles abandoned, many with the doors hanging open. Peyton realizes that even if the power were somehow restored soon, it would take days of around-the-clock work just to clear the streets. Her gaze drifts across the street to the shoe store. The stream of people entering the store has slowed to a trickle and Peyton doesn't know if it's the lack of available inventory or lack of interest. When Eric gets here to guard their supplies, she's planning on finding out with a firsthand look inside.

There are no bodies evident in the street or on the sidewalks and Peyton wonders what the results of the gunfire were. She glances to her left and her heart nearly seizes when she spots a group of ten or twelve heavily tattooed young men coming down the side-walk. Peyton hates to brand them gangbangers just by their looks because the last thing she'd ever want to be is racist, but there's no two ways about it—they're gangbangers. Several have guns tucked into their waistbands and those who aren't fortunate enough to own a pistol are armed with baseball bats, machetes, or tire irons. As they continue down the sidewalk, it looks like Moses parting the Red Sea as other walkers shift to the opposite sidewalk.

Peyton glances at the lobby entrance and feels the first real stab of fear. Yes, there had been gunshots fired, but this a different form of terror altogether. *All they'd have to do is push open the doors and waltz right in.* Peyton looks at her reflection in the glass. She's not a knockout, but she does consider herself attractive. With an hourglass-shaped body and a narrow waist, Eric tells her all the time that she's curvy in all the right places. *Or would they even care what I looked like? Would I be just fresh meat, ready for the taking?* As the group of hoodlums grows closer, Peyton's breathing quickens. *What if they come inside and discover I'm alone?* Peyton begins to tremble as images of a gang rape from some horrible film she'd watched as a teenager flash through her mind. She slowly slinks away from the glass and hurries across the lobby, ducking behind a chair.

Sliding around where she can see out the window, Peyton's rapid heartbeat is thrumming in her ears. *Should I run back to Ranjeet's store?* Peyton eases her head to the side, one eye and half of her face exposed beyond the edge of the chair. *He would be no match for one of those guys, much less an entire group.* The people on this side of the sidewalk start veering to the other side of the street and Peyton knows the group of goons is close. The tremble turns into a full-on shake and Peyton is on the verge of hyperventilating, her imagination out of control. *Stop it! Why would they want to come into an office building? Get a grip, Peyton. Jesus, they're looking for things to steal, not women to ravage.* Peyton focuses on her breathing. *Or are they looking for both? Just take whatever they want because they can? Where are they? Shouldn't they have already passed by?* Peyton moves to the other side of the chair and eases her head out for a peek. *Maybe they changed course.*

Peyton jumps when the loud crash of shattering glass echoes through the interior of the lobby. *Oh no. No, no, no. Not Ranjeet.*

CHAPTER 33

Chicago

Peyton is frozen with fear as laughter and chatter drift down the corridor from Ranjeet's store. She doesn't know if Ranjeet escaped or if he's now in a fight for his life. Either way, there's not a hell of a lot Peyton can do about it. Still hidden behind the chair, her eyes dart around the lobby, searching for a better—safer—place to hide. The circular desk in the center of the lobby where the security guards usually sit is an option, but it also might be a magnet for the thugs if they venture down the hall. Still scanning, her eyes land on the door to the stairs—her old go-to. *Would they have any reason to leave the main floor? Not much upstairs but offices, and the basement is just parking. What about those ritzy condos?* The residences start on the twenty-second floor and Peyton can't see them putting out all that effort when there's easier pickings on the street. *But if they get me in the stairwell they'll run me down like a cheetah chasing after an antelope.*

Peyton shifts her gaze to the lobby entrance, praying Eric will walk through the door. *Why? Eric's not going to be much help.* Peyton hears the squeak of tennis shoes on the polished marble floors and her heart, already hammering, redlines. She cups a hand around her ear and tilts her head, straining to hear as her brain screams for her to leave. More squeaks, then a loud bark of laughter. They're definitely heading her way. *Fuck!* Her eyes dart to the case of water, then to the stair door. *There's no time.* Peyton grows more frantic as the voices grow louder. Lunging to her feet, she grabs her bag and runs for the exit. Pushing on the dead automatic doors, she glances over her shoulder to see the group of thugs rounding the corner, their bats splattered with blood.

"Hey," one of them says. "Need some help?" Others in the group laugh as they move closer. "I bet you got a sweet li'l pussy on you, huh?" the man says, obviously the leader of this ragtag army.

Grunting, Peyton pushes on the doors with all her weight. She feels the left-side door give and she bears down, dropping the bag in the process.

"Hey, I'm talkin' to you," the leader says.

Sweat is dripping down her face and burning her eyes. She steals a quick glance back to see the group of thugs only a few feet away.

"I axed you a question," the man says. "If you're not goin' to answer, I guess we're gonna have to find out for ourselves. I call first dibs," the man says, eliciting more laughter from the group.

Peyton's body is trembling from the exertion and fear. With one final hard shove, the doors part just enough for her to squeeze through. She reaches back for the bag, but it's too large and won't fit through the opening. Tugging on the one handle she can reach, it rips off, sending her sprawling on the sidewalk. She glances up to see the leader pushing on the doors.

Scrambling to her feet, she takes off down the side-walk, running headlong into the crowd and screaming for help. The shattered glass rips through the soles of her bare feet, leaving a trail of bloody footprints in her wake. Her pleas for help go unanswered as the hordes of people trudge onward, ignoring her. She glances over her shoulder to see the group of thugs spilling out onto the sidewalk, carrying her bag and the water she'd worked so hard to get.

An older gentleman dressed in a suit stops and asks, "What's wrong, young lady?"

Out of breath, all Peyton can do is point at the gang-bangers now coming their way.

The blood drains from the man's face. "I'm sorry. There's little I can do to help," he says before crossing the street.

Peyton watches in horror as the leader reaches for the pistol tucked into his waistband. Her feet bloody and raw, she turns and hobbles forward, waiting for the bullet to pierce her back.

A shot rings out.

When she doesn't fall over dead, she feels momentary joy, thinking he had missed. Another shot echoes down the street and Peyton remains upright, still breathing. It's only when she lifts her head and looks ahead that she knows the guy didn't miss.

Advancing down the street are three members of the National Guard, rifles braced against their shoulders. "Everybody down!" one of the soldiers shouts as people dive for cover.

Peyton turns to see her tormentor dead on the street and her hope soars until one of the gang members fires off a shot that shatters the windshield of the car next to her. *Move your ass, Peyton.* She drops to her belly and crawls across the broken glass, taking cover behind the car. She peeks around the side to see the gangbangers scattering. A couple of bigger guys are slow to react and they pay for it with their lives.

The soldiers pass Peyton's location and continue down the street, their rifles at the ready. Peyton turns and looks longingly at the looted shoe store. *It'd be my luck to get shot for stealing a pair of shoes. But what if I sneak into Bloomingdale's? It's just right there.* She turns to look at the looted department store. *What are the odds the soldiers will come back this way?* Still arguing with herself, she pushes to her feet. Glancing back toward her office building, all thoughts of shoes flee when she spots a woman tiptoeing around the pools of blood to snag the case of water she climbed seventeen floors to get. "Uh-uh, bitch," Peyton, mutters, hobbling out from behind the car and up the street.

CHAPTER 34

Manhattan

There's bad news and then there's really bad news. The bad news is that the stock exchange software is infested with the malware and Paige wonders if they'll ever get rid of it entirely. Now, the really bad news—about half the database that records and documents stock trades is trashed. The final tally for the damage won't be known for months, but it figures to be in the trillions of dollars. To pile on, the redundant system out in New Jersey is also infested. But the fears don't end there. Paige is betting the broker-dealers who make trades on the exchange are also compromised. The malware turns out to be a worm, a nasty little piece of software and, like other worms, it propagates quickly, self-replicates, and requires no user intervention. As far as Paige can tell, the payload on this worm was designed for one purpose only—destruction. Paige turns to look at Hank. "What was the worm with multiple payloads that the Kaspersky Lab found?"

"A newer version of the Duqu worm. Newer even than Duqu 2.0. It was discovered on their system in early 2015, and the lab thought it was one of the most sophisticated pieces of malware to date. The hackers were clever enough to make slight variations to each attack, such as slight changes to file names or algorithms to avoid detection. The version they found had at least four compressed and encrypted payloads."

Paige shakes her head. "Who needs Google when I have you? Anyway, I've seen some of the Duqu source code and this isn't it. Not even close."

"Could it be an updated version of the Stuxnet malware?"

"If it is, there are some radical differences from the original code I saw. I'll send it to Natalie in a moment. I'm still having a hard time wrapping my head around the idea that all these attacks are linked to this one piece of malware."

"That's my hunch, Paige, but it doesn't necessarily mean I'm right. Couldn't they have multiple embedded and encrypted payloads? One for destruction and maybe another targetin' somethin' else?"

"It's possible, but extremely difficult to do."

"Whoever is behind the hack has spent years developin' this malware, Paige. Maybe we should reach out to the folks at Kaspersky."

"Hello? Do you watch the news?" Paige asks. "It's a Russian company. There's no way the FBI or the NSA is going to ask the Russians for anything."

"They have offices here in the States," Kent Fitzpatrick, the IT guy, offers.

"Yeah, probably to spy on us," Paige says.

Fitzpatrick shrugs. "We've used them in the past."

Paige swivels her chair around to stare at Fitzpatrick. "Yeah? And where did that get you?"

Fitzpatrick shrugs. "They've been very helpful to us in the past."

"Of course they were," Paige says, her voice dripping with sarcasm.

Hank's phone chimes and he pulls it out of his pocket to see a message from Elaine Mercer. He unlocks the screen and reads the contents before turning to Fitzpatrick. "Would you mind steppin' out of the room?"

"I'm not leaving the room until she unplugs her flash drive," Fitzpatrick says.

Paige scowls. "What? You afraid I'm going to copy some of your precious software?"

"It's my ass on the line," Fitzpatrick says. "Unplug the flash drive if you want me out of your hair for a few minutes."

"What if I plug it back in when you leave?" Paige asks, wagging her head back and forth with each word.

"If you do, I'll get a notification on my phone."

Hank feels like he's back in first grade. "Paige, pull the damn drive."

Paige pulls it out and waggles it in the air. "Satisfied?"

"Yes," Fitzpatrick says, his nose in the air as he exits.

"What an asshole," Paige mutters as the door closes. "What's the latest, Hank?"

"Nothin' good, that's for damn sure. Apparently one of our navy ships decided to take out half the fleet that's docked at Norfolk."

Paige rears back in surprise. "Jesus. How did *that* happen?"

"Accordin' to Elaine, they haven't been able to contact the ship. They don't know if the damn thing has been hijacked or what."

"Which ship did the shooting?"

"The new Zumwalt-class destroyer."

"Well, that makes sense. Talk about a piece of shit. They've worked a gazillion years on the damn thing and still can't get it right. The navy is trying to implement their new Total Computing something-or-other. The entire ship runs entirely by computer with about half the number of sailors as the current class of destroyers. I guess it's their way of saving money if you forget to factor in the billions of dollars already spent on development."

"The computer networks control everything? I've seen pictures of the ship, but that's it."

Paige nods. "Yes, from the ship's lights to her guns, it's all controlled by computers. I'm sure the network's partitioned so that the cooks don't have the capability to launch a missile, but I haven't seen any of the source code to know how it's structured."

"The structure doesn't matter because these hackers appear to have had abundant time to map every system on the ship."

"I think you're right."

Hank rereads the message from Elaine. "There's more."

"Of course there is. What else?"

"The Acela Express train derailed and slammed into other parked trains at Penn Station. Death toll unknown at present, but witnesses report seein' the train acceleratin' as it approached the station."

Paige leans back in her chair and grabs a strand of hair and twirls it around her index finger. "Huh. Now I'm doubly confused."

Hank leans forward in his seat, propping his elbows on his knees. "I've been thinkin'."

"That's dangerous," Paige says. "We don't want to get that big brain of yours overheated."

"Funny," Hank says, frowning. "We don't know exactly what happened with the aircraft, the dam, or all of the rest, but one thing sticks in my mind."

"Throw it out there. I'm game."

"Reports from the nuclear power plant suggested a water pump failure. The recordin' from Dulles pointed to an engine speed problem. The dam and power plants are producin' electricity. How? Through the use of turbines. Initial reports from the chemical companies were that their systems were overpressurized. The new warship's guns are run via computer. And witnesses say the train was speedin' up and not slowin' down as it should have been."

"Yeah. I like where you're going with this," Paige says. "You think they're targeting specific programmable logic controllers, such as the turbine speed controller?"

"I think so. Either that or they hacked into the SCADA systems and manipulated the controllers that way. Hell, if they've hacked the SCADA systems they could target not only the PLCs, but every other peripheral device connected to the network."

"What about the stock market?" Paige asks.

Hank leans back in his chair and crosses his right leg over his left. "I think it's a statement—a big fuck-you to America. You said it yourself. The worm here was designed for one thing—to do as much destruction as possible as quickly as possible. I think it's the anomaly out of the group. Everything else can be tied back to the various components that caused the disasters."

"Say you're correct in your theory. My question is, who and why? And why now?"

"Those are the big questions. How long is it goin' to take to create a program to delete the infected files?"

"Who knows? I need to send what I found to Natalie."

"Give me a ballpark?" Hank says. "If you haven't noticed, the country is going to hell around us."

Paige shrugs. "Hours, certainly, and that could stretch into days. We have to reverse engineer the worm before we can design a program to eliminate it."

"We need to shorten the timeline, Paige. Whatever it takes."

Hank's phone chimes again. He looks to see another message from Mercer. He swipes to unlock his screen.

"Mercer again?"

Hank nods as he reads through the new message. "Power's out in parts of western New York State."

"How long until they kill the power here in Manhattan?"

"Don't know. Probably sooner rather than later, especially since we've clamped down on their malicious activity here at the stock market."

"Can we leave before it happens?"

"That, I don't know."

CHAPTER 35

For the guards at the maximum-security prison Attica, the power outage in western New York happens when they're most exposed. With the early-dinner service under way, the mess hall is clogged with four hundred of the most dangerous prisoners in New York's prison system. Get in trouble at another prison and you get shipped off to Attica, site of the notorious prison riot that killed forty-three people in 1971.

The Attica Correctional Facility is one of only a handful of prisons in the country that has a permanent tear gas system installed. As long as the prison has power, guards can deploy tear gas in the mess hall and a few other select places throughout the prison at the touch of a button. Corrections Officer Brandon Spicer is standing just outside the mess hall staring at the rain streaking down the windows when the power goes off. With the threat of tear gas now gone and the lights off, the inmates are on him in seconds. Spicer is quickly thrown to the floor and the inmates begin kicking and stomping him. He wonders why the backup generators haven't started up, but before his brain can process possible reasons, several of the inmates start kicking him in the head like they're trying to hit a forty-five-yard field goal. He curls up in a fetal position, his hands over his head, as the beating intensifies. Bones crack with an audible crunch and Spicer shouts for help from his fellow officers between his gasps of pain. He glances across the floor and discovers why help is not coming—several of the other guards are lying on the floor, dead.

A sustained burst of rifle fire outside is the last sound Spicer hears before a violent kick to the head snaps his neck. Like a pack of rabid dogs, the inmates march through the prison, killing and maiming. Areas normally protected by electromagnetic locks are now fair game as the prisoners take revenge on the guards before turning on their own. The corridor leading to A-block is awash in blood as the carnage escalates.

The violence is not restricted to A-Block. Much of the same is occurring in the other three cellblocks. For Corrections Officer Lydia Darnell, the shrieks of the aggressors and the wails of those being attacked create a cacophony of sounds straight out of hell.

Inside the control room in Times Square when the power went off, Darnell's currently ducked down beneath the glass, trying to open the iron gate to the weapons locker behind her. Times Square is the small, secure booth that looks out over the hub of the prison where the tunnels from all four cellblocks meet. She doesn't know if the door to the booth is still locked now that the power is out, but the last thing she wants to do is rattle the knob or make any noise that will draw attention to her presence. She finally finds the right key—it's not a gate that gets used often—and quickly unlocks the door and darts inside. After relocking the gate, she grabs a shotgun and a box of shells and begins loading the weapon as she shuffles to the far corner of the room and sags to the floor. Once the gun is fully loaded, Darnell braces the shotgun against her shoulder, waiting for the inevitable.

CHAPTER 36

Out on the chopper deck of the USS *Stark*, Captain Hensley tried waving at the two Seahawks hovering off the stern to signal that the ship hasn't been hijacked. There have been no visual clues that the helicopter pilots understand, or they're wary it's all an act and the bad guys are holding the crew hostage. Admittedly, it's not normal for one navy ship to fire on other ships sailing under the same flag, but Hensley is running out of options on how to convey the message that he and the crew aren't under duress. And looking at all those Hellfire missiles hanging off the helicopter's stub wings is giving him heartburn.

He turns and scans the deck, looking for anything he can use to convey the ship's radio is broken. "Piece-of-shit ship," he mutters as he walks over to the helicopter hanger. He rolls up the door to find the space empty, not so much as a screwdriver in sight. Yes, the sea trials involving the helicopters are way down the road, but he's pissed they didn't build out the space. He curses the manufacturer and slams the door down. He walks back to the center of the helipad, fuming. Then

168   *Tim Washburn*

an idea pops into his head. Unclipping the useless portable radio from his belt, he rears back and slams the radio onto the deck. It breaks into pieces and Hensley steps back, gesturing at the shattered remains as if he were highlighting an item in the showcase showdown on *The Price Is Right*.

One of the choppers breaks from formation and edges closer. Apparently finally getting the message, the chopper pilot flies forward and hovers over the heli-pad, forcing Hensley to move out of the way. Once the helicopter settles on the deck, the back door opens and Hensley's bad day gets worse. Rear Admiral Richard Malloy, his commanding officer, climbs out with an angry scowl on his face and a sidearm strapped to his thigh. Hensley snaps to attention and salutes as Malloy approaches and the helicopter takes off. Malloy doesn't return the salute nor does he issue an order to stand at ease. He pins Hensley in place with a glare and steps forward until they're nose to nose. Once the helicopter retreats far enough away that they can have a conversation, Admiral Malloy says, "Captain Hensley, you are relieved of command."

Still at attention, Hensley says, "Yes, sir."

"What the fuck happened, Captain?"

"We're not sure, sir."

"Not sure? Half the goddamn fleet has been shot to shit and you don't know how it happened?"

"We're still dissecting the problem, sir."

"You're not dissecting shit, Captain. You'll be lucky if your ass doesn't get dissected by another inmate when you're shipped off to Leavenworth."

"Permission to speak, sir?" Hensley asks.

Malloy leans in closer. "What makes you think I want to hear some bullshit excuse?"

"Sir, we think the weapons systems were hacked."

"I did not give you permission to speak, Captain. And your goddamned weapons weren't hacked. This ship's fucking computer systems are bulletproof. I know because I've spent the last eight fucking years making sure that can't happen."

Rear Admiral Richard Malloy is in his early sixties and he has to look up in order to address Captain Hensley. With Malloy's dark, beady eyes, a sunken chin, and a slender build, Hensley can't get the image of a rat terrier out of his mind. Hensley wants desperately to wipe the spittle off his face yet he remains at attention. Finally, Malloy breaks eye contact. He steps back, removes his hat, and wipes the perspiration off his balding head as he gazes out to sea. He puts his cap back on, turns to face Hensley, and continues his tirade. "Why were your weapons even loaded, Captain?"

"We were scheduled for live-fire exercises, sir."

"Exercises means practice, Captain, not shooting up the fucking fleet."

Sweat is dripping into Hensley's eyes as he remains at attention. "Yes, sir." With his career probably swirling around the toilet bowl, he's tempted to tell Malloy to go fuck himself. But he doesn't. He stands rigid as Malloy circles him like a pit bull searching for the right spot to chomp down.

"Sir, how many ships sustained damage?"

"Did I tell you to speak?"

"No. Sir."

"To tell the truth, Captain, I don't think they've finished fucking counting." Malloy runs an index finger across the bridge of his nose and flicks the accumulated sweat onto the deck. With the ship stopped, there's not even a hint of a breeze and the afternoon sun feels like they're standing under a heat lamp. "Where's your weapons officer?"

"I'll take you to him, sir."

"You're not taking me anywhere, Captain. You're confined to quarters until I can get a handle on what the fuck happened here. Dismissed."

Hensley salutes and hurries to get back inside before Malloy changes his mind and puts him on one of the choppers. He steps through the door and nearly plows over his executive officer, Kat Connelly.

"How bad is it?" Connelly asks.

"Bad. I've been relieved of command and banished to my quarters."

"He can't do that. It's not your fault."

"He can, Kat. That's why he has those two stars on his sleeve. And, although what happened was out of our control, I'm the commanding officer."

"So, what, then? You going to your cabin to fall on your sword?"

Admiral Malloy comes stomping in the door and stops. "To your quarters, Mr. Hensley."

Kat comes to attention. "Sir, with all due respect—"

Malloy cuts her off with a wave of his hand. "Would you like to join him, Lieutenant Commander Connelly?"

"No, sir."

"That's what I thought." Malloy heads for the stairs. "Ms. Connelly, tell the sailor in charge of weapons to get them up and running."

Hensley clears his throat. "Sir—"

Malloy whirls around. "Why am I still looking at you, Mr. Hensley? You've been ordered to your quarters. Move your ass."

Hensley ducks through the hatch and heads down the corridor.

"Sir?" Connelly says.

"You're already walking a very fine line, Ms. Connelly."

"I know that, sir, but we immobilized the weapons systems."

"What the fuck do you mean, you immobilized them?"

"We disconnected them from the ship's computer, sir."

"How are we going to diagnose the problem if we can't communicate with the weapons computers?"

"We can't, sir."

"Fix it, Ms. Connelly. And tell one of those choppers to park their ass on the deck until I tell them otherwise."

"We can't, sir. The radios are inoperable."

"Then go stand on the deck and wave him in."

"Yes, sir," Connnelly says as she snaps off a salute and hurries out to the rear deck.

CHAPTER 37

Los Angeles

When people think about Los Angeles they often think of the weather, the movie stars, Hollywood, or the interminable traffic. For those with longer memories, thoughts of Los Angeles might trigger images of the Watts riots, the white Bronco chase through the city, or chaos in South Central. Very few people, other than those who work there, ever think about the sprawl of industrial properties that are situated fourteen miles east of downtown Los Angeles. Hemmed in by densely populated neighborhoods that have filled in over the years, the area known as Santa Fe Springs is home to an amalgam of chemical manufacturers that put nearly five million LA residents at risk if something were to ever go wrong.

One of those companies is CleanCal Industries. The list of items manufactured at CleanCal sounds innocuous—household cleaners, personal hygiene products, pool and spa supplies, automotive fluids, and general cleaning supplies. Nothing on the list triggers alarm bells and two of the most common chemicals used at

CleanCal are chlorine and ammonia—two ubiquitous products found in homes all across the world. Their presence at the plant doesn't move the danger needle for many nearby residents because most don't stop to contemplate the quantity of chemicals the company must store on site to keep the production lines humming along.

Separately, the two chemicals are relatively safe as long as they are used according to the labeled directions. But many people have discovered during everyday cleaning duties that if the two chemicals are accidently mixed—say, in a toilet bowl—it creates a toxic vapor that'll burn the sinuses and trigger a coughing fit.

The combination of the chlorine and ammonia creates chloramine vapor, a toxic substance that irritates the eyes, nose, throat, and airway. If inhaled, the vapor enters the bloodstream directly through the lungs and combines with a person's red blood cells, making them incapable of carrying oxygen. Prolonged exposure to the vapors could be fatal.

The people working inside the plant are properly trained and each and every employee is aware of the toxic hazards. To alleviate potential mistakes, the ammonia and chlorine are kept in separate areas of the plant and are isolated from each other by a series of pipes and valves that feed each chemical to the production line when needed.

In addition to the careful handling of chemicals, CleanCal prides itself on innovation. The plant is highly automated, using the company's computer networks to control almost every aspect of production. There *are* humans to act as oversight and the company also employs seven information technology people to keep the software up to date and to ward off the nearly continuous intrusion attempts on the facility's computer network.

But someone missed something somewhere and unbeknownst to those seven IT employees, the plant's network is now compromised.

Four blocks east of the plant is a dense neighborhood of smaller homes that contains nearly a thousand residents. Three of those residents are Loretta Ortiz and her two sons, nine-year-old Mateo and seven-year-old Gabriel. Celebrating their last few days of freedom before school starts, Loretta is preparing a late picnic lunch for them to share at the neighborhood park. The mostly Hispanic community is a fairly tight-knit group of families that have bonded over the years through interactions at the neighborhood elementary school adjacent to the park. Loretta steps over and switches on the small television in the kitchen, hoping to catch a quick weather update.

The area is experiencing an intense heat wave, thanks to a stationary high-pressure ridge stalled over the deserts to the east. Instead of the usual cooling easterly winds that blow in off the coast, Los Angeles is being blistered by westerly winds from the hot desert regions of the state. It's almost enough for Loretta to cancel the picnic, but the park offers plenty of shade and the boys have been cooped up in the house all morning. Loretta, an English teacher at the school, is hoping to run into other children from the neighborhood so the boys can burn off some of their rambunctious energy. And if it gets too uncomfortable they can always walk down the street to the library.

Loretta makes fairly good money as a teacher and her husband, Miguel, has a good job as a supervisor at a grocery distribution center just down the street. It's close enough that he can walk to work, allowing Loretta to keep the family car for emergencies and it also helps them avoid making payments on a second car. The plan had been for him to join them at the picnic, but he called earlier to say he's tied up.

Their small two-bedroom, one-bathroom home has an open living and kitchen area, thanks to the renovations that she and Miguel have made. They bought it in foreclosure, and Miguel and Loretta spent every weekend for months making the home theirs. They eliminated walls, remodeled the kitchen and bathroom, and repainted everything, both inside and out. Now it's a bright and airy home and Loretta loves it. The only downside is the boys have to share a bedroom. The backyard *is* large enough to add a third bedroom, but Loretta and Miguel don't want to overbuild and possibly end up taking a big loss if they ever decide to sell.

Loretta groans when a weather tease for the six p.m. newscast promises more of the same. She pulls her long, dark hair up off her neck, twirls it a time or two, and clips it up out of the way. A short, curvy woman with large, dark eyes and a dark complexion, Loretta prefers the natural look and rarely applies much makeup other than a dab of lipstick on occasion. Today she doesn't even bother with that. It's too hot. After turning off the television, she grabs her cell phone, her sunglasses, and the picnic basket. "Boys," she shouts, "time to go."

Mateo and Gabriel come running down the hall,

laughing. Loretta smiles and her heart flutters a little when she thinks how lucky she and Miguel are. She herds the boys out of the house and locks the door, having no idea she won't cross the door's threshold ever again.

CHAPTER 38

Pashat, Pakistan

March 6, 2006
TARGET: Al-Qaeda
CONFIRMED KILLED: 83
CIVILIANS KILLED: 37 (16 children)

Nestled in a fertile valley in the mountainous region of Pakistan and close to the Afghanistan border, Pashat is a beautiful small community surrounded by verdant fields planted with a variety of crops. Today the weather is pristine, making it a perfect day for a celebration. Dressed in all their colorful finery, the Ansari family is making final preparations for the day's main event—a wedding. Among them, and creating his fair share of mischief, is thirteen-year-old Hassan. A handsome dark-haired and dark-eyed young man, Hassan Ansari is taking great pleasure in playfully pestering his cousin, Ayesha, the future bride. Dressed in a long, beautifully embroidered, bright red dress and matching head scarf, Ayesha's dark eyes are alight with pleasure as she revels in her special day.

Hassan soon grows bored with the pestering and of

all the women fawning over the bride. He stands and gives Ayesha a peck on the cheek before hurrying off to play with his other cousins. A large family, the Ansaris have been productive when it comes to offspring. The event has drawn family from all over the area, many of them children ranging in age from toddler to teen. Hassan finds his cousin Nadeem, and together they set off to do a little exploring.

The wedding is taking place in the backyard garden of Ayesha's home on the outskirts of the city in the foothills of Hindu Kush mountains. Hassan and Nadeem escape the backyard to explore the neighborhood—what turns out to be a lifesaving choice.

As they venture down the block, chasing after a lizard, both are stunned when a ground-rattling explosion rips through the afternoon silence. Hassan turns to see what had blown up and his heart plunges into despair when he sees his uncle's house on fire. His chest tightening with fear, Hassan races up the street with Nadeem as dazed neighbors pour out of the surrounding homes. As the two boys near the house, the fire is so intense they can do little but watch.

In the aftermath, after the injured were treated or rushed to the hospital in town Hassan discovered that his immediate family survived, but sixteen of his cousins did not, including the beautiful bride-to-be, Ayesha.

Present day, somewhere near Boston

An ignited ember of anger still resides inside Hassan Ansari's gut and probably will until the day he dies. Sometimes it flares brighter and other times he does his best to ignore it, but today it's roaring as he remembers the horror of that day. Hassan runs a hand through his thick, dark hair and leans back in his chair. Right now, he's running a program on his computer to discover if he can access any of the other MOAB bombs deployed around the world.

They got extremely lucky with the one bomb in McAlester, Oklahoma, after the internal guidance computer connected to the local Wi-Fi network. While the computer hunts, Ansari stands and stretches before walking over to the small break room to pour a cup of coffee. He's been mulling over the confrontation between Jermar and Nazeri, and, for the first time, a small larva of doubt tries to worm its way into his brain. Hassan takes a sip of coffee then prowls through the cabinets looking for a snack.

Nazeri has been attentive to their needs up to now, bringing in food, snacks, and drinks during the long days of work. But it's now well past the lunch hour and there's no food in sight. Hassan finds a bag of Chex Mix, rips it open, and pours some in a bowl and pops a handful into his mouth. He pours the coffee down the drain and grabs a bottle of water from the fridge instead.

Nazeri also promised that Hassan and the others would be provided for after termination of the operation, yet gave few details. Hassan unscrews the lid on the bottle and takes a sip, his mind swirling with a mixture of thoughts. Everyone is working under the assumption that their chances of being caught are somewhere between slim and none, but Hassan wonders. He's worked an odd computer job here and there over the years and funneled that money into a savings account he opened on a trip down to Manhattan. And, if absolutely necessary, he could hack a bank or two for funds, but he doesn't like stealing. Then another thought hits him: *How bad is stealing after everything I've done today?* And for the first time he sees himself in a new light. One he's not particularly pleased with. From this day forward Hassan Ansari, if his actions are ever discovered, will be known as a cold-blooded murderer and will, most likely, be branded a terrorist.

That thought makes him somewhat nauseous. No longer hungry, he puts the bag of Chex Mix back in the cabinet and dumps the contents of the bowl in the trash. Then his thoughts drift to the friends he'd made over the years while in college. *Could any of them have died in today's attacks*? Mulling that over, he returns to his computer and discovers the software has found another active bunker buster bomb at a military base in Japan. He stares at the screen for a long time, his brain roiling with indecision. Looking up, he spots Nazeri walking his way and he quickly exits the program.

"Have you found other active bombs, Hassan?" Nazeri asks.

"No," Hassan lies, still staring at his screen.

Nazeri cocks his head to the side. "That's odd. You would think with all of the American military hardware scattered around the globe we would find additional targets. Did you allow the software time to complete its task?"

"Yes," Hassan says in his sternest voice as he glances up at Nazeri. "There are no more active bombs. Run the program yourself if you do not believe me."

"I just might do that," Nazeri says.

"Have a go. Do you need assistance pulling the program up on your computer?" Hassan asks, staring Nazeri in the eyes.

"Watch yourself, Hassan."

Hassan breaks the stare first and Nazeri turns and walks away.

Hassan leans forward and removes the tape covering the computer's camera then scrolls to the program that controls the camera and switches it on. He turns the monitor slightly until Nazeri's face is in the frame and surreptitiously snaps several photos and saves them inside an encrypted folder in the cloud. He replaces the tape and sits back in his chair, thinking.

Nazeri is the one who decides which portion of the power grids to take down. It wouldn't do to kill the power to a potential target—how are you going to blow something up if it's not up and running? Hassan has no doubt that by the time this is all over with most of the United States will be without electricity. Then he wonders what that means for his apartment here in Boston. He has enough food for a day or two, but the power's going to be out much longer than that due to the damage they're doing to the transformers. *Will I ever see my apartment again? My friends?* It's an unanswerable question and he tries to clear his mind. He turns to look at Nazeri, who is seated at the head of the table, grinning eagerly as his fingers fly across the keyboard.

"What are you doing, Nazeri?" Hassan asks.

Nazeri never looks up when he says, "I'm sending a gift to the people of Los Angeles."

Hassan shudders at his enthusiasm. Hassan, who became enchanted with the movie *The Wizard of Oz* shortly after arriving in the States, thinks of Nazeri as the Tin Man. But unlike the movie character, it appears Nazeri has no need for, nor does he want, a heart.

CHAPTER 39

Los Angeles

Loretta Ortiz leads her two sons into the park, pleasantly surprised to see several other families already there. It appears Loretta wasn't the only one who thought a picnic lunch would be a good idea today. Blankets dot the grass and food is laid out on platters as children flit in and out, grabbing a bite of food before hurrying off to play again. Loretta says hello to the other mothers and spreads her blanket out in the deep shade, next to her friend and fellow teacher Renata Rodriguez. After opening the basket, she lays some sandwiches out for the boys and both grab one and head out to join their friends.

Loretta smiles at Renata. "Ready for school?"

"I don't know about school, but I'm ready for a routine." Renata, mother to eight-year-old Sofia and six-year-old Sara, is a short, chubby woman who always has a smile on her face.

Loretta pulls her legs up beneath her as she scans the park, pinpointing the location of her two sons. "Me, too. Have you met the new principal?"

"No, but I hear good things about her. I was talking to one of my other friends who taught under her last year. She really likes her." Renata looks around to make sure the kids are out of earshot. "Hey, I brought a pitcher of frozen sangria swirl. Want some?"

"I would love some." Loretta fans herself with her hand. "Is this heat ever going away?"

"Someday, but this will help, today." Renata pulls out a plastic cup and pours some sangria swirl and passes it to Loretta. "I'm just glad the school is air-conditioned."

"Thank you," Loretta says, taking the cup. "Me, too." She takes a sip and smacks her lips. "This is perfect."

It's not long before other mothers drift over and they huddle together on the blankets, gossiping as the children play. Renata pours more sangria swirl for the new arrivals. They sip and talk and laugh as the children dart in for food before taking off again. As it turns out, two other mothers had thought ahead and packed containers of frozen adult beverages and, when the sangria swirl runs out, they break out a pitcher of frozen margaritas. Other than the heat, Loretta thinks, it's turning out to be an ideal afternoon.

Down the street at CleanCal, the day crew is trying to troubleshoot some balky pumps. Sitting in the plant's control room, Mark Perry, one of the plant engineers, is keeping a close eye on pump speeds and tank pressures. Watching a graphic display of real-time activity at the plant on a large video screen, Perry does not like what he's seeing. He turns to the shift supervisor for the regular employees, Dennis Nelson, and says, "Dennis, you're going to have to dial those pumps back."

Nelson is busy working a keyboard. "We're trying, Mark. The network is awfully sluggish."

"How long has that been going on?" Perry asks, concern in his voice. The last thing they need now is a sluggish computer network.

"The last hour or so. It's weird," Nelson says.

"You talk to the IT guys?"

"Yes. They're looking into it."

An alarm sounds and Perry looks up at the screen. "Pressure's too high, Dennis. Kill the power to the pumps at the ammonia tank."

"The computer isn't responding to any of my commands, Mark."

Perry snatches up a phone and dials a three-digit number, one of the plant's phone extensions. He wedges the phone between his shoulder and neck as he works the keyboard. "We need to bleed off some of the pressure, Dennis." The phone isn't answered until the sixth damn ring and Perry, hot under the collar, barks out an order to manually shut down the pumps to the ammonia tank. Perry knows he needs to bleed off some pressure, but now he's in a pickle. He risks serious injury to the plant workers if he bleeds off the ammonia vapors while they're in the area. Perry punches up a camera inside the plant to check on the workers' progress, as the pressure nudges into the red.

"They're working way too slow, Dennis. Get on the horn and light a fire under their asses," Perry says, his eyes glued to the video screen.

Nelson grabs a handheld radio and urges the employees to hurry it up.

Perry, watching the pressure continuing to build, stands from his chair. "Dennis, we're going to be in a hell of a mess in about fifteen seconds."

"We're trying, Mark."

"Then try harder." Perry, watching the workers on the camera, sees one of them shake his head. "Dennis, stand by to bleed the pressure." He reaches across the console and hits a button that sounds a warning horn throughout the plant. "Hurry up, damn it," he mutters as the workers scurry to safety. He glances up at the monitor displaying tank pressure. It's as high as he's ever seen it. "Now, Dennis," he shouts.

"The EPA is going to fine us," Nelson says, his finger hovering over the button.

"I don't care. Hit the fucking button."

Nelson does, releasing a cloud of ammonia into the air. The pressure in the tank begins to drop and Perry sags into his chair.

"Jesus," Nelson says.

"What?" Perry asks, his eyes scanning the large video screen, searching for problems.

"Look at the chlorine tank numbers."

Perry does and his stomach flip-flops. "What the hell is going on?"

"I don't—oh no," Nelson mutters.

Perry glances up at the big screen. "What?"

"Several of the bypass valves are opening and I have no control."

Loretta is buzzed. And that's something that surprises her because she is not a heavy drinker and she never drinks during the day. However, she is having a good time having adult conversations for once. She drains the last of her margarita and is reaching for the pitcher of strawberry daiquiris when she spots Mateo running up.

"Mom, what's that smell?" Mateo asks.

Loretta sniffs. "Smells like a cleaner or something." She glances over at the school to see if the maintenance workers are doing some work inside. They'll often do a thorough cleaning before school starts and during holiday breaks. But judging from the empty parking lot the odor is not coming from the school. Loretta waves a hand at her son. "Go play. It's nothing."

Mateo shrugs and takes off again.

Several moments later, Loretta notices the smell is getting stronger. She looks over at her friend Renata. "Do you smell that?"

Renata sniffs. "Smells like ammonia." Several of the other mothers begin to notice the smell.

"What is that?" someone else asks as several of the women stand.

Without warning, a siren blares from somewhere down the street. Loretta pushes to her feet and stumbles forward, grabbing on to Renata to keep from falling. She glances at the sky, thinking bad weather had crept up on them. But the skies are clear, no storm clouds in sight. Dulled by the alcohol, Loretta stumbles around, shouting for her sons, trying to get a handle on the situation. Other mothers begin yelling for their children.

The siren stutters and, a millisecond later, an immense explosion rips through the quiet afternoon, drowning out the mothers' pleas. Loretta looks to the east to see a cloud of smoke ballooning high in the air. She turns away and hurries across the playground, desperate to find Mateo and Gabriel. As the cloud of smoke drifts overhead, Loretta's eyes begin to sting and her sinuses begin to burn, her breathing becoming more labored.

Putting a hand up to shield the sun, Loretta slows, searching desperately for her sons. The ammonia smell is now laced with something else. Loretta tries to put her finger on what it is. Then she does and her blood runs cold. Chlorine! She's done enough cleaning in her day to know the dangers of combining ammonia and chlorine, but Loretta doesn't know the chloramine vapors are four times heavier or that the toxic mix is now sinking down over the park.

Unfortunately it's not only the chloramine Loretta needs to worry about. As the molecules from both the chlorine and ammonia continue to react, the ongoing chemical reaction spins off two other nasty substances—hydrazine and hydrochloric acid, making the falling mist of vapors a lethal fog of certain death.

Her vision blurry, Loretta stumbles across the open field. She thinks she sees Mateo on the other side of the field and she attempts to shout his name. But this time she can't inhale enough air to stimulate her vocal cords and the shout comes out as a croak. Still a good distance away from her oldest son, she moans with despair as Mateo clutches his throat and sinks to his knees. Loretta's brain is screaming for her to hurry as she closes her eyes and opens them again, furiously wiping her eyes in an attempt to clear her vision. Her foot catches on a tree root and Loretta tumbles to the ground.

Huffing and puffing, she pushes to her knees and starts crawling. The gravel and rocks bite into her palms and knees as she wobbles forward. Her lungs feel as if they're going to burn through her chest wall as she works her jaw, trying to keep her throat from closing.

But it's a losing battle, and seconds later, Loretta Ortiz collapses to the ground, the images of her sons flashing through her mind slowly dimming to darkness.

CHAPTER 40

Manhattan

Using her laptop, Paige logs in to her VPN and sends the malware to Natalie Lambert over at NSA. She gives Natalie a few minutes to peruse what she sent then makes a call. While she's doing that, Hank plugs Paige's flash drive into his laptop and pulls up the infected computer code. The first thing that is readily apparent is that the code appears very clean and well written. Usually when foreigners initiate a cyber attack, their code is riddled with misspelled words or the words are used in the wrong context. But here, it appears clean and concise. Hank digs a little deeper. As expected, the malware Paige found appears to be a rootkit, which allows administrator-level access to the network and is extremely difficult to detect. Hank leans back in his chair, thinking.

Could Natalie be right? Is an insider involved? Hank mulls that over for a moment. *If it's not an insider it's someone with a firm grasp of the English language. Have they spent significant time in this country?* Then his thoughts meander down another path. *What if the hackers aren't foreigners? Could a homegrown terror-*

ist cell be behind the hack? Hank realizes they're all unanswerable questions and they'll stay that way if they can't find any damn clues. Right now their batting average is nil with not much hope it's going to improve anytime soon.

Paige disconnects the call to Natalie and turns to Hank. "Natalie told me this malware is some of the most sophisticated software she's ever seen. But there is one bit of good news. The NSA has been working on developing several software tools that might kill it."

"What's the bad news?" Hank asks.

"It could take a while to reprogram the software to attack this particular piece of malware."

"What's your definition of 'a while'?"

Paige grabs a strand of hair and wraps it around a finger, delaying. "A couple of days if we're lucky."

"Hell, Paige, there may be nothin' left of this country in a couple of days."

"Natalie is going to call me back after she's had some time to closely examine the software. Maybe she can suggest a more reliable time frame. I know that's not the answer you're looking for, Hank, but this stuff is extremely complicated."

"Can we use the program you used to find the malware and quarantine it?"

"No. It's only a seek-and-find program."

"So, what? We sit on our hands, waitin' for the next tragedy?"

Paige lets the strand of hair fall and pushes to her feet. "I don't know, Hank. Maybe we shut the factories and power plants down for a day or two until we develop a fix."

"I can tell you right now that's not goin' to happen. No way in hell."

"Wouldn't it be better to save the remaining pieces of infrastructure so it could be restarted when we patch the software?"

Hank stands and walks over to the long glass wall that looks into the server room. The thousands of flashing green and red diodes are mesmerizing. "Think of the enormity of what you're suggestin', Paige. Jeez, you're talkin' about cuttin' off power to millions of people. That would plunge the country into chaos."

"I think we're already well on our way. What's worse? Losing power for a couple of days or a couple of months?"

"The main problem I see is that an overwhelmin' majority of power suppliers and industrial plants are private companies. What then? Does the FBI call them up and ask if they'd mind shuttin' down for a few days?"

Paige sighs. "I don't know, Hank. Maybe the president could declare a national emergency."

"That's a big step and one I've already suggested to Elaine. But I wouldn't hold my breath if I were you." Hank begins to massage his temples with his left hand. "What a fuckin' mess," he says as he walks back to his chair and sits. "I think you and Natalie need to be in the same room together. Maybe you two could bang out a solution quicker with the help from other people at both agencies."

"I agree, Hank."

"Wrap up in here and I'll go talk to Tomás to see if we can get a plane back to D.C." Hank stands and walks toward the door. As he reaches for the handle, the lights in the hallway flash off and almost instantaneously flash back on. He turns to look at Paige. "That's not a good sign."

"You think the generators just kicked on?"

"Yep."

CHAPTER 41

Chicago

With her lacerated feet, Peyton had zero chance of running down the woman who stole her case of water. She did, however, recover her backpack containing the canned food. Hobbling through the lobby door of her office building, Peyton is trying to dial up enough courage to venture down the hall to check on Ranjeet. With each step, the pain radiates up her legs and it takes tremendous will to continue moving forward. *I can't go any further.* The thought of having to walk all the way down the corridor to Ranjeet's store makes her nauseous. She stops and scans the lobby, looking for something—anything—to protect her feet. *What can I use?* The artificial fig trees scattered around the lobby aren't going to do her much good. The same applies to the wooden benches. Then her eyes drift to the upholstered furniture. *I can't walk around with large seat cushions on my feet.* Peyton studies the furniture for another moment and then comes up with an idea. She shuffles over, digs through her bag, and pulls out the scissors.

After a few minutes of cutting and trimming, Peyton

stands to test out her new shoes. They won't be seen on any fashion runways anytime soon, but they're adequate. After cutting the foam to fit her foot, Peyton used the material as an outer shell and wrapped everything up with the cushion's cording. She takes a tentative step. Definitely not Nike Airs, but they're not bad. The homemade shoes feel clumsy on Peyton's feet, but they are fairly comfortable to walk on. How long they'll last is anybody's guess and, as for style, they're not much to look at. But pair those with her shredded pencil skirt/loincloth, and Peyton looks like she's on her way to a Village People concert.

Glancing at her watch she sees it's nearly five-thirty. She turns to look out the window and discovers the stream of people on the sidewalk has slowed considerably, which could be a good thing or a bad thing. Good, because they'll have a little more freedom of movement without the crowds, but on the flip side there's safety in numbers. Peyton shivers at the thought of Eric and her walking home alone. Grabbing her bag, she stuffs the extra material for her homemade shoes in and shuffles over to the entrance to the corridor leading to Ranjeet's store and takes a peek down the hall. She really, really, doesn't want to do this alone. Her heart racing, she glances over her shoulder one final time, hoping to see Eric lumbering up the sidewalk. No such luck. She takes a deep breath and turns into the hallway, her senses on high alert.

At the entrance to the store, Peyton picks up a metallic scent. It's a familiar odor but she can't pinpoint the source. Street noise drifts through the shattered windows, making hearing difficult. She scans the dusky gloom, whispering Ranjeet's name.

No response or not one she can hear.

Her body trembling, she crosses over the threshold and enters the store. Ranjeet's once carefully arranged merchandise litters the floor and the shelving is over-turned. Peyton picks her way through the clutter, search-ing for her friend. There's no semblance of where an aisle began or ended, just one jumbled mess, like some-thing you'd see in an earthquake aftereffects video. Nudging items aside with her makeshift shoes, she ventures deeper into the dark store. The sun has pushed to the west and the street is now in shadow, making it that much darker inside. She picks up the metallic scent again and it's stronger. With the blood pulsing through her veins and her hands trembling, Peyton slips the bag off her shoulder and digs through it look-ing for the flashlight. Finding it, she clicks it on and gasps. Dark, rust-colored splatters are everywhere. It looks as if someone walked inside with a bucket of barn-red paint and sloshed it around.

Then it hits her. The metallic scent and the splatters can mean only one thing—blood. And lots of it. "Ran-jeet," she says a little louder.

No response.

Waving the flashlight back and forth and scanning the floor, Peyton moves toward the remnants of the front counter. She sees more blood, but no sign of her friend. The store is not large and it doesn't take long for Peyton to finish her search. She steps over to the glassless window frame and scans the sidewalk, look-ing for a trail of blood and hoping Ranjeet had some-how escaped.

No blood.

Peyton exhales a long, shaky breath. The only places left to search are the storeroom, the small office, and the restrooms, all located at the back of the store. Peyton picks her way through the mess and enters the hallway leading to the rear of the store. The women's restroom is first up. She eases the door open and waves the flashlight around, crying out when the cone of light bounces off the mirror and hits her in the eyes.

No blood and no Ranjeet.

Finding the men's restroom empty, Peyton approaches the door to the office, fear and dread racing up and down the length of her spine. She places her hand on the doorknob and twists, pushing the door open. She aims the flashlight into the room and screams.

The one quick glimpse is enough because the image will be seared in her memory for eternity—Ranjeet's severed head is resting on the desk, his dead eyes still open and staring back at her.

CHAPTER 42

Corrections Officer Lydia Darnell hears the sirens start up. Then the lights flicker and flash on.

Thank God the generators finally kicked on.

Darnell shuffles over to the gate and inserts the key, hesitant to open it. *Could some of the guards still be alive?* Darnell weighs the odds in her mind. *How long before help arrives?* None of the questions can be answered from here, she reasons. But if there's even one guard left alive, Darnell aims to save them.

Darnell grabs a handgun and tucks it into her waistband, then reaches for the shotgun and fills her pockets with shells. After grabbing a radio and several extra clips for the pistol, she turns the key and slips into the Times Square guard booth. She desperately wants to use the radio to call for help, but she knows the inmates probably have a few radios now, and the last thing she wants to do is announce that a guard remains alive. From there she quietly eases the outer door open and takes a peek down the hall. What she sees makes her blood run cold. Bodies litter the corridor and the uneven concrete floor is puddled with blood. With her hands trembling and the bile surging in the back of her throat, she tucks the shotgun to her shoulder and moves out into the hall.

The ponds of blood and the haphazardly scattered bodies make the footing treacherous and the going is slow. Darnell approaches the first guard and kneels down to roll him over. It's Bud Curtis, one of the nicest guards at the prison. His torso is riddled with stab wounds, but she checks for a pulse anyway. As she feared, Bud Curtis is long gone. She rises and places the shotgun to her shoulder as she continues down the corridor. She finds four more guards, all dead, before arriving at the door to cellblock A. Inside, bodies litter the concrete, one or two moaning in pain. She treads carefully, stopping to check on two people still alive. Both are inmates, but their faces are so badly beaten she can't identify them. She bends down to whisper that help is on the way before moving on.

Her head is on a swivel, trying to clear the cells as she passes. Other bodies are inside some of the cells and all appear to be dead. She exits A-Block and turns left at the next corridor. Her heart leaps into her throat when she finds one of her best friends on the force. Sueann is lying in a pool of her own blood, her uniform trousers down around her ankles and her top ripped open. Bite marks are visible on her breasts and they left a broken mop handle sticking out of her vagina. Like a lightning bolt, anger floods Darnell's system, washing away the residual fear and igniting an ember in her gut. "Fucking animals," she mumbles.

She quickens her pace, stepping around bodies, now searching for live targets. As she enters cellblock B an inmate rushes her from a cell. She swivels around, pulling the trigger as she turns. The buckshot hits the inmate in the chest, sending him back into the cell. Darnell racks another shell and continues on. At the exit to cellblock D she finds another female guard in the same condition as Sueann. She has bite marks, but instead of a broom handle, they used her baton. Bile surges into Darnell's mouth, and she bends over and vomits. When the spasm subsides, she wipes her mouth with the back of her hand and continues on, the shotgun up and braced against her shoulder.

Darnell finds fifteen more guards, all of them dead. The sadistic bastards had mutilated both male and female corrections officers, including two women who had their breasts sliced off and their genital areas mutilated. Darnell dry heaves and forces herself to turn away.

The slow burn in her gut is now a raging fire. Two inmates appear around a far corner, their shirts covered with blood. Darnell takes aim and drops the one on the left before jacking another shell and blowing a hole in the other's chest. There will be no surrender as far as she's concerned. At a door to the yard, she pauses to peek through the security glass. More bodies litter the yard, a mixture of guards and inmates. *Are guards still in the watchtowers?* She slips the radio from her belt and looks at it for a moment. It's not worth the risk.

She reattaches the radio to her belt and glances out the window again. If she goes out there the likelihood of being overpowered and killed is a near certainty. With a very low probability of finding any guards still alive, she decides to return to the armory and the safety of a locked door. Darnell makes it to the end of the corridor before she hears the squeal of the outside door opening. Then voices echo down the hall. She glances over her shoulder to see a large group of inmates turning the corner.

Darnell's first thought is that she didn't bring near enough shotgun shells. Yes, she does have the pistol and extra ammo, but trying to hit anything much beyond twenty feet is dicey and Darnell has no plans for them getting that close. She hugs the wall of cells and quickens her pace. She makes it to the end of the cellblock, sucks in a lungful of air, and hurries toward the center gate.

"Hey, bitch," one of the inmates shouts.

She turns and fires the shotgun, jacks another shell, and fires again. The inmates break for cover and she turns and hurries on, stepping over and around bodies as she feeds more shells into the shotgun. Another glance back reveals that the inmates have regrouped and are in pursuit. Darnell rips the handgun from her waist and squeezes off fifteen quick shots, scattering the inmates again. She hadn't been aiming at separate targets, just firing at the group. If she's lucky she wounded a few, but she's not hanging around to find out.

She ejects the magazine and slaps another in as she hurries along the cells in A-Block. She tries to hurdle a large puddle of blood and her plant foot slides out from under her. The shotgun skitters away as she braces for the fall. She hits the ground and rolls onto her stomach. *Where's the shotgun?* She glances around and spots it up next to a cell.

"Get her," a voice shouts from behind her.

She pushes up to all fours and attempts to stand, her feet seeking purchase on the slippery floor. She glances behind her to find the inmates now only about twenty feet away. She drops to her knees, pulls the handgun, and fires another salvo then ejects the magazine and replaces it with a full one. Carefully, she bear-crawls forward until her feet reach a portion of dry floor and she stands. She hurries to the shotgun, scoops it up, and fires a round down the corridor, and the inmate in the lead drops. Trying to jack another shell, her blood-soaked hands slip from the stock. She wipes her palm on her pants, pumps another round into the chamber, and fires. Another inmate spins away from the pack, holding his arm. The others break rank, seeking cover in the cells. Darnell loads two more shells into the shotgun as she turns and hurries on.

She makes it to the end of the last cellblock and slips in another pool of blood while trying to turn toward Times Square. She stumbles forward and the shotgun goes flying down the hall. *Screw it*, she thinks as she stumbles toward the door. With the power now on she'll need to enter the six-digit number into the electronic lock. *What's the combination?* Her brain is spinning through the possible combinations. *The code changed recently. What the hell is it?* This is not one of her normal work areas. She sneaks a peek down the hallway. Judging by the size of the group, the number of inmates has grown significantly, no doubt drawn in by the gunfire.

They're much too close and, as an image of Sueann flashes in her mind, she pulls the pistol and takes a shooter's stance with both hands positioned on the gun. Rather than spraying bullets this time, she takes direct aim and squeezes the trigger. Altering her aim, she fires again.

Two down and too many to go. She aims at four more prisoners and shoots then sprays a few more bullets into the group and switches out magazines. She's down to her last. She punches a series of numbers into the lock and tries the handle. No go. Another glance down the corridor reveals the inmates are regrouping. *What is the damn number?* She clears the last numbers and tries again. And still the handle doesn't turn. She resumes her firing position, and counts the shots as she fires. She wants at least one round left in the chamber, just in case.

The inmates scatter again as she turns back to the lock. *Think, Lydia. They announced the new code at morning roll call.* She steals another glance down the hall. The inmates are using the sides of the doorway for cover as they creep forward. *Damn it, Lydia. Punch in the right combination or prepare to eat your gun.* Clearing the last set of numbers, Darnell punches in a new set of numbers that pop into her head. She takes a deep breath, turns the handle, and the door opens.

She charges into the room and relocks the door as the inmates draw abreast. One snatches up the shotgun and takes direct aim at her. Although the glass is allegedly bulletproof, she wonders how many direct hits from double-ought buckshot it can withstand. The inmate fires and the glass fractures into a spiderweb of cracks. The inmate steps forward and places the barrel against the glass. He fires, and a small hole appears. He jams the barrel through and racks another shell. Darnell lunges inside the weapons locker and slams the gate shut as the shotgun roars again. She grabs another shotgun and begins loading while her mind spins. *Did I reload the shotgun? Yeah, I did. Three shots fired. Oh shit, two left.*

The sound of shattering glass echoes through the office. She braces herself behind a file cabinet and takes aim. A head pops around the gate door and Darnell fires, the head erupting into a spray of blood. With no doubt another inmate will pick up the shotgun, Darnell jacks another shell. Seconds later another inmate steps out, the gun tucked tight to his shoulder. Darnell ducks down behind the filing cabinet. Peeking around the side, she sees a pair of feet in the doorway. The dumb ass is just standing there waiting for her to stand up. *Can I get a shot off before he does? Maybe. But, maybe not.*

She ponders it for another moment before lying down on her belly. Silently, she eases forward until the man's legs come into view. She pulls the trigger and the blast in such a confined space temporarily deafens her. Pumping in another round, she pushes up to a squatting position and slowly duckwalks forward, the shotgun up and ready. The injured inmate's screams are echoing off the walls, but she does her best to block out the sound.

There's movement out of the corner of her eye and she lifts the barrel and fires just as the inmate pulls the trigger. The inmate shoots high, blowing one of the overhead cabinet doors off. Darnell sinks to her knees and takes a deep breath. If her calculations are correct, she will have to dodge death one more time before the inmates are out of ammo.

But time is not her friend. She has to eliminate the gun threat before the inmates get creative and try to burn her out. Once the gun is eliminated from the equation, Darnell will have free rein inside the armory to fend off any other assault attempt. She takes a moment to look around the room, searching for something she can use for a distraction. Her gaze is drawn to a rolling chair tucked under the desk with a Department of Corrections jacket draped over the back. Easing the chair out, Darnell runs through the sequence of events in her head as the injured inmate continues to wail.

Moments later, when the man with the shredded legs pauses to suck in a breath, she hears a loud crunch and the screaming stops.

Darnell can guess what happened, but she's trying not to think about it as she runs the scenario through her head again. Once she's satisfied, she shoves the chair toward the gate and quickly repositions the shotgun against her shoulder. An inmate beyond the door fires the last shot, shredding the chair and jacket. Darnell stands and starts pumping rounds into the room, as the inmates scatter.

Then, much like Jack Nicholson in *The Shining*, Darnell pushes her face up to the bars and shouts, "Who's next, motherfuckers?"

As the remaining inmates scurry away, Darnell retreats and takes cover behind the file cabinet. She pulls the radio from her belt and puts it to her lips, "Hello? Anybody out there?"

An answer comes back. "Ten-four."

Not knowing if it's an inmate or guard, Darnell triggers the radio and asks the man to identify himself.

"This here's Walt Taylor in watchtower one. Who's this?"

Darnell sags with relief. She triggers the radio and says, "This is Officer Lydia Darnell, Walt. Please tell me help is on the way."

"Help's coming, Lydia. The National Guard out of Buffalo should be here within the hour," Walt responds. "There are several state troopers on scene, but not enough to try an entry."

"Walt, are the outside gates secure?" The last thing they need is for any of these savages to escape.

"Ten-four, Lydia. They're being guarded by the troopers. What's the situation in there?"

"God-awful. All the guards here in cellblocks A and D are dead, as are a bunch of the inmates."

There's a long beat of silence, then Taylor says, "Lydia, you might want to find a place to hunker down until the troops arrive."

"I'm hunkered. Radio me when they arrive."

CHAPTER 43

Manhattan

Hank, Paige, and Tomás Morales exit the stock exchange building to find chaos. It appears Hank was correct in his assumption that the power is out in Manhattan. Nearby traffic lights are dark and traffic is already gridlocked as angry drivers pound their horns, creating a symphony of sound that's almost deafening. The situation is not much better on the sidewalks—already clogged with people. Workers continue to pour out of the now-dark high-rises, pushing pedestrians out onto the streets, further snarling an already terrible traffic situation.

"I don't think we're getting the truck out of the parking garage anytime soon," Morales says. "I guess we're hoofing it back to headquarters."

Hank puts the extra ammo clips in his front pocket and strips out of his FBI Windbreaker and crams it into his bag. "There's nothin' at the office for us, Tomás. We need that jet."

Morales points at the jammed streets and says, "How are you getting to the airport, Hank? You going to walk?"

"No, we're goin' to fly when you have a chopper pick us up at the Wall Street heliport."

"Hell, Hank, do you think I can just pull aircraft out of my ass?" Morales asks. "Even if I could find you a chopper it can't land there. The heliport was hit by a barge a couple of weeks ago and it's still under repair."

Hank pulls up a map of Manhattan in his mind. "Okay, then have the chopper pick us up at the East 34th Street Heliport. C'mon, Tomás. You're the assistant director in charge. You have ready access to all the agency's goodies."

"Why can't you two work here at the field office?" Morales asks. "We've got backup generators so the power outage shouldn't be an issue."

"We need some help with this if we want a fast fix, Tomás," Paige says as she slips out of her own jacket. "Back home we'll have access to not only our computer programmers, but those at the NSA as well. And face-to-face is always better for brainstorming, especially when we're dealing with such a sophisticated piece of malware." Paige wipes the sweat from her forehead. The temperatures are pushing the mid-90s and, coupled with the hot exhaust gases from the gridlocked vehicles and the body heat from growing crowds, it feels as if they're standing inside a giant oven set on broil.

Morales pulls out his cell phone and checks for service. He's surprised to see he does have it, but he figures it's not going to last long. "Cell service is going to be very spotty with the power outage. How are we going to communicate, Hank?"

"We don't need to communicate. We'll head to the heliport and you send the chopper."

"What if I can't find a helicopter?" Morales asks.

"C'mon, Tomás. What are the odds of that happenin'?"

Morales pulls a handkerchief from his back pocket and wipes the sweat from his face. "I'm not a magician, Hank. And this power outage could be an issue. Might temporarily limit available resources until it gets restored."

Paige glances around at the crowds then steps closer to Morales and lowers her voice, saying, "Tomás, it could be months before power is back on."

Morales rears back in surprise. "Wha . . . what?" he asks, furrowing his brow.

"Hank and I stumbled across some internal power company e-mails back in D.C. Apparently the hackers overloaded some of the large transformers and burned them up."

"Can't they just replace them?" Morales asks.

"Yes, if they had spares available, but many companies don't stock replacement transformers. They're too expensive. A single transformer costs millions of dollars, and the main reason for the delay is that most have to be shipped in from overseas."

"That figures. We don't make anything anymore. So you think the hackers have done the same thing to the power grids here in Manhattan?" Morales asks.

"Almost certainly."

"Jeezus." Morales glances around at the thousands of people now crowding the streets and sidewalks. "How are we supposed to survive?"

"Grab Cecelia and get on the plane with us," Hank says.

"Can't, Hank. I've got a field office and five resident offices to run." Morales's voice is subdued as he tries to get a grip on the enormity of the situation.

"Then send Cecelia with us," Hank says.

"She won't go without me, Hank."

"You're probably right, Tomás, but you might ask her anyway."

Morales shakes his head. "No, if things get too bad here we can always hop on an agency plane and head to our condo in Virginia. You two head out. I need to get a few things out of the Tahoe."

"Don't forget your service weapon," Hank says.

"I won't."

Hank puts a hand on his friend's shoulder. "Don't stay in the city too long, Tomás. Things up here could turn dangerous in a hurry."

"We'll be okay. You two head for the heliport and I'll find you a chopper to take you to the airport."

"What about our bags?" Paige asks.

"We're headin' back to D.C.," Hank says. "I don't think you're goin' to be hurting for clothes."

"I'll ship them to you as soon as I can, Paige. That sound all right?"

Paige nods, glad she'd slipped on her running shoes on the plane. They don't coordinate well with her outfit, but they're a hell of a lot more comfortable to walk in.

"Last chance, old friend," Hank says, squeezing Morales's shoulder.

"No. We'll be fine. But we need to catch these bastards and put a stop to this madness."

"That's what we're tryin' to do," Hank says. "See you around, Tomás."

The two men shake hands and Paige gives Tomás a hug. "Be safe," she whispers in his ear.

"Same to both of you," Morales whispers back. "Stick with Hank. He's pretty damn handy to have around."

CHAPTER 44

North Atlantic Ocean

Rear Admiral Richard Malloy continues to pace around the USS *Stark*'s Ship's Mission Center barking orders. The ship's weapon systems are being reintegrated into the computer network, and a majority of the sailors working inside the center are wishing they were elsewhere. No one knows what might happen next and those same sailors don't really care to know because it will inevitably be something bad. That's just the way it is aboard the navy's newest destroyer.

Malloy steps over to the weapons control station and asks, "How much longer, Lieutenant Griffin?"

"We're close, Admiral." Mike Griffin looks up from his computer screen, a pleading look on his face when he says, "Sir, we aren't arming the weapons, are we?"

"Not yet. We'll run the computer program through a few dry-fire exercises first. If those go as I expect they will, then we'll talk about rearming."

"Sir?"

"What is it, Lieutenant?"

"Well, sir, we didn't find any glitches in the systems

during our earlier computer simulations. It was only after we loaded the armaments that something went terribly wrong."

"What's your theory as to why that happened, Lieutenant? Operator error, maybe?"

Griffin's face turns crimson. "No, sir. It was not operator error."

"Then, what?" Malloy asks.

"I think the computer software has been compromised."

"Impossible. I've spent the last eight years of my career working with some of the brightest minds in the industry to implement this new concept of ship-wide computer integration. So this bullshit about the systems being compromised ends here. Do you understand, Lieutenant?"

Griffin sits up straighter in his chair. "Yes, sir."

"Carry on. Notify me when ready."

"Yes, sir." Malloy moves on to terrorize someone else and Griffin returns to the task at hand. What Malloy doesn't know is that weapons systems are up and ready to go and have been for some time. Griffin is trying to delay as much as possible, but that ruse will last only so long before the admiral demands action. Griffin looks around to pinpoint Malloy's location before reaching for the phone. He punches in the four-digit extension from memory and waits for the phone to be answered, all while keeping close tabs on the admiral's location.

Captain Hensley, still confined to quarters, answers on the first ring. "What's happening, Griff?"

Griffin cups a hand around his mouth and the phone and whispers, "How do you feel about mutiny?"

"Is Malloy rearming the ship's weapons?" Hensley asks.

"He plans to after a couple of dry runs. Can you contact Norfolk?"

"Hell no. The radio is still down."

Griffin spots the admiral looking his way. "Malloy's coming. Talk to the chopper pilot. See if he'll relay a message."

"I'll do that. Keep me posted, Griff."

Griffin hangs up the phone and returns to his computer screen, just as the admiral arrives at his station.

"Where are we now, Mr. Griffin?"

"The weapons have synced with the ship's computers, sir."

"Good. Deploy some targets. I want to see how well the guns track."

"Yes, sir." Griffin makes the call down to the deck and stands and stretches, waiting for the targets to be deployed. His mind is churning, trying to think of ways to sabotage the dry-fire exercises. *Am I willing to flush my career down the toilet?* Maybe, he decides. His wife, whose father rose to the rank of rear admiral during his time in the navy, would be none too happy. *But she's not here and I am.* Griffin sighs and retakes his seat as the admiral steps up to the raised platform at the front of the room.

For the next hour, the USS *Stark* performs flawlessly during the dry-fire drills. The guns track their targets with precision and the two gun barrels look as if they're performing a ballet on deck as they rotate, raise, and lower, never losing track. As for the missiles, the computers track simulated targets and deliver their pretend payloads on target every time. Even the two smaller 30-mm machine guns prove lethal as they destroy target after target with an accuracy not achievable when guided by human hands.

The admiral, grinning from ear to ear at the front of the room, declares the exercises an overwhelming success. He steps off the podium and works his way toward Griffin. "Mr. Griffin, load weapons."

"But, sir—"

Malloy cuts Griffin off with a wave of his hand. "Did you detect any anomalies, Lieutenant?"

"No, sir, but—"

"No *buts*, Lieutenant. Load weapons. And that's a direct order."

"Yes, sir." As the admiral departs, Griffin continues running scenarios through his head. *How much time can I buy?* He grabs the phone and dials Hensley again, who quickly answers.

"Let me guess," Hensley says, "the ship performed perfectly."

Griffin ducks down below the video monitors. "You got it. Did you get a chance to talk to the chopper pilot?"

"No. Malloy placed a guard on my door."

"Who is it?" Griffin asks.

"Petty Officer Perry."

"Can you order him to stand down?"

"I tried. No go."

"What's his usual job?" Griffin asks.

"Engine room and damage control."

"Damn it. Okay, let me think about it. Maybe I can talk the admiral into running a drill while the weapons are being loaded."

"Drag your feet for as long as you can, Griff."

"I'm trying. Keep checking your door and, when it's clear, make a break for the chopper."

"I will. And, Griff?"

"Yeah?"

"Hurry."

CHAPTER 45

Chicago

Peyton, still traumatized, looks out the front windows and spots Eric striding up the street. She wonders what he's thinking as he slows, trying to pick his way around the pools of blood and the dead bodies near the entrance.

"Are you okay, honey?" Eric asks, walking across the lobby.

"I don't know," Peyton says before breaking into sobs.

He wedges his way into the chair and wraps an arm around his wife.

"What happened out front?"

"The . . . National   Guard . . . shot . . . shot . . . some looters. What took . . . (sniffle) . . . you so . . . (sniffle) . . . long?"

"Aaron the asshole wouldn't let us leave. But, hey, I got tomorrow off."

Peyton burrows her face into Eric's chest. "You're probably . . . (sniffle) . . . going to have . . . (sniffle) . . . a lot of . . . tomorrows off."

Eric gently puts a hand under Peyton's chin and lifts

her head so he can look her in the eye. "What do you mean?"

Peyton runs the back of her hand across her dripping nose. "I had a . . . a . . . partial . . . conversation . . . with . . . with Paige. She told me to . . . to . . . get out . . . and then the call . . . dropped."

"Out of where? The office building? Our condo?"

Peyton shrugs and wipes the tears off her cheeks. "I think it was more."

"What? Like get out of Chicago?"

"Maybe."

"Why? They'll probably have the power back on before we get home."

Peyton shakes her head. "Paige's voice was . . . urgent. And she's in the know." Peyton wipes away the last of her tears and blows her nose into a fabric remnant she continues to lug around. "I think the power could be off for a long time."

Eric leans back in the chair, stunned. "How long?"

"I don't know, Eric. I don't even know if I'm right. It was just a feeling I got listening to Paige."

"Is that why you're so upset?"

"No, but I don't even know where to begin."

"Are you injured?"

"My feet are cut up pretty bad."

Eric leans forward to see Peyton's feet wrapped up in her homemade shoes. "What do you have on your feet?"

"My attempt at making shoes."

"Where are the new heels you bought?"

Peyton nods toward the coffee table on the other side of the lobby. "Over there. My feet were blistered something awful after climbing down the stairs."

Eric glances at her makeshift shoes again. "I don't think you'll win any design awards."

"Probably not." Peyton wants to tell Eric everything that has happened, but she can't. Not yet. She doesn't want to relive seeing Ranjeet's severed head on the desk. She pushes out of the chair and stands. "Can we go home now?"

"Of course." Eric gets his first glance at Peyton's tattered skirt. "What happened to your new skirt?"

"Another long story."

"How come you didn't hit one of the looted stores for a new pair of shoes?"

"That's one part of the long story. Can we just go?"

"Yes." Eric takes her hand, grabs her bag, and steadies her as they shuffle out the exit. Eric is struck with an idea when they arrive at a looted CVS on the next corner. He walks carefully across the broken glass and grabs one of the shopping carts and drags it back. After some cajoling from Eric, Peyton dumps her backpack in and climbs aboard.

It's frightening to see the looted stores that stretch on and on, block after block. Eric pushes the cart onto the DuSable Bridge and takes a short break at the midstream point of the Chicago River. Abandoned buses, trucks, and cars litter the bridge's surface and there's a steady stream of people, mostly business types, heading north to their homes.

"God, I'm thirsty. I wish we had some water," Eric says, using his already-saturated shirt to mop the sweat from his face.

"We did have some at one time, but it got stolen."

"Let me guess. All part of the long story?"

Peyton nods. "Let's just say it's been a very long day."

Eric steps over to one of the abandoned cars and puts his nose to the glass, cupping his hands around his face for a look inside.

"What are you doing?" Peyton asks.

"Looking for water," Eric says as he moves to the next car in line.

"Don't you think they'd take the water with them when they left?"

"You're probably right." Eric checks one final car and returns.

Peyton climbs back in the shopping cart and they continue their journey. Across the river the parade of looted businesses continues. "I wonder where the National Guard troops went?" Peyton asks.

"They're probably off marshaling their forces, waiting for the madness darkness will probably bring."

Peyton shivers at the thought.

Eric makes a left onto East Oak Street and they travel toward the setting sun. "How much further until we're home?" Eric asks, the sweat dripping off the tip of his nose.

"You want it in miles or blocks?" Peyton asks.

Eric groans. "That far?"

"I think. We never really see this part of Chicago because we always take the subway, but I've been coordinating street names with subway stops and we've still got a ways to go."

Eric groans. He pulls the cart to a stop and wipes his face again. "I'm taking a cold shower when we get home."

"I hate to rain on your cold-town parade, but we're not going to have any water at home."

"Damn, I didn't think about that. And that means no

air-conditioning, either. It's going to be a long, miserable night."

"Right now, we need to focus on getting home and worry about all that stuff later."

Eric has to push hard to get the cart going again. A short while later, the road they're on dead-ends into some type of medical complex. Feeling like a coxswain sitting in the shopping basket, Peyton raises her arm and points to the north. "That way, Eric. We should run into the road we're looking for."

"Are you sure that's the right way?"

Peyton knows Eric is terrible with directions—so bad he couldn't find his way out of a paper bag. "The sun sets in the west. That way's north," she says, pointing. "I promise."

Eric turns the shopping cart around and picks up North Crosby Street going the way Peyton pointed. Unfortunately, that road, too, ends at the next cross street. Peyton looks up at the street signs. "This is Division Street. There's a subway stop for it. I told you we're going the right way."

"Now which way?" Eric asks. "It's going to be dark here in a little bit."

"Let's go right and then take the first left. That'll put us back on course."

"You're the navigator," Eric says, straining to get the cart going again. Not designed for rough terrain, two of the cart's wheels have lost some rubber and it's now wobbling, making it that much more difficult to push. A block and a half down the street, a nearby burst of gunfire shatters the silence. Eric jerks the cart to a halt and grabs Peyton's hand. "Get out. We need cover."

There's more gunfire, this time a sustained burst from what sounds like multiple weapons.

Eric tips the cart over and Paige crawls out. Their options for cover limited, they scamper across the street to a vacant lot and dive to the ground. "Did you see where it's coming from?" Eric whispers.

"No, but I think I might have pissed in my pants," Paige whispers back. "And I lost one of my shoes."

Eric lifts his head a few inches, trying to see over the tall grass to find a spot that will offer better cover. "That's the least of our worries," he whispers. There are buildings on either side of them, but they're too far away to do them much good. Their only option is a half-dead elm tree in the far corner of the property. "We need to crawl—"

The last of his sentence is obliterated by more gunfire. And this time it sounds closer. Much closer.

He taps Peyton on the shoulder and points to the large tree. She nods and they both start crawling, hugging tight to the ground.

CHAPTER 46

After the call-up from the governor of New York and a hasty retreat to the armory for weapons and gear, sixty members of the New York Army National Guard out of Buffalo are now in a convoy rolling down Highway 354. All sixty are outfitted with body armor and battle helmets, and all are heavily armed for the dangerous mission that lies ahead. Call it luck or bad fortune, but it was proximity that determined today's call to duty. Situated along the eastern shore of Lake Erie and just downstream from Niagara Falls, Buffalo also happens to be the closest major city to a small village that lies thirty miles to the east—Attica, New York.

Captain Scott Butler, the unit commander, gave his men a briefing about their destination and the ongoing unrest at the Attica Correctional Facility, but little else. The reason the briefing was lacking in details is because that's everything Butler knows at the moment. More info is promised upon arrival at the prison but, deep down, Butler knows they're heading into a slaughterhouse. And that's not something a majority of his men see every day.

Butler glances out the side window at the tree-covered hills and sighs. Hell, to be honest, it's not something he's ever seen before. Every man in the unit—this is a mandated male-only mission—has a regular job and families that depend on them, Butler included. Yes, his group contains six police officers, five firefighters, and three paramedics who might work a bloody car wreck or a bloody crime scene every now and then, but that pales in comparison to what they might find inside one of the nation's most notorious prisons. Butler made a point to emphasize one thing before rolling out—they will be entering a war zone.

The power in Buffalo remains on, but no one is sure how long that will last. Butler, a dentist, had to cancel his remaining patients and, on his way to the armory, called his wife to tell her he wouldn't be home for dinner. The remaining members of the group made similar changes to their schedules along with similar calls to loved ones. His band of soldiers is a diverse group. In addition to the police officers, firefighters, and paramedics the group includes teachers, small-business owners, city employees, two auto mechanics, and several college students. Some have prior military experience, but many don't—relying on the two weekends a month and the two weeks of summer drills for training. Their socioeconomic status varies widely, as do their ages. Butler is the oldest at forty-two and Private First Class Shawn Turner is the youngest at nineteen.

While his team members are busy with their own thoughts as the trucks rumble down the highway, Butler is busy working the radio. The National Guard is unique in that they serve a dual role. Soldiers can be called up by state officials to manage a local crisis, or, as a reserve unit of the United States Armed Forces, they can be called up at any time by the federal government. If the feds activate a unit then most likely those soldiers are headed overseas to fight in the ongoing conflicts. And as the number of active military soldiers declines, more guard units are being activated. At the moment, Captain Butler would much prefer a flight overseas rather than this road trip to hell. Butler triggers his radio and says, "Say again, sir?"

"I said the schematics of the prison are in the e-mail I just sent you," Major General Lawrence Moore says. The adjutant general for the state of New York, he's tucked away in his office back at headquarters near the Albany airport.

"Roger, sir," Butler says. "Will we have reinforcements?"

"Unfortunately, no. With all that's happening, we're getting stretched mighty thin. There are state troopers at the prison and hopefully more on the way."

"I assume they will be under my command."

"That is correct, Captain," Moore says.

"Do we have *any* intel from inside the prison?"

"Very little. My understanding is it's a real blood— hold on a sec, the governor is calling."

Butler tries to imagine what the scene may look like, but he doesn't have any real reference points, having never served in combat.

After several moments General Moore comes back on the radio. "Are you there, Captain?"

"I'm here, sir."

"This is highly unusual, but the order comes directly from the commander in chief."

Or, in other words, he's talking about the governor of New York.

"Go ahead, sir," Butler says.

There's a long pause and then General Moore says, "Scott, I have to be honest with you. I don't know what to make of the governor's order."

"What is it?"

"He orders us to protect the remaining guards, but he also orders that we take no prisoners."

"What was that last part, General?"

"You heard me, Scott. Take no prisoners."

"Jeezus, Larry. No way. My men and I aren't going to prison for murder. And that's exactly what it would be. For Christ's sake, I'm a fucking dentist, not some hired mercenary."

"Scott, it's a direct order from the commander in chief."

"I don't care if it's a direct order from Jesus Christ himself. We aren't murderers, General. If the governor wants them killed tell him to get his ass on a plane and head this way. I'll save a rifle for him."

"Listen, Captain, I know the order is highly unusual, but if the power grids across the rest of the state fail, the last thing we want is for those murderers to be out on the street. Think about that for a moment."

"Okay, I've thought about it—no. That's the reason we have laws in this country. And what makes you think the rest of the grid is going to fail?"

"Just a hunch. Manhattan is currently without power and the governor called up other guard units to patrol the streets. Think about what those killers up there would do to a bunch of unarmed civilians."

"Manhattan is four hundred miles away, General. How are the prisoners going to get there? Walk?"

"Okay, they might not make it to Manhattan, but they sure as hell could make it to Buffalo. Do you want them loose in your town?"

"Of course not." Butler pauses and stares out the truck's windshield at the road ahead.

"To add a little more food for thought," General Moore says over the radio, "looting has already started in Manhattan and the governor issued a shoot-to-kill order."

Butler triggers the radio. "I'm not doing it unless we get a formal immunity letter from the attorney general that covers the entire unit."

"How far are you from the prison right now?"

"We should be there in fifteen minutes or so."

"There's no time for a letter, Captain."

"Then I'll assess the situation and run the operation as I see fit."

"Are you disobeying a direct order?"

Butler pushes the transmit button and says, "Butler out," before reaching up to turn off the radio.

CHAPTER 47

Chicago

Peyton and Eric make it to the elm tree and duck behind the tree's massive trunk. Upright, they now have a better view of the area. Neither has been able to pinpoint the location of the gunfire because it's difficult to do when you have your faces buried in the dirt. Eric leans forward and takes a peek around the base of the tree, zeroing in on the Target across the street. It's the only thing that makes sense. Everything else in the area looks to be residential buildings with a few small businesses occupying a smattering of the ground-floor spaces. The construction site next door obstructs Eric's view of the rest of the block, but from all appearances there's nothing here to spark a war other than that one large retail store.

As if reading his thoughts, Peyton asks, "Are they fighting over that store?"

"I don't know. It's hard to see anything from here."

Both jump when more gunfire erupts. Eric ducks back behind the tree just as a random spray of bullets chews into the tree's upper canopy, launching a storm of wood chips that pelt Eric and Peyton as they hug the ground. The gunfire ends as quickly as it began and Peyton exhales the breath she didn't realize she'd been holding.

"I saw bursts of flame from inside the store," Eric whispers, "but I can't tell who the other shooters are or where they're shooting from. You see anything?"

Peyton rolls onto her side and rakes her fingers through her hair, picking out the dead leaves that have accumulated there. "All I saw was dirt. I think we need to find a safer spot."

"Can't. We'd be too exposed trying to get there. And it sounds like they're using machine guns and that means they'll be spraying bullets everywhere." Eric tilts his head back and looks up at the tree's underlying branches. "In fact, I think a few bullets hit during that last round of fighting."

"All the more reason to find a safer place." Peyton rolls onto her belly, pushes into a kneeling position, and crawls closer to the base of the tree for another look. "What about that building under construction?" Peyton asks, pointing to the skeletal framework of a multistory building going up next door.

"It's fenced." This late in the day, the construction site is buttoned up for the night. Eric turns to look at the sun as it sinks lower in the sky. "Might be best to wait until dark to make our move—" Eric, hearing the rustling of footsteps on pavement, stops speaking and turns to see four police officers creeping down the street. All are wearing body armor and helmets, and all are loaded for bear. He turns and whispers to Peyton, "I think they're trying to flank the store."

"What do you know about military maneuvers?" Peyton whispers.

Eric shrugs and whispers, "Hey, I watch the History Channel."

"What does the History Channel say about being in the direct line of fire?"

Eric looks at the approaching police officers then the store, contemplating the angles. "Oh shit."

"Exactl—"

The last syllable of her word is clipped when the police open fire on the building again. Those inside start firing back and Eric pushes Peyton to the ground and crawls on top of her as a salvo of bullets zings by overhead. Glancing up for a peek, he sees bullets stitching across the dirt only yards away from their position. Eric, who hasn't been to church since Easter Sunday 2005, closes his eyes and begins mumbling the few words he remembers from the Twenty-third Psalm. But he doesn't get very far before his thoughts are interrupted by a loud whooshing noise that sounds like a giant bottle rocket being launched. Eric squeezes Peyton tighter, and a few milliseconds later an enormous explosion detonates, shaking the ground beneath them. Almost instantaneously, car alarms in the area begin wailing as the crash of shattering glass cascades down the block.

Lying on top of Peyton, Eric bears the brunt of the blast and is momentarily deafened by the explosion. Peyton, feeling like she's being suffocated, elbows Eric in the gut and he rolls off her. Pushing up to her hands and knees, she pulls up her shirt to wipe the dirt from her nose and mouth. She turns her head and says, "We need to go."

"What?" Eric asks, his voice about fifty decibels louder than it needs to be.

Peyton gives Eric a stern look before placing a finger against her lips.

Eric points to his right ear and says, too loudly again, "I can't hear."

Peyton emphasizes her point by angrily tapping her finger against her lips. She glances across the street to see a dozen police officers converging on the store. Or, rather, Peyton thinks, what's left of it. Flames are flickering from a half a dozen fires deep within, and the entire front facade is now nothing but a pile of rubble. Thinking the battle is over, Peyton turns her gaze back to Eric and slowly mouths the words, "Let's go."

"You're cold?" Eric asks in a loud voice, his brow furrowed.

Peyton shakes her head. She holds her left palm out flat and uses two fingers from her right hand to pantomime walking.

"Oh," Eric says. "Let's go?"

Peyton nods.

"Now?"

Peyton nods again.

"Okay." Using the trunk for support, Eric pulls himself to his feet just as the gun battle resumes. Still unable to hear, he turns and takes a step. Then another.

Peyton, horrified, lunges to her feet and tries to grab her husband, but she's not fast enough.

A stray bullet hits Eric midstride and he crashes to the ground.

CHAPTER 48

January 13, 2006
TARGET: Taliban
CONFIRMED KILLED: 22
CIVILIANS KILLED: 18 (5–6 children)

ocated along the border that abuts Afghanistan's
Kandahar Province, Chaman is a large city of
180,000 people in northwest Pakistan. Home to one of
the major international border crossings between the
two countries, the city is often used by the United
States military to move men and equipment into and
out of Afghanistan. Situated atop the high plains on the
Balochistan Plateau, Chaman's base elevation is nearly
1,400 meters and there's not much in the surrounding
area that provides protection against the cold winds
that come sweeping off the mountains in winter.

And today is one of those days. With a stiff wind out
of the north and light drizzle, it's downright miserable.
Twelve-year-old Sheezal Bukhari has his coat buttoned
up to his chin and his hood up as he makes his way

*home from school. His family lives in a small neigh-
borhood not far from the school on the south side of
the city. Just up the road is the home field for the city's
football team as well as the local cricket grounds. Initially, Sheezal dreamed of playing football there someday, but he found out early that he wasn't blessed with
an overabundance of athletic ability. He tucked that
dream away and applied himself to his schoolwork.
What he and others soon learned is Sheezal might not
be athletic, but he more than makes up for it with his
intelligence.*

*Currently first in his class, Sheezal spends summers
immersed in high-level learning programs at the
Balochistan University of Information Technology, Engineering and Management Sciences in nearby Quetta.
In addition to computer programming, Sheezal is taught
English, which he picked up quickly. At twelve, he's
hacked just about every network in Pakistan, both civilian and government. He doesn't do it for malicious
purposes, only to test his skills.*

*His backpack slung over his shoulder, Sheezal makes
the turn onto his street, hoping his mother has some hot
tea brewing for his arrival. Their home is at the end of
the block, near a busy thoroughfare known as College
Road that runs along the outskirts of downtown. With
the wind whipping and with him thinking about his
next hacking target, he has no idea a drone is circling
overhead.*

*Seconds later, there's a blinding flash and a ground-
trembling explosion. The pressure wave from the blast
knocks Sheezal off his feet and he lies there a moment,
stunned, his ears ringing. After a few minutes he begins moving his limbs, making sure all of his body
parts are still attached. They are, and he pushes to his*

feet. His vision blurry, he wipes a hand across his fore-head and feels something warm and sticky. He looks at his palm to see it covered in blood. After taking a mo-ment to wipe the blood out of his eyes, he looks up and screams. He stumbles down the street, yelling his mother's name until he reaches the spot where their home once stood.

Four days later, after his mother was laid to rest, Sheezal hacked into an American newspaper website and discovered that the drone was targeting an auto-mobile containing high-ranking Taliban leaders as it traveled east on College Road. For the first time Sheezal understood what the words collateral damage *meant when there was no mention of the eighteen civilians killed during the attack.*

Present day, somewhere near Boston

Today, Sheezal Bukhari has no qualms about the hell they're unleashing on the United States. Shortly after his mother's death, his father was driving a truck across the border as part of a convoy when they were ambushed and, at the age of twelve, Sheezal began his shuffle through the homes of various relatives, never quite fitting in. The one thing he didn't let lapse during it all was his education. He knew it was his ticket out, and when he received the scholarship offer, he jumped at the chance.

In the United States, he excelled in the classroom but lacked the social skills required to fully embrace campus life. It wasn't until grad school that he finally opened up some and made a few acquaintances who drifted in and out of his life, but nothing permanent. Instead of working on making friends, he focused on

232   *Tim Washburn*

his work, joined a gym, put on thirty-five pounds of muscle, and visited a whorehouse when he felt the need for carnal pleasures. Sheezal often wonders if his life would had turned out differently if his mother were still alive. But he refuses to retreat into that deep, dark hole, and returns to the task at hand.

Feeling sluggish, he stands and moves into the break room. He grabs an energy drink from the fridge and spends a moment stretching his back before opening the can. As far as he's concerned, the new American administration can shove those canceled student visas up their ass. There's nothing back home for Sheezal and over the years he has set himself up well. He has money and he has a half a dozen seriously back-storied identities that will allow him to move freely around the country.

No, the only stumbling block that Sheezal sees on the horizon is the arrival of that asshole, Basir Nazeri. And that's not an insurmountable problem, just one that will require additional thought. He drains the energy drink in three swallows and belches as he tosses the empty can into the trash before returning to his computer. "Hey, Nazeri," Sheezal shouts across the room, "how about some food? Is that on your agenda?" Sheezal is physically similar in size to Nazeri and he's the only member of the group willing to challenge Nazeri's authority.

"I have ordered some pizzas," Nazeri says.

"We've had pizza for three days in a row," Sheezal says, running his fingers through his wiry beard. "Order something else."

"Or what?" Nazeri asks, standing.

Hassan, fearing a confrontation, says, "Pizza's fine."

"No, it's not, Hassan. That shit he orders tastes like

cardboard," Sheezal says, pushing out of his chair. He and Nazeri engage in a stare-off.

After several seconds, Nazeri never breaks eye contact when he says, "What would you prefer, Sheezal?"

"Steaks, or hamburgers, or whatever. I think we've had our fill of pizza."

Nazeri calmly retakes his seat. "I'll see what I can do. In the meantime return to work."

Sheezal's stare lingers on Nazeri for an extra moment or two before retaking his seat. After examining the targets for a moment, Sheezal picks an oil refinery near a highly populated area. He likes the fact that he's targeting the one resource Americans can't seem to get enough of. More, more, more is all the Americans want, Sheezal thinks, leaving few resources for the billions of other people who occupy this planet. With tentacles stretching throughout the Middle East, the U.S. government sucks up the oil and is more than willing to go to war when their interests are threatened. No, Sheezal doesn't hate everyone in this country, but he does hate the politicians, the large corporations, and the hypocrisy.

Using the back door that Nazeri provided, Sheezal enters the company's network and searches through the database of attached devices. He can either target the PLCs that control the multitude of valves inside the plant, go after the pressure sensors, or attack the pumps that move the chemicals through the facility. Hoping an overheated pump might spark a fire, Sheezal chooses the pumps and launches the malware payload targeted specifically at the controllers that regulate pump speeds. Once he has control, he ramps up the speeds on the 142 pumps inside the building and sits back in his chair, waiting for disaster to strike.

CHAPTER 49

Delaware County, Pennsylvania

People drive by it day after day and never give the facility a second thought. Others might drift by the collection of tanks and towers and not wonder about their purpose as they cruise down the scenic Delaware River. And some people will buy or build their homes nearby, never knowing what goes on inside the plant across the road or down the street. There are no regulations or restrictions that prohibit the construction of homes in the vicinity, and most of the residents believe that if it's okay to build in a certain area, then it must be okay to live there.

If they only knew.

Located on the north bank of the Delaware River and about ten miles west of downtown Philadelphia, Clark Energy's refinery pumps out 180,000 barrels of refined oil products every day. The chemical elements, or hydrocarbons, in one barrel of crude oil can be used to make gasoline, heating oil, jet fuel, lubricants, waxes, and propane. Which specific product is produced is dependent on the refining process used. The most common procedure, fractional distillation, involves heating the crude to a certain temperature, forcing individual carbon atoms into a gaseous state where the atoms reform, creating a specific product. Further refining follows. The resulting products may then be cracked, reformed, or pumped into a cylinder for vacuum distillation in an attempt to further rearrange the fuel's molecular structure.

Some refineries, including Clark Energy, use a process called alkylation to boost the octane levels in gasoline. Some communities across the United States have banded together to try and stop this particular process because of the potential dangers to their towns and cities. It's not the end product that has them upset, it's the main chemical used in the processing—hydrofluoric acid. A very potent chemical, hydrofluoric acid will dissolve metal, rock, glass, and ceramic, making it a favorite in the movie industry for dissolving human bodies. The one thing it won't eat through is plastic and that's how Clark Energy stores this deadly chemical at the plant.

Stored as a liquid, if the hydrofluoric acid were to leak from a refinery, it forms a deadly vapor cloud when exposed to air. Any contact with the vapor cloud could produce serious, painful chemical burns, blindness, and death from asphyxiation.

Today the alkylation unit is up and running and thirty-three-year-old Nolan Carroll is inside the plant's control room keeping a close eye on the activity. Everything at the plant is computerized and, with a touch of a button or a click of the mouse, Carroll can make adjustments to keep the plant running smoothly.

Carroll and his wife, Melinda, welcomed their second child, a girl, to the world three months ago. It didn't take the family long to figure out their small apartment was no longer going to work. He and Melinda went house shopping and found a reasonably priced three-bedroom, two-bath home only a mile from the plant. After some negotiating with the sellers, a price was agreed to and the Carroll family moved into their new home two months ago. Working at the plant and knowing the dangers, Nolan fell in love with the selling price of the home and ignored his initial misgivings about the location.

A decision he will live to regret.

He rolls his chair a little to the left for a better look at the video screen that displays hydrofluoric acid levels inside the alkylation unit. The acid levels are rising and the pumps haven't shut off. Using his computer mouse, Carroll navigates through the company's computer network and clicks on the programmable logic controller that regulates the pump's speed and attempts to dial it back. He's surprised when the pump doesn't respond to the computer's commands. He turns to his coworker Jack Sandoval. "What's up with all the pumps?"

"I don't know," Sandoval says. "The computer won't allow me to adjust the speeds."

"Same here. Try killing the power to one or two of them and see what happens."

"I tried. The computer wouldn't let me do that, either."

Carroll feels a tingle of panic inch down his spine. Before he can decide on a course of action, the building is rattled by a large explosion that sends shrapnel shredding through the control room. Carroll grabs his cell phone and dives under his desk. After lighting the screen, he quickly punches the speed dial for his wife and waits.

"C'mon, c'mon, answer the phone," he mumbles as the first tendrils of the vapor enter the control room.

Still off work for her last few days of maternity leave, Melinda Carroll returns home after taking their three-year-old daughter to Mother's Day Out. Inside, she takes a long look at the mess in the kitchen and decides to rest a moment before tackling that chore. With the baby, Elise, sleeping in her car seat, Melinda sags onto the sofa, exhausted. Yesterday, Elise had been fussy and Melinda had spent a good portion of the night pacing the floors with the baby in her arms, trying to calm her. Melinda picks up a magazine, fans through the pages, and tosses it back on the coffee table. Eventually her eyelids grow heavy and she drifts off to sleep.

Sometime later, Melinda startles awake when her cell phone rings. Disoriented, it takes her a moment to find it. She digs it out of the sofa and looks at the screen to see Nolan is calling and answers.

Instead of his usual *hello*, Nolan says, "Get out of the house right now."

"What?" Melinda asks.

"There's been an accident at the plant. You have to hurry. Leave and head—"

"Nolan? Nolan, are you there?" Now in a panic, Melinda grabs her bag, picks up the car seat with the baby still napping inside, and hurries out of the house. She flings open the car's back door, snaps in the car seat, and climbs behind the wheel. Burning rubber, she backs out of the drive and gasps when she sees the fiery inferno at the refinery, just down the road. After dropping the car into drive, she slams on the gas. Quickly winding her way through the neighborhood, she glances ahead to see a white cloud of something hovering close to the ground and moving her way. She stops at the intersection and looks back at the plant, her heart hammering in fear for her husband's safety.

She sniffs and smells a funny odor as the cloud envelops the car. Seconds later, her eyes and lungs begin to sting. Elise wakes and immediately begins screaming as Melinda slams on the gas and steers onto the main road. Hoping to clear the odor and smoke from the car, she triggers her window down.

And that proves to be a fatal mistake.

The toxic cloud of hydrofluoric acid invades the car. Now unable to breathe or see, Melinda loses control of the car and it slams into a ditch. Dazed, she's wondering why Elise is no longer crying and that's her last thought before her body shudders one final time and goes still.

CHAPTER 50

Manhattan

Paige and Hank are moving north on Broadway, trying to make their way to the East 34th Street Heliport. And it's a tough slog. The sidewalks are jammed tight as teeth and no one seems willing to give an inch. Having visited the city many times, Hank knows New Yorkers can be brusque, but most of these people are downright surly and he gets the feeling things could spiral out of control at any second.

Passing St. Paul's Chapel, Hank's not surprised to see a steady stream of people filing into the church. He knows many people fall back on their faith during times of duress, hoping divine intervention will intercede on their behalf. But unless their deity knows how to fix the power grids, Hank thinks, they're probably wasting their time. He grabs Paige by the hand and leads her through the crowds and into the street. It's slightly less crowded, but the abandoned automobiles do allow them room to take a breath.

"How much further?" Paige asks.

"Sixty-two blocks. Goin' to make it?" Hank asks.

"Don't have much choice. How do you know it's

precisely sixty-two blocks and not sixty-one blocks or sixty-three blocks?"

Hank shrugs. "I just know."

"What? You just dial up a map of Manhattan in that big brain of yours?"

"Yeah, that's pretty much how it works."

"Do you ever get lost?"

"Sure, if it's a place I've never been to before or if I haven't looked at a map of a specific area."

Paige shakes her head. "Weird. Shoot, half the time I can't remember what I had for lunch yesterday."

"That's not uncommon for most people. But if you stop and think you'll eventually remember."

"Do you have to stop and think? Or do you just pluck it from memory?"

"It depends. In this case I did have to count the blocks."

Two blocks up, past a looted Staples and a ransacked Starbucks, people are lining up around City Hall, already chanting protests.

"What are they protesting?" Paige asks.

"I guess they want the mayor to wave a magic wand and make everything better. Most people have no idea how the power grids work. They just assume when they flip a switch that the light will come on. It's somethin' we all take for granted. But, unfortunately, there are no magic fixes."

"How long have we been without power? A few hours, maybe? And it's already this chaotic?"

"It'll get worse. Much worse," Hank says. "A day or two without water and food and this city will turn into a hellhole real fast."

"How are they going to survive?"

"Not my problem."

"That's rather cold-blooded. Don't you have empathy?"

"Of course I do. But there's not a damn thing I can do about it. The only thing we *can* do is try to prevent this from happenin' elsewhere."

"Do you think Tomás is going to come through with a helicopter?" Paige asks.

"It'll be there."

"You sound sure."

"I am sure. Tomás can pull a lot of strings."

"How did you two get to be such good friends?" Paige asks.

"We've worked on several cases, but I think the main reason is that we both came from similar backgrounds. He's half-Mexican and I'm half-Indian—or Native American if you're into bein' politically correct—and we both had to overcome multiple hurdles to get where we are today."

"He seems like a great guy."

"He is," Hank replies.

Three blocks up, they pass the Jacob K. Javits Federal Building, home to the FBI's New York field office. The building, a highly secure place on any normal day, is now even more so, with a dozen or more armed agents, wearing full body armor, guarding all of the building's entrances and exits.

"Are you sure you don't want to head inside and work from here?" Paige asks.

"I'm sure. Our best chance to crack this thing is back in D.C."

A few minutes later, while crossing Walker Street, Paige and Hank run into the first hint of real trouble when a fusillade of gunfire erupts in the middle of Broadway.

Daily News Website

—BREAKING NEWS—Norfolk Naval Station attacked! Significant damage reported.

Details are slow to arrive on the situation at Norfolk Naval Station. We do know the port and several ships were damaged. More details to follow . . .

—BREAKING NEWS—Reports of second chemical plant explosion near Los Angeles. More details to follow . . .

—BREAKING NEWS—Horrific train crash snarls traffic in Northeast Corridor. Acela Express train plows into Penn Station. Witnesses report train was speeding up when crash occurred.

First responders on the scene report significant loss of life. Cause still undermined. Witnesses report the train was speeding up as it approached the station. More details to follow . . .

—BREAKING NEWS—Massive explosion at army munitions depot in McAlester, Oklahoma. More details to follow , . .

—BREAKING NEWS—Stock trading halted because of computer irregularities. Experts fear loss of financial transactions. Monetary losses expected to be astronomical.

All stock trading has been halted due to some type of computer glitch. Officials believe computer issues may be deeper than first expected. Experts we've spoken to fear there could be a significant loss of financial transactions. More details to follow . . .

CHAPTER 51

Attica

If Attica Corrections Officer Lydia Darnell were willing to take her hands off the shotgun, she'd use them to cover her ears. She doesn't know exactly what's happening out in the prison, but judging by the howling screams and insane blubbering, it's bad. Real bad. It can't be fellow officers being killed because every guard she saw was already dead. But there's no doubt some old grudges are getting settled and in a barbaric way. And they have all the necessary tools to get the job done with ready access to every kitchen utensil inside prison walls. Still locked away in the armory, Darnell is trying to stay alive long enough for the cavalry to arrive. She'd love to have access to the prison's camera system, but that would mean opening the steel cage door, and that's not something she's willing to do.

Prisoners have been in and out of the Times Square booth, no doubt plotting ways to get their hands on the last remaining guard and the weapons inside. So far there has been no direct attack on Darnell's position—the bodies piled up at the door may be acting as some type of deterrent. But Darnell is ready if they do come.

She now has four fully loaded shotguns stacked up on the floor next to her, along with a nice selection of fully loaded pistols. The inmates' only chance to get to her would be to send in a wave of cannon fodder in hopes she'd run out of ammunition. And that's not entirely out of the question. With over two thousand inmates inside the prison walls, Darnell doesn't have enough ammunition to kill them all.

Her radio squelches and the tower guard, Walt Taylor, says, "Darnell, you there?"

Darnell takes one long look out the armory door before triggering the radio. "I'm here, Walt. Status?"

"National Guard is five minutes out."

Darnell exhales a sigh of relief. "How many soldiers?"

"That, I don't know. Hold on."

Darnell cranes her neck for another look. Still clear. Taylor is back on the radio seconds later. "Sixty soldiers are inbound."

Darnell clicks the talk button. "Jesus, Walt, that's not going to be enough. These savages will chew through sixty weekend warriors like they're having a midmorning snack. We need an overwhelming force if we're going to take this prison back."

"Lydia, these soldiers will be wearing body armor and will be heavily armed. The prisoners don't have any weapons, do they?"

"Some of these guys could make a weapon out of a piece of tissue, but, no, they don't have any firearms that I'm aware of," Darnell says over the radio. "But sixty men ain't no match for the monsters in here. Hell, Walt, six hundred soldiers might not even do the trick."

"If they don't have any guns I don't see it being a

big issue. Besides, *I* don't have the authority to call up more troops."

Darnell sighs. She taps herself on the forehead with the handheld microphone a few times, thinking it's a good thing Walt didn't decide to be a brain surgeon. She pushes the transmit button and says, "I know that, Walt. Get on the horn to the warden or the director of corrections and tell them we need more soldiers."

"Ten-four. I'll make the call, Lydia, but what am I supposed to tell these soldiers that are rolling up right now?"

"Tell them to contact me. Darnell out." She slings the handset over her shoulder and waits. Darnell takes up the shotgun again as the wailing of the wounded drones on. Her mind drifts and she wonders, briefly, which prison gang is now calling the shots. There's a long list to choose from. Ethnicity plays a major role in deciding who belongs in which gang, but there are also multiple gangs among a single ethnic group. Most of the Hispanic prisoners at Attica fall into three groups: the Mexican Mafia, the Nuestra Familia, or the Netas. Most African American prisoners retain their street gang affiliations, making the Bloods and Crips two of the largest prison gangs in existence. Not to be outdone, the Caucasian prisoners also have several gangs to choose from, but the overwhelming majority of whites here call the Aryan Brotherhood home. Yes, they're all diverse groups, but they do have one thing in common—each group despises the other enough to want to kill them.

Darnell startles when Walt calls to her over the radio. She drags the handset off her shoulder and answers, "Still here, Walt."

"Good to hear," Walt says. "I've got a Captain Butler here with me who wants to talk to you."

Darnell rolls her eyes. "Walt, hand him the radio."

A new voice sounds over the radio. "Officer Darnell, I'm Captain Scott Butler with the New York National Guard. What is the situation like inside the prison?"

"How do you think it is, Captain?" Darnell says.

"Bad?" Butler asks.

"Beyond your worst nightmare. Do you really have only sixty soldiers with you?"

"Yes, but they're all highly trained men."

"That might be true, Captain, but you're about to meet about two thousand of the meanest motherfuckers you've ever met. I suggest you bring lots of ammunition."

"We'll be prepared. How many other corrections officers are with you?"

Darnell sighs and clicks the transmit button. "Zero."

A lengthy silence follows before Butler asks, "Are any of the other guards still alive?"

Darnell blows out a long, shaky breath. "Not in cellblocks A and D. I don't know about the rest of the prison, but I haven't heard anyone else on the radio."

"What's your current location, Officer Darnell?"

"I locked myself in the weapons locker inside Times Square. It's situated at the crossroads where prisoners cross to other areas of the prison. Do you have floor plans?"

"I'm looking at them now," Butler answers. "Can you activate the doors so we can enter other areas of the prison?"

"Yes, but I'll be exposed. Call me when you need a door opened."

"We'll need more than one insertion point. Any suggestions?"

"Look, Captain, I don't want to tell you how to do your job, but I don't think dividing your forces is the best idea."

"Duly noted, Officer Darnell. Can you open the doors to the yard?"

Darnell groans then says, "Yes."

"Good. We'll finalize plans out here and I'll be back to you in a moment."

"Okay," Darnell says over the radio. "Tell your men to loosen up their trigger fingers, cause they're going to need 'em."

CHAPTER 52

Gardez, Paktika Province, Afghanistan

May 18, 2010
TARGET: Bomb makers for the Taliban
CONFIRMED KILLED: 33
CIVILIANS KILLED: Unknown

Decimated early in the war, Gardez, the capital of the Paktika Province, is slowly making a comeback after the war shifted to other parts of Afghanistan. The Americans still maintain a forward operating base nearby, but troop numbers have dwindled over the years. Surrounded by the mountains of the Hindu Kush, Gardez's current population has swelled to over 70,000 and the city, built at the intersection of two important roads, is the axis for commerce for a large swath of eastern Afghanistan.

With help from international aid organizations, the schools were rebuilt and the students returned to the classroom. Now at the local high school, seventeen-year-old Raahim Durrani is saying good-bye to his teachers for a final time. Small for his age and extremely shy, Raahim didn't have much of a social life in school, so he filled his time with reading, studying, and learning other languages. Fluent in six languages, including English, Raahim used his language-learning skills to master another form of language—computer programming. He can now program using SQL, Java, JavaScript, Python, C, Ruby, and many, many others.

Raahim says good-bye to his last teacher, grabs his backpack, and exits the school for a final time. With excellent ACT and SAT scores, Raahim, on a whim, applied to some of the most prestigious universities in the world with money he'd earned over several summers. But knowing his family would never be able to afford any of them, he enrolled in classes at Paktika University for the fall semester and accepted his fate. Weeks later, the acceptance letters began to roll in and Raahim would read them and put them away in a drawer as keepsakes. Days later he received a letter that would change his life. He had already been accepted to two prestigious universities in Boston, and the letter informed him that he would be awarded a full scholarship if he met certain conditions and agreed to work on a special software project. With very little thought, he signed the paperwork, canceled his enrollment at Paktika, and set his sights on Boston.

As Raahim makes his way back home, he runs through a mental checklist of what else needs to be done. He leaves in two weeks to participate in a special summer program at the university and has already started packing. Although excited, he has momentary bouts of sadness when his thoughts turn to leaving his family. The youngest of five children, Raahim will miss his two brothers and two sisters, but it's his parents he thinks about the most. It could be years before he returns home again and both of his parents are in their mid-

fifties—not that old, but like most Afghans they've had hard lives trying to eke out an existence in a country perennially at war.

Raahim tries to come to grips with maybe never see-ing his parents again as he crosses the bridge on his way to their neighborhood on the south side of the city. It's a beautiful day and Raahim pauses in the middle of the bridge to watch the clear, cold snowmelt trickle over the rocks as his mind churns with emotions. His two sis-ters are busy with their own families, and Raahim realizes he'll miss watching his nieces and nephews grow up.

Turning and leaning against the bridge, he allows the sun to warm his face. A moment later, he opens his eyes and notices a trail of smoke streaking across the sky. It's moving too fast to be an airplane and he won-ders what it is. With no obvious answers, he shrugs and turns for home.

As he's turning into his neighborhood something ex-plodes and the blast wave nearly knocks him off his feet. Raahim, stunned, watches as smoke rises from somewhere in the neighborhood and balloons across the sky. His heart now hammering, he begins to run.

Turning down the street he lives on, Raahim slows then stops when he discovers his home is no longer there. With tears streaming down his cheeks, he sinks to his knees and buries his face in his hands.

Two weeks later, after burying his parents and two brothers, Raahim shuffles through the Kabul airport in a daze, waiting for his flight to be called.

Present day, somewhere near Boston

Raahim closes out the web browser he had been looking at and sits back in his chair. Every few months he'll scan the Web to see if anyone has taken responsibility for killing his family and the results are no different today, eight years later. Raahim rubs his eyes. He's been going for twenty-four hours straight and is in desperate need of sleep. Pushing back his chair, he stands and walks into the break room and grabs an energy drink from the fridge. Already jittery, he knows the caffeine jolt is only going to make it worse. He puts the unopened drink back in the fridge and leans against the counter.

He made it through the plane crashes just fine, but as the day wears on Raahim is losing his taste for killing. He turns and searches the upper cabinets for some antacids. He finds a bottle of Pepto-Bismol with a couple of swallows left in it and unscrews the cap and drains it. Looking at the empty bottle he wonders if some of the others are having similar thoughts.

Tossing the empty bottle in the trash, Raahim exits the break room and heads for the room where they've been bunking the last couple of nights.

"Where are you going, Raahim?" Nazeri asks.

"I'm going to lie down," Raahim says.

"No, you are not. We have business to attend to," Nazeri says.

"It can wait," Raahim says as he walks past where Nazeri is sitting. Then he stops, turns, and glares at Nazeri. "Do you have a quota for the number of dead per day? If so, feel free to use my computer."

CHAPTER 53

Peyton kneels next to Eric, who's lying on his right side. Unsure if she should move him, she leans down and puts her ear on his chest, listening to see if her husband is still breathing.

He is.

"Eric, can you hear me?" When she gets no response she reaches out and shakes him.

This time there's movement as Eric turns his head and groans.

She crawls toward his head and leans down next to him, their noses nearly touching. "Where are you hit?"

"Don't know . . . for sure . . . upper . . . upper . . ." His words trail off as he grimaces with pain.

Peyton straightens and scans the part of his back she can see, looking for bloodstains or wounds. There's nothing readily apparent, so she looks over his legs and finds no blood there, either. She leans back down, next to Eric's face. "I don't see anything here, babe. Were you shot on your right side?"

"I don't—fuck, it burns like . . . someone . . . is . . . stabbing me . . . with a . . . hot . . . hot . . . poker."

Peyton reaches a hand out and wipes the dirt from his lips. "Do you think it's safe for me to roll you over?"

"I think . . . so."

"Can you move your hands and feet?"

Eric spends a moment trying out his right hand, then his left, before giving his feet a go. Everything appears to be functioning normally, yet Peyton is hesitant to move him. *What happens if there's a bullet lodged in his spine?* Peyton doesn't know what to do. *What if he's bleeding out while I'm sitting here thinking about it?* Peyton takes a deep, calming breath, trying to slow her rapidly pulsing heart. "Eric, I'm going to roll you over."

"O . . . kay."

She places a hand on his shoulder and gently rolls him onto his back. Eric shouts with pain and Peyton gasps. The entire right side of his white shirt is caked with blood and dirt.

"How . . . bad?" he asks before clenching his teeth and groaning.

"I don't . . . know. I need . . . I need to peel your shirt back." Peyton leans over and begins unbuttoning his shirt. Her hands are trembling, making the simple task that much more difficult. "I don't really know what I'm doing, Eric."

"Need to . . . clean . . . the wound."

"With what?" Peyton asks, finally finishing with the last button.

"Need . . . water."

A flash of anger flares in Peyton's gut for the woman who stole her case of water. But it fades almost as quickly as concern over Eric's health returns to the forefront of her mind. "We don't have any water, honey."

"You need—fuck, it hurts so bad, Peyton. Maybe . . ."

Eric takes a deep breath and winces with the pain. "Find one of . . . the cops."

Peyton glances across the street. It looks as if the fighting is over for now, as several police officers file into the store. "I don't want to leave you, Eric."

"No . . . choice. Only . . . option . . . we . . . have."

"Let me peel back your shirt to see how bad the wound is."

"Leave . . . it. Get . . . cops."

"Okay. I'll be right back." She leans over, gives Eric a quick kiss on his lips, and lurches to her feet. She takes a step and mutters a few curse words, having forgotten she's missing a shoe. The grit and gravel bite at the soles of her lacerated foot as she hobbles across the vacant lot. When her damaged foot hits the hot asphalt, Peyton yelps with pain, but she continues on. As she nears the store, some little niggle in her brain tells her she probably should put her hands up. She reaches for the sky and limps closer. As she nears the store, she spots a police officer standing near the entrance, his backed turned to her. "Sir," Peyton says.

The police officer whirls around, the barrel of his rifle rising as he turns.

"Don't shoot!" Peyton shouts, startling the other officers, who immediately spring into action and, within seconds, Peyton has a dozen rifle barrels pointed directly at her. "Please, please don't shoot," Peyton begs, her entire body now quivering with fear.

The closest officer, the one Peyton initially addressed, lowers his weapon. "Jesus Christ, lady. Are you trying to get yourself killed?"

He's a fairly young guy, probably late twenties, Peyton thinks, and he has a wild look in his eyes, no doubt hopped up from the recent gun battle. "I'm sorry. I didn't mean to startle you."

The other officers lower their weapons, several shaking their heads.

"I need . . . I need your help . . ." She squints, trying to read the name tape stuck over his right breast. "Officer Campbell."

Campbell waves to the burned-out store. "If you haven't noticed we're a little busy at the moment."

"Officer Campbell, my husband is injured. He was struck by a bullet during your . . . your shoot-out."

Campbell slings his rifle over his shoulder. "Okay. Where is he?"

Peyton turns and points to the vacant lot. "Over there by that tree. Please hurry."

Campbell turns and shouts, "Evans, you're with me."

Another police officer hurries out of the store and Peyton, now limping badly, leads them across the street.

"What's wrong with you?" Campbell asks.

"Feet are in pretty bad shape," Peyton answers.

"Hold up," Campbell says. He turns and barks out another name. Seconds later another officer hurries out of the store, this time a woman. "Janice, help her back to the station."

"I'm on it, Sarge," the woman replies, hurrying across the street.

"Ma'am, go with her," Campbell says. "We'll look after your husband."

"I'd rather stay," Peyton says.

"Ma'am, in all honesty, you're just slowing us down," Campbell says.

Peyton nods and Campbell and Evans take off at a jog.

Peyton looks at Janice, the female officer, and takes a second to read her name tag. "Where's the police station, Officer Jacobs?"

Janice points at a beige building on the corner, a little over a hundred yards away.

Even with all that has happened today—all of the turmoil, including the death of Ranjeet, the shoot-out, and now Eric's wounding—Peyton's first thought is that those were some really dumb-ass looters to hit a store next door to a police station.

CHAPTER 54

Manhattan

Paige and Hank are currently hiding behind a building at the northwest corner of Walker and Broadway as the gun battle rages on. The best Hank can tell is that it looks as if a group of nasty-looking characters are trying to stick up the big bank just up the block on Broadway. The store near where they're currently positioned, some kind of jeans and footwear place, has already been looted and empty shoeboxes and broken glass litter the sidewalk.

"Why are they trying to rob a bank?" Paige asks.

"Hell if I know. I guess because they think they can. What they don't know is the bank manager most likely put all the cash drawers in the vault and locked it up when the power went out."

"Then why don't the employees just walk out the back door and let them have at it?"

"I don't know, Paige. I'm not a bank manager or a bank robber. All I know is this is takin' up valuable time."

"You don't have to be so cranky about it."

Hank scowls then takes another peek around the

corner. Those people caught out in the open when the gun battle began are still crawling around through the broken glass, trying to take cover wherever they can. If he and Paige can just get across the street they'll be golden. Hank spends a moment studying the layout. They could backtrack and pick up another street, but every second that ticks off the clock is an opportunity for something else bad to happen. And their exposure to ricocheting bullets will be limited by all the abandoned cars clogging the street. Hank ducks back behind the building.

He glances at his watch and calculates the number of blocks ahead of them. By his calculation they've covered eighteen blocks, and if they can cover ten blocks every eight minutes they can be at the heliport in about forty minutes. He turns to look at Paige. "We're crossin' the street."

"Now?"

"Yes, now. Just stay low until you get behind those other buildin's across the street."

"You want me to go first?"

"It doesn't matter, Paige. We're wastin' time."

"Okay, you go first."

Hank sighs, bends over, and races to the other side.

Paige takes a deep breath and follows. When she's about midway across, the gangbangers on the street open up again and she has to dive behind an abandoned taxi. She looks to Hank for help. He holds up a hand as he watches the scene play out up the street. When he sees the bad guys duck back down, he waves Paige onward. Paige scrambles to her feet and duckwalks the rest of the way across, standing only when she's safely behind the building.

Hank takes one look at her once-elegant, expensive

clothing and knows to bite his tongue. Paige, noticing the expression on his face, looks down at her grease-streaked clothing and groans. "Well, hell. So much for this outfit."

"You've got plenty more back at your place. Let's roll." Hank turns and starts walking, setting a brisk pace.

Paige has to hurry to catch up, but once she does she has little trouble. With her long legs and taut muscles honed in the gym three days a week, Paige can match Hank step for step with limited exertion. But with the heat, humidity, and having to fight through the crowds, Paige can feel her energy draining away.

When they reach the next intersection, Hank pauses and pulls out his cell phone to check for a signal. He's disappointed—but not surprised—to find the phone has no service. "I wish we had some way to communicate with Elaine."

"We can use Wi-Fi when we get on the plane."

Hank glances at his watch. "That could be a while. And we've been out of contact with her for a good while already. There's no tellin' how many catastrophes have occurred while we've been incommunicado."

"Does it matter?"

Hank glances at Paige, a scowl on his face. "Yeah, it matters."

"Why? There's not a damn thing we can do about it. At least not until we find a way to eliminate that nasty piece of malware."

"Speakin' of that, do you think Natalie has made any progress?"

"I hope so. I'll call her when we get on the plane."

They cover the next ten blocks in less than eight minutes, much to Hank's delight. Or, rather, he's as delighted as he can be considering the ongoing crisis. Walker Street had merged into Canal Street five blocks back, meaning they're now only a few blocks from the East River. Over the years, billions of dollars have been spent on upgrading the city's sewage treatment plants in an effort to clean up the East River, yet it still remains one of the most polluted waterways in the country. A fishy, briny odor lingers over the area as Hank pauses to pull up the map of Manhattan in his mind. If they turn north on Allen Street, it's thirty-eight blocks to reach the East 34th Street Heliport. Hank glances at his watch and says, "If we can keep up this pace, we'll be at the heliport in less than thirty minutes."

"That's assuming we don't run into any more trouble," Paige says.

"No negative thoughts, Paige," Hank says, turning up Allen Street. When Paige catches up, he asks, "What do you think is next on the hackers' list of targets?"

"Who knows? I'm beginning to wonder if there's a computer network left in this country that they haven't hacked."

Hank wipes the sweat from his brow. "Let me rephrase the question. If you were hackin' to inflict the most damage, what would your next target be?"

"The most damage you could inflict on the largest populations would be to keep doing what they're doing—hitting the power grids. Cut the power and you cut off the water supply, the sewage treatment plants, and everything else that we've come to rely on to live."

"I agree," Hank says. "But I keep gettin' hung up on the motive. If it's a foreign nation or state they have to know we'll retaliate with overwhelmin' force. So what would they gain? A few days of pleasure watchin' us squirm before we obliterate them? That doesn't make any sense."

"It doesn't make sense, but I think this cyber attack is much too sophisticated for it to be anyone other than a well-funded nation or state group."

"I disagree. The hackers have spent years refinin' their attack, and if they have access to one or more supercomputers, say, at the larger research universities or major tech companies, then why not?"

Paige licks her lips, trying to generate more saliva. She's regretting not bringing along some of the bottles of water from the stock exchange offices. "Are you suggesting a group of college students or a few rogue employees are behind this hack?"

Hank, his shirt saturated with sweat, switches his backpack to the other shoulder. "I don't know what I'm suggestin'. Who hates this country enough to try and destroy it?"

"A lot of people, including the usual suspects, such as Iran and North Korea."

"But that takes us back to my original point about retaliation. All of those countries know—they absolutely know—that payback is a bitch. Who wouldn't be concerned with our response? A group of very smart people not affiliated with a specific country, but who also have deep-seated animosity toward the United States."

"Like a terrorist group?" Paige asks.

"No, not the usual suspects such as Al-Qaeda or ISIS. This feels different to me. I don't know. Maybe I'm just blabberin'. But my gut tells me this is straight-up retribution."

"For what?"

"That's what we need to find out."

CHAPTER 55

North Atlantic Ocean

Captain Bruce Hensley, still confined to quarters, sneaks up to his cabin door for another look through the peephole and smiles. The guard is gone. Not sure what Griffin had done to cause the guard to leave his post, or how long he might be away, Hensley opens the door and hurries down the corridor. He climbs down the stairs to the rear deck and pauses. If Admiral Malloy spots him prowling around on the rear-deck camera, Hensley could be charged with mutiny. He stares through the glass at the Seahawk chopper sitting on the deck, weighing his options.

Inside the USS *Stark*'s Ship's Mission Center, Rear Admiral Richard Malloy is champing at the bit to get the ship's weapons up and running again. Having spent the last eight years of his career overseeing the designing and building of America's newest warship, he has more than his reputation at risk. As the Department of Defense whittled down the number of ships it was willing to purchase, Admiral Malloy's stature inside the navy ranks was also whittled down. A proud man born to blue-collar parents, all his years of hard work and ass-kissing will be for naught if he can't prove that this new Zumwalt class of destroyers is just what the navy needs for twenty-first-century warfare. And after years of delay and budget-busting expenditures, it's now make-or-break time for both the ship and the man. Normally not one willing to take big risks, he'd considered sending the ship back to port for a bow-to-stern review. But with his fears that the USS *Stark* will never sail the high seas again and with a heavy dose of ego that his intimate knowledge of the workings of the ship will prevail, he's opting for an at-sea reboot and retry. Malloy turns to the ship's weapons officer and says, "Mr. Griffin, how much longer?"

Although the weapon systems are now operational, Lieutenant Mike Griffin says, "Sir, they're having some trouble getting the missile pods back on the rails."

"What about the guns?" Malloy asks.

Well, shit, what now? "Well, sir, uh . . ." Griffin sputters. "They're—" He glances up at one of the video monitors to see his captain racing across the rear deck toward the helicopter. "—Can I show you something, sir?"

Everyone in mission control can hear the admiral sigh before he marches across the room to the weapons station. "What is it, Mr. Griffin?"

Hensley swings open the rear door of the chopper and dives inside as the pilot and copilot turn in their seats.

"What the hell?" the pilot asks, none too happy about someone piling in his helicopter uninvited. He removes his headset and asks, "Who the hell are you?"

Hensley leans forward. "I'm Captain Bruce Hensley, commander of the USS *Stark*, Lieutenant."

"Yes, sir," the pilot says, sitting up a little straighter in his seat. "Why are you in my helicopter, sir?"

"I need to use your radio."

"With all due respect, sir, what's wrong with your ship's radio?"

"It's not working. I don't have time to go into all the details, Lieutenant," Hensley says, slipping a spare headset on. "Can you power up the radio?"

The pilot and copilot share a look, both wondering why the ship's captain is in their helicopter wanting to use the radio. The pilot turns to face Hensley. "Sir, we're here on orders from Admiral Malloy."

"Christ, I'm not asking anything out of the ordinary. All I want to do is make a simple radio call."

"I need permission from Admiral Malloy, Captain."

Hensley yanks off the headset, tosses it on the seat, and leans forward to look the pilot in the eye. "When the shells and missiles start raining down on Norfolk again, call Admiral Young at Fleet Forces Command and tell him to mothball this motherfucking ship. Got it, Lieutenant?"

Before the pilot can respond, Hensley pushes open the door and hurries toward the aft entrance.

Griffin's shoulders sag when he spots Captain Hensley climbing out of the helicopter only seconds later. He's served with Hensley long enough to be able to read the boss's body language and the captain's red face is a dead giveaway. Griffin turns back to Malloy and points at a schematic of the vertical missile launching system on his computer monitor. "That's the issue, there, sir. I think with some fine-tuning it'll work like a charm."

"Good eye, Lieutenant. And that's a minor fix." The admiral stands, places his hands on his hips, and arches his back. "Are we locked and loaded?"

Griffin picks up a phone. "I'll call down to the weapons room to make sure, sir, but I believe we are." Griffin waits for the admiral to move on, then dials Hensley's extension and waits for him to answer. He does on the third ring. "What happened?" he whispers into the phone.

Hensley is out of breath when he says, "They won't allow me . . . to make a radio call without . . . Malloy's permission. Where's my guard?"

"Engine room," Griffin whispers. "The admiral took my suggestion and ran a damage drill while we waited. What now, Bruce? I've stalled about as long as I can."

Hensley sighs. "I'm out of options, Griff."

"Mr. Griffin?" Admiral Malloy shouts across the room.

"Do you have a cell signal?" Griff whispers over the phone.

"No."

"Well, sit tight, because the shit show is about to start up again."

"Reset the power to the weapons, Griff. That'll buy us a little time."

"He'll skin me alive, Bruce. I'll try to think of something else." Griffin hangs up the phone and his fellow crew members turn to look at him, fear painted on their faces. He reaches for the power switch and says, "Admiral, we're locked and"—Griffin triggers the switch off then back on—"wait one, sir. The weapons are resetting for some reason."

"Goddamn it, Mr. Griffin. What the hell is going on?"

"Some type of power interruption, sir. It'll take a few moments for them to come back online." Griffin shoots a pleading look at Connelly.

"Sir," Connelly says, "maybe we should hold the live-fire exercises until we can diagnose this computer issue."

"There is no computer issue, Ms. Connelly. The systems performed flawlessly during the dry-fire exercises."

"I know, sir," Connelly presses, "but the weapons shouldn't just power off, should they?"

"The ship's computer is designed to reset itself if it discovers an anomaly. That's simply the case, here."

"But, sir," Connelly says, "wouldn't that be a major problem if we were in the heat of battle?"

Malloy waves at the monitors. "Look around, Ms. Connelly. Do you see any other ships on the screens?"

Connelly scans the array of video monitors. "No, sir. Not at present."

"Exactly. We're conducting sea trials. We'll have to make some minor tweaks to the ship before we send her out on patrol. We'll fix the computer issues. That you can be assured of."

Connelly has to concentrate to keep from shaking her head. "Yes, sir." She turns to look at Griffin and shrugs.

"How much longer, Mr. Griffin?" the admiral asks.

Out of alternatives, Griffin says, "Two minutes, sir."

"Good," Malloy says. "Bring up our list of targets."

Griffin types out a command on his keyboard and the list of deployed targets and their locations appears on the large screen at the front of the room. The mood inside the Ship's Mission Center is tense. Members of the crew are waiting for what they know is coming. The lights on Griffin's console flash green. He could kill the power again, but he would risk being court-martialed for insubordination. Griffin exhales a long, shaky breath and says, "Weapons online, sir."

"About time, Mr. Griffin. Sound battle stations. Helm, all ahead full. Let's start with the deck guns."

CHAPTER 56

Inside the police station, Peyton is offered a turn at the water cooler and she takes advantage of it, drinking cup after cup as Jacobs strips out of her body armor. Moments later, Campbell and Evans return, half carrying and half dragging Eric between them, his arms draped over their shoulders. Eric is conscious and groaning in pain. "Clear off one of the desks," Campbell orders, hauling Eric past the reception area and into the squad room.

Peyton and Janice Jacobs sweep the contents on the closest desk to the floor and Campbell and Evans lower Eric onto the desk as Jacobs hurries off to grab a first aid kit. Peyton walks over to the water cooler and fills a cup and returns to her husband, gently lifting his head and dribbling water into his mouth. "How bad is the pain?"

"Mostly numb," Eric mumbles.

Jacobs returns moments later, gloved up, masked up, and wearing a plastic face shield. She glances at Peyton and says, "I'm also the team medic, so your husband is in good hands."

"Thank you," Peyton says. Exhausted, she pulls over an office chair and sits, taking Eric's hand in hers. Campbell and Evans stack their rifles in the corner then unclip and remove their heavy armored vests.

Jacobs gently peels Eric's shirt back. "Tilt him onto his left side," Jacobs says.

Evans and Campbell roll Eric onto his side and Jacobs continues gently pulling the bloody, sweaty shirt away from Eric's torso, revealing a gunshot wound near the lower part of Eric's rib cage. She quickly cuts the remaining fabric and tosses the bloody shirt to the floor. She leans down for a closer look at the wound.

"Looks like a through-and-through," she says. "It missed the lung, but the bullet could have nicked his liver."

"How will you know?" Peyton asks.

"I won't. Not without a CT scan. But judging from the amount of blood lost, I'm leaning toward the positive that the liver remains intact."

"A through-and-through means the bullet passed through his body?" Peyton asks.

Jacobs twists the cap off a large bottle of saline. "Correct. He has both an entrance and an exit wound. Okay, guys, lay him back down and scoot him a little to the side so that the wound is beyond the edge of the desk."

Evans and Campbell do as instructed and Jacobs says, "Sir, this might sting a bit."

"His name is Eric," Peyton says.

"Okay, Eric," Jacobs says, "this is going to be cold and it might—oh hell—it will sting, but I need to irrigate your wound."

Eric nods.

After ripping open a package of gauze, Jacobs pours

about half the bottle of saline around and over the wound.

Eric winces and squeezes Peyton's hand as Jacobs dabs with the gauze, cleaning away the dried blood. She leans over and cleans the exit wound, dabbing and wiping with a new patch of gauze. A fresh rivulet of blood trickles out and Jacobs applies pressure to the wound. "Sorry if this hurts, but I need to stop the bleeding."

"It's okay," Eric says, clenching Peyton's hand again.

After several moments of applying pressure, Jacobs removes the gauze and checks for more bleeding. "I think we've got it stopped for now, but don't be surprised if you find some oozing."

"How will I know if it's too much bleeding?" Peyton asks.

Jacobs glances up. "You'll know. Just put some pressure on it. When I'm finished, I'll dress the wound with a hemostatic dressing that has a clotting agent in it. That'll help." Jacobs stands and says to Campbell, "Sarge, will you shine your flashlight down here?"

Campbell grabs a small tactical flashlight off his belt and clicks it on, focusing the beam on Eric's wound. Jacobs pulls out a pair of tweezers and leans in close. "Okay, Eric, I need to do a little probing here, looking for shirt fibers. I'll try to be as gentle as possible, but it's going to hurt."

"Go ahead," Eric says, clenching his body.

"Relax, Eric," Jacobs says. "At least try to relax your abdominal muscles. That'll make my job a lot easier."

Eric nods and tries to relax his midsection. But with the first touch of the tweezers, he clenches up again.

"It's hard, Eric, but try to relax," Jacobs says as she

continues to probe the wound. "There you are, you little suckers," she mumbles as she removes a few tiny
threads, laying them on Eric's chest. After several moments of digging around she says, "I think I got them
all."

Eric blows out the breath he had been holding.

Jacobs stands and drains the rest of the bottle of
saline over the wound. "Infection is going to be the primary concern." Jacobs turns to look at Peyton. "Do
you have any antibiotics at home?"

"I don't know," Peyton says. "Maybe."

"If you do, start them immediately." Jacobs returns
to dressing the wound and strips off her gloves.

Peyton stands and helps Eric up and he sits woozily
on the edge of the desk.

Jacobs snaps on a new pair of gloves. "Now, ma'am,
let me have a look at your feet."

"I'm Peyton, by the way," she says, sitting back
down and stripping off the one remaining makeshift
shoe.

"Nice to meet you, Peyton," Jacobs says, peering at
Peyton's attempt at a shoe. "Pretty good handiwork on
the fly. But I have to ask, where are your regular shoes?"

"That's a long story, Officer Jacobs."

"I bet," Jacobs mutters. She pats the desk. "Put your
feet up here where I can look at them."

Peyton leans back in the chair and props her feet on
the desk as Jacobs grabs another bottle of saline and a
fresh pair of tweezers. After several moments spent
picking out glass fragments and grit, Jacobs wets a
piece of gauze with the saline and wipes Peyton's soles
clean. "What size shoe do you wear?"

"Seven," Peyton answers.

Jacobs opens a tube of antibiotic ointment and

slathers it over Peyton's feet. "I wear an eight, but I've got an old pair of sneakers in my locker that are just a tad bit tight."

"I don't want to leave you shoeless," Peyton says, "especially after everything you all have done for us."

"Nonsense," Jacobs says as she strips off her gloves. "Sit tight. I'll be right back."

"Are you sure?" Peyton asks.

"Yes, I'm sure," Jacobs says before disappearing down the hall.

Peyton turns to look at Sargeant Campbell. She's dying to ask about the shoot-out, but instead says, "What do you know about the power outage?"

"Not much," Campbell says. "We're operating on a generator at the moment. Why? Do you know something different?"

"I don't know anything certain, but I did talk briefly with my sister, who's an FBI agent in D.C. She said something about getting out before the call dropped."

"Get out of where?" Campbell asks, taking a seat on the edge of the desk.

"I don't know. But her voice sounded urgent. I think she meant get out of the city."

"We haven't been told squat, but leaving the city is not a bad idea," Campbell says. "We've been without power for a few hours and it's already going to hell. I hate to think what tomorrow will bring if the power doesn't come back on."

Jacobs returns, carrying a beat-up pair of sneakers. She hands those and a pair of socks to Peyton. "They're well used, but they're a damn sight better than what you had."

"Thank you," Peyton says, gently pulling on the socks. "I don't know how we can thank all of you enough."

"We're here to serve," Officer Evans says. "Just doin' our job, ma'am."

"I think you've gone well beyond the call of duty," Peyton says, slipping on the shoes. "So, thank you very, very much." Peyton stands to give the new shoes a try. They're a bit big, but they're a hell of a lot better than the heels she started the day in and much better than those she created from the sofa cushion. She puts a hand on Eric's back. "Can you walk?"

Eric stands to test out his injured body. "Yeah, I can walk."

"I'd offer to drive you, but I don't think we'd get very far," Jacobs says.

"You're right," Eric says as he walks forward a couple of steps. "I don't know how you are going to clear all of those abandoned vehicles."

"That's not something we're going to worry about right now," Campbell says. "It'll work out, eventually."

Peyton steps over to Jacobs and gives her a hug, before moving on to Evans, and finally to Sergeant Campbell. She breaks the embrace and steps back. "Thanks again for everything."

Jacobs says, "Hold up a sec," before turning and heading down the hallway.

She returns moments later with a half a dozen bottles of water in a grocery sack and a T-shirt for Eric. She hands both to Peyton. "Eric, you need fluids. Try to drink as much of that water as you can."

After one final round of good-byes, Eric and Peyton venture out into the unknown.

CHAPTER 57

After studying the floor plans of the prison, Captain Scott Butler now believes that Officer Darnell is correct—the only safe approach is through the front door. Laid out in a square, the four cellblocks form a perimeter around four separate outdoor areas. They'll enter through cellblock A, which runs north and south with cellblock B on the opposite side of the prison. Cellblocks C and D run east to west, completing the square. To make matters more difficult, each cellblock has access to a tunnel that divides the four fields, with Times Square positioned at the intersection of the four tunnels.

Butler closes the lid on his military-provided laptop and runs a hand across his face. He knows his men are getting itchy and the longer they delay the more time they have to think about what might lie ahead. Butler steps over to the side window of the truck and places his computer on the front seat. They could plan for days and still not come up with a scenario where he and his men wouldn't have to enter the prison. After hitching up his pants and tightening his armored vest, Butler picks up his M4 carbine and walks over to the gathering of state troopers to coordinate radio communications.

Troopers from Troop A will take their long guns and head for the watchtowers that are situated on the four corners of the inside prison yard. Correctional officers will continue to man the watchtowers along the exterior wall and they are also armed with rifles. State policemen from Troops E and C, armed with shotguns, will accompany Butler and his men inside. The officers in Troop B will stand in reserve and all the external traffic will run through Major Clyde Pierce, the area commander for the New York State Police. Butler takes Pierce by the elbow and leads him away from the group.

"What have you heard from headquarters?" Butler asks.

"Concerning what, Captain?" Pierce asks. A short man at five-six, Pierce is built like a fireplug.

"Our orders." The commingling of troops hasn't been an easy process and Pierce has made it known that he's pissed his well-trained troopers are under Butler's command. Not that Butler gives a damn.

"Apparently you've received all the orders. They haven't told us shit," Pierce says, crossing his arms across his thick chest.

Butler, a head taller than Pierce, takes a step closer and lowers his voice, saying, "You better shape the fuck up, Major. We don't have any idea what we're going to run into inside those prison walls, but I'm not going to have you out here fucking up my mission. If you don't like it you can haul ass and I'll find someone else. Otherwise, be the leader you're supposed to fucking be." Butler takes a step back. "Understood?"

Pierce takes a moment, but eventually says, "Understood, Captain. You can rely on me."

"Thank you, Major Pierce. We've got a lot more serious shit to worry about rather than trying to mark our territory."

Pierce smiles, momentarily breaking the tension. "You don't talk like any dentists I know."

"That's because at this moment, I'm not a dentist. Today, I'm a soldier just like you and your men." Although they've reached some type of temporary truce, Butler decides to keep his orders to himself. He glances at his watch. "We're going inside in four minutes." Butler turns and makes his way over to a group of corrections officials who are huddled near the entrance to the administration building. "Four minutes," Butler tells them. He steps over to the prison's warden and asks for a word in private. The warden obliges and they move away from the group.

"Where am I likely to find the guards that might still be alive?"

The warden, Albert Diaz, takes a moment to think. "Inside the Times Square guard post and armory and the medical facility, for sure. Other than that, I just don't know."

Butler looks up at the sky. "It'll be dark soon. What's the fuel status for the generators?"

"They're tied in to a thousand-gallon fuel tank. Shouldn't be a problem." Diaz pauses then says, "But the generators are old, Captain. They can be cantankerous."

"Great. Put a couple of your maintenance men in there to baby them along. My plan is to lock down as many inmates as possible in the nearest cells available and I can't do that if the power fails again." Butler pauses as another ambulance passes by. Right now, there are more than fifty parked haphazardly around the entrance, waiting for the wounded. "Priority for the wounded will be staff first, followed by the injured inmates. The remaining staff will be sheltered in the auditorium."

"It sounds like you have a good handle on the situation, Captain. But, let me remind you that some of the meanest and most violent criminals ever convicted in this state are now loose inside the walls behind me. I don't say that to frighten you, but you need to prepare yourself for what you're likely to find. The safety and security of your men and any remaining staff is paramount and that should be at the forefront of your mind as you enter the prison."

Butler, finding the last statement odd, cocks his head to the side. "So you've spoken with the governor and are aware of his orders?"

"I have, Captain, and yes, I'm aware of his orders."

"And that's okay with you?"

Diaz looks down at his shoes for a moment before looking back up. "All I'm saying, Captain, is do what you think needs to be done."

"To be clear, Warden, we won't murder unarmed prisoners."

"I understand, Captain Butler, but be forewarned that most of the men you'll encounter inside would kill you at the blink of an eye without any hesitation."

"I understand, but that doesn't change my stance. Tell your two men with the keys to be ready." Butler turns and walks away. He calls the men going inside together for a few final words before telling them to get into position. As they file away, Butler looks for Walter, the corrections officer. He spots him with the group of prison officials and walks over. "Walt, can I borrow your radio?" Butler asks.

Walter hands it over and Butler keys the transmit button and says, "Officer Darnell, are you there?"

A moment later Darnell replies. "I'm still here, Captain."

"Sit tight. We'll be entering the prison in thirty seconds. Do you still have your weapons?"

"Locked and loaded, sir."

"Good. Butler out." He hands the radio back to Walter and starts walking toward the entrance. Then he stops and turns around. "Walter, can I borrow your radio for a while?"

"Of course, Captain." Walter hands the radio back to Butler, who clips it on his belt.

Butler retraces his steps and walks up to the entrance. He doesn't have butterflies in his stomach—it feels more like a hawk has taken flight instead. He takes a deep, calming breath as he joins his forces that are bunched up near the door. After one final deep breath, he says, "Remember your assignments, men. Go, go, go."

CHAPTER 58

Hassan Ansari looks at the clock in the right-hand corner of his computer screen then checks the position of the satellite. He'll have access to the ship soon. For computing power to carry out their attacks, the five Ph.D. students hacked their university's supercomputers and installed a back door that allows them administrator-level access. They tested it out over the previous few months to see if their activities would be discovered or if it raised any red flags and neither happened. They're certain because, as advanced students in computer-related fields, they receive e-mails and notifications from their universities about attempted intrusions, viruses, or other events that might harm the school's computer networks. So far there has been no mention of their activities. To mask their location, they are using a secure VPN that Nazeri has access to and from there the signals are routed through other servers all over the world.

Hassan might feel a tad squeamish about killing innocent civilians but he has no such qualms when it comes to an American warship launching missiles at

...e has no idea how
...ained, but he hopes
...ill bring the weapons
...now in a few minutes.

...*s and decides* to use the
...anding in front of the urinal,
...sef opens the door and slips in-
si... ...es up and the two huddle near the
sink. Havin... ...nd two cleverly disguised pinhole cameras in their sleeping quarters, Hassan is wondering if
Nazeri has placed listening devices in the restroom. Just
in case, he turns on the water and he and Yuusef talk in
muted whispers.

"What are we going to do about Nazeri?" Yuusef
asks.

"I do not know," Hassan says. "I think he has a different exit strategy for us than the one we have been
discussing among ourselves."

"What do you mean?"

"Once this is over he no longer has a use for us."

Yuusef's eyes widen. "What are you suggesting?"

Hassan leans against the counter. "The easiest thing
for him would be to cut the loose strings. Yes, we are
all participants, but we are also witnesses to his involvement."

"We know nothing about him. What threat are we to
him?"

Hassan debates telling Yuusef about the pictures
he'd snapped of Nazeri and decides against it. "How
do you see this ending, Yuusef?"

Yuusef shrugs. "I thought we would all go our separate ways."

Hassan shakes his head. "We are all criminals now,

CHAPTER 58

Hassan Ansari looks at the clock in the right-hand corner of his computer screen then checks the position of the satellite. He'll have access to the ship soon. For computing power to carry out their attacks, the five Ph.D. students hacked their university's supercomputers and installed a back door that allows them administrator-level access. They tested it out over the previous few months to see if their activities would be discovered or if it raised any red flags and neither happened. They're certain because, as advanced students in computer-related fields, they receive e-mails and notifications from their universities about attempted intrusions, viruses, or other events that might harm the school's computer networks. So far there has been no mention of their activities. To mask their location, they are using a secure VPN that Nazeri has access to and from there the signals are routed through other servers all over the world.

Hassan might feel a tad squeamish about killing innocent civilians but he has no such qualms when it comes to an American warship launching missiles at one of their own naval bases. He has no idea how much damage Norfolk has sustained, but he hopes whoever is running the ship will bring the weapons back online. Either way, he'll know in a few minutes.

Hassan stands and stretches and decides to use the restroom while he's up. Standing in front of the urinal, he looks up when Yuusef opens the door and slips inside. Hassan finishes up and the two huddle near the sink. Having found two cleverly disguised pinhole cameras in their sleeping quarters, Hassan is wondering if Nazeri has placed listening devices in the restroom. Just in case, he turns on the water and he and Yuusef talk in muted whispers.

"What are we going to do about Nazeri?" Yuusef asks.

"I do not know," Hassan says. "I think he has a different exit strategy for us than the one we have been discussing among ourselves."

"What do you mean?"

"Once this is over he no longer has a use for us."

Yuusef's eyes widen. "What are you suggesting?"

Hassan leans against the counter. "The easiest thing for him would be to cut the loose strings. Yes, we are all participants, but we are also witnesses to his involvement."

"We know nothing about him. What threat are we to him?"

Hassan debates telling Yuusef about the pictures he'd snapped of Nazeri and decides against it. "How do you see this ending, Yuusef?"

Yuusef shrugs. "I thought we would all go our separate ways."

Hassan shakes his head. "We are all criminals now,

CHAPTER 59

The first few minutes of the live-fire exercises go off without a hitch. The computer is tracking targets with precision and the large 155-mm rounds from the deck guns are obliterating the targets. Over at the weapons station, a tiny caterpillar of doubt is trying to worm its way into Lieutenant Griffin's head. *Had I been doing something wrong?* The more he thinks about it, the more he wonders. But then he replays the earlier event in his mind. *The weapons went wacky the moment they were initialized. Why then and not now?* Griffin turns to his computer and scrolls through pages of computer feedback on the weapons' operations. The deck guns are working exactly like they were designed to do. He glances up to see a grinning Admiral Malloy walking toward him.

"Mr. Griffin, let's try a missile or two," Malloy says.

"Yes, sir," Griffin says. Hoping to make the selection more difficult and to buy a little more time, Griffin refers to the weapons using their full designation. "Which missiles, Admiral? The RIM-66M Standard

Yuusef. Murderers. Nazeri's worst fear would be that one of us gets captured and points the finger at him."

"You believe he is going to kill us?"

Hassan nods. "Our only hope is to get away before he can."

"How long do you think this will last?"

"I do not know. The sooner we leave, the better."

"Tonight?" Yuusef asks.

"Maybe. In the interim, continue with your tasks." Hassan turns off the water. "I'll leave first and you wait a few moments before coming out. Nazeri does not need to know we have been talking."

Yuusef nods and Hassan slips out of the bathroom. When he returns to his computer he discovers that the satellite window is now open, allowing him access to the USS *Stark*'s computer systems. He sits, cracks his knuckles, and pulls up the coordinates for Naval Station Norfolk again as he waits for the ship's onboard cameras to come online.

Missile, the RIM-162 Evolved Sea Sparrow, the RUM-139 anti-submarine, or the BGM-109 Tomahawk?"

Malloy places a hand on his chin, playing it up for all it's worth. "Umm, let me see. Not the Tomahawks. Let's be creative. We'll fire a standard missile and then a few seconds later a Sea Sparrow to track and kill the first missile. Sound good, Mr. Griffin?"

"Yes sir," Griffin replies. "Give me a minute to set it up, sir."

"Notify me when ready," Malloy says before turning and walking away.

Griffin grinds his teeth as he enters the launch sequence for the missiles. Once that's completed, he ducks down behind the bank of monitors and picks up a ship's phone and makes another call to Captain Hensley, who is back in his stateroom, under guard. Hensley picks up on the second ring. "What's happening with the weapons, Griff?"

"Nothing unexpected." Griffin scans the area to make sure Malloy isn't hanging around before lowering his voice. "Did we screw something up during the initial exercise, Captain?"

"Tell me what you think," Hensley says.

"I don't know, Cap. I don't think we did, but it all happened so fast."

"Remember during the event when the computer wouldn't respond to any of your input?" Hensley asks.

"Yeah, I do remember. But why is everything working so flawlessly now?"

"I've been contemplating that exact question as I watched the video feed. The only thing I can think of that makes any sense whatsoever is that either the hackers can't access the ship's computers or the event was a one and done."

"I can't see it being a one and done," Griffin says. "Penetrating the ship's systems would have required enormous effort and I can't see them walking away from that. So that leaves us option one. The ship is cruising around in the middle of the Atlantic Ocean, and unless they're following us on another ship, their only access would be via satellite."

"Bingo. Weather could be a factor or it could be the satellite they're using is out of position."

"So we didn't fuck up?" Griffin asks.

"No, Griff, we didn't screw up. What's the admiral doing now?"

"We're preparing a missile test."

"Keep a hand close to the kill switch, Griff."

"I will, Cap. Later." Griffin hangs up the phone and reluctantly tells Admiral Malloy that the missile test is ready.

"Very well, Mr. Griffin. Fire when ready."

"Roger, sir." Griffin has the Sea Sparrow programmed to launch precisely three seconds after the launch of the first missile. He runs through the numbers again and positions his finger over the launch button. "Launch in three, two, one . . ." He presses the button and the first missile erupts from the vertical launching system. Three seconds later, the second missile blasts from its launcher. Griffin tracks the missiles and he gets a sinking feeling in his stomach when the first missile makes a long looping turn to the left. He checks the progress of the Sea Sparrow and that sinking feeling he felt is now a burning coal in his gut. Whatever the Sea Sparrow is tracking, it sure as hell isn't the target it's supposed to be tracking.

"Admiral, we have a problem!" Griffin shouts. He watches the screen as the first missile veers left again, taking dead aim at the USS *Stark*. "Incoming," Griffin shouts as more missiles roar out of their launchers. Everyone in the mission center dives under the desks.

"What the fuck are you doing?" Malloy shouts, racing over to the weapons station.

"It's the comp—"

His last words are obliterated when the first missile plows into the helicopter sitting on the deck and detonates. Shrapnel rips through the upper superstructure, shredding everything in its path. Griffin hammers the now-inoperable kill switch with his palm before diving under his desk. He catches a glimpse of the forward deck camera on a video screen and cringes as more missiles roar out of the launchers.

The admiral is the only person still upright, as he pounds on the keyboard above Griffin's head. Shrapnel continues to zing around the room, tearing through video monitors, computers, and those unlucky few who chose the wrong spot to hide. Malloy seem oblivious to all of it as he pounds the buttons on the weapons center console. "Kill power to the goddamn ship!" Malloy shouts at the top of his lungs.

Within seconds, the control center is plunged into darkness and the barrage of missiles stops. Only then does Griffin hear the moans of the wounded. The battery-powered emergency lights kick on and Griffin climbs out from beneath his desk as others do the same. The admiral is standing and staring into the distance as if in a trance. "Are you injured, Admiral?" Griffin asks.

Malloy turns to look at him. "What?"

"I asked if you were injured, sir."

"No, no. I'm not injured," he answers in a flat, lifeless tone.

Medical personnel rush into the room and begin triage. Griffin pulls a chair over and positions it behind Malloy. "Sir, why don't you sit down for a moment?"

The admiral nods and slumps into the chair as Captain Hensley hurries into the room and says, "Mr. Griffin, disable the weapons." Hensley takes a second to survey the damage then turns to his executive officer. "I need a ship-wide damage assessment, Kat."

She nods and hurries away to carry out the captain's order, as Hensley starts barking out more orders. The injured members of his crew are either being carried out or being helped out by medical personnel and taken to the infirmary. Luckily, no one inside the mission center appears to have sustained any life-threatening injuries. Hensley doesn't know if that's true for the entire ship or not. He won't know that until Connelly returns with the damage report. He walks across the room and squats down next to Malloy's chair. "Are you okay, Admiral?"

Malloy turns to look Hensley in the eyes. "No. I'm not okay. What the hell just happened?"

Hensley wants, badly, to shout *I told you so, you arrogant bastard*, but he doesn't. "The same thing that happened to us during the first live-fire exercise. This computerized piece of shit has been compromised, Admiral."

"What were the missiles targeting?" Malloy asks.

"We won't know for sure until we power the ship back up, but I'd assume they were targeting the same thing as before?"

"Norfolk?"

Hensley nods.

"Jesus Christ. What a nightmare. I need to talk to Admiral Young," Malloy says, referencing Admiral Ronald Young, the commander in chief of the U.S. Atlantic Fleet.

"We continue to have communication issues, Admiral," Hensley says. "We can't make a radio call, a phone call, or send an e-mail."

"Don't you have someone aboard who can fix it?"

"We're trying, sir. Am I to assume, sir, that I'm no longer confined to quarters?"

Malloy takes a moment, looking at the damage inside the room. "You are correct. We'll be lucky if either of us has a job after this clusterfuck." Malloy pauses, then turns to look Hensley in the eyes. "It's a little late now, but I owe you an apology, Captain. If I'd listened to you and your crew, this would have never happened."

Hensley is momentarily taken aback by the admiral's honesty. It's not often that a two-star admiral admits fault—the old adage that "shit rolls downhill" is usually the prevailing attitude in the navy. Hensley is just hoping the admiral's story doesn't change between now and their inevitable date at the general court-martial. Hensley, unable to come up with a meaningful answer, simply says, "Thank you, sir."

Malloy nods. "Power this ship back up and take us back to port, Captain."

CHAPTER 60

Cushing, Oklahoma

Cushing is a sleepy little town of 8,000 residents that lies about an hour northeast of the capital city, Oklahoma City. The town is not much different from other small cities across the country. They have a school, a grocery store or two, local restaurants, a pharmacy, and doctors' offices. But Cushing has one thing those other towns don't. Known as the Pipeline Capital of the World, Cushing is home to one of the largest oil-storage facilities on the planet. With up to eighty million barrels of crude oil in storage, the town is a major strategic player in U.S. energy policy—and a potential terrorist target.

Over the last few years, the companies have erected tall fences topped with concertina wire and fortified the ingress and egress routes with guard shacks. Security cars patrol around the clock and the employees are on constant lookout for new strangers to town who might have nefarious purposes in mind. With the exterior fortifications in place, no one gave much thought to what happens on the inside—specifically the supervisory control and data acquisition (SCADA) systems that interface with the computers.

With over three hundred storage tanks scattered around the area—many large enough to fit a 747 jet inside—there are just a handful of companies that control how the oil flows in from the drilling fields or out to a refiner downstream. And everything is controlled with the click of a computer mouse. Working for Black Gold Energy, shift supervisor Sadie Turner sits at one of the banana-shaped desks, her eyes darting back and forth among the eight video screens stacked horizontally on the wall. Arrows indicate which way the crude oil is moving and red and green tank icons indicate whether the tank is emptying or filling. Beneath the tank farm are hundreds of miles of pipelines that Sadie controls by electronically opening and closing the valves. The crude is pumped at pressures as high as 1,000 psi, and Sadie also keeps a close eye on the pressure readings for each section of pipeline.

Four other similarly shaped desks take up the rest of the control center, each manned by one of Sadie's coworkers. Being the only girl on the team, she's learned not to react to the raunchy jokes or the constant revelations of sexual escapades that occurred the night before. Sadie glances at the video monitor on the upper left and winces. "Jackson, what's your monitor showing for fill line F8-331?"

Jackson, occupying the desk next to her, scoots his chair closer to the desk and clicks on his computer mouse. "It suggests the pressure's too high, but I bet it's a sensor error."

"What makes you think sensor error?" Sadie asks.

Jackson shrugs. "What else could it be? If the pressure is really that high, we'd be watching a real-life gusher."

Sadie snatches a radio from her desk and stands. "What if it's not a sensor error? Open the backflow valve. That'll tell us whether it's a sensor error." As Sadie approaches the window she uses the radio to direct one of the field workers to the trouble spot.

"Sadie, I'm getting no response from the backflow valve," Jackson says, his voice edging higher.

"Kill the pump, then." Sadie watches as the field worker approaches tank eight.

"The computer won't let me shut down the pump."

"What the hell do you mean *won't let you*?" Sadie hurries across the room and knees Jackson's chair away from the desk, grabbing for the keyboard. "Is the valve not responding?"

"No, the *computer* is not responding."

Sadie's fingers dance across the keyboard. "Brian, is your computer responding?" she shouts to one of the other workers. A bead of perspiration trickles down her back.

"No, I can't—"

A dozen alarms begin to sound. "What the hell is going on?" Sadie shouts. "Someone try to reboot the system." Sadie hurries back over to the window, the radio to her lips. "Anything out there?"

Before the field hand can answer, oil explodes out of the ruptured pipeline, slicing the worker in half. Other workers rush to the site. Two run to the main valve for a manual shutoff but never make it. Horrified, Sadie watches as other pipelines rupture. Sadie's coworkers rush to the window in time to see four other workers cleaved in half. Before they can react, the oil hits an overheated pump and ignites. With multiple ruptures now occurring, the fire spreads into a conflagration so intense the heat can be felt inside the building. The wall of fire creates its own wind and the swirling flames race across the landscape, now heading directly toward them.

Sadie spins around, searching for shelter. Her eyes dart across the room, finding nothing that could survive the approaching storm.

"The cellar," Jackson shouts. It was built for protection against Oklahoma's many tornadoes and the group rushes for its outside door.

"Wait," Sadie shouts. "We're going to need water." They race to the communal fridge and grab all the water they can carry. Sadie glances out the window to see the flames only a few feet from the building. "I don't know if we can make the cellar."

"We don't have any choice," Jackson shouts. The noise from the fire sounds like something straight out of hell. Jackson grabs her hand and pulls her toward the door. They burst outside and the heat is so intense it's like walking on the surface of the sun. They race toward the cellar and Brian arrives first. He flings the large steel door open and the others race for the steps.

"Hurry," Brian shouts.

Sadie is the last to enter and Brian nearly knocks her down as he dives in behind her. He reaches for the cord to close the door but the wind is too intense. "Help," he shouts. The oil is raining down as liquid fire. Jackson races up the stairs and together he and Brian pull the door shut and slam the bolt home. The heat in the confined space is suffocating. They begin to strip off their clothes as they burrow deeper into the cellar.

What they don't know is the cellar is not airtight. It was designed that way to keep those in the cellar from suffocating. Sadie, kicking herself for not bringing a flashlight, feels something drip onto the top of her head. She touches it with her hand and it feels oily. She takes a sniff and her gut clenches. "We have to get out of here!" Sadie shouts. "Oil's coming in!"

"There's nowhere to go," Jackson says.

The drips soon turn into a river and seconds later Sadie can see flames licking down the wall. Sadie is two words into her prayer when the oil inside the cellar ignites.

CHAPTER 61

Attica

Butler had thought he had prepared himself for what they might find inside the prison. But he was wrong—very, very wrong. Just walking through the prison is a treacherous task because of all the blood. Bodies litter the corridors—both guards and inmates. Several of the bodies have been disemboweled and the stench—oh Lord—the stench is god-awful. A few of his men have already vomited and Butler is working overtime to keep the bile surging up the back of his throat in check. And the worst part is—they haven't even entered the cellblocks yet. So far they haven't found a single living thing.

After entering the prison and passing through the administration building, half the team went left toward cellblock C and half the team, including Captain Butler, went right toward cellblock A. The plan is to sweep the cellblocks and meet somewhere in the middle before clearing any of the outbuildings, such as the mess hall and recreation center. Butler clicks the radio that's clipped to his vest and positioned near his mouth. "Lieutenant Clark, what's your status?"

Lieutenant Gary Clark, a loan officer at one of the local banks in Buffalo, responds, "Still proceeding toward cellblock C, sir."

"Any friendlies?" Butler asks.

There's a long pause before Clark responds. "Negative, Captain."

"None here, either. Butler out."

The prison has dozens of windows, but they don't offer much illumination as the sun sinks lower on the horizon. The windows do, however, offer a slight breeze that allows the troops a breath of fresh air occasionally. When they come to the end of the corridor, Butler, walking point, holds up his hand and the troops come to a stop. He turns his head and says, "Johnson, Foster, scout ahead, but not too far." Two men break from the ranks and walk to the corner and take a peek down the hall. One moves out and the other steps out to cover him, the rifle braced to his shoulder. To watch them work you wouldn't know that Wayne Johnson owns a tree-trimming company or that Kevin Foster teaches middle school math.

While they search ahead, Butler orders the man with the keys, Art Robinson, front and center. Around the corner and down the hall about sixty feet is the gate that leads into cellblock A. Butler says to Robinson, "Unlock the gate, but don't open it. We'll do that. Got it?"

Robinson nods, the keys rattling slightly in his trembling hand.

Johnson and Foster return seconds later, their faces ashen. "Clear to the gate, sir," Johnson says. "But—"

He's interrupted when Johnson groans and leans over and vomits, splattering the shoes of everyone nearby. Again, Butler has to tamp down the urge to join him.

Butler dry swallows a couple of times and says, "Continue, Mr. Foster."

"It's bad, Captain. A couple of the guards we are decapitated and . . . and . . . it looks"—Foster pauses and takes a deep breath and then another before saying—"it looks like whoever killed them . . . played kickball with . . ." Foster blows out a shaky breath and bends over and puts his hands on his knees.

Butler puts a hand on Foster's back. "I get the idea. Take it easy, Kevin. Take some deep breaths."

While they're waiting for Foster to recover the lights suddenly flash off. That's followed a second later by a chorus of groans from the troops.

"Mount flashlights," Butler orders. The M4 rifles have a mount on the barrel where each soldier can attach a tactical flashlight. While they're doing that, Butler makes a radio call. "Major Pierce, generator status?"

"Hold on, Captain," Pierce replies.

While he waits, he radios Clark. "Butler to Clark, over."

"Clark here."

"What's the power situation over there?"

"We still have power here, sir."

"Roger. Be prepared in case it goes out."

"Ten-four. Mounting flashlights now, Captain."

"Roger. Butler out." He waits a second and then says, "Major Pierce?"

"Pierce here. I was waiting on an update from the maintenance people. The generator that powers cellblocks A and D overheated."

Butler's brain is clicking through a long line of obscenities as he pushes the transmit button and asks, "Timeline?"

"Unknown, Captain. Apparently they don't get used very often."

Butler takes a deep breath and releases it. "Roger. Keep me posted. Butler out." Butler turns around to make sure everyone has their flashlights mounted. "Squads one and two move out. Squad one, you're point." Butler had separated his team into four-man squads so they wouldn't all be tromping around as one large group. "Squads three and four, you're next." He nods at Robinson to go with them.

As the eight men brush past, Corporal Reed stops and asks, "Rules of engagement, sir?"

Butler sighs. Reed is only twenty-one and he's been known to jump at his own shadow. "Keep your finger off the trigger for now, Todd," Butler replies. "The last thing we need is you shooting someone in the back."

"Roger, sir," Reed says before disappearing around the corner.

"Everyone else, hold your position," Butler orders before proceeding around the corner. The flashlights are dancing all over the place—looking like some kind of funky light show at a disco inside the gates of hell. From the jittery movement of the beams, it's readily apparent to Butler that his team is either juiced up or stressed to the max. As he draws closer to the gate, he sees it's already open and that squads one and two are already working their way forward. He grabs Robinson by the elbow. "I told you not to open the gate."

"I didn't, sir. It was already open when we got here."

"Fuck," Butler mutters. He triggers his radio. "Squads in reserve, watch your six." Then he says, "Butler to Foster."

"Foster here," Foster says over the radio.

"Kevin, when you were scouting ahead, was the gate to the cellblock open or closed?"

"It was closed, sir," Foster replies.

Butler turns and shouts to the men ahead, "Halt! Maintain your positions."

CHAPTER 62

Manhattan

Hank is berating himself for not grabbing a flashlight from his go bag. With the sun now diving toward the horizon, they're moments away from absolute darkness with twenty blocks still to go. Growing up in a small town in Oklahoma, Hank is accustomed to the dark. Back home he could drive two miles out of town, kill his lights, and be absorbed inside the inky darkness of night with a blanket of stars and the occasional moon providing the only glimmers of light. But it's altogether a different thing to be in a lightless city with millions of other humans, many of them confused and angry. And that's not including the predators who prefer the gloomy obscurity for fulfillment of their heinous appetites. Yet, even they will find life difficult with the total absence of light, Hank thinks.

Hank and Paige cover two more blocks in their journey to the heliport before the last of the sunlight fades. Surrounded by towering buildings, it turns dark fast. Even at high noon, many of the streets in Manhattan are shaded, but navigable. Not now.

Hank and Paige slow down, trying to minimize the risk of running into something.

"This is ridiculous," Hank says. "At this pace it's goin' to take us all night to even get to the heliport, much less back to D.C." Hank stops. "Hold up, Paige. Stay right where you are for a moment."

"Why? It's only getting darker," Paige replies.

"I have an idea. Just sit tight." Hank veers left. There's just enough light that the outlines of the abandoned vehicles are still visible. He works his way around the nose of a sedan and tries the door. Locked. After thinking for a second or two, Hank pulls out his pistol, grabs it by the barrel, and smashes the driver's side window. He reaches inside and clicks on the car's headlights. A few people on the street stop to applaud while others follow his lead and, within seconds, the street is awash in light. Spotting a delivery truck ahead, Hank walks up to it and opens the door, searching for a flashlight. After searching the door's side pocket and coming up empty, he climbs up into the cab and pops open the glove box and finds a flashlight buried under a mountain of food wrappers. He clicks it on to make sure the batteries are good and finds that they are. He climbs out and rejoins Paige on the sidewalk.

"The person that owns that car is not going to be happy," Paige says.

Hank shrugs. "I hope they have auto insurance. That won't cover the dead battery, but it might cover the glass."

With the sidewalks now lit, they make good time. Either someone had the same idea that Hank had or word spread, because block after block is now lit with automobile headlights. Paige sidles up close to Hank and asks in a quiet voice, "Where are all these people going to sleep?"

"I guess they'll head for their apartments or wherever they live and hope they can get a window open. Otherwise, it's goin' to be a long, hot night."

"What are they going to do for a bathroom?"

"That open window will be handy, I guess. Or there's always the fire escape on these older places." Thinking of that, Hank steers Paige away from the buildings and toward the street.

The farther north they walk on First Avenue, the more it opens up. Most of the buildings in this area run in size from four to six stories with a few taller buildings interspersed, but nothing like the colossal skyscrapers that New York City is famous for. As they approach East 14th Street, the silhouetted redbrick towers of Stuyvesant Town come into view. Hank had read about the place but this is the first time he's been in the neighborhood. New York City's answer to a postwar housing shortage, "StuyTown," as residents call it, consists of eighty-nine large residential buildings all crammed into a small, eighty-acre parcel. Add in Peter Cooper Village, Stuyvesant Town's sister development just across 20th Street, and the number of residential buildings grows to 110, with over eleven thousand apartments and more than 25,000 residents. What that means to Hank is that there are more people in these thirteen blocks than there are in all of Ada, Oklahoma, a town that covers fifteen square *miles.*

They pass StuyTown and Peter Cooper Village and on the next block they discover a long line of people trying to enter the VA hospital. The why is unclear— most appear upright and walking—but as far as Hank's concerned if a person served this nation then he or she is entitled to all the benefits the Veterans Administration offers. It doesn't matter that the city is without power. There wasn't any electricity in the foxholes they manned, either, Hank thinks.

They pass the City University of New York and several hospitals, and they're now on the homestretch, only three blocks from the heliport when they walk past a looted restaurant and hear a woman screaming inside. Paige comes to an abrupt halt but Hank never misses a stride. Paige hurries to catch up and grabs Hank by the elbow, pulling him to a stop. "Aren't you going to do something?"

"What? It's not our fight, Paige. Besides, we've got a helicopter waitin'."

"You're just going to walk on by?"

"Yeah."

"That is not acceptable, Hank," Paige says, stomping her foot. "Give me your damn gun and I'll go."

"You can't have my weapon."

"Then get your ass in there and stop it."

"We don't even know what *it* is. How do you know it's not some people playin' around?"

"Did that sound like a woman"—Paige makes air quotes—"'playing around'? Huh? Did it?"

When Hank doesn't answer, she says, "Then I'll go handle it without your damn gun." Paige turns on her heel and Hank grabs her by the arm.

"Stop it." He sighs. "Stay here."

Hank walks back to the restaurant and tries to get a peek inside. The automobile headlights do a decent job lighting the street and sidewalk but very little of that light spills into the surrounding buildings. He can see some movement inside yet little else. Then the woman

screams again—a heartbreaking wail that spurs Hank
into action. The restaurant appears to be fairly shallow,
but other than the woman who's screaming, he doesn't
know if there are two or twenty people inside. Access
isn't a problem because all of the glass has been shattered and it now litters the sidewalk, making a silent approach impossible. Hank draws his weapon, pulls out
the flashlight, and sidles up to the edge of the building.

The only safe approach, Hank reasons, is to hit it hard
and fast. After taking a deep, calming breath, Hank steps
over the lower glass frame, brings his weapon up, and
clicks on the flashlight. What he sees makes him both
nauseous and furious. Two men have a young girl bent
over a table, her skirt puddled on the floor. One of the
men, his trousers around his ankles, has his hand on
the girl's neck, grinding her face against the table surface while the other stands behind her, his dick in his
hand. And that's exactly how he dies. Hank doesn't
shout a warning, or *FBI*, or anything. He pulls the trigger twice and the man behind her drops to the floor.
Hank swings the gun left and double taps the second
man in the forehead. It's all over in about five seconds.

Hank turns his head to the side and shouts for Paige.
When she arrives, Hank steps outside and replaces the
partially used clip for a new one. Several minutes later,
Paige helps the now dressed sobbing young woman
outside and Hank's anger burns hotter when he sees
that the girl is maybe fourteen years old at best. Paige
wraps her arms around the girl and spends several minutes trying to comfort her. Eventually the sobbing subsides enough to find out the girl lives in an apartment
building just up the street. Other questions about how
she ended up in the restaurant or how long she'd been

there go unasked—they're pointless questions and the answers aren't going to change what happened.

Hank and Paige walk the girl home and continue on to the heliport in silence. Paige doesn't ask about the shootings and Hank doesn't ask for any specifics about the girl's injuries. Both know exactly what happened.

They find the promised helicopter waiting and climb inside. The pilot revs up the engine, and seconds later the chopper lifts off with Hank staring out one window and Paige staring out another, both wondering about evil and why it exists and, in the back of their minds, both are wondering what's next.

CHAPTER 63

Hassan Ansari sighs when he loses the link to the USS *Stark* again. This is the second time the crew has taken the ship off-line, and now that he has lost access to the ship's onboard cameras, he can only assume that they've powered the ship down. He doubts they're dumb enough to bring the weapons online a third time, so he makes a note to check on the ship later, once it's closer to port.

Hassan leans back in his chair and takes off his glasses, giving his eyes a momentary rest. He spots Nazeri pacing on the other side of the room, talking on the one landline phone in the building—a phone that Nazeri unplugs and keeps under lock and key when he's not using it. Hassan wonders whom Nazeri is talking to and whether their discussion concerns his fate and that of his fellow students. He replaces his glasses and leans forward, opening a program Jermar created that allows the five to communicate inside an encrypted chat window and away from Nazeri's prying eyes. At this point, Hassan doesn't trust Sheezal and he decides to leave him out of this chat. Hassan types: **We need to** know whom Nazeri is communicating with and what is being discussed.

Jermar replies first: Hack phone company?

Yuusef joins the conversation: Be easier to tap the phone line here. We need another phone. Check all the closets?

I will do it, Raahim types, now back from his short nap. Cover for me.

Raahim stands and heads for the door to the corridor just as Nazeri hangs up the phone and shouts, "Where are you going, Raahim?"

Raahim stops and turns, saying, "I'm still not feeling well. I think some fresh air will help."

Nazeri points at the window. "Open that if you want fresh air."

"I would prefer to walk around outside for a moment," Raahim says.

"And I would prefer you stay here," Nazeri says.

"Are we not allowed outside anymore?" Raahim asks.

"What is it with you, Raahim?" Nazeri asks. "You just returned from a nap and now you want to go for a walk? We are behind schedule. You will sit down at your computer and resume your work."

Raahim crosses his arms in defiance. "Or what?"

Nazeri reaches behind his back and pulls out a pistol, and all five of the hackers gasp. He holds the pistol up high for all to see and says, "Playtime is over. Everyone back to work."

Raahim returns to his seat as the others, eyes wide, continue working. Hassan is not that surprised that Nazeri has a weapon and it only strengthens his resolve to discover more about the man and whom he is working for. He opens a web browser and searches for phone providers in the area. He finds three companies and he clicks open their websites. Infiltrating the companies is not a problem, but without the specific phone number he's shooting in the dark.

Stuck, Hassan closes the browser and pulls up the team's list of targets. As he scans the list, his sour stomach roils. It's a smorgasbord of death and destruction that includes additional power grids, chemical plants, dams, nuclear power plants, and oil refineries. And that's just on the first page. From there it's on to the water treatment plants, sewage facilities, and other vulnerable infrastructure elements.

Hassan leans back in his chair, thinking. After several moments, he opens a new chat window and, again, takes Sheezal off the list of participants. He types: **Jermar, can you hack Nazeri's computer?**

Jermar responds: **Remotely?**

Hassan nods as he types: **Yes. Can you do it?** They all have excellent computer skills, but Jermar's hacking ability is a thing of beauty.

Sheezal, working on power grids, proudly announces that another power outage is on the way.

"Where?" Hassan asks.

"The Midwest," Sheezal says, smiling.

Hassan frowns as he glances down at his screen to see Jermar's answer pop up in the chat window: **If he is signed on to the network, maybe. I will try.**

Hassan types out a response: **Hurry!**

CHAPTER 64

While Paige and Hank wing their way to the airport, the employees of Heartland Energy in Little Rock, Arkansas, are hard at work. Nestled in the pine trees west of Little Rock is an unassuming low-slung building that is set back from the main road and hidden behind a mass of large-scale commercial stores. The only thing that differentiates this building from others in the area is the number of exterior cameras and the razor wire that encircles the property. It's not a difficult place to find, if you know what you're looking for— but good luck getting inside. In addition to the razor wire, there are a multitude of other external security features to prevent and repel possible threats from terrorists looking to do the country harm.

But the security doesn't end there. Inside, the company's computer networks have all the necessary firewalls, the redundant systems, and the people who know how to operate such networks. In fact, the facility operates much like other businesses with one exception— 18 million people depend on the second-by-second decisions made by the employees working inside the average-looking building.

Heartland Energy plays a role in managing the largest machine ever built by humans—the power grid. Heartland oversees the flow of electricity to homes and businesses in all or part of fourteen states, serving 18 million customers. It's a highly automated process that's managed from the state-of-the-art control room that looks more like a NASA rocket launch facility, with a wall of large video screens displaying weather, news, and the current status of the grid. With 790 member power plants, 65,000 miles of transmission lines that stretch from West Texas to the Dakotas, it's a massive job just to keep it all up and running the way it was designed to do every day, 365 days a year. Heartland harnesses the power from multiple utilities and independent power producers and feeds that power out to the grid. It's a hodgepodge of different entities, both public and private, with each usually having to conform to a different set of rules depending on jurisdiction, making the task that much more complicated. To help, a network of computers performs a majority of the control center's tasks, but humans are involved, too. One of those humans is night shift supervisor Jackie Gentry.

At twenty-eight, Jackie's attention to detail and her dogged determination led to a promotion to supervisor, surpassing many long-term employees who still harbor resentment. Jackie could care less what the old-timers think—her ultimate goal is to someday run the company. She's not rude or mean—in fact, she goes out of her way to include everyone whenever decisions are made—but some people aren't happy no matter what you do. And, for Jackie, that's fine—just do your damn job.

Tall at five-ten, Jackie grew up in northern Minnesota,

where the harsh winters sometimes had an effect on the power grid and she knows that a power outage can have disastrous consequences, even loss of life. With long, wheat-colored hair, blue eyes, and a slender build, Jackie has many of the traits of her Nordic ancestors. Tonight, her hair is gathered into a high ponytail as she takes a seat at her workstation. Inside the control room, as many as twenty people are working to monitor voltages, line outputs and inputs, power plant status, electricity demand, and, of course, a second-by-second look at wholesale energy prices. After all, Heartland Energy is a business and the number one goal is profits, with performance and customer service tied at a distant second. Millions of dollars are made every day by buying and selling electricity either through other companies or by purchasing futures and options on the open market. Jackie understands all of this, but her primary objective is to keep the lights on, regardless of the circumstances.

Using her computer, Jackie dims the room's lights a bit more and gets on with her daily tasks. Summer is peak demand for electricity, and August often ends up being the winner most years as temps across the region soar past 100 degrees most days. Even the nights are hot, rarely dipping below 80 in most places, and all those energy-gobbling air conditioners cutting on and off put a tremendous strain on the power grid. This time of the year, Jackie likes to keep a close eye on the power plants. They had received the urgent messages about the other power outages, but there's little they can do but focus on keeping the lights on for their customers. During most months of the year the power plants operate below peak capacity—not so during the summer months. Most every plant is churning and burning and, coupled with light winds that often idle the big wind farms during the hottest months, it's a tightly choreographed dance to keep the grid running.

The folks at Heartland Energy take their jobs seriously. To ensure the power continues unabated they built an exact replica of this facility on the other side of the Arkansas River. There, the crew and computer systems mimic everything Jackie and her staff do and are capable of taking over power grid operations at a moment's notice.

Jackie opens the program that monitors the plants and pages through the real-time results that show capacity, power generated, and current status. All looks normal until she lands on a natural gas–fired plant in the Nebraska Public Power District. She glances up from her screen and scans the room, looking for one of the engineers. She spots Isaac Armstrong and calls him over. "Have you seen the turbine speeds at the Early Power Plant in Fremont?"

Isaac pulls up a chair and sits. "They're fluctuating a little, but it hasn't triggered an alarm."

"Yet," Jackie says. "They're really ramping up. I bet we'll get an alarm—" Her last words are drowned out by an audible alarm as one of the video screens flashes red.

"There you go, Isaac. Find out what the problem is, please."

Isaac gives her a mock salute and returns to his workstation. Now Jackie has to find a way to reroute power while maintaining consistent voltages and frequencies. She scans through the list of power producers, trying to find one or two who aren't operating at capacity. "Damn it," she mutters. It doesn't help that the few nuclear facilities she has access to were ordered off-line earlier in the day after the disaster at Calvert Cliffs.

Another alarm sounds and more screens flash red. Turbine speeds at eight more power-generating plants are redlining. If she takes them off-line all at once, it could lead to a precipitous drop in voltage, which would trigger automatic shutdowns all across the region. She begins removing the troubled plants from the grid one at a time and replaces them with spinning standbys—power plants that are up and running but not sending power to the grid. The one major problem that all power grid managers have to deal with is the fact that there is no energy storage to draw from. If you want power then you have to get it from a power-producing plant at the exact moment you need it. By the time Jackie is finished replacing the troubled plants, she's out of spinning standbys and all available plants are now operating at max capacity to pump out power during one of the day's highest peaks for demand as people enjoy dinner and rest comfortably in their nice, cool homes.

Jackie swivels her chair around, searching. "John," she shouts across the room to her coworker, "call the other interconnects to see if we can buy some additional capacity."

John waves to let her know he heard her and picks up the phone.

"No, no, no," Jackie mutters as turbine speeds at other plants ramp up. "What the hell is going on?" she mumbles as a cascade of alarms sound around the room. The current status of the grid is displayed on a very large screen hanging on the front wall and Jackie looks on in horror as several grid segments flash from green to red. Red is the one color that makes a grid controller's blood run cold and it feels as if ice is running through Jackie's veins as she watches the avalanche of power failures continue. Within seconds the entire map turns red and 18 million people are left in the dark.

CHAPTER 65

For most of the 18 million people caught off guard when the power goes off, it's an irritant and an inconvenience. But it's much more than that for the Thornton family, who live on the Kansas side of the border that cuts Kansas City in half. Thirty-nine-year-old Todd Thornton fumbles through the dark on his way into the kitchen to grab a flashlight, all the while talking to his thirteen-year-old daughter, Grace. "I'll be right there, sweetie. I just need to find a flashlight."

"I'm okay . . . Dad," Grace says, exasperated.

He shuffles into the kitchen and starts opening drawers, feeling around for a flashlight. He knows he has a half dozen of them scattered around the house for situations such as this, but finding one is a different story when there's no hint of light inside a darkened house. His callused fingers light on a cold, steel cylinder and he pulls it from the drawer and clicks it on, waving the beam around the room. "I found it," he says to Grace.

"I can . . . see that."

Todd moves around the breakfast bar and walks

over to where his daughter is and kneels on the floor. He finds the button that displays the battery level and punches it. His heart sinks when he sees the indicator in the red.

"We're good for a while," he says, climbing to his feet. "I don't know why the generator didn't kick on. Guess I need to go see what's wrong with it."

"What's . . . a while?" Grace asks. Using her mouth to activate the sip and puff functions on her wheelchair, she spins around to look at her father.

"Don't worry, Gracie," he says, taking a seat on the couch.

In the car with her mother when a drunk driver swerved across the centerline and plowed into their car on a sunny afternoon last summer, thirteen-year-old Grace Thornton survived and her mother, Sharon, did not. But for Grace, who is now a quadriplegic, Todd knows there are days when she wished she hadn't, and that's something they have to get through together. Unable to breathe on her own, Grace has a tracheostomy and relies on a ventilator to keep her alive.

What was once a family of three is now a family of two. Todd, who works full-time as a carpenter, has home-care providers to help with Grace's care round the clock, but he prefers time alone with Grace a couple of hours during the evening so that he and Grace can chill in privacy. The settlement they received from the drunk driver's insurance company pays for Grace's care and there's probably enough money to allow Todd to cut back on his hours. But his plan is to use that money to send Grace to college, an opportunity he was never afforded.

Todd is a tall, broad-shouldered man with a keen eye for detail. His carpentry skills are in high demand

and his work appears in some of the most expensive homes in Kansas City. He and Sharon had bought a three-bedroom Craftsman bungalow in desperate need of repair the year before Grace was born. Sharon and Todd laughed and loved as they ripped out old flooring, installed new hardwood floors, and shopped for new appliances. Devastated after the accident, Todd worked through his grief as he widened the doors, built an entry ramp, and remodeled the bathroom—all to accommodate Grace's wheelchair.

"Are you . . . going to check . . . on the . . . generator?" Grace asks. Most patients with a tracheostomy are unable to talk, but in Grace's case she can still swallow, so the doctors decided on another type of trach tube that allows some air to pass through her vocal cords, allowing her to speak.

Todd glances at his watch. "I want to wait until Doris comes. She should be here in the next ten minutes or so." Doris Martinez is the night caregiver who spends five nights a week staying at the Thornton home.

The ventilator's battery level isn't usually a concern. But Todd had taken the day off and he and Grace ran around town buying supplies and a few new outfits for school that starts next week. He wonders what's wrong with the generator now. It's used so infrequently and the last time it didn't come on, Todd discovered that rats or squirrels had chewed through the plastic housing and went after the wiring. But he has to have it. Without that generator the hospital will not allow Grace to live at home. As an added precaution, Todd registered his daughter's ventilator use with the local power company, making their home a priority for return to service.

"Will you . . . check to see . . . how much . . . bat-tery . . . I have left . . . on my iPad?" Grace asks.

"I will. Would you like to read?"

"Yes."

"Be right back." Todd stands and returns to the kitchen to grab Grace's iPad. While he's there, he opens the cabinet where they keep Grace's supplies and pulls out the manual resuscitator and places it on the counter, where it'll be within easy reach. When he returns to Grace's side, he lays the flashlight in her lap and mounts the iPad holder on her wheelchair and pops in her tablet. He then straps on Grace's head-mounted stylus pointer, which she uses to turn the pages. "Is the headband too tight?"

"No . . . it's fine . . . quit worrying . . . Dad . . . and go fix . . . the generator."

Todd is torn. He would like Grace to experience as much independence as possible, but he hates leaving her alone, even for a second. There are just too many things that could go wrong—a ventilator hose could kink or slip off her trach tube and without the use of her hands, Grace would be unable to fix it on her own. Todd grabs the flashlight and kneels down to check the ventilator's battery status again. It's still in the red, but Todd doesn't know how accurate the indicator really is because he has never allowed it to reach that level. He sits back on his heels, wondering if he can afford to wait any longer.

CHAPTER 66

The good news is the ship's engineers have finally fixed the USS *Stark*'s radio. The bad news is the radio now works. Both Admiral Richard Malloy and Captain Bruce Hensley received a tongue-lashing from the commander of the Atlantic Fleet unlike any the crew had heard before. Both are now relieved of duty and Executive Officer Kathleen Connelly is at the helm as they limp back to port. Only one of the engines is back online, but that's okay with most of the crew. No one is in a real big hurry to find out what punishments may await back at the naval base.

As a steady stream of damage reports from Norfolk continues over the radio, Captain Hensley reads through his own damage report. He has been relieved of command, however, he hasn't been banished to his quarters. The upper superstructure of the ship sustained heavy damage and they're damn lucky no one was killed. Many of the injuries were superficial and most of the crew are back at work after being treated and released by the ship's medical personnel. Hensley lays the report aside and stands, making his way across the room to where Malloy is seated. He pulls up a chair and sits.

"We should have canceled the entire Zumwalt program," Malloy says.

"Why didn't you?"

"Money. The navy had to have something to show for those billions spent over the years."

"What happens to the ship now?"

Malloy shrugs. "I doubt any of the three will see the open sea again." Malloy sighs. "Maybe we tried to do too much, too soon."

"How so, sir?" Hensley asks. Talking helps him not think about *his* dismal future.

Malloy looks around the mission center. "The ship's computers. No matter how hard you try, someone is always waiting to exploit a weakness. Maybe we would have been better off if we'd compartmentalized more and not tried to create this total ship computing environment." He turns to look at Hensley. "Hell, I grew up watching three television channels. What the hell do I know about computers? But, I will say, we had some of the brightest people in the business working on this project and we still didn't get it right." Malloy looks away, staring at something in the distance. "What a mess."

They sit in silence for a few moments, watching the crew work in what was supposed to be a state-of-the-art Ship's Mission Center. Most of the debris from the helicopter explosion has been cleaned up, but there are still several shattered video screens hanging from the ceiling at odd angles. Hensley thinks how lucky the helicopter pilots were to have come inside for chow only moments before their chopper was obliterated. Then his thoughts turn to the damage Norfolk sustained. The deaths haven't been tallied yet and, according to the radio, search and rescue operations are ongoing. Hensley looks at Malloy. "Admiral, have you served as a member of the court during a general court-martial?"

Malloy blows out a long, shaky breath. "Many times. It comes with the job."

"What do you foresee happening?"

Malloy glances at the captain. "To you and me?"

Hensley nods.

"I don't know." He thinks about it for a moment then says, "I believe my punishment will be much harsher for not listening to you or your crew." Malloy looks down at the floor. "But you wouldn't believe the tremendous pressure we were under from the higher-ups to prove the viability of this ship."

"I felt the pressure, too, Admiral."

"I know you did, Bruce, but it was my name attached to this project." He looks up at Hensley. "So to answer your original question, I'll probably be stripped of rank and drummed out of the navy. I don't believe you will be facing the same type of punishment. You didn't know the computer systems were compromised. Oh, they'll raise a stink, but I think you'll be okay in the end."

"Does 'okay' mean I retain my current rank?"

"If I have anything to do with it, you will. I've been in the navy for a long time, Bruce. I've made a lot of friends and a lot of enemies along the way. Fortunately, most of my enemies have retired or they're pushing up daisies. I'll do everything for you that I can."

Hensley takes a deep, calming breath. "Thank you, sir."

"You're welcome, Captain." The admiral slowly

pushes to his feet, looking as if he's aged ten years in a single day. "How much longer until we dock?"

Hensley looks at his watch and quickly calculates speed and distance. "An hour and a half or somewhere thereabouts."

"Mind if I use the officers' wardroom for a bit to make some calls?"

"It's all yours, sir."

"Thank you." Malloy shuffles out of the mission center and disappears down the corridor.

CHAPTER 67

Todd Thornton found a few candles buried at the bottom of a drawer, lit them, and placed them around the living room. Now he's standing at the front door, waiting for the flare of headlights that will announce the homecare provider's arrival. He glances at his watch—again. Doris is late. With no electricity and no cell service, he has no way to contact her to find out if she's on her way or, if she is, how long before her arrival. He hears something beeping and he turns to look for the source. It's coming from Grace's wheelchair.

He hurries across the room and kneels down next to Grace's chair. As he feared, the beeping is the low-battery alarm for Grace's ventilator. He's read the ventilator directions a dozen times, but he can't recall how much time is left once the alarm sounds. It's not something he's ever had to worry about.

He silences the alarm and stands.

Grace looks up from her iPad. "What . . . is it?"

Grace may not be able to move her limbs, but her mind is as sharp as ever. And Todd has never lied to her and doesn't plan to start now. "Your vent, Gracie. I'm going to run outside and start the generator."

"Okay . . . I'll be . . . fine, Dad," Grace says.

Todd leans down and kisses Grace on the forehead. "I'll be back in just a second."

Gracie nods. Todd grabs the flashlight, takes one more look around the room to make sure the candles are safely placed, and hurries for the door. Having second thoughts, he stops, turns, and says, "Gracie, come sit by the front door so that I can talk to you." He can't see her face, but he knows his request probably earned him an eye-roll from his daughter. With her dark hair and big, beautiful, blue eyes, Grace is the spitting image of her mother.

Grace rolls over by the door and Todd props it open with one of his boots. "Shout if you need something, okay?"

"Jeez, Dad . . . you're just going . . . around to the side . . . of the house."

Todd sidesteps the ramp and walks down the porch stairs and cuts around the side of the house. After popping the lid on the generator enclosure, he puts the flashlight in his mouth and checks the wiring first. None of the wiring looks frayed and he moves on to the gas connection. Tied into the natural gas line that runs into the house, the generator allegedly has an infinite supply of fuel, but Todd knows the gas company could also have a problem. He pushes the manual start button and nothing happens. He mutters a string of curse words as he pulls off the front panel to check the battery connections. There's a clock ticking in his head and he hurries around the front to check on Grace. He nearly blinds her with the flashlight. "Everything okay? Still getting a good supply of air?"

Kansas City

"Yes, Dad," Grace replies. "What's wrong . . . with the . . . generator?"

"Battery, I think. I need to get some tools out of the garage and pull the battery out of my truck." Todd opens his truck door and hits the garage door opener then remembers the power's out. "Can anything ever be easy?" he mutters as he jogs back in the house. He ducks into the garage, pops the latch on the opener that will free the door, and groans when he lifts it overhead.

He grabs some wrenches from his toolbox, hurries back to his truck, and pops the hood, one ear listening for the low-battery alarm again. He climbs up on the bumper to loosen the battery cables and lifts the battery out and carries it around to the generator. "Gracie," he shouts, "how ya doing?" He kneels down and starts loosening the bolts on the dead battery, waiting to hear from his daughter. When she doesn't respond, he shouts, "Gracie!" and waits for her response. The low-battery alarm hasn't sounded again or he would have heard it.

When she doesn't respond a second time, Todd scrambles to his feet and races around to the front of the house and shines the light on Grace. His heart plummets when he sees her slumped in her wheelchair. Todd lunges up the steps and shines the flashlight on the ventilator to see a message that takes his breath away: VENTILATOR INOPERATIVE.

Todd sidesteps the wheelchair, hurries into the kitchen to grab the manual resuscitator, and rushes back. He puts the flashlight in his mouth and gently pulls the ventilator tubing from her trach tube and attaches the resuscitator. Todd squeezes the bag, pumping air into his daughter's lungs. "C'mon, Gracie," he moans, scanning the street for Doris's approaching headlights.

But the street remains dark and there is no response from his daughter.

Reaching across, he nudges the chair's joystick into reverse and backs Grace into the living room. Placing a hand on her neck, he feels for her carotid artery, and moans when he discovers she has no pulse. Unbuckling her seat belt, Todd gently lifts Grace out of the chair, stretches her out on the floor, and kneels down beside her. He gives the bag a big squeeze as his other hand searches for her sternum. When he finds it, he places his other hand on top and begins chest compressions. After thirty hard, fast pumps, he squeezes the bag to inflate her lungs.

Thirty minutes later, Todd is dripping sweat and tears onto his daughter's chest as he continues to try and resuscitate her . . .

. . . An hour later, Todd, his arms trembling from exertion, sits back on his heels, buries his face in his hands, and weeps.

CHAPTER 68

Chicago

As they near their condo, Eric is struggling mightily and Peyton slows to help him along. They had retrieved Peyton's bag from the battered shopping cart, which they left behind. "How are you doing, babe?" Peyton is lighting the way with the flashlight she'd taken from the goody closet at work hours ago.

"I'll live."

"You're the last person on the planet I would have expected to end up with a bullet wound."

"Especially with your sister being an FBI agent. I guess I'm just lucky that way." Eric looks up at the lightless sky. "I can't believe how damn dark it is."

"It doesn't feel like we're in the city at all. And listen to the silence."

"Yeah, dark and silent. Just like a scene out of a horror movie before the bad guy fires up his chainsaw," Eric says. "How much farther?"

"A couple of blocks." Peyton shifts her heavy bag to the other shoulder. "What's the plan when we get home?"

"Rest and sleep. See what the morning brings."

"You don't think we should try to get out of the city while we can?"

"I'm beat, Peyton. We both need rest. We'll take stock of what we have and get a fresh start in the morning. But, even then, I don't see how we're going to make it all the way to your mother's place in Champaign. Hell, it's a two-hour drive on a good day. How long is it going to take us to walk that far?"

"I don't know if we have any other options, Eric. What are you suggesting?"

"I don't know. But we're looking at four or five days of hard travel with God knows what now running around out there. I think we'd be better off to wait it out here."

Knowing Eric is dealing with a good amount of pain, on top of being exhausted and hungry, Peyton bites her tongue. A fight is not what both need now. "Let's see what the morning brings."

"Deal," Eric says.

They turn onto their street and, moments later, climb the stairs up to their third-story condo. When Peyton opens the door, it feels as if she has stuck her head in an oven.

Eric shuffles past. "Jesus, it's like a furnace in here," he says, sagging onto the new leather sofa they bought last month.

Peyton and Eric purchased the recently renovated two-bedroom condo last year. Located on the top floor of a three-story redbrick walk-up, the condo is open and airy with one large space that features the living room and kitchen. Down the hall is the master bedroom, the lone bathroom, and another, smaller bedroom. Altogether, it's a little over 1,900 square feet, more than twice the size of the apartment they rented downtown. The first two floors of the original home are owned by the Singleton family, which includes two school-aged daughters. The Singletons lucked out because they're away this week on a short, end-of-summer trip up north.

Peyton props the front door open, drops the bag on the kitchen counter, and walks around the condo with the flashlight, opening windows. A feeble evening breeze drifts through, but does little to dissipate the heat. In the bedroom, Peyton peels off her tattered skirt and blouse and slips on a pair of gym shorts and a T-shirt before returning to the kitchen.

She lights a few of her scented candles and scatters them around the living room.

Back in the kitchen, she pulls down their small basket of medications from over the stove and paws through the bottles, searching for antibiotics. She finds a bottle of amoxicillin that expired three years ago and unscrews the cap to see four furry tablets inside. She dumps two into her palm, grabs a bottle of water, and takes them to Eric. "Take both of these pills. Maybe we can get enough onboard to stave off an infection."

"How many pills are left?"

"Two."

"Maybe I should space these out. Take one now and another later."

Peyton brings a candle from the kitchen and places it on the coffee table before kicking off her borrowed tennis shoes and dropping onto the sofa. "I think two together would be better, but do what you want." Peyton carefully peels off the blood-spotted socks and with the flashlight takes a closer look at her damaged feet.

"I guess I'll take both now."

"Good choice." A few of the cuts have reopened and are oozing bloody pus. Peyton's mind flashes back to the filthy sidewalks. "Didn't you have some antibiotics left over from your root canal?"

"If I did, they'd be in the medicine cabinet in the bathroom."

"I'll look in a minute, but first I want to check your wound."

Peyton scoots closer as Eric peels up his T-shirt. She leans in and wrinkles her nose. "You stink."

"Thanks, but your body odor doesn't remind me of a bouquet of spring flowers, either."

"Touché." Peyton pulls back one edge of the gauze covering Eric's wound. "I see a little blood, but it's not much. I think it's best to leave it alone for now."

"Sounds good. Now, go back to your side of the sofa. It's too freaking hot to snuggle."

Peyton scoots back to her side. "Hungry?"

"Maybe. What do we have to eat?"

"On the menu this evening, we have our room-temperature chicken noodle soup or our carefully selected slices of minced ham with locally sourced crackers."

"Enticing. Cold soup or Spam? That's a tough decision." Eric takes a deep sniff. "I smell sugar cookies. Please tell me you didn't light *that* candle. You know we both start craving cookies every time you light that thing."

"It's not like we're blessed with an overabundance of candles. That's the best I can do if you don't want to sit around in the dark. So, soup or Spam?"

Eric groans. "I bet the Singletons have peanut butter and jelly and bread that we could borrow."

Each family traded keys in case of emergency once they got to know one another.

"We are not raiding the neighbors' pantry."

"The bread will be stale before they get back," Eric whines.

"No, Eric."

Eric shifts around on the sofa, trying to find a comfortable position. "It's too damn hot to eat anyway."

"I agree. Besides, I think I drank too much water back at the police station." Seeing her husband's discomfort, Peyton asks, "Would it be more comfortable if you stretched out on the bed for a bit?"

"Maybe."

Peyton stands and helps Eric off the couch. She grabs the flashlight from the kitchen counter and lights their way down the hall to the bedroom. Eric kicks off his shoes, slips off his slacks, and flops down on the bed. Peyton decides to stretch out for a few minutes to give her aching feet a break. She lies down beside him and clicks off the flashlight. The heat, mingled with their exhaustion and the dark, is a recipe for sleep and, within moments, both are snoring.

Sometime later, Peyton stirs awake, an alarm going off in her head. She sits up and that's when she smells it. Smoke! She jumps off the bed and races down the hall, the smoke growing heavier and filling her lungs with each breath. She turns into the living room and her heart stutters when she discovers the living room engulfed in flames.

She screams Eric's name and turns, racing back to the bedroom. "Eric, Eric, get up. The condo's on fire. Hurry, Eric. Wake up! We have to get out!" She scrambles to find the flashlight and clicks it on to see the room filling quickly with smoke.

Eric struggles to sit up. "Call 911!"

"We can't." She grabs Eric's hand, helps him off the bed, and pulls him down the hallway.

"My shoes," Eric says, trying to free his hand.

"No time," Peyton shouts, giving his arm a hard tug. "C'mon."

Entering the living room, Peyton discovers that the fire is spreading rapidly, with two walls now engulfed and flames flickering across the ceiling. With smoke stinging their eyes and filling their lungs, Peyton grabs Eric's hand and pulls him out the door. When they reach the ground, they stagger onto the front lawn and collapse to their knees, coughing, as the fire roars behind them.

CHAPTER 69

With much work to do, Hank and Paige snap out of their melancholy moods as they board the agency plane at the private jet terminal at Newark International Airport. That location was chosen for one reason— New Jersey still has power. Hank follows Paige up the jet stairs. The pilot takes one look at Paige's grease-stained clothes and says, "Rough day?"

"You could say that," Paige says, dumping her bag on one of the seats and plopping down. This is a different jet and a different flight crew from this morning's flight. Hank steps inside and offers his hand. "How ya doin', Michelle?"

"Still waiting on my phone to ring, Hank. You?" Michelle Miller asks.

"Been a long day. I still have your number, I just haven't had the time."

Michelle smiles. "You're a busy man, Hank. Are we going back to Davison?"

"No, Baltimore. Is that a problem?"

"No, I just need to modify the flight plan. We loaded

on some food. You two make yourselves comfortable and we'll be in the air momentarily."

Hank ducks his head inside the cockpit and the copilot, Carlos Torres, turns in his seat. "Damn, Hank, you travel more than the president."

"You may be right, Carlos. You doin' all right?"

"Living the dream, Hank. Living the dream."

Hank walks deeper into the cabin and drops his bag on the floor and takes the seat diagonally opposite from Paige. This jet has seating for eight with two clusters of four leather chairs that face one another.

"How do you remember all their nam—never mind. Forget I asked. But, hell, you can't do that, either."

Hank offers her a tired smile as he digs out his cell phone. "There's food."

"I heard. Don't have much of an appetite at the moment."

"Can't blame you for that." Hank powers on his phone and finds a dozen missed calls and ten text messages, most from Elaine Mercer, but a couple of the recent calls are from Nana. He decides to return her call first. He touches Nana's picture, puts the phone to his ear, and the call goes straight to voice mail. He disconnects and tries her home phone, but the call won't go through. Worried, he scrolls quickly through his text messages and finds out why Nana isn't answering in Mercer's last text. "Looks like the hackers have been busy."

"What now?" Paige asks.

"They've taken down more power grids. This time they hit the heartland."

"Figured that was coming sooner or later."

"Yeah, me, too. Do you think they're going to take them all down?" Hank asks.

Paige pulls out her smartphone and turns it on. "I don't see why not. Anything else from Mercer?"

Hank scrolls through the messages. "Looks like they hit two more nuclear power plants, one in Arkansas and the other in San Diego." Hank tosses his phone onto a nearby seat and stands. He steps over to the small galley area, grabs two bottles of water from the mini fridge, and hands one to Paige. "You callin' Natalie?"

Paige takes the bottle, unscrews the lid, and takes a long drink. "Yeah, as soon as I recharge my batteries a bit. I'm physically and mentally exhausted."

"We both need to eat somethin'." Hank drains his water, screws the lid back on, and walks back to the small galley area. He pulls open the warming drawer and the doughy, cheesy aroma from the pizza inside instantaneously triggers his hunger button. He pulls the large box out and lifts the lid to see a half-dozen different slices of deep-dish pizza inside. He grabs a couple of plates from the overhead cabinet and carries it all back to his seat. After handing Paige a plate he offers her first choice and she selects a slice of sausage and mushroom.

"Change your mind about bein' hungry?"

"I didn't think I was hungry until I smelled the pizza," Paige says, scrolling through her e-mails, hoping to see one from her sister, Peyton. No such luck.

"Works every time." Hank grabs a slice of meat lover's, closes the lid, and returns the box to the warming drawer. He grabs two beers from the fridge and returns to his seat, passing a cold brew to Paige. Once they've eaten their fill and drained their beers, both pull out their laptops and sign on to the jet's secure Wi-Fi network.

Paige shoots off an e-mail to Natalie while Hank

does a little digging into the operation of the nation's power grids, hoping to prove his theory that the hackers are targeting specific PLCs. What he finds only reinforces his original theory. No matter the fuel source—coal, natural gas, nuclear—the heat they generate is used to create steam that powers a spinning electrical generator, most often a steam turbine. And the same principle applies to hydroelectric facilities although the movement of water is the fuel that spins the electrical generators. But, no matter the source, they all rely on some type of controller to regulate the speeds of those spinning devices and those controllers are interfaced into the facility's computer networks for ease of use.

After a little more digging, Hank discovers that only a handful of companies actually make the PLCs that are used to manufacture everything from dog food to the power that enters a person's home. Hank sits back and thinks about that for a moment. He glances at Paige and says, "What do you know about programmable logic controllers?"

"Other than the fact that they control almost everything on the planet, not much."

"Easy to hack?"

"Of course. They're simple devices that operate on a few lines of code. Are you back to your theory the hackers are targeting PLCs?"

"It's the only theory that makes sense."

"I agree, but that's not going to tell us how they did it or who's doing it. Until we know those two things we have no way of stopping them."

"And you're tellin' me it may be a while before we know that information. I'm tryin' to find ways to mitigate further damage. Maybe we can prod some people to take their critical systems off-line."

"Funny, when I mentioned that you said, rather adamantly, it was absolutely impossible," Paige says.

"I still don't think it's a realistic scenario, but I don't like sittin' on our hands waitin' for the next disaster."

"I e-mailed Natalie. She has dozens of people working on the malware and they're making progress."

"What does that mean?" Hank asks.

Paige shrugs. "Progress is progress, Hank. It's going to take time."

"That's the one thing we don't have."

Daily News Website

—BREAKING NEWS—SECOND attack on Naval Station Norfolk! Further damage reported. Attackers unknown. President raises threat level to DEFCON 3. More details to follow . . .

—BREAKING NEWS—Power outage occurs in large swath of the Midwest. As many as 18 million people may be affected. More details to follow . . .

—BREAKING NEWS—Power out in parts of New York State. Manhattan included in outage.

New York governor calls up National Guard to patrol streets on NYC. More details to follow . . .

—BREAKING NEWS—Possible prison riot at Attica Correctional Facility in western New York State. More details to follow . . .

—BREAKING NEWS—Numerous National Guard units activated to quell chaos.

The governor of Illinois has activated the National Guard for the greater Chicago area. We have unconfirmed reports that the governor issued a shoot-to-kill order to curtail widespread looting. More details to follow . . .

—BREAKING NEWS—Massive explosion at army munitions depot in McAlester, Oklahoma. Damage extends nearly one mile from plant.

Sources tell the *Daily News* the bomb that exploded at the McAlester depot was a GBU-43/B Massive Ordnance Air Blast (MOAB) bomb. Used recently in the war in Afghanistan, the bomb is better known as the Mother of All Bombs. The MOAB is the largest nonnuclear weapon in the American arsenal. More details to follow . . .

CHAPTER 70

Attica

The gate to the cellblock being closed and then opened has Captain Scott Butler rethinking his strategy. Although heavily armed, his force of nearly a hundred men, including the state troopers, is severely outnumbered. Yes, some of the inmates would die if they tried to ambush Butler and his troops, but they wouldn't get them all before being overwhelmed. Butler makes a radio call to Lieutenant Gary Clark, who's leading the second team toward cellblock C.

"Clark here, sir."

"Hold your position."

"Roger, Captain."

Butler pauses to allow Clark time to pass on his order before saying, "Gary, was the gate to cellblock C open or closed when you got there?"

"It was open, Cap."

"Okay. Gary, you need to maintain situational awareness at all times."

"We are, sir. I have guards posted around our perimeter."

"Good. I'll be back to you in a minute. Butler out."

He tosses the radio handset over his shoulder, thinking. He turns, spots Corrections Officer Art Robinson, and waves him over. When he arrives, Butler says, "Art, do all the guards carry radios and keys?"

"Radios, yes. But not everyone carries keys. The cells are opened and closed electronically, and those working the blocks don't carry anything that could be used as a weapon."

"Thank you, Art. Next question. If the inmates were planning an ambush where would they do it?"

Robinson thinks about the question for a moment. "Probably in the transitions between cell blocks, the mess hall, the entrance to the tunnels, or the area around Times Square—the place where all four tunnels interconnect. They could hide down one tunnel and hit you when you funnel into the choke point. In fact, that might be the most logical place to do it."

"I think you may be right, Art. Thanks for your help."

Butler unclips the prison radio from his belt and looks at it for a moment, debating his next step. He puts the radio to his lips and presses the transmit button. "Captain Butler to Officer Darnell."

A couple of seconds later, Darnell answers.

Knowing now that some of the prisoners are most likely listening in, Butler has to be extremely careful or he'll be putting her life in jeopardy. He changes his mind and says, "Sit tight for now."

"Roger, Captain," Darnell replies, confusion in her voice.

Butler turns back to Robinson. "If Darnell is inside Times Square, can she see down all four corridors?"

"No, sir. She can only see down two of the corridors and the entrances to the other two."

"Thanks." Robinson turns to leave and Butler squats down and leans back against the wall, considering all of his options—none of them good. After several moments, he glances up and calls over Lieutenant Fred Parker, a social worker by trade. A tall, barrel-chested African American, Parker slings his rifle and walks over as Butler slides up the wall to his feet. "Freddy, you work out complicated social situations all day long. Do you think you could reach out to the inmates over the radio and convince some of them to turn themselves in?"

"I can try, Scott, but they're going to want some type of reassurances or concessions."

"I can guarantee you the governor is not going to offer them squat. Surely some of them don't like what's happened in here." Butler kicks at something on the floor with the toe of his boot then looks back up. "Hell, Freddy, they can't all be bad men."

Parker takes the radio from Butler and spends a moment gathering his thoughts. Butler makes a radio call to Lieutenant Clark and passes on the plan.

When Parker is ready, he places the radio to his lips and announces his name and position before beginning his plea. "I know some of you don't like or approve of what has happened today. It's not our place to judge you or your actions. Our only job is to secure this facility. If you surrender you will be treated with respect and will be afforded due process under the laws of the state of New York. We have troops stationed at the entrances to cellblocks A and C. Surrender with your hands in the air and I will guarantee your safety." Parker pauses and looks at Butler, who gives him the nod to continue.

Parker, having given them the carrot, now offers the stick. "For those of you who refuse to surrender, there

are zero guarantees concerning your survival. We will
find you. Whether you live or die will depend on the
decisions you make. But, to be honest with you, I don't
like your odds. We will offer no warnings. We will
offer no pleas. And, just to make my point clear, we are
authorized to shoot to kill." Parker pauses to let that
thought sink in then says, "Men, the ball is now in your
court." Parker hands the radio back to Butler.

"Well done, Freddy," Butler says. "Now we wait."

But they don't have to wait long. Prisoners, their
hands in the air, begin streaming into the corridor. Butler orders two squads to search the prisoners as they arrive. "And make sure you find all the damn keys," he
tells them. Now Butler has to find a place to put them.
With no power the cell doors are inoperable. He asks
Art Robinson, and Robinson suggests the school. Butler relays that information to the team over at cellblock
C and orders them to do a head count.

As the prisoners are searched, Butler takes to the
radio again, talking to Major Pierce, who is outside the
prison walls. "Major, have your troopers escort some
of the prison personnel inside so we can start identifying these men." He passes on the details of where to
take them and asks Pierce to round up some coffee.
Butler, who started drilling teeth at eight this morning,
is running on fumes with a long night still ahead of
them.

It's pushing midnight by the time they finish searching and identifying those prisoners who surrendered.
Every member of Butler's team is hungry and exhausted, but they still have work to do. Some of the
prison staff brewed several large pots of coffee in the
administration building and that's helping. But Butler
needs his men clear-eyed and focused. He steps over to

the coffeepot and pours another cup as the warden, Albert Diaz, approaches.

"Captain," Diaz says, "we have a somewhat accurate head count."

"How bad is it?" Butler asks.

"We have no way of knowing how many inmates have been killed in other parts of the prison, but we have two hundred and eleven inmates unaccounted for," Diaz says.

Butler sighs and sets his coffee cup on the table. "Okay. We need to root them out."

Diaz holds up a finger. "One more thing, Captain. Ninety-eight of those missing inmates are from the SHU."

"What the hell is a SHU?"

"It's our Special Housing Unit. It's the place where we house the troublemakers and our most violent inmates in solitary confinement."

CHAPTER 71

There are no approaching sirens, no firemen hurrying to deploy hoses, and no hope as Peyton and Eric, still coughing from the smoke, watch their home go up in flames.

"It was those damn candles of yours," Eric says, staring at his wife.

Eric and Peyton are standing in the middle of the street as people stream out of nearby homes to watch the destruction unfold. "Those candles were the only light we had," Peyton says.

Eric lowers his voice. "Then you should have blown them out before lying down."

"I wasn't planning on—you know what?" Peyton says, cocking her head to the side, "Fuck you, Eric." Peyton turns and walks away from her husband.

A few of the neighbors wander up and offer conciliatory condolences, but it's clear they're more concerned about the risk to their own property as the embers from the fire drift onto their roofs. It's not long before murmurs of irresponsibility drift through the crowd. Peyton hears them and can feel heat creeping into her cheeks. Her friend from two houses down, Allison Bailey, walks over and gives Peyton a hug. "Don't listen to those assholes," she whispers in Peyton's ear. "They all had candles burning, too."

Peyton nods and, unable to keep the floodgates closed any longer, bursts into tears. "Oh God, Allison. This has been the worst day of my life," Peyton says, clinging to her friend as if she's the last life preserver on a sinking ship. "And now, we . . . we don't have anyplace to live."

"Shh, don't worry about that now," Allison whispers. "We'll figure it out."

Peyton continues to sob. "What happens . . . when . . . the . . . the Singletons come . . . back? Now their . . . home . . . is gone . . . too."

"That's why we have home-owner's insurance, Peyton." Allison steps back and takes Peyton's hand. "Let's go back to my place and open a bottle of wine. What do you say?"

Peyton nods and wipes the tears from her cheeks before following Allison down the street. Their house is now fully engulfed and the roof is teetering on the edge of collapse as a shower of red-hot embers continues to rain down. It's bright enough for Peyton to see the angry looks she receives, but she does her best to ignore them. Still angry with Eric, she walks by him without a word and follows Allison up the steps to the front door. Allison's husband, Jordan, works in software development and is often away, as he is this week. Allison holds the door, and Peyton brushes past and sags into the closest chair, wiping the last of the tears from her cheeks. She can't help but notice that Allison, too, has candles burning.

One of the smaller homes on the block—a two-bedroom, one-bath Craftsman style—the Baileys have this place all to themselves. Allison returns from the kitchen, carrying two glasses of red wine and passes one to Peyton before sitting. "I thought Eric would follow."

"I'm glad he didn't," Peyton says. "And he can stay out there as far as I'm concerned."

"Uh-oh, trouble in paradise?" Allison asks, tucking her feet up under her. A real estate agent, Allison is short at five-two, with shoulder-length blond hair and green eyes. And like Peyton and Eric, she and Jordan are also in preliminary discussions about starting a family.

Peyton takes a sip of wine and says, "He blames me for the fire."

"They're called *accidents* for a reason. He'll snap out of it. In the meantime, you two can use the guest bedroom."

"I'm not sure I want to sleep in the same room with him at the moment." Peyton drains the glass in one long swallow.

"Oh hell, Peyton, that's all heat-of-the-moment stuff. You two will kiss and make up." Allison stands, returns to the kitchen, and comes back with the opened bottle of wine. She tops off Peyton's glass, puts the bottle on the coffee table, and retakes her seat. "And you can borrow some of my clothes if you need to. My jeans and pants will be way too short on you, but you have free access to my shorts and shirts."

"Thanks," Peyton says, staring into her wineglass. "I can't believe I'm sitting here drinking wine while my house burns to the ground."

"There's not a damn thing you can do about it. We

can't call the fire department, and even if we could, they'd never get a truck here in time."

Peyton sniffles, on the verge of tears again.

"Is there anything in your home that can't be replaced?"

Peyton shakes her head. "Not really."

"No, there's not. And look on the bright side, it'll give me a chance to ring up more commissions when I find you a new home."

Peyton attempts a halfhearted smile. There's a knock on the glass storm door and Eric sticks his head in and asks, "Can I come in?"

"Of course," Allison says, standing up.

Eric walks gingerly into the house. He's holding his side and wearing nothing but his boxer briefs and the T-shirt from the police station.

"What happened to you?" Allison asks as she passes by on the way to the kitchen.

"I was shot earlier today?"

Allison stops and turns, her eyes widening in surprise. "Do what?"

Eric starts to tell the story, but Allison cuts him off with a wave of her hand. "Hold that thought. This is going to require another bottle of wine."

Eric takes a seat on the edge of the sofa. "I'm sorry, Peyton. I love you."

"I love you, too. But not when you're an asshole."

"I know. It's been a long day, babe." Eric settles back on the sofa as Allison returns with a fresh bottle of wine, a glass for Eric, and clothing for both of them, which she puts on the coffee table before sitting.

"No offense, you two," Allison says, "but I'm not into the campfire scene. Change clothes and toss what you're wearing outside. There's some bottled water in the garage that you can use to rinse off."

"I'll change clothes," Peyton says, "but we're not wasting your water. You need to hang on to all the water you can, Allison."

"Why?" Allison asks. "I can always run to the store when the power comes back on."

"There's a problem with that scenario," Peyton says, standing. "The power could be out for a while."

"Like what? A couple of days?" Allison asks.

"Longer," Peyton says. "Maybe much longer."

CHAPTER 72

Attica

If the stench inside was vile when Butler and his men entered the prison, it's now, after hours of fermentation, gag-inducing repulsive, and most of the troops have resorted to using makeshift masks to cover their noses and mouths. Captain Butler had a heated argument about removing the bodies with folks from the Department of Justice and lost. Crime scene preservation was their excuse and Butler wishes he could bottle the foul odor and ship it to them for a little taste of what he and his men are now enduring. Butler takes a deep, calming breath and immediately regrets it. He coughs and turns his mind back to the mission. At this point, he just wants it over with as quickly as possible. But he knows without a doubt that's not likely to happen.

Butler had called up the state troopers in reserve to guard the prisoners who surrendered and to provide protection for the prison personnel on-site. Now he looks up and scans the area, searching for Lieutenant Fred Parker. He spots him over by the coffeepot and calls him over. "What do you think, Freddy, should we offer the remaining inmates another chance to surrender?"

Parker shakes his head. "I don't think so, Cap. They've had hours to consider their options."

"I concur," Butler says. "As my grandfather used to say before stepping into the hog pen with his pocketknife—it's nut-cuttin' time." He turns to the men around him. "Squads one and two, move out and keep your heads on a swivel." He makes a radio call to Lieutenant Gary Clark over in cellblock C and passes on the order. Once the two squads have cleared the cellblock gate, Butler orders more squads on the move. Parker takes off to be with his men and before slipping down the corridor Butler orders squad seven to remain as a rear guard. He unslings his rifle and braces it tight to his shoulder, his index finger caressing the trigger guard.

He's six steps into cellblock A when a barrage of rifle fire from up ahead shatters the silence. Butler hurries to the front to see two inmates bleeding out on the floor.

"They tried to jump me, sir," Corporal Todd Reed, one of the young firemen, says.

"It's okay, Todd. Drop back and let me take point," Butler says, knowing the young man, a jittery person on a good day, is going to start spraying bullets at everything that moves. "And, Todd?"

"Yes, sir?"

"Try not to shoot me in the back." Butler notices that Reed's hands are trembling. "As a matter of fact, Todd, why don't you join squad seven at the rear? Make damn sure nothing gets past you."

Reed salutes. "You can count on me, sir."

As Reed retreats, Butler and his men move forward

to discover the horror show continues. They find seven inmates and six more guards dead, their coagulated blood pooled into a red lake that spans the width of the corridor. Butler turns his head and whispers, "Watch your footing." But he finds the task difficult while trying to keep his gaze centered on the area ahead. He holds up a hand, deciding to switch tactics. "Squads one and two on me."

When the men arrive, he has them form a circle with their backs to the center. He joins the circle and they proceed down the corridor in a rugby scrum formation and make the turn into cellblock D. They find more of the same—bodies and blood. Finding no one alive, Butler is beginning to doubt the warden's head count.

When they reach the center of cellblock D and the iron-barred gate that separates the two sides, Butler holds up a hand and the scrum comes to a halt. The gate is centered in a concrete block wall with four feet of empty space on either side—making it a perfect hiding spot. And unfortunately for Butler and his men, the opening is fairly narrow, meaning they'll have to enter side by side rather than using Butler's preferred formation. Butler puts a finger to his lips, trying to hear movement or other signs of life from the other side of the wall. But the heavy breathing of his men wipes out any chance of hearing anything.

Butler points at two men, Jack Coleman and Steven Perez, and waves them forward. Coleman and Perez usually spend their days patrolling the streets of Buffalo in their police cruisers. Butler motions them closer and whispers his instructions. "Go together, one left and one right, just like you're breaching a house." Coleman and Perez both nod and take up positions on either side of the opening. Both ditch their rifles and pull out their pistols. In such a confined space, a rifle is unwieldy and there's a chance the bad guys could grab it by the barrel and rip it out of their hands. Butler holds up two fingers, signaling that the squad members are to form up in pairs, then he waves the troopers with the shotguns up to the front. Once everyone is in position, Butler nods at the two by the gate.

They hit the doorway together and one swings left, the other right.

And that's when all hell breaks loose.

Coleman and Perez begin firing almost immediately, sustained bursts, one shot after another as fast as they can pull the trigger. Butler has no idea if they're facing five inmates or fifty. "Troopers, up," Butler shouts. Two state troopers armed with riot shotguns step through the doorway and immediately open fire, the booms from the shotguns almost deafening. Two more troopers step through the door and open fire.

The pistols have fallen silent and Butler's wondering what happened to his two men. He steps over to the door, braces his rifle against his shoulder, and clicks off the safety. He turns into the corridor to see inmates everywhere. It's dark as hell, making it impossible to make an educated guess on their number. Butler sees them trying to overpower the state troopers and opens fire. He shouts for squads one and two to deploy as he moves the barrel from target to target, squeezing the trigger. The copper slugs of the 5.56-mm cartridges are deadly at a distance, but up close they're absolutely lethal.

One of the inmates tries to grab a shotgun from a trooper's hand and Butler drills him right between the eyes, launching a spray of blood, bone, and brain matter. Butler can hear other M4s firing, but still nothing more from the pistols. He takes a quick peek at the floor to see his two men on the ground. He looks back up as a large man comes charging toward him. Butler fires and the man drops like a sack of cement. With the gun lights and the muzzle flashes, it looks like a dance with the devil.

About a dozen inmates turn and try to make a break down the corridor, one carrying a shotgun. Butler sights in on the middle of his shoulder blades and squeezes the trigger. The man drops and the shotgun flies out of his hands. The rest of the inmates make it about six steps before they're all cut down. Butler checks for other bogies and, not seeing any, shouts, "Cease fire."

The gunfire stops, but Butler still hears a roar in his ears. He puts the radio to his lips and shouts for the paramedics then tells his men to secure any other firearms. He hurries over to the closest man and kneels down, gently rolling him over. It's Coleman, and his throat has been slit from ear to ear. Butler checks for a pulse anyway and, as expected, doesn't find one. He stands and hurries to the next man. This time it's one of the state troopers. He has been bludgeoned to death, his face unrecognizable. His blood boiling, Butler stands and hurries over to Perez, who's curled up next to the wall. Butler kneels down beside him. "Steve, can you hear me?"

He's rewarded with a groan. Butler doesn't see any apparent external injuries but he's afraid to roll him over to look, fearful of doing further damage. Butler puts a hand on his shoulder. "Hang in there, Steve. Medical personnel are on the way."

Butler stands and asks one of his men to stay with Perez until help arrives. Butler looks at Parker. "Body count, Lieutenant Parker?"

"I count seventy-three inmates killed in addition to thirteen correctional officers in cellblocks A and D, sir."

Butler does the math in his head. He has no idea how many inmates Lieutenant Clark and his men have encountered, but he hasn't heard much in the way of gunfire from that side of the prison. "Listen up, men," Butler shouts. "We have over a hundred more prisoners to find. From here on out, it's shoot first and don't even worry about asking *any* fucking questions later. Understood?"

CHAPTER 73

With all commercial aircraft grounded, it seems strange to look out the window and see one of the busiest airports in the region devoid of activity. There are no baggage handlers rushing to load on luggage before a plane departs, no fuel trucks zipping across the tarmac, and no food catering companies with their scissor-lift trucks loading on snacks and booze. Although all is quiet outside, Hank can only imagine the chaos going on inside the terminal.

The pilots taxi the jet to one of the air charter terminals and park. Hank stands and stretches.

"Do we have a ride?" Paige asks, sliding her laptop into her bag and standing.

"Yeah, someone from the Baltimore field office is pickin' us up and drivin' us down to Fort Meade." Hank glances out the window at the terminal building. "Why do you think the hackers haven't hit Baltimore yet?"

"No idea. I haven't been able to figure out if there's a method to their madness. You can bet they have access to the computer networks, but why they're choosing to crash some power grids and not others is a mystery."

"Think it's significant?"

Paige shrugs. "No clue. You told me earlier that we'd eat and we'd sleep. We've eaten. When do we get to sleep?"

"Yet to be determined." Hank grabs his bag and slings it over his shoulder as Michelle Miller lowers the jet stairs.

"Hank, are you two headed to Meade?" Michelle asks.

"Yeah."

"Mind if we tag along?"

"Not at all. Are you two bunkin' at the base hotel?"

"I guess. Power's out at my place in D.C. and we couldn't get to Carlos's place even if we tried. Anyway, we have a flight scheduled out of here in the morning so we'll make it work. Give us a couple of minutes to finish and lock up."

"Will do." Hank walks down the stairs and takes a deep breath, picking up a hint of the ocean in the briny breeze blowing off Chesapeake Bay to the east. Located twelve miles south of downtown Baltimore, the airport sees a lot of traffic from Fort Meade, which is located only ten miles down the road. Paige climbs down the steps and joins him.

She looks down at her ruined clothing. "I wished I had another outfit."

"I don't think anyone's goin' to care what you're wearin'."

"I know. Maybe Natalie will let me borrow something from her locker."

"That'll work. You two are about the same size."

"She's a little bigger on the top end."

Hank takes a moment to study Paige. "Maybe." That statement gets Hank an elbow in the ribs.

Michelle and Carlos climb down, fold up the stairs, and lock up the jet. They walk around to the front of the building and pile into the idling Suburban at the curb for the short drive to the base. Once there, they badge their way past the guards and drop Michelle and Carlos at the hotel before the driver drops them off at the National Security Agency. They quickly discover their badges aren't sufficient to get them inside the building and they wait while the guard makes a call to their host. A minute or two later, Natalie Lambert arrives to escort them inside. After clearing security—Hank had to relinquish his weapon and both surrendered their phones and backpacks—Natalie gives them both a hug before leading them to the elevator. They take the elevator down and exit, walking down the corridor to a plain wooden door absent of signage. Natalie positions her face in front of a nearby retinal scanner and the door pops open and they enter into a large workspace brimming with people.

It's not the NSA's National Security Operations Center, but there are enough computers, video monitors, and televisions inside to fully stock a half a dozen sports bars. Natalie leads Hank and Paige to her desk and pulls up two extra chairs. Hank's butt has barely touched the seat when Natalie launches into her spiel about what they've discovered so far about the malware.

Hank holds up a hand to stop her. "Do we have any idea about who's behind the hacks?"

"Not yet," Natalie says. "They're clearly spoofing

and are routing their attacks through servers all over the world."

"How long before we get a bead on them?" Hank asks.

Natalie sighs. "I don't know, Hank. Maybe never."

Hank leans forward in his chair. "That's not goin' to work for me, Nat."

Natalie throws her hands up. "I'm sorry, Hank. Right now we're focusing on how to stop the malware from spreading and how to eradicate it."

Hank won't let it go. "They've hacked a navy ship at sea. The only way they can do that is via satellite."

Natalie thinks about that for a moment. "Good point." She lifts the desk phone and makes a call to someone else inside the agency. She passes on Hank's suggestion, listens for a moment, and hangs up. "Signals is going to attempt to find your satellite. But don't get your hopes up yet, Hank. I can guarantee you they're spoofing their communications, too."

Hank leans back in his seat. "All we can do is try."

"Agreed. Now, can I continue with our findings?" Natalie asks.

"Please," Hank says, smiling. He listens with one ear as Natalie continues. He's competent with a computer, but Paige and Natalie operate on an entirely different level. Mentally, he runs through the list of the hackers' targets, trying to find other avenues of investigation. *Could they be using cellular networks to carry out their attacks?* He mulls that over for a few minutes.

Hank interrupts Natalie again to ask another question. "Would these hackers be workin' together as a group? For instance, would they be together inside a single facility?"

"I would think so," Paige says.

"They don't necessarily have to be," Natalie says. "They can communicate online."

"I think that's too risky," Paige says. "These people are extremely clever. They know we are capable of intercepting their communications. I believe, for security reasons, they are working within the same physical space."

"But there are a hundred different ways to communicate online without being swept up in the NSA's nets," Natalie says, turning to look at Hank. "What do you think, Hank?"

"I agree with Paige. It's a much simpler process if they're workin' together as a group. And it eliminates the threat of havin' their communications intercepted. I have a couple more questions and then I'll let you two get back to work. How many people are we talkin' about?"

"I think a dozen or less," Natalie says. "It's extremely difficult to keep anything secret if you have more people than that."

"Paige?" Hank asks.

"Natalie's right. Initially, there could have been a large number of people involved, but once they hit the operational phase, the fewer people, the better."

"Last question," Hank says. "Do you think they're havin' external communications with someone on the outside who's callin' the shots? Or is it all in-house?"

Natalie grabs a strand of her honey-colored hair and wraps it around her index finger. "I don't think we have enough information to hazard a guess. I do think they had a game plan going in. It could be they're just sticking to the script."

"Even if they are communicating with someone on the outside," Paige says, "you can bet they've covered their tracks."

"Unless they make a mistake," Hank says.

"I wouldn't count on these people making many mistakes," Natalie says.

Hank runs a hand through his dark, wavy hair. "We don't need many. In fact, I'd settle for just one."

CHAPTER 74

Chicago

Peyton takes a sip of wine and studies her friend over the rim of the glass as Eric finishes his story about how he was wounded. It's obvious Allison's having second thoughts about inviting them to stay after finding out the power could be off for an extended period of time. And Peyton can't blame her. She knows how empty her own pantry was before the house burned to the ground. But the thought of trekking all the way to her mother's house in Champaign makes her ill. Peyton drains the last of her wine and, deciding she's had enough, sets the glass aside and asks Allison, "Where's Jordan this week?"

Allison leans forward and adds more wine to her own glass. "Seattle. He was scheduled to come back tomorrow, but I don't know what's going to happen now that all flights are grounded."

"Did they ever say what happened to cause all those airline crashes?" Peyton asks.

"They don't know," Eric says. "What's strange is that the jets, from the little I heard, were all 737s."

"Is that significant?" Allison asks.

"Maybe. I think something hinky is going on with the jet crashes and the power outages."

"Why? What do you think is happening?" Peyton asks, her anger with Eric now on extra-low simmer.

"Peyton, remember me telling you about that book I read recently? The one where it proves people have already hacked into our power grids?"

Peyton nods. "I remember. How could I not? That's all you talked about for several days."

Eric takes a sip from his wineglass. "I talked about it because the book scared the hell out of me. Anyway, I think someone hacked our power grids and maybe even those jets."

"But who?" Allison asks.

Eric shrugs. "Who knows? Probably the damn Russians. It looks like they've hacked everything else in this country."

"What would Russia have to gain?" Allison asks. "They'd have to know that we'd respond in kind. Hacking an election is much different than cutting off power to millions of people."

"I don't know," Eric says, "but you make a good point." Eric braces his left hand against the arm of the sofa and groans as he pushes to his feet. "Maybe it's not the Russians. Maybe it's a terrorist group." Eric bends to the left, trying to stretch his right side. "Regardless of who it was, we're screwed."

"Speaking of that," Allison says, "my offer still stands. You two can stay with me. There's no telling when Jordan's going to come home. And, to tell you the truth, I don't like the idea of me being in this house all by myself after your story about the shoot-out at Target."

"Let's see what tomorrow brings," Peyton says.

Eric walks over to the front door and steps out onto the porch.

Allison looks at Peyton. "I'm serious. I'm terrified to stay here alone."

"What are we going to do for food and water?"

"What were you going to do at your mom's house?"

Peyton shrugs. "We haven't thought that far ahead."

"Your mother lives alone. How much food is she going to have on hand?"

"Good point. But after everything I saw today, I don't know if we'll be safe anywhere in this city."

"You're a hell of a lot safer inside this house than you would be traipsing all across the country," Allison says.

Eric comes back inside and closes the front door. "Looks like the fire's almost out."

"Does it look like we'll be able to salvage anything?" Peyton asks.

"Uh, no," Eric says. "It's all gone. I bet the Singletons are going to be pissed."

"Did they drive on their trip up north?" Allison asks.

"Yes," Peyton says.

"Judging by the clogged roads, it's going to be a while before they return."

"You're probably right." Eric runs his hands across the top of his head, massaging his skull. "I'm beat. I'm going to bed."

Peyton stands. "Me, too."

Eric looks at Allison. "Do you have any weapons in the house?"

"Jordan has a shotgun that he uses to go bird hunting. Why?"

"Might be best if we get it out and load it up, just in case."

CHAPTER 75

Somewhere near Boston

Hassan leans back in his chair, removes his glasses, and rubs his eyes. When he enjoys the work Hassan can go long stretches and never notice if his eyes are bothering him. Not so, today. In addition to blurry vision, he can feel a wicked headache coming on. And he hasn't had one of those in months. For the last two hours Hassan has been cherry-picking the least lethal targets to attack, although he doesn't know how much difference there is between two deaths or twenty. Dead is dead.

After cleaning the lenses with the tail of his T-shirt, Hassan puts his glasses back on and opens the chat program on his screen. Unfortunately, Nazeri has been on his computer since ending his phone call and Jermar hasn't had a chance to apply his hacking skills. Nazeri has access to everything Hassan and his team do, except the chat program, and he appears to be taking great pleasure sowing death and carnage among the American people. Hassan closes the chat window without sending a message, knowing what Jermar's answer would be. Standing, he walks into the break room and grabs a bottle of water, thinking about Nazeri. They're running out of time.

Opening one of the drawers, he pulls out a bottle of ibuprofen and pops three pills and washes them down as his tired brain continues to churn. His mind drifts from Nazeri to his own predicament. *If I can get out, where do I go?* Hassan has lived in the Boston area since his arrival in the United States, but he hasn't had a lot of free time nor a real desire to do much exploring. *Would it be better if we all left together?* Hassan thinks about that for a moment. They'd be much easier to find as a group. And if one gets caught it could spell doom for the rest. But that spurs another thought. *How much energy would Nazeri devote to finding us?* Hassan realizes that's the one answer he needs yet he has no idea how to obtain it. He looks up as Yuusef steps into the break room.

Yuusef hurries over and whispers, "You saw the gun. What are we going to do?"

Hassan scans the ceiling, looking for cameras. He doesn't see anything obvious, but the ones they found in their sleeping quarters were well hidden. And a microphone can be placed almost anywhere. "Go back to your computer," Hassan whispers.

Yuusef's facial features scrunch in anger. "Why?"

Hassan points to his ear and then the ceiling.

Yuusef nods. He grabs a drink and heads back to his computer. Hassan waits a moment then follows. At his computer, he pulls up a chat window and stares at the names, trying to decide whom to include in this conversation. He clicks on Yuusef's name only and types: **How well do you know the city?**

Hassan watches Yuusef read the message and sees a

confused look wash across his face. Hassan types: **Need place to hide.** When Hassan looks up he sees Yuusef nod.

Yuusef's message pops up on Hassan's screen seconds later. **Know city well. When do we leave?**

Tonight, Hassan types. **When Nazeri sleeps.** Hassan pauses then types: **How much effort will he devote to finding us?** Hassan sends the message and waits.

The telephone rings and the loud clanging startles everyone in the room. Nazeri stands, tucks the pistol behind his back, and walks across the room to answer. Hassan coughs to get Jermar's attention. When he looks up, Hassan nods toward Nazeri's computer.

Jermar nods and begins to type.

Yuusef's reply pops up on Hassan's screen: **We must burrow deep.**

Hassan silently curses in his native tongue. He's surprised a moment later when Nazeri hangs up the phone and strides out of the room. Usually Nazeri's conversations last much longer. Hassan jumps up from his chair and hurries around to Jermar's side of the table and whispers, "Any luck?"

"My program was running in the background while Nazeri was using his computer," Jermar whispers. "I'm in but everything on his hard drive is encrypted."

"I can crack it," Sheezal says, joining the conversation.

His willingness to help lessens Hassan's distrust of him. And, more important, Sheezal is a wizard at opening encrypted files.

"Can you copy it to the cloud?" Sheezal asks.

"Working on that now," Jermar answers.

Sheezal turns to Hassan. "We need to escape as soon as possible if we wish to remain alive."

"I concur," Hassan whispers. "We leave when Nazeri sleeps."

"If he sleeps," Sheezal says. "If not, we need another pla—"

Their conversation is interrupted when Nazeri returns. "Plotting, are we?" he asks, looking at Hassan. Nazeri smiles. Seconds later three additional men enter the room, all heavily armed with pistols at their waists and rifles slung over their shoulders.

Nazeri smugly crosses his arms. "Hassan, did you really believe turning on the water in the restroom would mask your words?"

Hassan sags and has to grab Jermar's chair to keep from sinking to his knees.

Nazeri switches his gaze to Raahim. "Raahim, I can assure you there are no more phones in the building. And," Nazeri says, turning his gaze back to Hassan, "yes, I do plan on sleeping. I cannot say the same for you."

Hassan, stunned at this sudden turn of events, shuffles to Nazeri's vacant chair and sits.

"Oh, one more thing," Nazeri says, holding up a finger. "Jermar, I know you're very clever, but you are wasting time copying my hard drive. There is nothing on it. I store everything on a private server in the cloud."

Jermar's shoulders sag and he takes his hands off the keyboard and leans back in his chair.

"I am now implementing a new set of rules," Nazeri says. "One: If these three men ask you to do something, you do it. And two: If you attempt to escape you will be shot. Any questions?" Nazeri pauses and looks gleefully around the room. "Good. Gentlemen, let's move to target 1-A before I bid you good night." Nazeri nudges Hassan out of his seat and sits as the three armed men take up positions around the room.

CHAPTER 76

Attica

Captain Scott Butler takes off his helmet and wipes the sweat from his brow. With the power still off and all the fans silent, it's hotter than hell inside the prison, and combined with the adrenaline coursing through his system, Butler is sweating like a whore in church. He puts his helmet back on and refastens the straps. The floors are awash with fresh blood as he orders his men to move out. It's early morning now, and they still have much work to do.

As they creep deeper into cellblock D, Butler makes a radio call to Lieutenant Gary Clark, who's running the show over in cellblock C. "Gary, keep your eyes open. Watch the choke points."

"I am on it, sir," Clark replies. "Sir, you didn't say during our earlier discussion, but did any prisoners survive the ambush attempt?"

"No, they did not," Butler radios back. "We're now facing some of the most diabolical, evil men on the planet, Gary. Do not hesitate. Have your finger on the trigger at all times and shoot to kill."

"Yes . . . yes, sir."

Butler hears the fear in Clark's voice yet he doesn't say anything to dissuade it. A little fear will help to keep Clark focused. And, to tell the truth, Butler's dealing with his own fears. It's hard not to when you're surrounded by dead bodies and you know that the next man you encounter will kill you without compunction. A few moments later, Butler startles when he hears gunfire from the other side of the prison. Rather than short bursts, it's continuous bombardment and Butler wonders if his men on that side have encountered another ambush attempt.

When the gunfire slows to a few sporadic shots Butler triggers his radio. "Butler to Clark." He waits a moment for Clark to respond. And waits. "Butler to Clark, over," he tries again. A tingle of dread slithers down his spine. "Men," he shouts, "hold your positions."

"Captain," an anxious voice says over the radio, "this is Sergeant Tyler Fields. Lieutenant Clark is injured."

"How badly, Sergeant Fields?" Butler asks.

"Bad, sir. He was stabbed in the neck."

Butler's shoulders sag. He takes a deep breath and triggers the radio. "Put pressure on the wound and get him to an ambulance. Any other injuries?"

"Yes, sir," Fields replies. "We're trying to sort it out now, sir."

"Roger. Status of the prisoners?"

"Dead, sir."

"How many, Sergeant Fields?"

"A bunch, Captain. They hit us when we entered the chow hall."

" 'A bunch' doesn't tell me much, Sergeant."

"Stand by, sir."

Butler looks around at his men and says, "Move out,

men. Remember my instructions." Butler's brain clicks through the list of personnel on the other side of the prison. Lieutenant Marvin Maxwell, a social studies teacher, is with that group, but he's a tad skittish and that's the last thing Butler needs at the moment. His mind continues to run through the list. He clicks his radio and says, "Sergeant Vasquez, you are in command." Hugo Vasquez is an Erie County sheriff's deputy.

"Roger, sir," Vasquez replies. "Inmate body count is twenty-seven, sir."

A moment later, there's another voice on the radio. "Maxwell to Butler, over."

Butler sighs. He clicks the transmit button and says, "Lieutenant Maxwell, now is not the time. Vasquez has command. Roger the twenty-seven, Sergeant."

"But, sir," Maxwell whines over the radio.

Butler is exhausted, hungry, and angry. "That's a direct fucking order, Lieutenant. Butler out." He clicks the handset back in place and follows his men as they move deeper into D-Block. Finding no living people, it doesn't take them long to clear the empty cellblock. Now it's time to clear the tunnels. They return to the entrance inside cellblock D and make their way toward Times Square.

Butler removes the prison radio from his belt and puts it to his lips. He'll be announcing their location but he wants to give Lydia Darnell a heads-up. "Officer Darnell, almost to you."

"Roger, Captain," Darnell radios back. "Visitors at three o'clock."

Butler pulls up a mental map of the prison. The three o'clock position would put prisoners in the tunnel from cellblock B. "Stay sharp," Butler tells his men. "Bogies to your right when we clear the tunnel." He quickens his pace and moves to the point.

A few moments later they're approaching the intersection of the four corridors and Times Square. Butler holds up a hand and everyone comes to a stop. Moving into the center of the group, Butler whispers directions. Unsure if there are other prisoners in the adjoining tunnels, he orders squads three and four to clear those while squads one and two swing into the tunnel to cellblock B. "Hard and fast," Butler tells his men. After positioning a rear guard, Butler orders the men to move out.

The four squads fan out at once. The eight members of squads one and two hit B tunnel hard and fast, firing as the group of prisoners attempt to push forward. Butler edges out and starts picking off the prisoners at the back of the pack. The door to the guard booth swings open and Butler gets his first look at Corrections Officer Lydia Darnell as she steps out, the shotgun tucked tight to her shoulder. She fires two rounds at the group of inmates and walks forward, mowing down any inmates left standing. Within fifteen seconds, it's over.

"Cease fire," Butler shouts. Smoke and the acrid smell of spent gunpowder linger in the air. Butler orders a body count then turns to Darnell and offers his hand.

Darnell bypasses his outstretched hand and leans in for a hug. "Thank you, Captain Butler."

"You're welcome." He looks at the shotgun in her hands. "Payback?"

Darnell nods. "I lost some good friends today."

"I know you did. Hopefully this is almost over."

"Thirty-nine inmates dead, Captain," Lieutenant Fred Parker shouts.

Butler does the math in his head. If the count is right they've whittled the number of remaining inmates down to somewhere around thirty. At this pace, there's a good chance they'll be able to leave this godforsaken place before daylight. His thoughts are interrupted by a radio call from Sergeant Vasquez.

Butler clicks the transmit button. "Butler here. Go, Vasquez."

"Sir," Vasquez says, "we have a hostage situation at the infirmary."

Butler mutters a string of curse words. "Roger, on my way." He looks at Darnell. "Most of the prison staff is at the school with the other prisoners."

Darnell shakes her head. "Uh-uh. I'm going with you."

"Works for me." Butler turns to his men. "Freddy, with me. For everyone else, Sergeant Gibbs is now in command. We're almost home, men. We still have around thirty prisoners to find. I'm betting a good number of those inmates are inside the infirmary, but be careful as you clear the rest of the prison. Good work, men."

As the men move out by squads, Butler glances at Darnell and says, "You better grab some more ammo for that scattergun of yours."

CHAPTER 77

Hank Goodnight is working the phones as Natalie, Paige, and the crew continue to work on unraveling the malware. Natalie has the NSA scouring for any scrap of information, but Hank is taking it a step further by contacting his sources at a little-known agency inside the Justice Department called the National Security Analysis Center (NSAC). Started shortly after 9/11, the agency was originally tasked with keeping tabs on foreign nationals. But the agency's role has expanded over the years and they now have access to over 130 databases and over two billion records. Of those records, half are unique to the agency and can't be found in other government databases. Able to access every intelligence database in the U.S. government, the agency also has access to law enforcement data and can access many commercial companies that collect data on American residents. In comparison, the NSA is limited to intercepting only domestic electronic *communications* while the NSAC has no such limits. It's Big Bother personified.

It doesn't feel like an inside job to Hank, but he's

covering all the bases. It would be much faster and easier if he had a name, however, for now, he's having them search for any mention of the ongoing cyber attack and he's having them compile backgrounds on known hackers both inside and outside the United States. That last part of his request will likely be a bust because most hackers never reveal their true identities and he'll end up with a bunch of screen names with little attribution. But it feels good to be doing something.

Hank leans back in the chair and runs a hand across his face, feeling the stubble. It's been a long, long day. He pushes wearily to his feet. "I think I'm going to find somewhere to stretch out for a bit."

Paige looks up from her computer. "Oh, is this the sleeping part you were talking about?"

Hank shrugs. "I suppose. You're a big girl and I figure you'll sleep when you want to sleep."

"I'm too wound up anyway," Paige says.

"Hank, there's a couch in my office," Natalie says.

"Which is where?" Hank asks, looking around.

Natalie points to a door on the other side of the room. "Thanks, Nat. I promise not to slobber."

Natalie smiles. "And no farting, either."

"That, I can't promise," Hank says. "Anyplace to get a cold beer around here?"

"Check the small fridge in my office. I think there's a few cans in there."

"They let you drink on the job?" Hank asks.

"We work some long hours. It's not encouraged but it's also not discouraged. So until they say no, I'll have a beer or some wine when I'm working late."

"Want me to bring you and Paige a glass of wine?"

Natalie looks at Paige. "Want some chardonnay?"

Paige shakes her head. "If I drink a glass of wine, I'll crash and burn."

"I'll pass, too. Thanks for asking, though."

"Hey, it's your wine. I was just going to be the delivery boy."

"And a cute one at that," Natalie says, giving Hank a wink. She clucks her tongue three times and says, "Oh, think about the fun we could have had, Hank Goodnight."

Thinking it's best to leave that alone for now, Hank waves and heads for Natalie's office. Inside, he kicks off his boots, kills the light, and stretches out on the couch. It's about a foot too short for Hank's long frame, leaving his feet dangling off the edge. He stares at the moonlight slashing across the ceiling, wondering about Natalie. They'd done some fooling around, but nothing that involved shedding clothes. They were close, though, and it probably would have happened on that next date until Hank screwed that up. It's been a long while since he's had a relationship and he wonders if Natalie is currently attached.

But just as soon as he thinks that, his thoughts drift from Natalie to Paige. Both women are extremely intelligent and both are easy on the eyes. Both are curious and both are strong willed. Paige seems a little more refined and Hank doesn't know if that's a good thing or a bad thing. Although he's a small-town boy from Ada, Oklahoma, Hank has seen a lot of the world yet he remains somewhat culturally stunted. He hates opera and can barely tolerate the symphony. But he loves college football and Jason Aldean. He sighs and rolls over to his side, trying to turn off the spigot of thoughts crowding into his brain.

*   *   *

Paige felt a little uncomfortable during that exchange between Natalie and Hank and she spends a moment contemplating why. She's known Hank for all of one day. One extremely long day, yes, but all she knows about him is he has a grandmother he calls Nana and he's from a small town in Oklahoma. Then her mind flashes on that incident in Manhattan. Maybe she knows more about him than she originally thought. Hank had been calm and collected and it's obvious he has a strong moral foundation, evidenced by his actions in the looted restaurant. But then Paige wonders if he went too far. Was there another way that didn't involve the killing of two people? Not that those two men didn't deserve it for what they were doing to that young, innocent girl, but Hank made the conscious decision to be judge, jury, and executioner without, apparently, a second thought.

"Earth to Paige," Natalie says.

Paige startles and looks at Natalie. "Sorry. I guess I drifted off to la-la land."

Natalie smiles. "Was Hank there?"

Paige blushes. "What's the story between you two?"

"There's not one. We went out a few times and that's about it."

"Still interested?"

"No, I've moved in another direction."

Paige doesn't know what that means and she allows the conversation to die as the two return to dissecting the malware. Whoever created it knew what they were doing. It's a sophisticated piece of software and as they drill down deeper, they're beginning to find what the targets are. Hank is correct. Most of the payloads are designed to gain control of various industrial control systems. What's stunning is that the software is able to infiltrate a large number of different control systems, meaning that whoever created it spent years adding to its capabilities.

How the malware initially penetrated these various computer networks remains a mystery for now. It could have been an infected flash drive, a spear phishing campaign, an infected e-mail attachment, or a host of other methods the hackers use to gain access to a computer network. The answers will eventually come, but it will take a good amount of detective work to interview employees and to study the various companies' past history of software changes, updates, or additions. It's a long, tedious task that could drag on for months.

Right now, Paige and Natalie aren't concerned with how the malware arrived. They're more interested in how to kill it while also searching for digital fingerprints that might tell them who is behind the attack.

Natalie looks up from her computer. "You were right, Paige. I've found a self-destruct sequence buried in one of the payloads."

Paige leans back in her chair, thinking. After several moments, she says, "Why don't we write a piece of software to target and trigger that specific payload?"

Natalie contemplates that for a moment "Jesus, could it really be that simple?"

"Why not?" Paige asks.

In her excitement, Natalie leans forward and pecks Paige on the lips. "You're brilliant."

Paige is momentarily taken aback. But now she thinks she knows what "another direction" means.

CHAPTER 78

Chicago

Sometime later, Peyton wakes and sits up, momentarily confused about her surroundings. Then she remembers the horrors of a few hours ago and why they're now sleeping at Allison's house. But that wasn't what stirred her from sleep. It was a strange sound that registered somewhere in her subconscious. And it wasn't Eric's snoring. She's grown accustomed to that. No, it sounded like a cat scratching on a door and she knows Allison doesn't have a cat. She's allergic to them.

Peyton slides out of the bed and feels her way toward the bedroom door in the darkness. There was no way in hell she was going to leave another candle burning unattended. She cracks the door open and sticks her head out, straining to hear. *Maybe it's a limb scraping against the side of the house.* When you're in a strange home, you don't know what noises in the night to expect. Peyton knows that at her house the blower for the air conditioner had a slight rattle to it. Maybe Allison has a tree limb that brushes against the house when the wind blows.

Peyton hears a different noise and this time there's

no mistaking it for a tree branch. Someone is rattling the knob on the front door.

Peyton turns and says in an urgent whisper, "Eric, wake up. Someone's trying to break into the house." Peyton feels her way around the bed and shakes Eric. "Wake up."

"What?" Eric asks as he rolls onto his back.

"Shhh, keep your voice down. Someone's trying to break into the house."

"It's probably a tree limb or something," he whispers to placate his wife.

"A tree limb is trying to open the front door?"

"Fuck, is this day ever going to be over?" Eric mutters as he gingerly climbs out of bed. "Where's the shotgun?" he whispers to Peyton.

"You left it by the front door."

"That wasn't very damn smart, was it? Flashlight?"

"Hold out your hand," Peyton whispers.

"No, you keep it. I can't handle the gun and the light at the same time."

"What do you want me to do?"

"Click on the flashlight and light the way, but stay behind me. Once I have the shotgun, you take cover and turn off the light."

"What are you going to do?" Peyton whispers.

"I guess I'm going to open the front door."

"And do what?"

"Hell, I don't know, Peyton. I work at a goddamn bank. I guess we'll play it by ear."

"How are you going to see who's at the door?"

"When I shout 'Now' you hit them with the light."

"Okay," Peyton whispers. She clicks on the flashlight and covers most of the lens with her hand.

They exit the bedroom and creep down the hall as

Allison opens the door to her bedroom. "What's going on?" she whispers as she pulls on a robe.

"Someone's trying to break in," Peyton whispers.

Allison gasps. "Are you sure?"

"Yes, I'm sure," Peyton says.

Allison falls in behind them. At the entrance to the living room Eric spots the shotgun leaning against the wall. He walks carefully across the hardwood floor, hoping there are no creaks to announce his presence. After he picks up the shotgun, Peyton kills the light. Eric can't remember if he chambered a round or not. He feels around the trigger guard and finds the button that unlocks the chamber and slowly racks the slide. He feels around inside the chamber and finds a shell already seated. Slowly, he slides the chamber closed and steps over to the door. Holding the shotgun in his right hand, he reaches out his left, turns the lock, and flings open the door.

"Now," Eric shouts.

Peyton clicks on the light as Eric raises the shotgun, his finger on the trigger. The beam lands on a man standing at the door, and Eric is a second away from pulling the trigger when Allison screams and the man shouts, "Wait! Don't shoot!"

Eric looks down the gun barrel at the man before him. "Jordan?"

"It's me. It's me." Jordan bends down and puts his hands on his knees, on the verge of hyperventilating.

"What are you doing here?" Eric asks, lowering the gun. Allison brushes past and wraps an arm around her husband.

"I guess I could ask the same thing," Jordan says. He stands up straight and Allison leads him inside. "What happened to your house? I saw some embers still glowing," Jordan says as he sags onto the sofa, still trembling.

"Long story," Peyton says, taking a seat in one of the side chairs. "We thought you were in Seattle."

"I was. There were five of us from Chicago out there and the company decided to charter a plane to fly us home. I had to walk all the way from the damn airport in the dark."

Allison takes a seat next to her husband. "Why didn't you use your key to unlock the door?"

"My keys are at the office." Jordan looks at Eric. "I thought you were going to blow my head off."

"I almost did," Eric says apologetically. "Now that you're home, you can take over gun duties."

Jordan nods. "How long has the power been off here?"

"Most of the day," Allison says. "And Peyton thinks it might be off for a while."

Jordan looks at Peyton. "How long?"

Peyton shrugs. "I don't know. Weeks, maybe."

"How do you know this?" Jordan asks.

"My sister called, but the call dropped. Basically all I heard was 'get out.' "

"Of the city?" Jordan asks.

"That's my interpretation. Was the power still on in Seattle?"

"Yeah, it was. But flying in we saw a lot of darkness. I'd say most of the Midwest is without power."

"How did you land at O'Hare if it was dark?"

"It was dicey. We didn't have much choice. The plane was low on fuel. Luckily the pilots fly out of here all the time and they know the airport well. I'm sure they violated a page-long list of regulations, but it was either land or crash." Jordan stands. "We can talk more in the morning. Right now, I'm wiped out."

Eric stands and Jordan takes the shotgun from him.

"Were you going to pull the trigger?" Jordan asks.

Eric thinks about it for a moment. "Yeah, I was."

CHAPTER 79

Attica

At the entrance to the prison infirmary, Captain Scott Butler calls his senior officers together. Luckily the generator is still running on this side of the prison, allowing them a chance to see what's going on inside the hospital. From what they can tell there are at least fifteen inmates inside with four hostages, all located inside the main room on the hospital's second floor. "I don't want to get involved in a long standoff," Butler says. "What are our options?"

"We put snipers with thermal image scopes on top of the buildings on either side of the hospital," Sergeant Hugo Vasquez says, "then kill the power."

"How are they going to tell the good guys from the bad, Hugo?" Butler asks.

"Those FLIR scopes have excellent visual contrast, Captain. They should be able to tell the difference by the clothing the people are wearing."

"And if a prisoner happens to put on a lab coat or takes clothing from the hostages to put on?" Butler asks.

"Are they that smart?" Vasquez asks.

"The inmates may not be brain surgeons, but they're cunning as hell. Someone will have thought of that."

"What about tear gas?" Lieutenant Fred Parker asks. "This is a prison. They'll have tear gas out the wazoo."

Butler thinks about it a moment, then calls Officer Darnell over. "Does the prison have tear gas guns?"

"Yes," Darnell says. "And there are certain areas of the prison where tear gas can be deployed with the push of a button."

"I assume the hospital isn't one of those locations?"

"No, it's not. That's what the guns are for."

"Masks?"

"Oh yeah. Plenty."

"Do you have access to the equipment?"

"Sure do. We keep it in several places throughout the prison, just in case."

Butler turns to look at Vasquez. "Hugo, go with Darnell to grab some tear gas gear."

"On it, sir," Vasquez says, falling in behind Darnell as she takes off down the corridor.

While they wait for the tear gas, Butler begins formulating a plan. If he sends more than two squads inside it'll get crowded in a hurry. But having never been exposed to tear gas, he wonders how effective it will be. He scans the crowd and calls over one of the state troopers who is milling about.

"I'm Trooper Ellis Goodman, Captain," the man says.

"Scott Butler, Ellis. Nice to meet you. Have you ever been exposed to tear gas?"

"I have, sir. Not a pleasant experience."

"Describe what it's like."

"It's bad, sir. It feels like your nose and eyes are on fire. It'll make you cry like a baby and then the sneezing and coughing starts. And it's hard to breathe. Something in the gas triggers the mucous membranes and your throat will start to swell. I've only been exposed in an outdoor environment and I assume effects would be much more concentrated in a confined area. You thinking about gassing the inmates holed up in the hospital?"

"It's an option. Did you feel incapacitated? Or could you still function?"

"When you get gassed you can't do shit, sir."

"Thank you, Ellis. Do you want to be part of the takedown team?"

"Hell, yeah. I've trained with the trooper SWAT teams several times."

"Any other state troopers here who have done the same?"

"Sure. Want me to organize a breach team?"

"Yes, but limit the number of shotguns to two. We must keep the hostages alive."

"Yes, sir. How many men, you figure?"

"Eight."

"That sounds about right. Get too many people in there and bad shit starts to happen."

Ellis pauses then says, "What do you want us to do about the inmates, sir?"

Butler thinks back to his original orders. "If they're incapacitated, cuff them. If someone tries to harm you or the hostages, take them out."

"Yes, sir. You might want to have some medical people on standby for the hostages."

"They're already on the way. Put your team together and then we'll finalize the plan."

"Roger, sir."

Ellis takes off to assemble his team and Captain Butler steps over to talk to Parker.

"Freddy, think we should try to talk them out of there?"

Parker shakes his head. "We're back to the original problem. We don't have anything to negotiate with. They aren't going to get reduced sentences or time off for good behavior based on the things we've seen in here today. They're fucked and they know it."

"What if we offer them their lives? That's worth something, isn't it?"

"To me and you, yes. I'm not sure it means a hell of a lot to men who will most likely be behind bars for the rest of their lives." Parker takes off his helmet and mops his brow with his sleeve. "Did you ever expect to see anything like this in here?"

Butler sighs. "No. It's hard to believe what one human can do to another. I know there are men inside this building who didn't participate in the killing, but I don't know how they're going to weed those out from the rest of them."

Parker puts his helmet back on. "Not our problem, Scott. We're here to secure the prison and then get the hell out. And it can't come soon enough for me." Parker glances at his watch. "Hell, I'm supposed to be at work in about three hours."

"Tell me about it. I have a full slate of patients scheduled."

"I'm glad you're not going to be drilling on my teeth this morning."

Butler gives his friend a tired smile. "I think I should probably cancel the morning patients. A few will bitch and moan, but they'll get over it. It's better than drilling a hole in someone's cheek."

Parker chuckles. "That wouldn't feel real good. On a serious note, Scott, you might want to talk to the general about having some counselors available for these men."

"It's already on my to-do list, Freddy. We're all going to be having nightmares about this place."

Darnell and Vasquez return with the tear gas gear. Once the masks are divvied up, Butler goes over the plan a final time with Ellis Goodman and his fellow troopers, many of whom are busy tightening their bullet-resistant vests. Darnell loads two of the tear gas guns and passes one to Butler. The plan is for Darnell and Butler to fire the tear gas canisters through the door window that leads into the hospital. Goodman and his men will then enter the space and secure the area. Once that's complete, National Guard troops, under the leadership of Lieutenant Parker, will recover the hostages and take them down the stairs to be treated by medical personnel while the inmates are cuffed and led out of the room.

Butler and Darnell climb up the stairs with Goodman and his men on their heels. At the top, there's an open space that's about six feet deep that runs the width of the building, with the door to the hospital centered on the far wall. Goodman and his troops take up positions on either side of the door and Darnell and Butler follow. Not knowing the accuracy of the weapons, they're hoping for a point-blank shot through the door glass.

Butler nods at Darnell and she tucks the tear gas rifle to her shoulder and stands while Butler braces for the shot. Darnell ducks back beneath the window a second later and whispers, "It's security glass. They must have replaced it recently."

Butler nods, curse words zinging around inside his brain. He thinks about it for a moment and comes up with a new plan. He gets the attention of Goodman and mimics turning the knob.

Goodman nods. Butler and Darnell position themselves near the doorframe and wait for him to open the door. Carefully, Goodman turns the knob and opens the door about six inches. That's all Darnell and Butler need. They jam the barrels inside, fire the tear gas canisters, and step back. Goodman and his team have their pistols out in a firing position as they stagger their entries through the door, one right after another. Once they're clear, Butler and Darnell pause fifteen seconds and enter.

In their haste to end the hostage situation no one considered the difficulty of being able to see through the cloud of gas vapors. Butler clicks on a flashlight to find that only makes visibility worse, much like car headlights in the fog. He kills the light and tucks it into a pocket of his vest. Sweat is dripping down his forehead and onto the mask, making a bad situation worse.

Somewhere on the other side of the room, a shotgun roars and then roars again. Unable to communicate with the others, Butler has no idea what's going on. He jumps when someone fires a pistol right next to him. Tracing the direction of the muzzle flash, Butler peers through the lessening fog, trying to find out what the target was. While he's looking, he's nearly bowled over a moment later when someone backs into him. Butler whirls around and his heart stutters.

The inmates also have gas masks.

Butler pulls the trigger three times and backpedals as the man lunges for him. After two steps the man begins to falter and collapses to his knees. Butler puts a bullet through the top of his head and begins searching for more targets. It's still hard to see, but the cloud is dissipating. He can see another inmate creeping up behind someone over by the windows. Butler takes aim and fires two quick shots, hitting the man center mass.

The inmates might have masks, but they don't have body armor.

Other pistols bark and the shotgun roars again. Butler wonders how many inmates are really in the room. Someone latches on to the wrist of his gun hand and Butler tries to twist his arm away, but it feels like it's trapped in a vise. For the first time today, fear rears its ugly head as Butler fumbles for his knife with his left hand.

The man keeps twisting Butler's arm and it feels as if his shoulder joint is going to give out any second. Feeling the pistol slipping from his grasp, Butler burns through his last reserves of energy trying to maintain his hold on his weapon.

If he doesn't, he dies.

Butler flinches when someone fires a pistol right next to his head, the muzzle flash nearly blinding him. The man's grip on his arm slowly begins to loosen and Butler eventually yanks his arm free. He switches the gun to his left hand and starts scanning for targets again. Someone had propped the door open and the cloud of gas is rapidly retreating.

After several moments of chaos and terror, Butler makes his way over to a window and cranks it open. That helps with the vapors, but it doesn't do much to alleviate the pain in Butler's right arm—the arm he uses to fill cavities and set crowns. With the guns now silent, Butler works his arm in a circle as he surveys the damage. Bodies and spent shell casings litter the floor and Butler's hoping his men were successful in rescuing the hostages. Deciding that's the most important question, Butler hustles out of the room and down the stairs. He takes off the sweat-filled mask, takes a breath of fresh air, and makes a radio call. "Butler to Parker, over."

A couple of seconds later, he responds. "Go for Parker."

"Status of the hostages?" Butler asks.

"Two males accounted for, sir."

Butler mumbles a curse word or two. "What happened to the other two?"

"They were gone long before we arrived, Scott. Two females. And they didn't die pleasant deaths."

Butler stares out the window at the faint smudge of orange along the horizon and blows out a shaky breath as tears shimmer in his eyes. The long night is over, but the nightmares will linger long after. He puts the handset to his lips. "Roger, Freddy." Butler wipes his eyes, takes a deep, calming breath, and sends out a radio call to Sergeant Vasquez.

"Vasquez, here, sir," he answers a second later.

"I need a body count from upstairs."

"Already on it, sir. I'll have the number in a moment."

"Roger," Butler says. He looks up to see Lydia Darnell slowly descending the stairs. When she strips off her mask Butler can see tears are streaming down her cheeks. He steps over and meets her at the bottom, wrapping his arms around her. "It's over, Lydia," Butler whispers in her ear.

"It'll never be over for me . . . Captain," Darnell says between sobs. "I worked . . . with those people . . . laughed with . . . those people, and cried with those . . . people. And now . . . they're all gone."

CHAPTER 80

Target 1-A is a hack none of the grad students have performed before. Hassan doesn't know if the same is true for Nazeri, but he wouldn't be surprised if he had—probably more than a few times. They won't know if this particular attack has worked for several hours or even days because they don't have eyes on this target or any real-time access. What is assured is that every member of the team, if discovered, will be hunted to the ends of the earth if they're successful, and that thought makes Hassan Ansari nauseous, especially in light of what he's planning to do. If he could stop it, he would. But he can't and there is no way for help to arrive in time.

If Hassan had any doubts about Nazeri's intentions, they evaporated when the three armed men appeared. Dressed in tan fatigues, their uniforms are absent of any insignia and offer no clues as to their allegiance. All three men are dark haired with dark, olive-colored complexions, and all three look as if they were cut from the same cloth. If Hassan had to guess their origins he'd lean toward them being Iranian, or somewhere around that region. Regardless of their nationality, they're here now, and Hassan and his cohorts must find a way to mitigate their presence.

And Hassan has a plan. A plan he can't share with his cohorts now that Jermar's chat program has been compromised. It will spell doom, but it just might save their lives.

"Have you acquired the device?" Nazeri asks Sheezal.

"Almost," Sheezal replies.

Hassan is amazed that the general public remains uninformed about the dangers of their obsession to acquire wireless devices. They can't seem to grasp that if something connects to the Internet, it's hackable. Despite the continuing drumbeat of hacked databases, hacked nanny cams, or stolen usernames and passwords, their insatiable appetite for wireless devices continues unabated. Not only are consumers connecting wireless devices to their home networks, they are also allowing the implantation of wireless medical devices into their own bodies.

And it's one such device that is the target of Nazeri's current attack.

Unbeknownst to the general voting public, America's newly installed president relies on a pacemaker to keep his heart in rhythm. It is a closely held secret to prevent the public from believing their new leader is infirm. Hassan has no idea how Nazeri received the information, but he has it, along with the precise serial number of the device implanted in the president's chest. With that information, and access to the wireless network the device communicates with, Nazeri can alter the device's settings to speed up the heart rate, drain the battery, or turn it off altogether. Hassan knows that Nazeri's plan is to choose the speediest outcome and, in this case, he's planning to accelerate the president's heart rate.

Hassan thinks it's odd that Nazeri is acting as if nothing has changed as he and Sheezal work in tandem. But on another level, Hassan understands. This is the one target they all yearned for. Not only has the new president continued the merciless drone attacks, he has accelerated the program, dropping bombs all over the Middle East. Yes, this attack is about retribution, but Hassan hopes the elevation of the vice president to the highest office in the land will bring some sanity back to America.

While Nazeri and Sheezal make final preparations, Hassan is making his own plans. He checks the time to make sure the satellite window to the ship is still open then takes a moment to visualize his plan. It's not foolproof. The signal could go unnoticed or, to the other extreme, it could result in a bomb being dropped on their heads. But Hassan can find no other alternatives.

"What are the odds the president's pacemaker has the new firmware update?" Sheezal asks Nazeri.

"It doesn't matter," Nazeri says. "I have other vulnerabilities we can exploit."

Hassan is not surprised. Where Nazeri came up with all of the zero days, including the one that allows Nazeri access to the White House's wireless network, is still a mystery. But hopefully it won't remain a mystery for long. Hassan launches one of his programs that he created long ago and refined over the years. The software scans deep into the hard drive, searching for spyware or keylogger programs with administrator-level access. Hassan will not underestimate Nazeri again. He has no doubt now that Nazeri is monitoring their computer activities somehow and he has to find out how for his plan to work.

Within moments, Hassan's software produces a list containing two items. One is a keylogger and the other sends a chill down his spine. It's an encrypted file that Hassan has never seen before. It's obviously a file Nazeri has placed on his computer, but he has no idea of the contents. It could be a self-destruct mechanism or it could also be a dossier detailing every aspect of Hassan's life, including his family, friends, and a list of crimes he has committed. Hassan might be able to crack the encryption if he had enough time, but that's the one thing he doesn't have.

Hassan tries to put it out of his mind as he examines the keylogger. He doesn't want to remove the software, fearing its absence will trigger some type of alarm. What he would like to do is either blind it to his activities or simply turn it off for a few seconds.

"I'm in," Sheezal announces.

Hassan tries to tune them out, knowing that time is his greatest enemy. The attempted killing or the actual killing of the president could be the culminating event that will lead to their demise. Luckily that information won't be readily available, buying them a little more time. Hassan finds a way to momentarily disable the keylogger and does. With a clock ticking down in his head, Hassan logs out of the VPN they've been using and logs back on to the wireless network, unmasked. Navigating to the satellite, he types in a set of instructions and pulls up the USS *Stark*'s shipboard cameras.

Using his keyboard and mouse, he spends a few seconds manipulating the cameras then kills the connection. After logging out, he immediately logs back in to the VPN, enables the keylogger, and sits back in his chair. All he can do now is wait.

CHAPTER 81

Fort Meade

Natalie Lambert drains the last of her energy drink and tosses the empty can into the trash under her desk. Outside, dawn is breaking—a fact she knows only by glancing at the clock. There are no windows in the room and there will be no warming from the sun's first rays of the day. Paige is working on an adjacent computer as they continue writing a program to target the malware's self-destruct payload. It sounds easy, but it's not. The sophistication of the malware only makes it more difficult.

Natalie nearly jumps out of her chair when the office phone on her desk rings. She lifts the handset and says, "Lambert." She listens for a moment then says, "Oh shit. Really?" She listens for another moment as she pushes to her feet. "Okay. Hold on." She lays the handset down and races across the room.

"What is it?" Paige shouts after her.

Peyton glances back over her shoulder. "Signals. They got a hit on a satellite."

Natalie flings open the door to her office. "Hank, get up."

Hank rolls over and sits up. "What is it?"

"Signals got a hit."

Hank rubs his eyes as he stands from the sofa. "What and where?"

"They want to talk to you."

Hank grabs his cell phone and blinks against the bright lights as he follows Natalie back across the room. Paige stands and walks over as Hank grabs the phone. "Goodnight."

"Agent Goodnight, I'm Sheryl Wilkins, an analyst in signals. We picked up some satellite communications that might be of interest."

"I'm listening," Hank says.

"The communications originated in Boston and were relayed over one of our satellites."

"Where did the signal terminate?" Hank asks.

"A ship in the North Atlantic. I can't tell you specifically which one."

"Are you able to decipher what the communications were?"

"They're encrypted. We'll eventually decode it, but it might take a while."

"Have you picked up any other communications from that location?"

"Negative."

"Do you have the address and the coordinates for the ship's location, Sheryl?"

"Yes. Do you want to grab a pencil so you can write it down?"

"No, just tell me."

Wilkins relays the info and Hank passes on his cell phone number. "I need that decryption as soon as you get it. Thank you, Sheryl. You've been a big help." Hank hangs up the phone, pulls over a chair, and sits.

"Are we going?" Paige asks.

"This is my end of the deal. There is no 'we.'"

"Bullshit," Paige says.

Hank holds up a hand. "Hold up. Let me think this through for a minute. We don't know for certain it's them. She couldn't identify which ship received the communications. Hell, it could be a food warehouse ordering more tuna from a fishing boat."

Paige takes a seat at her computer. "You asked for the ship's coordinates. Tell me what they were."

Hank recites the coordinates and Paige enters them into the computer. After pulling up a map to locate the general area, she scrolls through the list of satellites, trying to find one that will provide a visual. Since it's dark, she'd prefer an infrared image, so she clicks on several different weather satellites, but they don't offer the image resolution she's seeking. She glances up. "Natalie, do you have access to images from the NSA satellites?"

"Yes," Natalie says, taking a seat in front of her computer.

Paige pedals her chair over while Natalie logs in. "Hank, what were those coordinates again?" Paige asks.

Hank rattles off the numbers again.

"How does he do that?" Natalie whispers.

"I'll tell you later," Paige says. "Pull up any satellites that cover the North Atlantic."

It looks like it's going to take them a while to find what they're looking for, so Hank rolls the latest information around in his mind. He wonders why this is the only communication the NSA has flagged from that address. He runs several scenarios through his brain, but none make sense. After all, these are sophisticated hackers and if they've camouflaged their activity to this point, why the aberration? Could it be a simple mistake? Hank wonders. The one thing he failed to ask Sheryl Wilkins was the duration of the signal. Hank stands. "Natalie, how do I get back in touch with Sheryl Wilkins?"

"Pick up the phone and dial star-639. That'll get you to signals analysis."

Hank picks up the phone and makes the call. He reconnects with Wilkins and finds out the answer to his question—forty-nine seconds. Hank sits back down and runs through the process of how that might happen. He tries to visualize the actions that would be required to transition from a secure private network to a secure, but less private one—one that would allow the NSA to intercept their communications.

"Got it," Natalie says. She turns her monitor so that Hank can see. "This is an accelerated video loop of the last thirty minutes that covers the coordinates Wilkins provided."

Hank leans forward in his chair. "Play it." He watches it all the way through and leans back in his chair.

"Do we need to replay it or enhance it?" Paige asks.

"No. There's only one ship currently at sea that has that bow and superstructure configuration."

"Which ship is it, then?" Paige asks.

"The USS *Stark*."

Paige and Natalie dance a little jig. "Hot damn. We've got the bastards," Paige says.

"Not yet, we don't," Hank says, pushing to his feet. "For some reason they wanted us to find them."

"Who?" Natalie asks.

"Someone on the inside of their operation."

"Why would they do that?" Paige asks.

"I don't know. That's what we need to find out."

Hank runs a hand through his hair. "Natalie, you finish up with the fix for the malware. Paige, find some clean clothes and gather up your things. I need to make some calls."

Daily News Website

—BREAKING NEWS—United States facing cyber attack? More details to follow . . .

—BREAKING NEWS—SECOND attack on Naval Station Norfolk. Further damage reported. Attackers unknown. President raises threat level to DEFCON 3. Multiple ships sunk. Many confirmed fatalities.

The military has confirmed that several ships have been sunk. Military leaders think the nation's latest warship, the beleaguered Zumwalt-class destroyer, may have been hacked. Search and rescue operations are still under way. More details to follow . . .

—BREAKING NEWS—Power outage occurs in large swath of the Midwest. As many as 18 million people may now be without electricity.

Several power company executives report their computer systems have been compromised. Hackers have apparently targeted several supervisory control and data acquisition (SCADA) systems. More details to follow . . .

—BREAKING NEWS—Power out in parts of New York State. New York City included in outage. National Guard troops called up in city.

After multiple reports of looting, the governor of New York has called up the National Guard to patrol the streets of New York City. We have heard unconfirmed

reports that the Guard has been ordered to shoot to kill.
More details to follow . . .

*—BREAKING NEWS—Possible prison riot at Attica
Correctional Facility in western New York State. Reports
confirm significant loss of life. National Guard troops
said to be entering prison. More details to follow . . .*

CHAPTER 82

Roger Rinsky had a miserable night. Yesterday, soon after leaving the golf course, it felt like he had a bad sunburn, but by dinnertime blisters had cropped up on his arms, face, and legs. At bedtime the vomiting began and for the first time, he wished he'd evacuated when they told him to. Deep into the night, the diarrhea started and Rinsky ending up messing the bed, forcing him to move to the sofa in the living room. This morning it has all coalesced and he hasn't left the bathroom in two hours. With daylight breaking, Rinsky knows he needs help or he's going to die hugging the porcelain throne.

He's severely dehydrated, his movements are sluggish, and standing or walking is out of the question. So Rinsky begins to crawl, desperate to reach the cell phone on his nightstand. After his wife died three years ago, Rinsky moved into an apartment in a small retirement community across the Patuxent River in Lexington Park. As his grief waned over the passing of his wife, Rinsky started playing golf every morning and chasing the ladies in the afternoons and evenings. And that led to his current predicament. His girlfriend, Dorothy, moved out last month after she walked in on Roger and her best friend, Susie, participating in a little afternoon delight. Now Rinsky is alone and it's looking like he might just die that way.

Rinsky makes it to the entrance to his bedroom and he can see his phone on his nightstand. The distance is maybe seven feet, but to Rinsky it looks like a mile. After taking a deep breath, he begins to crawl again, his guts roiling and cramping. He can feel the diarrhea coming, but there's little he can do about it as he crawls forward another foot, leaving a brown trail in his wake.

His addled mind drifts. He wonders how much radiation he was exposed to when the Calvert Cliffs nuclear plant exploded. *And what about Moretti and the others? Are they shittin' and pukin' their guts out?* Rinsky shakes his head in an attempt to clear his mind. But that triggers another round of nausea, and he pukes. There's nothing left in his stomach except bile, awaiting its turn to break down his next meal, a meal that's now in doubt. Rinsky wipes his mouth with the back of his hand and crawls forward another two feet. He raises his hand in a feeble attempt to reach the phone and he realizes it's just out of his grasp.

With one last surge of energy, Rinsky lowers his head and crawls, bumping his head against the nightstand. He exhales a stuttering breath and reaches up for his phone. He punches the button to light the screen and nothing happens. Rinsky screams with frustration, fumbles around for the power cord, and plugs in the phone. Rolling over onto his back, he waits for the phone to power up. He pokes and prods the blisters on his face, then looks at the ones on his arms. Some of his skin is turning black and that puzzles him. Jesus, it's not like he was inside the plant when the damn thing blew up. Hell, they were at least four miles away. He lowers his arms and stares at the ceiling, berating himself for not listening to Moretti. If he hadn't been so damn stubborn they could have made it back to the clubhouse when the sirens first sounded. And that might have allowed him time to set things right with Dorothy. But then his mind turns to Susie and their recent tumbles in the hay and all thoughts of Dorothy disappear. It's Susie and her magic mouth that take center stage in his mind. But he's now in such poor shape he can't even get a hard-on.

He checks the phone again. It's not charging and that's when he remembers the power is out. Rinsky mutters a string of curse words that would make a sailor blush and rolls over. He pushes himself up to his hands and knees and starts crawling again. His only hope now is to crawl outside and hope someone is around to help him.

Exiting the bedroom, he pauses to vomit again. He's as weak as a day-old kitten, yet once he clears the bedroom his sole focus is the front door. A Galápagos giant tortoise moves slowly, but today it would win a race against Rinsky, hands down. Halfway across the room, he falters, collapsing to his belly. His shoulders are burning and his knees are a bloody mess from the popped blisters. Rinsky rests for a moment, then uses his forearms to drag himself across the floor. With sweat dripping from his face and his throat parched, he finally makes it to the door.

Grimacing against the pain, he reaches up and turns the knob. Unfortunately, the door opens inward so he has to push himself back to gain clearance, the skin on his knees shredding on the tile. He eventually gets the door open wide enough to get through and he slithers out onto the concrete stoop. He looks around hoping to spot a neighbor, but there's not a soul around. This time Rinsky doesn't even have the energy to curse when he remembers the evacuation order and his refusal to leave.

After resting for a while, Rinsky pulls himself farther down the sidewalk, hoping to get out of the shadow of his apartment building in case someone comes by looking for him. He snakes his way across the wet grass and into the scant shade of a recently planted oak tree.

He's there three hours later when he coughs a final time and gasps a final breath.

CHAPTER 83

Calvert Cliffs

Inside the Calvert Cliffs Nuclear Power Plant, crews wearing hazmat suits are working in fifteen-minute shifts to reduce their radiation exposure as they attempt to stop the second reactor from melting. Inside the environmentally sealed control room, David Roark and Charles Lewis are thirty hours into their eight-hour shift. Pumps and generators were brought in overnight along with more staff, but there's major concern about the integrity of reactor two's enclosure. Reactor one is toast and the fire department is dumping an enormous amount of water on it to limit the release of more radiation as crews struggle to get the new pumps working. Once the pumps are operational, employees will need to pump millions of gallons of water every day from Chesapeake Bay just to keep the melting core cooled and to prevent more explosions. And, worse still, all of that water will now be contaminated, creating another massive headache of how to store a gazillion gallons of radiated wastewater.

The CEO of the corporation that owns the plant, J. Harold Houston, arrived this morning, screaming about lawsuits and lost investments. Roark and Lewis are doing their best to stay out of his way. With reactor one down, they're keeping a very close eye on the instruments measuring the health of the second reactor. If it blows, a wide swath of land around the plant—a nineteen-mile radius——will be uninhabitable for generations. And a large evacuation might still be needed if they can't contain reactor one. Roark and Lewis are also helping a team of suits from corporate do a thorough inspection of the plant's computer systems, which are still up and operating. It will be an arduous task that could take months or years. Roark has already started thinking about employment alternatives because the last thing he wants to do is sit next to a melting mound of radiated metal for the next however long it takes.

As everyone knows after watching YouTube videos of the Fukushima disaster, they're in for a long slog. The Japanese are years into the aftermath of their disaster and they still don't have a good handle on how to stop the escape of ionizing radiation. And the Russians could never find a solution for Chernobyl and eventually had to entomb the destroyed reactor in a sarcophagus of concrete and lead. No one here knows for sure what's in store or what to expect. The best thing to do would be to shut everything down and order the plant decommissioned, but that's impossible now after the explosion of reactor one. Now the company's responsible for the outcome and the costs could soar into the billions of dollars.

If those problems weren't enough, the company also owns two more nuke plants and no one here knows exactly how this disaster occurred. Someone obviously hacked the plant's computer network and the fear is the other plants are now at risk. And they're not out of the woods here in regard to reactor two. Could the sabo-teurs be waiting for another opportunity to destroy the second reactor? It's a question with no answer. The smart thing to do would be to shut the company's computers down, but they can't. All mechanical operations of the plant are controlled by computer via the PLCs and the second reactor is still operating—for now.

"Uh-oh," Lewis says.

"What?" Roark asks as a bead of sweat trickles down his spine.

"The steam turbine speeds are ramping up."

"We've seen this movie before. Shut that son of a bitch down."

"The turbine or the entire reactor?"

"The whole damn thing."

"No!" someone shouts behind them. They both turn to see Houston, the CEO, standing in the center of the room.

"Sir, this is exactly how the failure of reactor one started," Roark says.

"Just dial the turbine speed back a little. We must have that reactor up and operating."

"We can't dial back the turbines," Lewis says. "Which part of 'the computers have been hacked' do you not understand?"

"Have someone inside the plant take manual control of the turbines," the CEO says.

"The last time we tried that," Roark says, "eight people died. And that was yesterday."

"Well, come up with another plan, then. We are not, I repeat NOT, going to shut down the second reactor."

Roark and Lewis share a look. They've both had more than enough. Roark stands, reaches across the console, and slams his palm down on the emergency release button that drops the control rods into the core of reactor two, stopping the fission process. He turns and walks toward the exit, looking at Houston. "I quit. Good luck managing your disaster."

CHAPTER 84

Attica

Captain Scott Butler steps outside the prison and takes a deep breath, his first taste of fresh air in what seems like forever. If he never sees Attica again it will be too soon. The final tally of the dead is grim. Other than Lydia Darnell and the two hostages they rescued from the hospital, every correctional officer or staff member inside when the power went off—all 167—are dead. The death toll for the inmates is considerably higher at 421. Of that number, Butler and his team are responsible for 198 of those deaths, the others killed by their fellow inmates. The plan now is to transfer the remaining prisoners to other facilities while law enforcement personnel work the massive crime scene. But the *who did what* might never be determined.

Butler walks over to the truck and tosses his helmet inside. He leans his rifle against the door and strips off his armored vest, spreading it out across the hood to dry. Butler's camo shirt is soaked with sweat and he tugs it away from his torso, hoping it will eventually dry. His troops are scattered around the parking lot, stripping off unnecessary equipment. Several have cigarettes dangling from the corners of their mouths, the smoke curling around their sweaty faces in the still air. Butler glances at his watch and curses. His first patient is due in the office in forty-five minutes. He pulls out his cell phone and attempts to call one of his dental hygienists to cancel his morning schedule, but the call won't go through. Butler reasons that the power is now out in Buffalo.

The cadre of ambulances is gone and in their place is a swarm of media vehicles from all over the state. The warden mentioned something to Butler about holding a news conference, but he wants no part of it. All he wants is a hot meal and a bed. He walks around the back of the truck, lowers the tailgate, and sits. Switching to a military satellite phone. Butler dials directory assistance to get the phone number to the hospital. He calls the hospital and becomes angry and frustrated when the medical staff won't release any information about his injured soldiers. The hospital isn't allowed to, according to the HIPAA law. He would like to call the families of those injured, but he can't do that until he knows the extent of their injuries. It's a quandary he'll have to find some way to wade through.

Butler hasn't smoked a cigarette in twenty years, but for some reason he has a sudden desire to have one. He stands and walks over to one of his soldiers and bums a smoke. After lighting it, he takes a deep pull and allows the smoke to curl out of his nostrils. Then he starts coughing and decides that's enough of that and he tosses it to the ground and grinds the cigarette out with his boot heel. He instructs Lieutenant Fred Parker to start rounding up the men, then studies the keyboard of the sat phone for a moment or two, dreading the call he must now make. He keys in the number for Major General Lawrence Moore and puts the phone to his ear. The call is answered on the second ring. "It's over, sir," Butler says. "The prison is secure."

"You disobeyed a direct order, Captain Butler," Moore says.

"No, sir, I managed the situation as I saw fit as the commander on the ground."

"No, Captain, you disobeyed a direct order from the governor himself."

"I guess we can agree to disagree, sir."

"This isn't a disagreement, Captain. Your fate will be determined at a later date."

Butler's cheeks redden with anger. "How about we decide my fate right now? I resign."

"Resignation denied. I want a full written report on my desk by the end of the day."

Butler blows out a breath, trying to keep his temper in check. "You'll have it along with my written resignation letter. Is that all, sir?"

"No, that is not all, Captain Butler," Moore says. "Do not waste your time drafting a resignation letter. It will not be accepted during a period of martial law."

"Who declared martial law?"

"The governor did last night. A majority of the state is now without power."

"We'll resolve this issue later. I better get started on that report, sir."

"I am not through with you, Captain."

"Sir, with all due respect, I'm exhausted and hungry. My men and I have been at this all night."

"I'm sorry the world doesn't conform to your schedule, Captain Butler. We have multiple reports of looting in Buffalo. You and your men will return to Buffalo and you will patrol the streets and return the city to order."

Butler pulls the phone away from his ear and mutters a string of curse words. He takes a deep breath and puts the phone back to his ear. "Is that all, sir?"

"That is all, Captain. Do not forget my report."

When the general hangs up, Butler tosses the phone in the truck and mutters a long string of curses.

CHAPTER 85

Now three miles from Norfolk, Captain Bruce Hensley heads to his stateroom to shit, shower, and shave and to change into his dress uniform. Filled with apprehension, he has no idea what to expect upon their arrival. Downstairs, he ducks his head into the officers' wardroom. "Admiral, we'll be docking in a few minutes."

Admiral Malloy nods. "I've made several calls on your behalf, Bruce. I believe things are going to work out just fine for you." The admiral returns to staring at the table, as if studying the wood grain.

"Thank you, sir." Hensley wants to ask Malloy about the outlook for the admiral's situation, but decides against it. "You can use Lieutenant Commander Connelly's quarters if you'd like to freshen up, sir."

Malloy never looks up from the table when he says, "Thank you, Captain."

Hensley ducks back out of the room and closes the door. After entering his stateroom, he flips on the shower and strips out of his sweaty clothes. Once he finishes up in the bathroom he puts on his dress uniform, grabs his phone, and takes a seat on the edge of the bed. He pulls up his wife's phone number and stares at the picture he'd snapped of her laughing. He liked the photo so much that he attached it to Maggie's number so that it comes up every time she calls. Now, with his career likely over, he wonders where they'll settle down. That is, if he doesn't end up in the brig. Though, from what the admiral says, that's probably not going to happen, but Hensley knows there are no guarantees. He touches Maggie's photo and puts the phone to his ear.

Maggie answers on the second ring. "Bruce, what in the world's going on? Somebody bombed the hell out of the base."

"I know, babe. Believe me, I know."

"Who did it? The Chinese? The Russians?"

"No, someone much closer to home." Hensley sighs. "It was us."

"What?" Maggie shouts over the phone. "What do you mean, 'It was us'? Our own navy?"

"To be more specific, it was the USS *Stark*."

"Oh Jesus. What happened?"

"Someone hacked the computers on board."

"How and who?"

"We don't know the answer to either of those questions."

"Okay. I can understand that. It's going to take a while. But how did the base get bombed not once, but twice? Didn't your crew learn the lesson the first time?"

"It's a long story, Mags. I had no control over the second bombing."

"What in the Sam Hill are you talking about, Bruce? You're the captain."

"Admiral Malloy came out on a chopper. He's—oh hell, I'll explain everything when I get home. If they let me come home, that is."

"Jesus, Mary, and Joseph. What's going to happen?"

"I don't know yet. We'll be in port in a few minutes."

"I'm coming down there."

"No. Stay home. I'll let you—"

A gunshot echoes through the ship. Hensley jumps to his feet.

"Was that a gunshot?" Maggie asks.

"Yeah. I gotta go. I'll call you back." Hensley kills the call and slides the phone into his pocket as he hurries to the door. He opens it and hears footsteps hurrying down the stairs, then Kathleen Connelly comes charging down the hall. She pulls up short when she spots Hensley.

"Thank God. I thought you'd gone and done something stupid."

"Not me. Where did the shot come from?"

"I don't know."

With a sinking feeling Hensley walks over to the officers' wardroom and opens the door. Admiral Richard Malloy is slumped in the chair, his blood dripping down what's left of his face and onto his shoulder. The pistol he used to shoot himself is lying on the table. Trying not to disturb the scene, Hensley steps carefully into the room to check if Malloy has a pulse and finds he doesn't. Not that he expected to find one, based on the size of the exit wound and the blood and brain matter splattered on the wall. Hensley exits and closes and locks the door. He looks at his executive officer. "Kat, please post a guard on the door. No one is to enter the room until the military police arrive."

"I'll handle it, Bruce. Are you okay?"

"Yeah. I knew he was despondent. I should have taken his service weapon."

"He wouldn't have let you take it even if you'd tried. He was a stubborn man."

"He was that." Hensley sighs. "A complicated situation just became far more complicated. I don't know what's going to happen when we dock, Kat. I assume I'll be taken in for questioning and that means that you are now in command. You better get back to the bridge so you can help dock this piece of shit."

"We were all a part of it, Bruce. And I'm sure we're all going to get grilled. But the one thing you need to remember is there was nothing we could have done. No one knew the ship's computers were compromised."

"I know. But the navy will want someone to pay."

Connelly points at the door to the wardroom and says, "I think someone just did."

Thirty minutes later the ship is docked. Captain Bruce Hensley steps out on the deck and salutes the two military police officers awaiting him. They return the salute and take Hensley in for questioning. During the interrogation process Hensley is told the final tally. His shoulders sag and he begins to weep when the military police inform him that six ships have been sunk, several others have been damaged, and nearly eight hundred sailors have been killed.

It's dark by the time the captain is released. He steps outside the headquarters building into the warm night, still unsure of his fate. That won't be decided until a thorough investigation has been completed. He walks to his car and climbs in. When he arrives home, Maggie meets him at the door with a cold glass of his favorite bourbon and a warm hug.

Daily News Website

—BREAKING NEWS—Multiple high-ranking officials confirm country facing cyber attack. Could be weeks before attackers identified. More details to follow . . .

—BREAKING NEWS—Finally a bit of good news on what has been the worst day in this nation's history.

We have just learned that the floodgates at the Glen Canyon Dam have been closed. The worries about the possible collapse of the Hoover Dam have abated for now. More details to follow . . .

—BREAKING NEWS—Reports confirm USS Stark *is responsible for attack on Norfolk Naval Station.*

The new Zumwalt-class destroyer, the USS *Stark*, is now docked at Norfolk. We still have no news about what occurred and a full damage assessment of the naval base is now under way. There is no word about the fate of the crew aboard the beleaguered warship or any word about the ship's future. Military experts say the investigation into the cause could last for months. More details to follow . . .

—BREAKING NEWS—Update on Seattle chemical plant explosion. Multiple fatalities confirmed at nearby water park. One mother is being hailed a hero.

We can now confirm that multiple fatalities have occurred at the WaveFront Water Park. Located a short distance from the chemical plant explosion, many of the deaths at the park were the result of chlorine poisoning.

The exact number of fatalities is still unknown, but one mother killed is being hailed as a hero after she directed several children to climb to the top of the park's tallest attraction to avoid the highly concentrated chlorine gas hovering near the ground. Included in the group of children are the woman's own son and several of his friends. We are happy to report the children are all recovering at a local hospital. Names of the dead are being withheld until the next of kin can be notified. More details to follow . . .

CHAPTER 86

Chicago

Peyton stirs awake and rolls over to find her husband propped up on an elbow and staring at her. "What are you doing, weirdo?"

"Looking at my wife," Eric says. He leans down and kisses her on the lips. Last night they'd made love and it was extremely emotional and tender after all they endured yesterday. "Ready for round two?"

Peyton playfully pushes him away, "You tie that thing in a knot."

Eric lies back down. "What do we do now?"

"Do you think Allison has changed her mind since Jordan is home?"

"I have no idea. What I do know is that it's a long walk to your mother's house. And with your lacerated feet and my bullet wound it's going to be a slow, painful journey."

"No one said we had to leave today," Peyton says, rolling over to spoon with Eric.

"We might not have a choice."

"I don't think they're going to kick us out on the street."

Eric runs his fingers through Peyton's hair. "They might. And I don't know that I would blame them. It's a hell of a lot easier to feed two people than it is to feed four."

"Knowing how much Allison hates to cook, I'm betting they don't have much food to begin with. It might be easier if we work together to find food."

"You can count me out if you're thinking of looting a store," Eric says, lifting the gauze to check his wound.

Peyton leans over for a look. "Your wound looks clean and dry. Let's hope it stays that way. Anyway, back to the food. It doesn't have to be a store. We can look for empty houses or even the schools."

There's a soft knock on the door and Allison announces that they're up.

Eric climbs out of bed and begins dressing. "How are you going to know if a house is empty?"

Peyton throws back the covers and Eric stops what he's doing to stare at her nude body. "I told you to tie it in a knot," Peyton says, climbing out of bed and pulling on her borrowed panties. "I guess we'll have to stake it out for a while before we attempt to go in." Peyton pulls on the gym shorts and the shirt. "I really need to pee."

"Bathroom's down the hall."

"We can't use the bathroom, Eric. There's no water to flush the toilet."

"Damn, this is going to be hard, isn't it?"

"Yes." Peyton opens the door and hurries down the hall. She says good morning to Allison and Jordan in the kitchen and slips out the back door and squats behind their garage. Coming back in, Eric slides by and heads outside to do his business.

"We're going to need to figure out the bathroom issues," Jordan says.

Peyton joins them at the table. "What? Like an outhouse?"

"Yeah, or something like it. Things will become unsanitary in a hurry if we don't bury our waste."

"I just had to pee," Peyton says, slightly embarrassed to be discussing this topic. "I thought urine was sterile."

Eric comes back in and takes a seat at the table.

"Urine is not sterile," Jordan says. "Anyway, we're off topic. We need to think about digging a latrine or something."

"We?" Eric asks. "You guys aren't kicking us out?"

"Hell, no," Jordan says. "If what Peyton believes is true, we're going to have to band together if we're going to make it. We'll have to come up with a set of ground rules so we're not tripping all over ourselves, but foraging for food and water will have to be done in teams of two, just so someone can watch the other person's back. Besides, Allison and I would kill each other if we're stuck in this house together with nothing to do."

"What's the food situation look like?" Peyton asks.

"Grim," Allison says. "We have some peanut butter, a couple of cans of corn, one can of green beans, and a box of cake mix. Everything in the fridge is spoiled."

"Pretty slim pickings," Peyton says. "Who do you know that was out of town yesterday?"

"The Wallace family from down the street flew out to California the day before yesterday," Allison says.

Jordan pushes to his feet. "I guess we'll start there. Eric, will you go with me?"

"Of course."

"Don't be so quick to answer. Are you willing to pull the trigger on the shotgun if you need to?"

Eric thinks about it for a moment. "I think so. I guess we won't know until we face that situation."

"By then it will be too late," Jordan says.

"What about you, then? Would you pull the trigger if it meant killing someone?" Eric asks.

Jordan nods. "If one of our lives were at stake, yes. In a heartbeat."

Eric runs his fingers through his hair. "Maybe I should be the gatherer and you should be the hunter."

Jordan shrugs. "Works for me. Let me grab the shotgun and some extra ammo and we'll take off."

CHAPTER 87

After hijacking the flight Michelle Miller and Carlos Torres *had* planned, Paige Randall and Hank Goodnight are now on the ground in Boston. Both had crashed as soon as the plane had taken off and they're far from well rested, but they are functioning. Hank looks out the side window as the driver from the Boston field office turns into an industrial area north-west of downtown Boston. The driver badges his way past the police barricades and pulls the Tahoe to the curb just down the street from the FBI's special weapons and tactics (SWAT) team's van. Parked two blocks from the target building, it will be the staging area for the upcoming assault on the building. Piling out of the car, Hank smiles again at how tight Natalie's jeans are on Paige. She catches his smile and shows Hank her middle finger.

Hank shrugs. "Hey, at least you got them on."

"I'm glad you find that humorous, asshole."

They make their way to the van in search of the guy running the show and find him sitting at the rear of the truck watching a video feed from the exterior of the building. He stands and steps down out of the van. "Hank Goodnight, as I live and breathe."

"How ya doin', Cliff?" Hank asks, extending his hand.

"Just waiting on you, Hank," the man says, pumping Hank's hand.

"Cliff, meet Paige Randall from cyber. Paige, this is Supervisory Special Agent Clifton Reiley from the agency's Critical Incident Response Group."

Once the introductions are finished they get down to business. "What do we know, Cliff?" Hank asks.

"We tried a camera under the door but they're in a different room inside the building. So we put the drone up and grabbed some video footage through a grimy-ass window. We did a thermal scan and counted eight living bodies inside."

"Did you run the photos through the NextGen ID system?" Hank asks.

"Quality's not good enough. Climb up in the van with me and you can watch the video," Reiley says.

"Is the drone still up?" Hank asks.

"No. We recorded video of the entire exterior of the building. What else you looking for?"

"Did you cover the roof?" Hank asks.

"Hey, this ain't my first rodeo. Of course we videoed the roof. It might be our best entry point."

"Did you scan for wireless networks, Cliff?" Paige asks.

"Yep. They have one, but good luck getting access to it."

"Encrypted?" Paige asks.

"Yeah, by something my tech guy says he's never

seen before. You'll have to talk to him. I struggle to keep my damn e-mail working right. Let's go look at the video."

Paige and Hank follow Reiley up the back steps and into the van. After watching the various video feeds, Hank sits back in his chair. "Did it look like those three armed men are guardin' the safety of the hackers or are they guardin' the hackers themselves?"

"That's an interesting way to look at it," Reiley says, rocking his chair back. "Are you saying those young guys are being coerced?"

"Maybe not originally. Remember, this thing had to be in the works for years. Be hard to ride herd on a group of folks over that length of time. It could be one or two got skittish once the people began dying. But, someone in there sent out an SOS when they logged on to the satellite from inside that buildin'. Will you play the interior footage one more time?"

Reiley does a double take. "Hell, Hank, is that brain of yours drying out? I don't ever remember playing a video for you more than once."

"I'm lookin' for confirmation, Cliff. I know what I saw, but I didn't get a real clear look. Any audio?"

"We're trying, but there doesn't seem to be a lot of talking going on in there," Reiley says, running back through the video that's stored on the hard drive. He stops on the interior shots from the drone and hits play. Inside are five people scattered out around a large table similar to one you might find at a church potluck. There's nothing fancy about the table or the fold-out chairs they're sitting in. Three other men, their rifles slung over their shoulders, are positioned around the room in a crescent-shape formation.

Hank leans forward. "Stop. Can you zoom in on that face?" he asks, pointing at the screen.

Reiley works the trackball, pushes some buttons, and the man's face fills the screen.

Hank points at the face and says, "His name is Hassan and he's originally from Pakistan. He never told me his last name, but when I met him he was a student at MIT.

"Where did you meet him?" Paige asks, amazed at Hank's recall—again.

"An Internet security conference two years ago. We had a brief conversation about various encryption methods. Nice guy. I can't believe he's tangled up in this mess." Hank startles when his phone buzzes in his pocket. He pulls it out and lights the screen. "Uh-oh, a 911 text from Mercer to call. Paige, visit with Cliff about a plan. I want you inside the buildin' as soon as it's cleared to preserve as much evidence as possible. And we know these guys love to deploy self-destruct payloads." Hank stands and steps down the stairs, waiting for the call to Elaine Mercer to go through. It does and she answers before the first ring is finished.

After a few moments of conversation, Hank kills the call and climbs back into the van. "Things may have gone from bad to worse for those guys inside the building."

"How so?" Paige asks.

Hank looks at Paige. "Did you know our new president has a pacemaker?"

"No. I don't recall hearing about that during the campaign," Paige says.

"I don't, either," Reiley says. "What about it? Did it crap out on him or go haywire?"

"Apparently his havin' one was a closely guarded secret," Hank says. "But, yeah, Cliff, somethin' went haywire. They don't have all the details yet, but the doctors believe someone hacked his pacemaker and accelerated his heart rate. Elaine believes it's all tied into these attacks."

"Is the president dead?" Reiley asks.

"Not yet. He's hangin' on for now. But that's another reason we need to be extremely careful about handlin' the evidence inside that building. How long until we make entry, Cliff?"

"The snipers are in position," Reily says. "Whenever you're ready, we're ready. One question, though. Do you want the snipers to take out the three armed suspects when we breach the door?"

Hank pauses, thinking. After a moment or two he says, "What are the odds that those guys on the computers are workin' on a class project and not hackin' into every computer network in the country?"

"Less than one percent," Reiley says.

"Have the snipers take out the guys with weapons," Hank says.

CHAPTER 88

The local police have blocked all traffic within a
four-block area of the building and have evacuated
the nearby businesses that wouldn't attract the attention of those inside the building. The assumption is
that the five men on the computers are unarmed. But
the FBI doesn't know that for a fact. They also don't
have the floor plans for the building. Reiley sent
agents to the courthouse but they came up empty. In
the end, it's not a large building—maybe eight to ten
thousand square feet—and the surveillance and thermal scans have detected no other humans so Reiley is
not that concerned about not having the building plans.

One of Reiley's men plotted out an approach that
will allow them access to the front of the building
without being seen. It's a roundabout way, but maintaining the surprise element is key. There was some debate about breaching through the roof but the only way
to get to it is via ladder, leaving the men exposed for
too long. Reiley also thought about dropping some
agents down from a helicopter, but that could spook
the bad guys and maybe lead to destruction of evidence

before they could get to them. So a hard, fast breach through the doors is plan A. Hank, wearing an armored vest and a FBI Windbreaker, is one of the eight men who will make entry into the building. Other agents will guard the building's other exits and will not be part of the breach team.

Now bunched on either side of the entrance, Hank and his crew are waiting for the demolitions man to finish applying the charges to the door. Three of the men have flash-bang grenades in their hands and will toss them inside as soon as the door is blown. Everyone takes a step back when the guy placing the charges nods. He holds up three fingers and counts down. When his fist is closed the door explodes into the building and the three flash-bangs follow.

The flash-bangs explode with a flash of intense light and sound and the team enters the building, their rifles up in firing position. Hank didn't hear the rifle fire from the snipers, but he assumes they were successful. Leapfrogging one another in twos, the well-rehearsed team makes entry into the target room. The three armed men are still armed, but their guns are silent, all three dead where they fell. Hank and the other members of the team work to quickly search and secure the remaining five men as other troops enter to clear the rest of the building.

Hank grabs the man he knows as Hassan and throws him facedown on the floor. He buries a knee in his back and pulls the man's hands behind him and zip-ties his wrists. When the all clear is given, the five men are separated and taken to other parts of the building for interrogation. Hassan is mumbling something Hank can't hear, his ears still ringing from the grenade blasts. As Paige and other computer experts swarm into the building, Hank grabs a chair and drags it into one of the smaller offices and forces Hassan to sit. Only then does he hear what Hassan is saying. He triggers his radio and says, "One bogie still unaccounted for." Then he turns to his suspect.

Hassan is trembling, his crotch wet where he pissed himself. Hank takes a couple of calming breaths, allowing Hassan a moment to fully grasp the situation, then crosses his arms and leans against the wall. "Hello, Hassan."

Hassan, his eyes wide in surprise, takes a close look at Hank and shakes his head. "How do you know my name?"

"We met at an Internet security conference two years ago. You never told me your last name."

"It's Ansari." He looks down at a spot on the concrete for long few seconds. "He was going to kill us."

"Who was?" Hank asks.

"His name is Basir Nazeri. Your men have to find him."

"Was Nazeri callin' the shots?" Hank asks.

Ansari nods. Over the next hour, Ansari lays out the entire plan, providing names, dates, and the other details of the attack. Hank does not take notes, nor does he record the conversation. It's just he and Hassan speaking, man-to-man. Yes, it was Hassan who logged on to the satellite and yes, it was Nazeri who produced all of the zero-day vulnerabilities and mapped networks. As the story continues to unfold, Hank realizes that Basir Nazeri is a very dangerous man. Hank grills Hassan about Nazeri and is not really surprised to learn that Hassan doesn't know much about the man.

"I have his picture," Hassan blurts out.

"Where?" Hank asks.

"In an encrypted folder I keep in the cloud."

Hank helps Hassan to stand and leads him back to the room where they had been working. The place is a whirlwind of activity with Paige standing in the center of the room calling the shots. He calls her over and explains what he needs.

"Where in the cloud?" Paige asks Hassan.

He explains how to find the folder and gives Paige his log-in credentials. Paige assures Hank she'll send the pictures out immediately and Hank takes Hassan back to his chair. Hank learns about the drone strikes on Hassan's family and the other four families and finally begins to understand some of the reasons for their actions. Once Hassan finishes his story, Hank probes for more information about Nazeri, digging for the tiny scraps that might provide a clue about his identity.

"When did you first meet him?" Hank asks.

"I told you. Six months ago. He showed up, called us together, and we started refining the malware." Hassan goes on to explain about the scholarships and receiving the software during his final year of undergrad study. He ensures Hank that the story is the same for the other four members of the team.

"And you hadn't met the other four students until six months ago when Nazeri arrived?"

"No," Hassan says. "I knew we were developing malware, but I had no idea of the purpose. Three days ago, we arrived at this building and that is the same time we discovered Nazeri's list of targets. We've been here since that day."

"Who targeted the president?" Hank asks.

"So you know?" Hassan asks, arching his brows. "Nazeri. Is the president dead?"

Hank debates whether to tell him, but Hassan has been divulging information and nothing he's said triggered Hank's bullshit meter. "The last I heard he was still alive."

"Good," Hassan says.

"Anything else you can tell me about Nazeri? Where he's from or who he was in contact with?"

Hassan shakes his head. "I attempted to find out more information about him and could not. Maybe you can find out by looking at the phone records."

"What phone records? Was he in contact with someone else durin' your stay here?"

"He was. He used a landline phone and some type of scrambler. I doubt you will find much in the way of content, but you might find whom he was calling. Nazeri is resourceful and extremely intelligent, but he could have made a mistake somewhere."

"What about accents? Did he have one?"

"I did not detect one. He spoke perfect English."

"American English?"

"Yes. I did notice that he did not use many contractions, if at all. That is common for some nonnative English speakers. My sense is that he has spent some time here in the States."

"Anything else you can think of about Nazeri?"

Hassan shakes his head. "You have the pictures."

"That was smart thinking on your part. What made you decide to do it?"

"A feeling. He became more belligerent as time went on. Yesterday, he told us he owned us. What do you do with something you own and no longer need?"

"Throw it away?" Hank asks.

"Yes. When the armed guards appeared, I knew our

time was short. I did not know Nazeri had left the premises."

"If you had to guess his origin, Hassan, what would you guess?"

"Middle Eastern. Maybe Iran, or Saudi Arabia, or another Gulf state." Hassan looks up at Hank. "What happens now?"

"You and your cohorts will be transported to separate locations where the interrogations will continue."

"Will I be killed?"

Hank hesitates for a moment then says, "No, Hassan, I don't believe so. You'll likely end up in prison somewhere."

"Guantanamo?" Hassan asks.

"I don't know, but I don't think so. Sit tight for a minute, Hassan," Hank says. He waves over another FBI SWAT team member and asks him to keep an eye on the prisoner. He returns to the main room and pulls Paige aside.

"You wouldn't believe the list of targets these guys were going after," Paige whispers. "Yesterday was only the tip of the iceberg."

"Did you e-mail those photos of Nazeri to headquarters?"

"I did. Who is he?"

Hank sighs. "The mastermind. And we may never find him."

"I'm sure the agency is blanketing the world with his picture as we speak. Did you ask that terrorist you're interrogating for details?"

Hank winces at her use of the word *terrorist*, but when he stops to ponder it a moment he realizes that's how they'll be branded. "Yes. He doesn't know much about him. Which is not surprisin'. Will you show me the picture?"

"Hoping to imprint it in that big brain of yours?" Paige asks as she leads Hank over to one of the computers.

"Somethin' like that," Hank says. Paige pulls up the photos of Nazeri and watches Hank's facial expressions while he scrolls through the images.

"You haven't seen him before, have you?" Paige asks when Hank finishes.

"No."

"I could tell by reading your expression."

"What? We've been together a couple of days and you now know all my tells?"

"Not all of them," Paige says. "I've seen sad, angry, and slightly excited. Haven't witnessed your happy yet."

"Good to know," Hank mutters. "Do you need my prisoner to help with any of their computer stuff?"

"I'd like for him to hang around a bit. Right now, we're taking inventory of everything and then we'll put it on a plane back to Fort Meade. We'll wait to dissect most of it back there. Did you ask him if they've inserted any booby traps or anything else we need to be aware of?"

"No. C'mon, you can ask him yourself."

Hank leads Paige back to the room and introduces her to Hassan. He finds another chair for Paige and drifts out of earshot while the two of them talk. While he's waiting, he calls Mercer and fills her in on the latest.

"Is the president still among the livin'?" Hank asks.

"Yes. Who knew someone could hack a pacemaker?" Mercer says.

"Anything connected to the Internet—"

"Can be hacked," Mercer says, finishing Hank's sentence. "I know, I know, Hank. But damn, it has to stop somewhere, doesn't it?"

"I doubt it. What's to stop them?"

"I suppose you're right, as always. How did our star programmer work out?" Mercer asks.

"She's good. Terrific, in fact."

"That's good to hear, Hank." There's a long pause and Mercer says, "Umm . . . oh, never mind. When are you coming back?"

Hank knows exactly what she was going to say. "You're worse than Nana, Elaine."

"You aren't getting any younger, Hank."

Hank nips that conversation in the bud and tells Elaine of his plans then kills the call.

Paige stands from her chair and walks over. "If I didn't know he was responsible for thousands of deaths, I'd think he was a nice, pleasant young man."

"Yep," Hank says. "He got in over his head and didn't know how to get out. Do you want him to hang around?"

"Yes, for a while, in case we hit a snag." She glances back at Hassan then turns to look Hank in the eye. "What's going to happen to him and the rest of them?"

"They'll be taken somewhere for further interrogation."

"And after that?" Paige asks.

Hank shrugs. "Not up to me. Prison somewhere, most likely."

"Are we flying back to Fort Meade together or are you staying here?"

"I'll most likely be here until we can run this Nazeri guy to ground. How much longer are you goin' to be here?"

"Most of the day, probably."

"I guess I'll either see you at the airport or I won't. You did good, Paige." Hank turns, walks over to the other guard, and tells him to keep an eye on the prisoner for a little while longer, and heads outside to confer with Reiley.

Paige watches Hank's retreat and her emotions go all over the place. Rather than try to sort them out, she walks back to the main room and returns to the task at hand.

ONE
WEEK
LATER

CHAPTER 89

Chicago

Peyton was correct in her assumption—it's a week later, and the power is still out in Chicago. Eric and Jordan have done a good job with gathering food, but it's water they're struggling to find. After spending all their lives taking it for granted that water will come out of the tap when you turn it on, it's a shock when the tap runs dry. Being without electricity is a major inconvenience, but being without water is an absolute life-or-death matter.

Now it's early afternoon and, after a lunch of canned chili cooked over a wood fire on Jordan's gutted gas grill, the four are seated in the living room discussing strategies to address the critical water situation.

"What about the vending machine at the school down the street?" Peyton asks. Her feet are slowly healing, but it still hurts to walk. Luckily she wears the same shoe size as Allison, and, more important, Allison is willing to share.

"Already looted," Eric says. "We checked." His bullet wound is healing nicely and he's dodged infection for now.

"What about the concession stands at Wrigley?" Allison asks.

"Same story," Jordan says. "They were probably cleaned out by day two."

The discussion drags on. Moments later, Peyton is struck by an idea. "We've been focused on finding bottled water and we haven't contemplated other sources. We live blocks away from one of the largest freshwater lakes on the planet. Why not take water from the lake?"

That stirs a debate about E. coli, salmonella, giardiasis, cryptosporidium, and a long list of other nasty bacteria and microorganisms. Once that's exhausted, the discussion moves to radium, lead, mercury, PCBs, arsenic, and other natural elements that might be present in the waters of Lake Michigan. But in the end, they are out of options.

"We'll boil the water to purify it," Peyton says.

"We need to run it through some type of filter first to filter out the larger debris," Eric says.

"How long do you have to boil the water?" Allison asks.

Without thinking, Jordan pulls out his cell phone he keeps charged with a small portable solar panel to Google the question. Then he remembers they have no cell service and no Internet. Old habits are hard to break. "I don't think you can overboil it, can you?"

"I don't think so," Peyton says. "But I think once the water is hot enough to boil that'll kill all the bad bugs."

"One other important question," Eric says, "is how are we going to get the water from the lake to here?"

"We'll have to carry it," Jordan says. "I have some five-gallon buckets from Home Depot in the garage."

"Five gallons of water is heavy as hell," Eric says. "We need a wagon or something."

"Didn't we see a wagon in the Wallace family garage?" Jordan asks.

"We did," Eric says. "Grab the shotgun and we'll go get it. Peyton, will you and Allison gather up the buckets?"

Jordan stands and retreats down the corridor to their bedroom to grab the shotgun.

"Yes. We'll make it a pleasant afternoon trip to the lake."

"I don't know about pleasant," Eric says.

"Probably wouldn't hurt if we got in and rinsed off, too. We'll take a couple of towels."

Eric sniffs under his arm. "You don't like my manly odor?"

"Uh, no," Peyton says. "Although I don't smell much better. I'll grab some soap and shampoo, too. We'll bathe like the old-timers used to do."

Jordan returns with the shotgun and he and Eric take off to grab the wagon. Although they carry the shotgun whenever they go out, they haven't needed it—yet. That will most likely change as the days stretch out and they have to widen their search for food. There has been no sighting of the Singleton family and they don't yet know their home no longer exists. Eric dreads that upcoming confrontation, but there's not a damn thing he can do about it.

The still-absent Wallace family lives just down the street and it doesn't take Eric and Jordan long to grab the wagon and return. Allison and Peyton meet them in the front yard with the buckets, towels, soap, and shampoo. They pile everything in the wagon and head for the lake, twenty-one blocks to the east.

When they reach the lake they're amazed by all of the tents staked out along the shore. The area is jammed with people, pets, and garbage for as far as the eye can see. If they were concerned about the water quality before, now they're doubly concerned. They spend several moments discussing the issue, but find no alternatives. They must have water.

Smoke lingers along the beach from the many campfires, and thousands of people are lounging around their campsites, swimming in the lake, or standing along the shore, fishing. That's something Eric and Jordan hadn't thought of and they file it away as a future food source. The afternoon is hot and humid and it doesn't appear that any clothing standards are in force. Many people are walking around in their underwear and just as many have shed their clothing altogether. Most of those would have been better served, Peyton thinks, if they had chosen not to discard their clothing.

Eric takes the shotgun and stands guard over their pitiful little wagon while the other three strip down to their underwear, grab the soap and shampoo, and wade out into the water. Because of his bullet wound, Eric and Peyton decided that the risk of infection outweighs his need for a bath so he takes a seat on the sand and people-watches. Fearing conflict, he avoids speaking to anyone as he surveys the crowd, his gaze continually returning to Peyton and Allison as they bathe. Jordan can take care of himself, however, Eric fears for the women's safety in this new world they're living in. He's not sensing any danger at the moment, but he knows that could change in a heartbeat.

The three eventually return and Jordan carries the buckets out to deeper water to fill them. Eric, still carrying the shotgun, helps Jordan lug the heavy buckets back to the wagon. Once everyone is dressed, Eric hands the shotgun off to Jordan and grabs the wagon handle, groaning to get it moving. It's a struggle in the sand, but the situation improves dramatically when they hit the asphalt.

"You three go ahead," Jordan says. "I'm going to make sure no one follows us."

"You really think someone would come after us?" Allison asks.

Jordan points at the wagon laden with buckets of water. "The buckets and the wagon are hot commodities about now. Plus, where would you rather sleep? In a tent surrounded by thousands of others or in a comfy bed with some privacy?"

"Point made," Allison says. "Don't linger too far back."

"I won't," Jordan says.

Eric takes up the wagon again as they begin their journey back home. What the future holds is unknown. All they can do is survive.

CHAPTER 90

Buffalo

With the power still out in Buffalo, Dr. Scott Butler hasn't had to worry about patients. Taking a break from drilling teeth day after day is a relief yet he remains busy despite the closing of his office. He and his troops continue to patrol the few city streets that are passable, although most everything that's worth having was looted days ago. The mindless, endless driving allows Butler's mind to drift and that's not a good thing, especially with the images from inside Attica still freshly imprinted on his brain. Three times this week he has awakened in the middle of the night because of recurring nightmares. His wife, Linda, keeps asking if he's okay and that only pisses him off. No, he's not okay and may not be for a long time. But he can't describe what they encountered at the prison to his wife, who has no concept of what one human can do to another.

"Cap, I see somebody walking in a store up the street," Lieutenant Fred Parker says from behind the wheel.

"What store?" Butler asks.

"I think it's a shoe store."

"Maybe they need a new pair of shoes," Butler says.

"Want me to stop?"

"Hell no."

"If we're not stopping at the shoe store to check for looting, what are we doing out here?" Parker asks.

"We're quelling the violence."

"I don't see much violence, Cap."

Butler shrugs. "We're out here because we've been ordered out here. And if General Moore has anything to say about it, we'll probably be driving these same streets at the same time next year."

"What did you do to piss him off?"

"I disobeyed a direct order."

"Why in the hell did you do that?"

"Because I didn't agree with it, that's why."

"What was the order?"

"It doesn't matter now." Butler stares out the side window for the next two blocks. He and Parker are alone in the truck. Other trucks from their unit are out and about, but Butler decided two people per truck is all this mission requires, allowing him the ability to rotate troops through while also allowing them time at home. He turns to look at Parker. "Are you having trouble sleeping, Freddy?"

Parker nods. "Some. I keep waking up in the middle of a nightmare."

"The same one?"

"No. Different nightmares, but same subject."

"Attica?"

"Ding, ding, ding, give that man a prize," Parker says

in his best game show host voice. "Are you having trouble sleeping?"

"Some. I have the same issue you do."

"Is the Guard going to spring for some counseling?"

"Yeah, but with the power off no one's working."

"The general approved it?" Parker asks, surprise in his voice.

"Nope. I went over his head to the governor. That's just one more reason he's pissed at me."

"Yeah, well, fuck him. He's probably sitting on his fat ass up at headquarters."

"I imagine you're right." Butler checks the side mirror to see if anyone is coming up behind them. There isn't and that's not surprising. The first part of the week the unit cleared a few of the main roads, pushing vehicles out of the way with their large trucks. But not many drivers are out on the road because there's not really anywhere to go. Hospital staff come and go, but the rumor is their fuel supply is almost gone. Butler wonders what'll happen to the patients when that happens.

Thinking about the hospital makes him thirsty for a cup of coffee. "Freddy, swing by Buffalo General so we can check on Clark and Perez." Lieutenant Gary Clark is still hanging on and Perez ended up with broken ribs and a ruptured spleen the doctors had to remove.

"We checked in with them this morning and both are doing fine. You just want another cup of coffee."

"Guilty," Butler says. They ride in silence for a while, looking out at the looted stores. Their first day on patrol was hectic as they chased down looters and put them in jail, despite the shoot-to-kill order. But the jail filled up quickly and, by day three, they pretty much gave up on arresting anyone else. It's hard to take a person to jail—or, God forbid, kill someone—when they're starving and scavenging for food. Butler's food situation is okay for the moment after divvying up all the MREs and other food supplies at Guard headquarters. They won't be flush with food forever and, according to word passed down through the ranks, it could be a while before the power is back on. Butler knows he'll be scrounging for food somewhere down the road, but that's a worry for another day.

Parker pulls into the hospital parking lot and kills the engine. They pile out and head into the hospital, stopping at the coffeepot on the way. In the ER they run into Linda Butler, the captain's wife, who's volunteering while the dental office is closed. Parker says hello and then makes himself scarce.

Linda gives her husband a hug. "I scavenged a few sleeping pills for you," she whispers in his ear.

"I don't need any damn pills," Scott angrily whispers.

"We're not going to argue about this, Scott. You're exhausted and grumpy as hell," Linda says before breaking the embrace and stepping back. "I still love you, though." She reaches out and tenderly places a hand on her husband's cheek. "You need to put what happened in that prison behind you, babe."

"How exactly do I do that?" Butler asks.

Linda lowers her hand. "By talking it through. If you're not going to talk to me, then talk to Freddy or someone else who endured that hellhole. Keeping it bottled up inside is not an option. And you know that."

Butler nods. "I know, but if I talk about it I'm afraid I'll relive it."

"Maybe some of it. But right now, you're reliving it every night. Maybe you should go talk to Tracy Green. I thinks she's in the hospital today."

"I'm not talking to a shrink. Hell, that woman's got more than one screw loose."

"Shh," Linda says, looking around to see if anyone overheard. "Okay, not Tracy, then."

Linda sighs in frustration. "There has to be someone you can confide in. What about your brother?"

"I can't call him because there's no phone service. I'll get it worked out."

Linda steps in closer and lowers her voice. "Bullshit."

Butler holds his hands up about shoulder high. "Okay. I'll talk to Freddy about it."

"Good. Do I need to clue him in in case you forget?"

"No. I won't forget."

Linda leans in and gives Scott a peck on the lips. "If I didn't love you I wouldn't care."

"I know. And I love you, too." Butler takes a sip from his coffee cup. "What are we having for dinner?"

"Tonight I will be heating up the beef ravioli in meat sauce."

Butler rubs his belly. "Sounds yummy. Can't wait."

Linda laughs. "I have to run. Love you, babe."

"Love you, too. See you tonight."

Butler takes off in search of Parker and finds him where he thought he would—at the nurses' station. "Ready to roll, Freddy?" Butler asks.

"Yeah. Did you check on Clark and Perez?"

"We'll come back later."

"You mean when they brew a fresh pot of coffee?"

Butler shrugs. They make their way back to the truck and climb in. Freddy takes the wheel again and fires up the truck and pulls out of the parking lot. A mile down the road, Butler says, "Freddy, we probably ought to talk through some things . . ."

CHAPTER 91

Despite a worldwide manhunt, the man known as Basir Nazeri remains at large. How he slipped the quickly closing net is still unknown. FBI agents viewed vast quantities of traffic and pedestrian camera footage in and around Boston and have yet to find any trace of Nazeri. Current thinking is that he may have slipped onto a ship in Boston Harbor, and with his computer skills could have easily erased or covered his tracks some other way. The FBI is still trying to trace the calls from the landline phone inside the building. The calls were bounced around the world several times and whom Nazeri was communicating with remains unknown. In fact, much remains unknown about the man who caused so much death and destruction.

The one spot of good news, depending on a person's political perspective, is that the president will fully recover after having his pacemaker replaced with one the authorities say is unhackable. Paige has been working around the clock with others from the NSA to dissect the computers captured in the raid and to unravel the worm that has compromised a large number of the nation's computer networks. The dissection is almost complete, but ferreting out the malware is a job that will take months, if not years.

Now back at her spacious condo after many days away, Paige Randall closes the lid of her laptop and returns to the kitchen for another cup of coffee. She's been running on coffee and energy drinks for days on end and she knows she needs to slow her intake of acidic drinks to give her roiling stomach a break. After taking another sip of coffee, she pours the rest down the sink, vowing to stop the caffeine cascade this very moment.

As she cleans the coffeepot she wonders what Peyton and Eric are up to. After Paige reached out to the FBI's Chicago field office, a couple of agents were sent out to find her sister. It didn't take them long to locate Peyton and Eric, who were still in the neighborhood, staying with one of her sister's friends. Paige was shocked to learn about their house burning down, but the agents insisted her sister and brother-in-law were doing just fine and Paige had passed that information on to her mother, Frances. Surprisingly, Champlain still has power and cell service. Paige had been so busy that she and Frances have talked only briefly during the week, but her mother did let on that she might be seeing someone.

Paige smiles at that thought as she puts the carafe back in place. She's happy for her mother. Exiting the kitchen, Paige walks down the hallway, enters her bedroom, and turns into her closet, searching for the perfect outfit for today's lunch meeting. After pawing through the rows of slacks and jeans, she turns in another direction and selects a simple skirt and a sleeveless top and pulls out a pair of Tory Burch three-inch espadrilles. After laying everything out on her bed she slips into her spacious bathroom to shower. She doesn't know what to expect from today's meeting, but she's hoping it turns out well.

Across town, Hank Goodnight steps out of the shower in his apartment and grabs a towel. He had spent most of the week in Boston searching for any clues that would lead to the capture of Basir Nazeri. But the clues are few. If Hank and the FBI didn't have a picture of him they would think he doesn't exist—a ghost. However, they do have a picture of the man, thanks to Hassan Ansari, and it's been plastered on newscasts and newspapers all across the globe.

Ansari and the other four members of the terrorist gang are still being held at undisclosed locations and the interrogations are ongoing. Their lives and past actions are undergoing intense scrutiny while authorities debate which legal forum would be best for prosecution. Regardless of which court forum is eventually chosen, all five will never enjoy a single day of freedom for as long as they live. There have been murmurs of prosecutors wanting to seek the death penalty, and Hank won't be surprised if that does occur, but he'll fight to keep Hassan away from the needle.

Hank wraps the towel around his waist and runs a comb through his hair. He has a few butterflies about the upcoming lunch meeting only because he doesn't know what to expect. The power is still out in D.C. and many other cities and towns across the country. Some portions of the grid will be repaired much quicker than others and the thinking is the electricity in the nation's capital could be restored within days. He spoke with

Nana earlier today on a landline phone at tribal head-quarters. Her generator is still humming along and the Chickasaw Nation still has a good supply of fuel.

The stock markets are still a mess and it will be months before active trading begins again, if ever. The malware destroyed millions of documents and what money belongs to whom may never be sorted out. Hank opens the closet door and doesn't spend a long time worrying about what to wear. He grabs a pair of jeans, a button-down shirt, and his cowboy boots. Elaine Mercer, his boss, hasn't decided where his skills would be put to the best use, so Hank will continue his hunt for Nazeri until something new pops.

After slipping on his jeans and pulling on his shirt, Hank takes a seat on the edge of the bed to put his boots on. To say he was surprised about Natalie's reve-lation that her sexual preferences have changed would be an understatement. Not that Hank cares. He's a firm believer in *love who you want to love* and he's happy that Natalie is happy. He has no tolerance for those people who denigrate another person's choices. His biggest pet peeves are intolerance and hypocrisy and he's not shy to let people know that. Hank stands and, after checking the mirror to make sure his shirt is not on inside out, he grabs his keys, his pistol, and exits his ground-floor apartment.

His Shelby Cobra chirps when he presses the key fob to unlock it. Stopping to inspect a suspicious stain on the hood, he discovers it's a grease spot and he rubs it away with his thumb. With little thought, he wipes his thumb clean on his jeans and climbs behind the wheel. It's hot outside and it's about thirty degrees hot-ter inside, thanks to the black leather interior. Punching the start button, he fires up the massive engine and flips the air conditioner to max cold. After putting his pistol in the glove box, he reverses out of his parking spot and shifts the transmission into first gear, goosing the gas and steering the Mustang out of the parking lot. He shifts to third gear then fourth when he hits the main road. Traffic is light because most of the residents in McLean work in the now-dark D.C. area.

After weaving through traffic he pulls into the parking lot of One Westpark and motors up to the entrance. He can't help but smile when Paige exits and walks to the car. She opens the door and climbs in. "Hi, Hank," she says, strapping on her seat belt.

It takes Hank a moment to pull his gaze away from her tanned, toned legs. "Hi, Paige. Nice outfit."

"You like it so you can ogle my legs."

"Nothin' wrong with starin' at your legs. You have very nice legs. Legs a man might like to run his hands across."

"Lunch, Hank. We're going to lunch."

"No dessert?" Hank asks.

"Yet to be determined."

Hank eases his foot off the clutch. "I like a woman with an open mind."

ACKNOWLEDGMENTS

The first round of thanks, as always, is reserved for you, the readers. If it weren't for you I couldn't do what I love doing. Thank you!

A special thanks to two people who are often overlooked—my production editor, Arthur Maisel, and my copyeditor, Randie Lipkin. I happen to think both are two of the best in the business. Thanks for finding my mistakes!

Thanks to my terrific editor and friend, Gary Goldstein. Thanks, Gary, for taking a chance on an unknown writer and for the dinners and adult beverages we've shared.

Thank you, Steven Zacharius, for giving us a place the writers can call home. Thanks, Lou Malcangi, for another great cover. I'm eternally grateful to all those who work at Kensington, including: Elizabeth (Liz) May, Lynn Cully, Lulu Martinez, Vida Engstrand, Kimberly Richardson, Lauren Jernigan, and Alexandra Nicolajsen. Welcome to the team, Lauren Vassallo! I look forward to working with you. A fond farewell to Morgan Elwell. Good luck in your future endeavors and thanks for being an advocate for my work.

Thank you, Jim Donovan.

Thanks to those who hold a special place in my heart: Kelsey, Andrew, and Camdyn Snider, Nickolas

Washburn, and Karley Washburn. I love you all very, very much. Camdyn is our first grandchild and, yes, we do everything we can to spoil her.

This book is dedicated to my parents and to Tonya's parents. Thank you for everything.

And lastly, to the woman who decided to share her life with me, Tonya. I love you forever and always.